# When Souls Unite

By:

Amanda Heit

Science Fiction

Teen/Young Adult

Heit, Amanda.
When Souls Unite / by Amanda Heit.
1st edition.

Paperback
ISBN-13: 978-1-949858-24-2
Ebook
ISBN-13: 978-1-949858-25-9

Printed in the United States of America
August 2022
10 9 8 7 6 5 4 3 2 1
First Edition

# Contents

# 1

When faced with eternal heartbreak some people give up and cry. Others melt away like wax wings flying toward the sun. Klast had long ago decided to stare the pain directly in the face. That's what he was doing right now. While the heartbreaker hadn't looked at him since being forced into the cage, Klast could hardly break away. The snowy gray coat, silky black ears, and brown booted limbs were a masterpiece. The intellect was mesmerizing. The eyes could transport him to warm, safe places where he had hidden as a child, but only when those eyes chose to. Five years of rebuttal paved for a strained relationship.

"Into the pits of the forge," Klast mumbled.

He threw the collection bill in his hand into the trash as he continued to stare out the window. Three months of unpaid rent on his apartment and he was being tossed out on his rump. If he had a bit more padding in that area, it wouldn't hurt so much, but he'd lost weight, and the rump was turning brittle, liable to snap. Klast pictured his belongings being chucked into the apartment dumpster. One sleeping bag, five cans of food, and toiletries gave his landlord not much to worry about. Klast, on the other hand, was holding a newly sharpened pocket knife covered in acid. His desperation couldn't be trusted.

"Think the world can be patched together with silly putty?" Klast asked more to himself than the heartbreaker he was watching. "We'll goop it together and you'll miraculously decide that I'm the best thing on earth since canned sardines instead of your personal curtain wall."

A cough came from behind him causing Klast to quickly wipe his eyes. His pupils had not been getting teary. Not in the least. No one needed to know how eager he was to rid himself of the rest of his possessions in the next three days. This was his second month of cutting his food into thirds so he could feed the IB dogs. They were grown and they ate a lot. He couldn't sell a scrawny Imprinting Bodyguard dog. These dogs linked into a man's soul and safeguarded it. Who would trust his soul to an emancipated thing? Klast shivered at the thought of having his soul torn asunder by a skeleton. The shiver came from experience.

"What?" Klast asked, briefly checking his reflection in the window to make sure he didn't look all red in the face. The glow of the yellow luminaire outside was pale enough that his reflection smoothed over the three-day black stubble. Scraggly. The hair on top of his head played the part of being born on Hyphas, but most of his genes came from the planet Lexia, including the wide flare of his nose. He stood there, a testament to hiding in plain sight.

"Bronze ordered pizza to celebrate," Mike answered.

Mike. Klast didn't feel so bad about being overheard pinning over a dog when it was Mike there. He understood. He'd lost three of his imprinted dogs before. Klast had only lost one, but he'd never been able to get over it as Mike had done. Imar liked to tell Klast that if he cheered up some, he'd get another IB. Klast ignored him. His IB was dead. Had Klast known that Shadow was going to get into a kennel fight within his first year and die, he would have spared his heart the later bleeding. He'd have shot Shadow first. That way he could control the moment his soul ripped out. It wouldn't have been such a large shock and wouldn't have revealed his Lexian characteristic to shift between worlds if he saw it coming.

"That was nice of Bronze," Klast said as casually as he could.

He turned from the window and then hunched forward as the object of his affection sent him a nasty bark. The devil. Klast didn't know why he still kept Deek except that he loved him. Four years at the arena and Deek had not imprinted. His high intellect was the problem. He couldn't settle his restless energy by falling in love with an idiot. When Klast contemplated giving the dog up for good, Deek would look at him and smile like he knew the thoughts in Klast's head. Klast would glare back and not do it. He couldn't reward *that* sort of behavior.

"You put the devil in alone?" Mike asked, stepping forward to look.

Sheltered in the heart of the arena, Klast's dogs were in caged rows of impenetrable steel with keyed locks and concrete floors. They couldn't dig out. They couldn't bite out. They couldn't claw out. They could, however, spray acid on the metal and work a hole into it by daybreak, which was why

Klast wondered if he was going to get any sleep tonight. The usually resistant Deek had been extra testy this year. Mike couldn't see it, but Klast was sporting a brand-new rip in his abdomen, compliments of Deek, the show floor freak. Most dogs enjoyed show days. They took it as a challenge to find their hearts' desire. Deek screamed.

Klast nodded, waiting for Mike to tell him to kill the dumb dog soon, or perhaps advise that he not leave the beast alone. Normally, Klast paired Deek with Tasha, but he didn't want Tasha staying up all night to calm the overconfident male. He wanted her alert and smiling for tomorrow. She was going to sell whether she imprinted or not. He needed her to, which would only mean that Deek was going to get worse. Way, way worse.

"Pizza!" Mike cheered, grabbing Klast by the arm and pulling him toward the door. Klast didn't miss the glance Mike gave the trash can. The golden trophy presented to Klast for being part of this year's breeder class had never had a better use. It's belly now held one wad of chewed gum, fingernail clippings, an old bag of dog poo, and a late rent notice. Klast would sell everything he had and come home to nothing.

"You're going to have a good season," Mike added with a pat as he let go of Klast's arm to open the door.

The aroma of baked bread, sauce, and three cheeses, excited the saliva in Klast's mouth. He'd been living off trail food, wishing that he could keep a few dogs when he'd only brought the ones that needed to go. All of them. It was a very dangerous thing to do, particularly with a bunch of IB dogs that hadn't claimed a master. Most breeders didn't dare go anywhere near their adult litter without their own IB beside them, but Klast didn't have that sort of protection anymore. The only safety he had was the rule of the pack. They learned, played, and worked together until those imprinting senses kicked on. Once that happened, the real test to his training stood before him. Had he done a good enough job of connecting with the dog so it wouldn't kill him when it wanted to break away?

So far the answer was yes. Klast looked forward to and dreaded showings at the same time. Not so much for the money, even if he needed it, but because he liked to see the animals discover that first spike of love. All it took was one sniff or one sound or one look, and an IB picked a lifelong partner till death intervened. Going to an IB showing wasn't for the faint of heart. You had to go knowing you might leave with a trained guard dog who would move the elements of creation to get their way.

"He can do it. He's got it in him," Klast said about Deek.

"If you say so," Mike shrugged.

Klast scanned the side of Mike's face. Handsome enough that he got dates anywhere, Mike was currently thoughtfully biting his lower lip, sucking in his tanned skin. His black hair was short, with a few strands of sneaky white, compliments of stress instead of his age. He was a flirty thirty. Klast was fast approaching Mike's age.

"Maybe next year you could just leave him home," Mike suggested.

Absolutely not! Where Klast went, Deek had to go. He had to be watched at all times or he was bound to cause some horrible trouble, the likes of which no one had contemplated an IB doing before.

"Last time I went to the dentist and left with him Sue, he bought a remodeled sports car with her stock money."

Mike laughed like it was a joke. If only. Deek came with him to the dentist now. Klast had had the hardest time getting Sue to watch the dog when he had suffered a dislocated shoulder two years later. She'd only dog sat with a lot of begging, some in tears, and had said it was the last time she'd ever watch Deek. Sue was currently watching his breed dogs, Tuff and Morgal, but the two of them didn't hold a match to Deek's flame even if Deek was their pup. Tuff and Morgal let Klast treat them like dogs: playing fetch, going for runs, and sneaking through the woods on rabbit hunts. Deek treated Klast like an overlord on good days, or his personal servant on bad ones. Today was a bad one.

"Maybe next year you could find me a lean and clean lady to date," Klast hinted.

He'd not had a pleasant distraction in some time. Once Deek sold (this had to be his year), Klast would have a ton of free time to slip into new habits. Possibly too much free time. What was he going to do without Deek? Be free?

"As if a woman would want anyone as unkempt as you," Mike teased.

Klast laughed like he thought the sentence was funny, and then he pushed past Mike into the room with the others, hiding his hurting insides. It was better that Mike had turned him down anyway. He hadn't the money to pay for a date. No woman wanted a loser, especially one that smelled of dog breath and two-week-old body odor. Not helping matters, Deek took up wailing like he was stabbed in the toe.

"If your dog keeps all the others up tonight, I'll shoot him." Sahafi's smile beneath his turban wasn't as shielded as Klast's fake laugh had been.

Sahafi had been in the dog breeding business the longest, with a solid twenty-five years under his belt compared to Klast's seven. Any threat he said wasn't a light one. Not anymore. Deek continued to wail. Klast kept his head up still waiting for the right moment to wow the world. One day, Sahafi would respect him like Mike and Bronze did.

Klast zoned toward the food table. It squatted in the center of the rectangle rig that contained five beds and seven stools. The room attached to the small office Klast had just left where each breeder could take happy dog owners to finalize business deals. Most never used the room for that purpose. For Klast, it was his spy window. His portal to witness what tired trail dogs did on their first night in an arena. If it wasn't for Deek, he'd ditch the window and the rig and take off to see a movie.

Sahafi had sauce on the side of his bearded mouth, proving that he'd already eaten at least one slice of pizza. Bronze, who looked like an ancient Roman hero, was busy scrolling through his contacts list muttering to himself if he should sell such-and-such a dog to so-and-so. Maybe if Klast took in some of Bronze's business tips, he wouldn't be hurting this bad. He'd sell more instead of waiting for the animal to love someone. It was going to hurt selling the dogs, not knowing if they were going to good people or not. A dog never picked wrong. They knew what they wanted. They got it. Wouldn't it be nice to be a dog?

"Klast?" Imar complained. The blond glared toward Deek even if he'd only shared a rig with Klast twice.

Mike and Bronze had endured Deek's antics longer. They'd met four years ago when Deek was a puppy at an IB agility training park, aka an abandoned athletic center. All of them had broken in separately to use the field, and since that day, they had booked showings together. Klast had already stood by the rig window for the last two hours so that Deek could see where he was and not cry. The dog hadn't looked at him once, but if Klast moved away, all tarnation broke out. Deek loved to humiliate Klast on trips. He was as silent as a spy at home.

"I got it. Cater to the baby," Klast answered as he opened one of the pizza boxes, saw that it had half a pizza left, and snatched the whole box.

He grabbed the book off his bed next, ignoring the protests for taking half a box with him. Spoils! If they wanted the dog quiet, they had to give up a pizza. The door slammed as he stomped over to Deek. The waist-high pest was barking in the direction of one of Bronze's dogs, trying to make the pet rile. Bronze had put his dog in the middle of Klast's zone. Most people would be offended by that because it meant that business deals would be happening on his turf, but Klast allowed it because the dog in question was Isa. As far as IB's went, she was tame. Her response to the bout of bad talking was to yawn and pretend to sleep while Deek yapped. He rammed the side of his cage, trying to reach her.

"Shut up, you dumb thing," Klast said, irritated. "All I wanted was a quiet night—"

Deek stopped talking mid-bark. He gave Klast a wide grin and inched toward the front of his cage as if Klast would toss in a pepperoni.

"No snacks for you." Klast opened the box and ate a slice right in front of the dog. Deek licked his lips. Klast ate another.

"A quiet night on the bed over there," he continued. "Not one sitting out here beside your cage making my rump sore while I read to you and make my throat hoarse. Can't I get a break? It's not… It won't be easy on me tomorrow."

He whispered that last part, but he had to roll his eyes as his dogs perked up trying to pick apart his silent thoughts. He refused to tell them. If he voiced that he needed them to move on so he got money, every single one of his dogs would pick a new owner, even if they faked the whole connection. That's the sort of smart they were. The downside to that was once they got over the loyalty to the pack perk and had left Klast's side, they'd turn into terrors in their new home and get shot. That's not the life he wanted for them. He wasn't selling them to die.

He'd muddle through somehow. If only he hadn't that hospital bill for his shoulder, the rent settlement that was sure to come, the property taxes for a burnt-down home, the dog food, and the vet bills to get the dogs legally show worthy, he'd not be doing too poorly.

"It won't be easy because I'm tired," he added.

He'd brought eight dogs with him. Three two-year-old's from last year and the rest nearly one from this year's litter. He'd sold one dog last year. One had died of an infection. The other had been hit by a car. He couldn't keep this many dogs without an income. Well, he'd taken up the part-time job at the power plant to pay for food and shots, but he hated it. Deek had to sit in the car the whole time. It was super boring for both of them. Klast measured electrical output against expected numbers. He rotated valves or took them apart and replaced pieces. The worst part was crawling through the tight structures getting fiberglass splinters, wishing he didn't have the job he did. He'd much rather be teaching his dogs how to find a cat in a thunderstorm.

"Forget the thunderstorm," Klast mumbled as he put his back to Deek's cage and sank down to accept his fate. "It's a tornado."

Deek whined. Klast finished the pizza, glad that at least he'd have that to go on in the morning, and started to read. He remembered reading about two pages before the full stomach lulled him to sleep.

# 2

"They don't let the breeders sleep with their dog inside the hut thing?"

That was the question his brain registered as Klast woke up. It was a female voice and not particularly close. Klast hazily recalled Deek howling a few more times during the night and maybe Mike coming out to check on him because Klast had been given a pillow and blanket. Klast sat up and glanced behind him to take in Deek's state. His earlier helper was not Mike. Bronze had come to his aid. He'd moved his dog Isa into Deek's pen to shut the devil up. There they were with Isa curled up and Deek's head resting on her back.

It was a wonder that no one questioned Klast about why he'd not put Tasha in with the trouble dog. Maybe they knew. Maybe they had all gathered around to read the mail he'd tossed in the trophy trash. Afterall, he had one impressive landlord. Miles away and Klast still got the late rent notices. The mail had been handed to him first thing as he checked in. Perhaps his landlord knew exactly the situation Klast was in right now. The three months of unpaid rent was all the grace he was going to get even if he was finally at the event that would change his balances. Too little too late.

There was one other letter he had received at check-in. He hadn't bothered to look at it since it was from his mom. He expected it to be worse than the rental notice. Not in a monetary "you are doomed" sort of way, but worse in the "I waste my time on frivolous postage to send you a picture of a hedgehog hugging an orange" kind of way. That letter was still in his pocket.

He scooped up the empty pizza box beside him and tiptoed toward the office, doing his best not to wake up Deek. Everyone was going to know of his failures soon enough. The best he could do was start his day with a good attitude. That would have been easier to do if his shoulder wasn't killing him from sleeping on rock-hard ground all night. Even after the surgery, it still acted up at times.

"Most breeders have a pet of their own, and yes, they normally sleep with their bestie, but no, none of them are allowed in the hut thing," a male voice incorrectly answered the earlier female question in the corporate office.

No one was going to stop a breeder from taking a dog into the sleeping rig. That's where they took "snapped" dogs to die out of sight of the moving crowds. It was easier to put the dog down than handle the law suit if a dog caused a riot. Plenty of riots happened in the outer ring. Klast was glad to move up in the world, dragged behind the glory of Bronze and Mike. They got top positions in the inner circle of the arena where the better dogs were located. He didn't have to worry about stepping into the rig's office to find dead dogs.

The layout of the arena was simple. Cages were all along the walls circling inward with the sleeping rigs next and the office in the center of that. The talking was coming from the corporate office, which proved Klast was up early enough to file whatever desperate claims he wanted without a ton of other breeders judging him for it.

"Why?" came the inquisitive voice as he moved closer to the doorway.

"They'd fight. Those are all guard dogs. They claim random specs of space and won't back down."

The office was smaller than the rigs. It was made mostly of windows so that everyone could see in once they got past all the cages of anxiously barking, excited dogs, and the sleeping rigs. Inside was a set of two tables. One where the hosts of the event logged everything and helped with transactions, and the other table for registration. Klast could make out four people inside even if the sign said "closed."

Two men he recognized since they had welcomed him the day before. Of the two strangers, one was a man who was probably an investor, and the other was the woman who was asking questions. Klast guessed she was the investor's secretary. The door was open, so he slipped in, ignoring the looks designed to prick his conscience.

"Normal policy on if I change my mind about imprinting versus selling?" Klast asked as he reached for the stickers that he was to put on his cage doors. The selling stickers were longer and included a space for bidding. A couple of good bids and he'd be able to buy a tent to live in by his starving dogs. Starting bids early was in his best interest if that's the route he was going to go, but most of his dogs hadn't ever seen a showing before. He wanted to give them the benefit of the doubt. He wanted them happy to leave the pack instead of otherwise.

"You selling this year? I'll take the lot. You had eight?" asked the interested investor before anyone told him to scoot.

Klast gave the man a nod without looking up. He carefully counted out eight selling stickers and eight imprinting stickers, unsure which way he wanted to go. Maybe the three two-year-olds would sell. They were level-headed enough that it could work. That left four newbies to watch out for.

"He also has the devil dog," prompted a host.

"I know who he is. That devil dog can read. People swear it."

"All my dogs can read, sir," Klast answered. "Normal policy?"

"All final decisions must be made before one," came the answer. "Klast, are you sure about this?"

He gripped the stickers in his hand, hiding the selling tags between imprinting ones. If he let his dogs see them, they'd know. Tightening his grip to force himself to plop on the bidding stickers, Klast looked up at the investor to determine what he might get out of a fellow when Klast refused to make up his mind until the last minute. The man didn't look very rough, which meant that he was in this for a turnaround sale. He'd inject the batch of dogs with a chemical substance that would turn off their ability to imprint so they would be more docile, and then he'd sell the litter together as a pack of trained guard dogs to watch some rich man's house or some facility that was building something sketchy.

Klast gripped the papers tighter. There was good and bad about that. The dogs would stay together. They were a formidable force together. However, they wouldn't be able to experience the joy of imprinting. They also never would do the same thing Shadow had done and die in a kennel fight. It wouldn't matter if another dog called their human fat or whatever had happened that had killed him. They wouldn't feel loyal to only one person.

"No, I'm not sure yet. That's why I was checking."

There was no telling what an injection would do to Deek. Would he calm down? Would he get worse? He was born to imprint. He was born to defend with every fiber of his being. The desire ran so strongly through him that it turned him crazy. The poor dog was nervous about being left behind again and watching his mates move away.

"All *eight* dogs can read?" the investor asked. "I can make you an exceptional offer—"

"The demon dog is not for sale." Klast surprised himself with how harsh he was with the words. It simply came out of him. Sure, Deek scratched him and drove him crazy, and he had every intention of selling him, but they were a team all the same. He had promised to look after Deek, and he had to uphold that promise or the dog would never respect him in his way.

Besides, they'd reached "the point." While not imprinted to each other, Deek could look at him and read his mind. He knew what Klast thought without him needing to say it. Klast had proved it. Two nights ago, he'd looked at the dog and thought to him to fetch something good. Deek had come back with two rabbits that he ate once Klast gave his permission. Klast wouldn't need to feed Deek out of pocket as long as they were in the woods. He wasn't allowed to tell the dog to go hunt in certain zones, and he had to make sure that the animal realized eating pets was never allowed, but Deek could help him hold things together. He was the dog that got the misbehaving pups to regain order again. However, he was emotionally needy.

"Alright. So the other seven—"

"Will get a chance to imprint before I subject them to torture. Good day sir," Klast cut him off yet again as he turned toward the door, ready to slap up the imprint stickers before his dogs woke up to read them.

"Why were you sleeping in front of the cage?" the woman asked.

He slipped out the door, but the investor and his lackey would not shake easy.

"The devil dog gets lonely. I didn't pair him with his pal last night because if she sells, he'd get aggressive. I don't want to have to separate that."

"There are two dogs in the cage," the lady pointed out.

"There are. One of them is not mine."

"And they don't fight?" the investor asked, interested even more.

"It's Bronze's dog. We traveled up here with a group. They've been together for the past two weeks learning to get along as a travel group. They don't fight."

"Never?"

"Don't go insulting them to find out," Klast huffed.

He was lucky to be this close to the office. Lucky that his friends always got a high turnaround when it came to selling and imprinting both. The really good breeders were in this inner circle where Klast was placed. The fair ones ran the loop at the middle and the newbies sat at the edge of the arena. Going off his sales, he'd never make it here, but Bronze, Mike, Sahafi, and Imar were seasoned professionals. They had bragged him up here. To be honest, Klast's dogs did compare to theirs. In some aspects, they were far better.

Klast started with Volt. The dog was still sleeping in his funny way with his brown legs stretched out and draped across a pillow. Klast had brought that pillow a long way. Volt loved that thing. Peeling off the back of the sticker on the imprinting sheet, Klast put it on the cage door and then walked over to Tasha.

The investor pulled out a pen and scribbled on the top of the sheet.

"Hey! That's an imprinting sheet. You can't write all over it when you feel like it!"

Klast shoved the man out of the way to read the message. "Will buy - Lawrence Petra."

"You can't—"

"I just did," Lawrence replied as he capped his pen and tried to look intimidating.

The talking woke Volt up. He scrambled off his pillow and came to sniff at the barrier of the cage. From the pushy manner of Lawrence, Klast half expected Volt to snarl and wake up the entire arena by barking threats, but he didn't. He barked out a short "morning" grunt and then sat down, waiting for breakfast to show up. Volt was one of the two-year-olds. He'd been through this before and knew what to expect. Klast would get exceptional behavior out of him today. He gave Volt a wink for his good behavior.

"If you already know you might change your mind, then it means you need the money. I'd make you an acceptable offer. I've only ever heard good things about you and your dogs, Klast Burma. I'd see they are taken care of. Not abused. That's a promise. I'm not trying to swindle you. Only help."

The smooth-talking alien. Klast stepped around him, flinching as he accidentally bumped into the secretary on the way to Tasha's cage so he could plop up the next sticker. Klast wanted to punch Lawrence Petra. He wanted to unleash Volt and tell the dog to chase the guy off. Volt would do it without question. So would Tasha, for that matter. All his dogs would except for Deek. Deek contemplated every command and action as if each one had a lasting consequence and it was up to him to decide if he was going to follow the order or not.

"I understand that the bond between breeder and animal is a strong one. You want what's best for them and I respect that."

"Why are you trying to buy guard dogs?" Klast asked, putting up the sticker and watching as Tasha woke up. She shook her snowy head speckled with gray and smiled up at him. Then she tilted her head to the side as if she was trying to figure out his thoughts around his tense posture.

"Sleep well, Angel?" he asked her. She nodded and then glanced toward Deek. "You let me worry about him. You don't need to." Another nod. He was going to miss her. He turned away before she could spot him tearing up. As he did, he found himself looking at the secretary lady for what felt like the first time.

Gorgeous. Absolutely gorgeous. Cinnamon sideswept bangs joined into the longer layers of her hair which cascaded past her shoulders and ended in a natural wave. A few of the red-toned strands brushed against the rose tint of her lips and across her pointed chin. Arched eyebrows rose above eyes so light brown they were the color of cashews. If those were the windows to the soul, he'd better stop right there, because they were exquisite. Looking at her was like looking at Deek. It made Klast feel sad and happy at the same time, like the way a love song reminded him of a good experience that would never come again but was the best while it lasted.

"I'm Peyton," the woman introduced.

"Pleasure," Klast replied.

He stepped around her yet again and slapped up more stickers. The corner of his eye told him he'd already lost the battle with Deek. The dog was up. A wiser man would have said something more to Peyton like perhaps "want to see a dog do a trick?" or "would you like to get dinner?" He hadn't the time for either of those things right now. Not if the scheming dog was awake. And he was scheming. Anything else and Deek would have barked. He'd woken up the arena every year he'd been here. An early riser who never slept and argued with any dogs that passed him. He earned his nickname well. The guards knew him on sight and groaned when Klast had Deek at his heel.

Klast rubbed on the other stickers, saving Deek for last. The battle was going to come. Sure enough, when Klast raised his hand to put on a sticker, the growls started up. Isa pretended not to notice by looking up into the air. Ignoring the behavior never changed it.

"It's a sticker, mate," Klast said.

Deek lunged at the edge of the cage and sprayed acid. It didn't come out of his mouth but his belly, and was the worst insult a dog put toward a human. The yellow-green liquid wouldn't kill anything, but it stung like crazy. Klast had expected something mean, but not quite *that*. He barely had time to pull the secretary lady out of the way. Lucky for him, Lawrence was still writing all over the imprinting papers so he'd not been in any danger.

"Darn you, devil!" Klast shouted. "I have to clean that up. I don't have the time this morning for your antics. If you want to express your dissatisfaction, you need to find a different way because—"

He stopped talking to pour the rest of his angry tirade at Deek silently. There was no use alerting all the dogs to his incredibly sour mood. Staring

Deek directly in the eye, he gave his order. No acid. Klast couldn't afford to pay to fix the cage. If Deek did that again, Klast would have to shoot him.

It was the first time he'd ever given that threat to a dog, even if he'd been thinking it the entire way over here. If Deek couldn't imprint, and Klast couldn't stand to let him go, the dog would have to die. Deek sank away from the edge of the cage, right into the corner, where he whimpered and cried. Isa moved toward the door and whined next to be let out.

"Did you soul-link with him?" Peyton asked, carefully avoiding the acid as she got closer. Klast grabbed her arm and dragged her backward again.

"Do not get close to that. He's mad at me."

"Is he yours?"

"He's nobodies," Klast sighed, earning a round of howls from the back of the cage. Deek even snarled. He was a bad-tempered thing at these events. At least he'd never broken out of his confines and hurt anyone. Already Klast could make out the arena guards stepping closer, picking out the troublemakers. They were armed with tranquilizer guns and they'd shoot the fur off his dog if Deek upset their delicate military training.

"But did your soul talk to him with your thoughts?" Peyton asked again.

Deek howled louder.

"Can you stop?!"

He got louder. Other dogs around the arena, not the ones who had traveled with the loud-mouth thankfully, woke up and yelled back. Great way to start the morning. Everyone was up now and they'd be glaring at Klast for bringing a bad dog.

"They'll shoot you, you know!" Klast hissed at him torn between fetching sand for the acid before it melted a hole and staying near the frightened dog so he'd be quiet.

Deek nodded at him and then offered another grin, as if to say, "You told me to express my displeasure."

"So I did. Then I told you to stop."

"Isa wants out," Deek barked the words at him.

Klast rolled his eyes and then glared again at Deek to behave before he trudged over to the sand barrels. The barrels were not close. Most of the well-trained inner circle dogs knew better than to spray acid around here. Deek knew better. That was the height of rude. The ultimate rejection to Klast being in charge of him, and it pained Klast to have those thoughts as he shoveled up sand, doing his best to ignore the mean comments from trainers who were stumbling out of bed.

By the time he returned, Bronze, Mike, Sahafi, and Imar were feeding their dogs breakfast. One of them had plopped down a thin layer of safety sand and put up a caution sign. Isa had been let out of the cage. It was remarkable that Deek would turn a blind eye to the open door when he begged for freedom, but if there was anything regarding doggy order, he was the first one to uphold the rules. Isa wasn't where she belonged, so off she went. Nice and easy. Too bad he didn't hold the same standards to his behavior.

Lawrence and Peyton hadn't spooked yet. Peyton was staring at the acid as if she wanted to put it into a test tube and discover its chemical composition. Lawrence was following Bronze around and asking him questions. About Klast's dogs.

"How can they be humans in a different form?" Lawrence asked, eyeing Hero.

"Ask Klast. I have no idea what training methods he uses, but his dogs are little humans. Brilliant, the lot of them. I've not met a single one I didn't like yet, and that's saying something."

Klast snorted. Bronze loved every IB dog he came across. He was so full of talk he could float to the moon on it.

"You seem like a reasonable man. Maybe you can talk Klast into selling the litter."

"Not with that approach," Bronze answered. "He's got two litters. Three if you count the demon dog."

"What's wrong with that one?"

"Nothing," Bronze lied as he glanced at Klast and the bucket of sand.

Klast tossed it down and stirred it around with the shovel, letting it soak up the mess. It was Bronze's easy nature toward trouble that had first impressed Klast. He rode on top of every blaze without getting burned. Klast took in a deep breath trying to force the calm into his jittery body.

"That dog is the smartest dog I've ever met. It takes a really strong personality to train intelligence like that when it doesn't want to listen to you because you're not imprint mates. I tell you that without Klast, that animal's full potential would have been ruined years ago. Klast is the best thing that ever happened to that dog. Regardless of the fight, Klast always handles the situation correctly. Always. He's a better man than many of us and the best trainer there ever was. I'm not making that up."

"What's his name?" Peyton asked.

"And yet he might sell him." Lawrence pointed to the bidding stickers that Klast had dropped in his haste to get the secretary lady out of the way. Bronze took one look at the notices and pretended he wasn't concerned.

"Nah," he said. "That dog needs to imprint."

"What are you selling for?" Mike asked Klast, stepping away from his dog cages to get closer to the conversation.

First bidder of the morning. Klast hadn't expected it to be on him. He wasn't ready, and neither were his dogs. All of them looked and smelled like they'd not done anything but hike for two weeks.

"Klast needs the money," Imar called down the rows. "His house burnt down and he can't afford to pay for a missing house and an apartment. Haven't you seen him starving himself so he could feed the dogs instead?"

"Shut up!" Klast howled at him.

How did he know that?! He hadn't told anyone. One rent notice in the trophy trash wasn't enough to tell Imar that he was starving. No. It was the actual starving that did that part. Imar had no doubt looked up a report of the burnt-down house. It had been in local papers, so if anyone felt up to snooping, there it was.

"That's why he ate half a pizza last night," Imar continued.

The man glanced down at his trained, imprinted dog by his side before meeting Klast's gaze. Coward. Imar wasn't brave enough to talk unless he had his dog there to ward off potential anger. Thinking of which, Klast didn't have anger issues. Why was he shouting at everyone? He needed to chill. Mellow down. Fizzle out. Gather his inner calm. Some demon was lurking at the edge of his senses waking up, ready to snap its unwanted jaws.

"I'm fine," Klast insisted, glancing over the cages of his dogs.

What was it? There was a sense of impending doom hovering over his head. Normally he could shake such a thing easy enough, but today? Something was coming his way, and he'd better be ready for it. His instincts were all in tangled knots, and Deek wasn't helping him any.

Klast looked at Imar's dusty gray dog, Trog, who eyed him with intention. Klast wasn't about to engage with a protective IB. At least the dogs Klast had brought looked back at him unconcerned as if everything was normal. Why wouldn't they? They followed the mentality of the pack still. Sacrifices were made for the safety of the whole. If Klast chose to starve, they would let him.

Only Deek didn't look back at him. Deek who had to know all of this already and was screaming, all the same, making his life worse. Deek realized that a dead human would mean the rest of the pack didn't get food anymore. They'd be sold and injected and lose their nature-born right to imprint. At least the rest of them would. Deek would never let anyone do that to him. He'd rather die fighting, and that's how he was going to go. Unless it was Klast who killed him. Deek would stand there and watch if it was Klast who...

"How did your house burn down?" Mike looked aghast. "That was the renovated one with the gorgeous pillars and sweeping patio, right?"

"Lightning hit an electrical line and it zipped right into the house and blew it up. We'd just stepped outside to train in the mud when it happened. So we're all fine. Thanks."

For now. Tomorrow they wouldn't be. Some of the dogs would be gone. Each litter he'd gone through seemed smarter and more amazing than the last. This group of dogs was his absolute favorite. Klast busied himself with scooping up the acid-soaked sand amid the exclamations of surprise.

Lightning striking the house through a wire was unreal, they claimed. Surely there could be something salvageable or some funding available to rebuild such a previously historical house.

The sand was heavy against Klast's sore muscles. He kept scooping.

"What's his name?" Peyton asked again.

Klast glanced up to find her staring at Deek. The dog was still looking away from everyone in an effort to not state his mind, but he was panting with the effort as if he fought a large internal battle he couldn't put to rest. His brown paws were planted firmly on the floor, his white and gray fur was turning fluffy, and his black ears were down. If Klast had to take a guess, Deek was thinking on repeat, "I'm doing my best not to make Klast mad."

"You never ask that," Mike answered her. "The name of an imprinted bodyguard-dog holds power. You know its name and you're one step closer to getting the animal to listen to what you say. Since these creatures will jump out of a plane if you tell them to, we don't pass around names. At least not until they're imprinted, because then they wouldn't listen to you anyway."

"A cheerful and exuberant morning to you all!" One of the host's voices came over the loudspeaker. "Doors open in half an hour to excite the crowd that has gathered outside. I know it's earlier than planned, but seeing as how we're all up…"

He paused and let the crowd outside the office chuckle. Klast grit his teeth. They were making fun of him and Deek for waking everyone up with barking for another year in a row.

"We're in for a real treat today. Five squadrons vying to get inside. Six hundred pre-bought tickets. Crowds lining up past five blocks already waiting to purchase entrance. It's a hot market today. Feed those dogs and get ready."

Ugh. He hadn't fed his dogs. He hadn't washed them either or brushed their coats. It wouldn't matter so much if they were all imprinting, but for those potential buyers, the animals had to look good. Plus, it was a kindness to those who did imprint that they take home a well-cared-for dog.

"Five squadrons?" Mike whistled. "They don't usually send more than two. Must be a high demand for dog-related training."

It was bitter-sweet news. There was a greater chance that the dogs would find someone they liked. Someone who could continue to teach them so they wouldn't get bored and go stir-crazy. Someone who would love them back. However, there was a higher chance the dog could die.

Oh, what use was it going in circles like this? Klast wasn't in the military and his dog had died. Maybe if he had been smarter, he'd have known better than to let Shadow into the same kennel as Morgal and Tuff. He never told anyone who had killed his dog. Klast's breed dogs had killed him. He never left his breed dogs alone anymore with dogs they had not given birth to themselves. The desire to be in charge was too strong.

"Shake some of that dirt off," Klast ordered. "No time for a bath, but you're all getting a brushing, even you, grumpy pants." He directed the comment to Deek as he finished cleaning up the sand and wheeled the bucket away.

Three more slaps and he'd finished hanging his stickers; although he left Deek's cage alone. Behind him, he heard Peyton giggle. When he turned to look, he grinned too. All of his dogs were jumping around on their hind legs, waggling to shake off dirt.

"You forgot the dance steps and the forward flips."

Four of his dogs started to solo waltz. Two did a flip. Deek leapt into the air and performed a double backflip. Klast smiled. That was his dog. His beautiful, incredible, amazing dog. Showing off only when it suited him. It had taken two years to get the move right. Even then, Deek didn't often use it. It scared him, but since he was scared about everything right now, maybe he thought it appropriate.

"When you change your mind and are ready to sell, call me," Lawrence insisted as he thrust a business card into Klast's hand.

The card got shoved into Klast's pocket right beside the letter from his mom that he'd not opened. Later. He had too much to do right now. Half an hour wasn't enough time to get all the dogs fed and brushed. Lawrence turned to collect his secretary lady friend, or whatever she was, only to slam his mouth shut and shiver. Klast looked at Peyton to figure out why. There wasn't anything wrong with her that he could see. Nothing that suggested cruelty or malice. Now that the sand and acid were out of the way, Peyton pressed up against Deek's cage, watching him sidestep. Klast had to hand it to him. Deek was a charmer when there was a woman to impress.

"That has to be where I'm failing," Klast mused to himself.

Women! He hardly talked to women, and Deek rather loved them. What that dog needed was a woman keeper. Finding one would be a challenge, but maybe today would be his lucky break with the extra big crowd. Klast would have to keep his eyes open, or take the easy path and engage with the other fellows.

"Yo, Bronze!" Klast exclaimed, skipping to him and taking the pooper scoop that he'd just finished with. "You know lady people."

Already Bronze was laughing at him for his awkwardness. Bronze had a wife and Mike had far too many girlfriends. Klast was better with dogs, but he was plowing onward. For Deek.

"Women. The devil likes them. Female dogs. Female humans. Can you do me a favor and keep an eye out for the female type of life form that might tickle the demon's fancy?"

"You're an embarrassment," Bronze teased before glancing over at the investor and shrugging.

Lawrence was still too busy studying Peyton with a frown on his face to reveal what he thought about this new reverse on Klast's abilities. Once again, Klast looked the interesting woman over, noticing how her black slacks had a dirty handprint on the right leg. Her shoes had a white stripe circling the gray fabric, which she had recolored orange like a teen. The shoes didn't match her cream undershirt and business-like collared blue shirt. Maybe she wasn't a secretary, but a curious sister or something.

"You sir, are the pro I aspire to be," Klast answered Bronze. He moved to take care of Deek first before the dog lost his good mood.

"Scoot, scoot." Klast pushed Peyton to the side as he reached for the key. A chill ran through him that he ignored in favor of being fast.

"He'll hurt you!" Peyton wailed, grabbing onto his arm as he clicked the lock.

Super weird. The girl had been inside for at least half an hour already and her hands were as cold as a glacier. He'd not noticed when he pulled her out of the way earlier. Maybe Lawrence was after a group of dogs to protect himself from the very women he'd brought with him, because jeepers she was cold! Klast glanced up at the hand and arm that were touching him, squinting when he came across a blue mark poking out from beneath Peyton's sleeve. It was only the tip of a point, but he knew exactly what it was. The tip was the edge of the triangle for death. Above that would be a tilted square representing the physical form, or body, that housed a swirl representing the soul. Two dots within the body cried out for power—the power over death.

Peyton quickly pulled away from him when he noticed, and looked at him wide-eyed as if he'd say something about it. Klast kept his expression neutral in the face of his enemy's lackey. It was a shame that such a stunning person had nearly died. A downright shame.

"The dog won't hurt me," Klast smiled at her. "He might not like the idea of being labeled for the show, but even he understands that he's a filthy monster and needs a good brushing. Pardon our funky smell. We were hiking for two weeks without bathing. Hopefully, I find the time to wash the dogs before they go storming off with newly infatuated hearts."

Peyton shook her head at him as he slipped into the cage and kicked it shut behind him. Deek sat down right away, submitting to looking more appealing.

"Good boy. Who's my good boy?" Klast praised. "Most gorgeous dog there ever was."

Deek sneezed at him. When he was like this, Klast never worried about Deek's behavior. Feeding and cleaning were not things he fought for control over. It was doing things contrary to what he thought should happen that got him riled because he couldn't always say what was on his mind.

"Question," Deek barked as he waited.

"What's the question?" Klast asked.

"Pretty. Thought. Feeling." The dog struggled to turn barks into words.

"What?" Klast wasn't making sense of the jumbled attempt to communicate. "Want to attempt saying that to my head?" He whispered as he looked in the dog's eyes and waited.

Soul talking wasn't anything that happened unless the soul was open to the experience. It had been six years since Klast had a dog's thoughts directed into his soul for his understanding. Six years since Shadow had died. The soul usually resisted the infiltration, but if there was any dog that was going to figure out how to get around a block in his way it would be Deek. If there ever was a moment that Klast needed a fast answer it was now. Things still felt wrong.

*"You think she's pretty."*

Oh. Heat rose to Klast's cheeks as he glanced once more toward Peyton, still watching the show. That's how it was going to be all day long. People he didn't know would press in around him to chat about his dogs. Klast grinned both because of Peyton, and because Deek had done the impossible. They were not an imprinted pair, but Deek was talking to him through his soul!

"Maybe," Klast answered, ruffling Deek's black ears for the fun of it. The dog hated that. Deek sent him a playful growl and rammed his head into Klast's arm.

"Question!" Deek barked out again as Klast moved to brush his side. His talking was usually muted and quiet, but he was getting riled and loud again. Klast brushed faster.

"What?"

"Pretty. You. Girl. Girl. You. No. Question!"

"Don't make too much out of it," Klast insisted.

It wasn't like he was going to ask the cold-fingered girl out on a date. He found lots of girls to be pretty, but timing was everything in relationships. Besides, if he asked her out, he'd have to face Lawrence trying to buy his lot of dogs again. Not to mention that Peyton didn't have her own life anymore. Everything she did was for the sake of science. She had no free will to agree to a date. Why did the enemy always get the good ones?

"Question! Question! Question! Help!" Deek demanded as Klast rose.

"Look, I've got to get eight dogs brushed and fed in under half an hour. I don't have the time for questions. If you can find a way to ask so I understand, then fine, but I'm a bit busy right now."

"Blue!" Deek barked as Klast closed the cage. What did blue have to do with anything? Klast sent Deek a shrug. "Blue. Pretty. Feeling. Klast!"

"In a minute," Klast answered with a shake of his head. He stepped around Peyton right as Lawrence got over his shivers and waved at her to follow him. Klast felt a peculiar chill sweep across the back of his neck.

# 3

"What do you think?" Lawrence asked Peyton as they stepped out of the way of the scrambling dog breeders so they could tend to their charges.

"He won't sell them. He'd rather starve himself first," Peyton pouted. "It would be better to find some other dogs that are not in the inner circle."

"I only want the good dogs. Not the ones that will turn on me," Lawrence snorted at her. "Klast's dogs are excellent. Mad and they don't turn on him even if they don't think he's in charge. They find creative ways to express their views. That's what everyone says about his dogs. I didn't go through all the trouble to hunt down a recommendation only to hear you tell me to look someplace else because it's too good. That dog he sold last year is the best in its field, even if I find his owner to be mediocre. We need a dog like that."

Peyton looked back at the one barking dog in the line of cages in her sight. The silver coat looked exceptionally creamy now that it was brushed out like a field of wild grass. The black ears accented the dog's sad, brown eyes. The creature had brown on its paws, traveling halfway up each of its legs like it was wearing socks. Adorable. It nearly broke her heart to see him hopping around demanding help with forming a question.

She had no idea what the dog was saying, but it impressed her all the same that Klast seemed to know. Or tried to know. The way he tended to the animals proved that he cared, and that was what held them all together. It wasn't a special training technique. It was love. He genuinely cared and they knew it. He wasn't about to sell them without a struggle. She admired that while it made her steaming mad at the same time.

She wanted his dog. The barking one. Yes, she understood that the animal was deadly. It could kill her and shoot her with acid. The dog was so impressive that even his anger took the form of careful calculation. From the puddle size of the acid spray, it never would have hit her or Klast. She'd feared Klast's retribution more.

Klast's absolute tenderness against the threat astounded her. No abuse. Only a reprimand and an explanation for why. Peyton was instantly drawn to his tolerant nature, and had been since she first saw him sleeping in front of the dog cage. Something about Klast Burma made her want to figure him out in an excited, sick-to-her-stomach sort of way.

She had nearly vomited when Klast took one look at her and decided she wasn't good enough for his dog. There was nothing wrong with her! Well, apart from the dying part. If she didn't get back across the doomscape at the end of the month to retrieve what she'd dropped there, she was going to die. Since imprinted dogs died when their human did, no one was going to sell her a dog to watch it die at the end of the month with her. But Klast didn't know what she needed to reach. With the dog, she could live. It could protect her. She wanted that unmatched, intelligent, silver dog.

Could the animal be a Prince or a Calvin? It looked older than the other show dogs, apart from the breeder's animals. Each breeder had his or her imprinted dog hooked on their belt. For some reason, Peyton couldn't see Klast hooking a dog to him like that. No. He'd strap the leash to his wrist or hand. It was a more breakable appendage, but easier to release. He looked trusting like that.

"Why doesn't Klast have a lead dog?" Peyton asked.

"It died, according to sources," Lawrence shrugged. "Most imprinted people don't come back from that. An imprinted connection isn't something to be taken lightly. You live and die with your dog. Rumor has it that Klast was found several times in dangerous places right after he lost his dog. Standing on a train track, staring into the water over a bridge, eyeing electrical wires. Watching him carry on afterward is rather hard to do. No one is sure why he didn't decide to die with his dog, but my source informed me that no one tried to persuade him either way."

Peyton rolled her eyes. That was a sad thing to know that no one was going to tell you to stick around because they would miss you despite a dog dying. Watching Klast carry on was super *easy* to do. He glided through the routines praising his animals and leaving them with large sloppy smiles on their faces just in time for the first impatient wave of people to crowd the cages.

"Does he have a family?"

"Mom, dad, a brother in the army, a sister who flies planes. I think I heard he had a pet goat for a time. Nothing too unusual."

He sounded normal, but he wasn't. She could see the same thing that Bronze had been going on about. Klast treated his dogs like they were all a little human. He expected them to be brilliant. Snippets of his words filtered her way through the scooting crowd.

"It's just like we talked about. They're here to look. You are not obligated to do anything or like anyone. If you do think someone is special though, just let me know. I'll take care of you, I will. We'll make sure all those other humans know what you're thinking. You simply tell me and I'll put it into words for you."

"You going to stand here all day?" Peyton asked, eyeing Lawrence with annoyance.

She didn't need him to babysit her. She hated the way he looked at her when she wasn't "looking." Peyton had known Lawrence for only a few days, but already she could tell they would never be friends. He had been a recommendation to her from her best friend Cindy. When all others stopped talking to her because of what happened, Cindy held strong against the rules. She'd come through again sending Peyton to Lawrence, who suggested getting an IB dog to save Peyton's life. The problem with Lawrence was that he treated her like she was already dead. She would *not* die. She was going to live. With that dog. The one that was still barking, demanding an answer to his question.

"How do I get the dog?"

The barking dog wouldn't run away from a tough fight. Since Peyton had been to the doomscape before, the demons there now had her scent. If she went back, she was done for. Cue defender dog. A pack of dogs would be great, but if not, she wanted that one.

"Steal it," Lawrence muttered. "And no, I'm not going to stand here all day. I'm going to find the refreshment stand and search for a backup option.

I'll come back just before one o'clock to see if he's changed those tags. You coming?"

"I'm going to stand here all day."

She was going to watch Klast. There had to be some sort of weakness she could pick out about him that would make him give her a dog. Klast made his way back to the barker's cage, whispered it something, and the dog lay on the floor twitching its tail impatiently as its eyes swept back and forth following everywhere Klast went. The dog watched him like they were an imprinted pair, even if they weren't. They thought to each other like they were too. Taking that thing wouldn't come easy even if did come down to stealing. The dog clearly liked him.

Peyton scanned both ways for the flow of traffic and then merged into it, coming to a stop beside a group of men in uniform that were looking at a different one of Klast's dogs. This one had a red coat with black legs and a striped tail making it look similar to a red panda. They were snickering about that, questioning if it was a dog or bear. The dog ignored them, staring across the way to where Klast was talking with another person, all attention riveted on its leader. All his dogs were doing that, watching him walk up and down except for the fluffy brown one that stood on all fours, snout in the air.

"Going to be a long day for you," Peyton muttered to the dog before her.

Searching dog eyes flashed against her own causing her step back as the panda dog gave her a soft bark before returning it's attention to Klast. What did that mean? She looked at the nearby soldiers. They didn't even notice. Surely someone else had to have seen Klast's dog talk to her. A further scan had her eyes latching onto a man who seemed to know what he was looking for. He wore a hat pulled low over his head, the kind that usually proved he was hiding a bald spot or scar. He'd come with a leash attached to his belt all rolled up as if he expected to imprint or buy a dog today.

"Hey," Peyton sidled up to him. "Can you tell what a dog says when it barks?"

"You were looking at the Burma dogs? Nope. No one can understand those dogs except for him unless they imprint and then people swear the things they hear their dog say is a miracle."

"A miracle how?"

"Complete sentences. Trigonometry. That sort of thing. Who teaches a dog trigonometry in the first year of its life? Apparently, Mr. Burma. Hold on. Any minute now. I want to see this."

"What?" Peyton asked, trying to match the gaze of the prepared man.

"That dog. See how it's no longer looking at Mr. Burma?"

"The brown one that stopped staring at Klast? Yeah."

"It imprinted. That means it won't listen to him anymore. Won't listen to anyone but the person it set its heart on. Problem is that it imprinted by a scent so the person it wants, it can't see. When a normal dog does that, it howls like its heart is going to break and wails and wails. Brings a powerful rush of people hoping that the dog wants *them*. Makes a huge mess. Fights break out more often than not, except around the pens of Mr. Burma. There's a reason people pay extra to get cages by his. Something about him gets all the dogs to not act like heart-stricken idiots. Not that he's noticed, I hear. He only looks at his own. If you see a fight start up, don't linger. The crowds are thick today. You could die."

"He holds back crowds by magic?" Peyton guessed. She chose to ignore the dying comment. She refused to plop over in a crowd that was trying to reach a caged dog. She had larger problems than that.

The brown dog took its snout out of the air, looked at Klast, and growled. It looked at the crowd, whimpered, and then barked. Klast pushed away from his current conversation so fast that Peyton nearly missed it. She didn't see him move, but she heard his words ringing through the air like a spark of joy had jolted down her cold, dying heart.

"No way! That's amazing! I'm so excited for you! So, so excited! What are you waiting for? Grab the leash. Let's go. Let's go find it!"

It felt like he was talking directly to her. Chills ran down her legs at the bound of joy that couldn't be squashed. *If only*. When Peyton's eyes caught sight of where Klast had teleported to, she found his face beaming. She couldn't look. It hurt too much. She wanted *him* to look at her like that. Instead of watch him, she looked at the crowds. The people parted out of his way. The dogs perked up, all except for the demon dog, who growled. Klast shot the growler a demanding look so chilling that Peyton felt that too. Had he threatened her dog??

The dog turned his face away from Klast to look at her instead. Peyton inhaled. Demon dog smiled as if Klast hadn't thought anything mean when she knew the truth. Note to self: the dog she liked was a liar. The animal blinked to clear her from his vision and returned to watching Klast after making one vain attempt to converse.

"I will get to your question later," Klast promised as he finished reaching the brown dog.

The hallway in which they all stood had gone quiet. Whoever she had spoken with was right. Klast didn't notice. He was super focused on his dog that wasn't his anymore. It had obediently scooped up a leash that was sitting inside the pen and was wagging its tail, looking at Klast like they were still best buddies instead of hasty enemies. Peyton had been hesitant to come to the IB showing because she'd heard bad things about open cages and trained killer dogs tearing apart everything in their way to get what they wanted. It made the news sometimes. Man pays ten thousand in damages for run-a-way imprinted dog.

Klast didn't seem to have read any of those headlines. He hummed as he unlocked the cage and grabbed the offered leash. His dog didn't bolt to reach what it wanted. It waited for him.

"I hope it's cute for your sake because I'm going to find it be super ugly," Klast teased. The brown dog laughed. "Oh, yup. It's going to be a weird one with a peg leg and seven warts. Maybe twenty."

It barked something at him that made him laugh as he finished connecting the leash. Then he casually led the dog out of the cage with one stern command. "No pulling."

That was the only command he gave. It caused a few people nearby to wince as if the dog would turn around and bite Klast's face for telling it what to do. It didn't. No pulling didn't include no jumping, because the excited dog jumped into the air a few times and howled a call so chilling that the next few rows of cages went quiet too. That's when she heard the running feet. People began stampeding to find the calling dog, but Klast was already off with it racing through the crowds himself, causing people to come to stumbling halts as they realized they had missed their chance and the dog wasn't looking for them.

"He put the leash in the death hold."

After the hallway was so quiet, the voice felt loud against her ears. Peyton glanced over, unable to keep her eyes on Klast and his excited hunting dog through the crowds. The speaker was another breeder who paid extra to lodge his dogs near Klast's. Blond with a gray dog brushing his side, he looked particularly annoyed.

"Yup," the breeder who'd introduced himself as Bronze earlier answered. "You know he only doubled the leash on Tasha because of demon dog. Tasha would never rip Klast's arms off. Horrible that she was the first to go, but that's Klast for you. He must have known it somehow. He'd already kept them apart."

As one, the two speakers both looked at the silvery dog Peyton wanted even more. What was wrong with him? Why did everyone keep calling him a demon? Why had those guys revealed the brown imprinted dog's name before Tasha had found the person she was looking for? It seemed a few minutes too early to get a loose tongue.

"Well, we won't be getting any sleep tonight," a third dog breeder stepped up to the other two. He was the tanned and dark-haired fellow. She was pretty sure that Bronze had called him Mike. Bronze and the other breeder groaned and then turned away from Klast's cages to focus on their own. That was until her dog started growling and hissing and banging into the side of his cage.

Peyton couldn't move. She couldn't understand it. Once adorably fluffy, the animal now looked like a demon. Teeth bared, spit sizzling, all warmth from his earlier dancing drained away. He had turned into a destructing force that was bent on destroying the metal cage that held him. He was doing a good job at it too. It was starting to dent, and they had assured her that those cages couldn't do that when she first arrived.

People backed away from the cage as fast as they could go, only stopping when Klast reappeared, oblivious to the fact that he was being chased by a confused soldier barely holding onto a leash that led to Tasha. That made even more people back away as if the unrestrained dog would leap after them for some unknown vengeance, but the brown animal was too happy strutting to be thinking anything of the sort. If demon dog was a bodyguard-dog in a rage, Tasha clearly wasn't.

"Bud!" Klast called out to her dog. "I know, dude, but she's so happy. All love is like that. You enjoy it while you have it and muddle through after it breaks your heart. You can do it. I *believe* in you."

Her dog howled back at him and stopped hitting the cage. Peyton shut her eyes. It wasn't her dog. It wasn't. She had to stop thinking of the creature like he was beautiful and see him for what he was. He was incredibly volatile. A beast of power that was going to crush her apart for the smallest desire to touch his perfectly silky, smoky fur.

"Are you even all that mad about Tasha, or are you mad about me getting out of sight again?"

It barked. He answered.

"But I don't understand your question. I told you I don't have the time to figure it out right now. You're going to have to—"

Another dog howled. A brown and white one that wasn't one of Klast's. Klast still looked at it anyway and smiled. "Bravo!" he cheered at the dog. "You make me want to be you, kid. All sure of yourself. You're amazing!"

"Let's talk," the breeder singled out the person the dog was looking at with a smile that verged on relief. "You got yourself a dog, sir."

Klast in the meantime had turned back to his barking, upset, question-forming dog, only to be distracted again when Tasha and her soldier tapped him on the arm, not at all scared about the newly dented metal a foot away from them.

"I didn't come here to get a dog. I can't afford it."

"The military will pay for it," Klast answered, glancing down at Tasha with clenched teeth as if he wanted to chew her out for picking a person who couldn't pay.

"Sorry, but I'm not active right now. I only came to support my friend who wanted to go see the dogs. I never expected this."

"You don't step into an arena without being prepared," Klast said in a voice that verged on not sounding as upset as he was.

"You'll have to take her back." The soldier held the leash out to Klast. Klast looked at it with blinking eyes before he looked down at Tasha.

"I knew you'd pull a number on me," he told her. "Just knew it. Listen." Klast put an arm around the soldier's shoulders. "She won't listen to me anymore. You came unprepared, but you won't leave that way. We'll go over everything you need to know and discuss payment options later. You'll be able to afford it. I promise."

"I can't," came the strained reply.

"You can," Klast smiled at the man. "You're going to start right here." He passed the guy a business card. "Watch all these training videos. Go over the commands with her. You can use her cage for an out-of-the-way place to practice." He pointed to where Tasha had just been. "Whatever you're going through, she's going to get you through it. She knows what it is, and she's got what it takes to pull you out of it."

"How can a dog—?"

"She totally knows," Klast insisted as if there was nothing to debate about. "Tell her to follow you. Off you go." With that, Klast turned away from them to chase down his breeder pal named Mike and ask him about finance options for inactive military men.

That earned the soldier a lot of jealous looks. He stood there unsure of what to do. Then he shook his head and dropped the leash, which was literally against the rules. They all had to sign a set of fifteen rules when they came in. No letting go of a leash was in the top five. That was one of the worst dangers of all, but his new dog didn't do anything wild about it. She didn't even chase the soldier when he walked off on her. She sat there looking at him with a tilted head and then she lay down and waited. When Klast noticed the dog sitting there alone, he rolled his eyes, told her she was a good girl, and put up caution signs, so everyone walked around her.

Peyton didn't want to walk around Tasha. She wanted to walk up to her and pet her, but when she took a few steps forward wanting to comfort the dog that got left behind, the animal gave her such a jarring look that she didn't dare. It was only a dog. The animal couldn't read her mind, right? And she only wanted to help! She wanted to make sure that the dog wasn't left to be brokenhearted, because Peyton knew all about abandonment. Left to decide her own fate. Left to die.

She couldn't let that happen. Peyton gave Tasha a nod and then strode out into the crowds, determined to find that soldier and bring him back for her. Behind her, she heard Klast going off again in rowdy praise. "You're going to have so much fun with this! Let's go find that sound! I hope it's the sound of intense burping followed by an ouch of a tongue biting. Gotta love a sound like that one."

He was ridiculous. She could picture it already. He'd go to his dog, get the leash, and hunt down a love match that would never be for him. He'd be left behind. Always left behind. On the thought, a few tears came to her eyes. Her demon dog howled. It was at that moment that she understood why he howled. He saw it too. The inner pain Klast had to feel every time he gave away a dog. There he was, looking happy to be left behind. Those who couldn't stand the thought of being left behind, or rather leaving him behind to deal with that all alone, felt like wailing.

Peyton shook her head. What was she *thinking*? She didn't know that much about the man. She couldn't prove anything. All her thoughts were speculation, but she walked faster, determined to not let the soldier get too far. If she couldn't make anything useful out of her own life at the moment, then the least she could do was help to make something good for somebody else. Maybe that's how Klast thought.

She was losing it. She didn't need to think this much about the man. All she wanted from him was the dog. She already had something to help him if she could put a better spin on it than Lawrence did. She could pay him. Get his house back together or something. She had company money that she could fall back on. If that failed, there was always a loan, and what did it matter if she didn't pay it off because she died? However, Klast didn't really want the money. She needed something else. Something he wouldn't want to refuse, but what?

It was impossible to not scan the crowds as she went and wonder if any of the people who walked past, ran past, or shoved through knew anything about Klast that would give her better insight into how to get his dog away from him. Demon dog was scary in a way that made her feel completely safe. Maybe that's why Klast kept going with dogs after losing one. He felt safe with them when the rest of his emotions were unsteady. Maybe.

The outer row came up before she knew it. No soldier. He had to be here somewhere. Lucky for her, she had a secret weapon to help her hunt him down. All it took was a tight grip and careful intention, and she could locate anyone she had met before. Clenching her hands into fists, she turned to the left and jumped when a loud bark sounded at her heels. A deep brown IB dog was on a leash, and the thing didn't like her. Its hair was standing up. Did it know what she was just about to do? Sparkle hunting wasn't illegal. Not in this city. She'd checked. However, the dog might not know it, and now it was snarling at her. Peyton brought her face to the owner, looking as clueless as possible.

"Uh…" she stammered as she backed away.

"Got something illegal in your pocket?" the guy guessed.

He looked as suspicious of her as his dog did. Hard blue eyes bored into her. They were so intense that she couldn't pay attention to any of his other features, but if she had been able to, she would have seen the sweat creeping up on his black hair, the hand that reached for a gun, and the way his dog's ears perked up at the sound. She would have realized that her good intention to find a soldier running from a dog was now a very bad intention, one that was going to get her neck bitten.

"No," Peyton said, but it was already too late.

The dog lunged at her. Her first reaction was to be impressed at how these creatures could come from nowhere looking so innocent one second and then taking her down the next. Her second thought was she was going to die. She hadn't the time to scream, but from across the arena, she could somehow make out the sound of demon dog screaming. The black dog hit her down, but right as its jaw started to open, it got slammed from the side. A sickening crunch of a fist smacking a jaw echoed the sound of her head connecting against the hard concrete. All thought escaped her brain except for the sound of the demon dog barking. Wow! He was loud!

"What are you doing?! Stay down if you want your dog to live. That's an order! No brawling in the hallways. We don't need that crap around here."

Klast. She wasn't sure if she thought the name or whispered it in confusion, but as soon as she did, the barking stopped. Everything was out of focus so it took a moment for her to sit up and look at a cream-colored puppy that had one gray paw on the back of the deep brown dog's side its teeth on the front of the much older dog's throat. That was the dog that Klast was escorting around next. It was cute.

"I'll handle this. Whatever it is. She's with me."

Klast had punched the other breeder down to the ground. The breeder was livid, but for the sake of his trapped dog, he didn't get up. Soldiers were crowding around them, some whining about not getting a better fight to watch. Peyton could only sit there, stunned that she'd been rescued at all. *By him.* The thought filled her up, making water come unbidden to her eyes. She didn't know this man, and here he was saving her instead of leaving her behind. Saving her like he saved all those dogs. She completely loved him for that.

He yanked her to her feet, disregarding the throb of her head and the unsteadiness that produced as she stumbled into him, doing her best not to reveal how little life she had inside of her. He dragged her down the hallway. Only then did he look back. His puppy ran at him with the leash in its mouth, waiting for Klast to take it to make their venture down the halls legal again.

"Jeez, Volt," Klast breathed out when he took the leash again and dropped her arm. Peyton stumbled, still trying to gather her balance. Demon dog was back to barking.

"Here I thought you'd gotten your direction wrong the first time, or that your quarry had moved, so you got all flustered and started to rush. We rescue Peyton now? Since when? You felt like it?" Klast complained back to the animal. "She must have done something, though. What did you do? Don't think you're getting out of this easy." He directed that last part to her.

Peyton shut her eyes and spread her feet farther apart. Don't throw up! Everything was woozy. Klast's intense gaze tunneled beneath her senses flooded with annoyance. Super weird. It wasn't like her to feel so much. She wasn't a guard dog.

"Well, out with it. My dogs can sense the truth, so don't bother lying. That will only make it harder on you. What were you going to be bleeding for?"

"I was only trying to help," Peyton whispered.

"Pardon?" Klast had to get closer to her to hear, and Volt was tugging hard on the leash impatient.

"That soldier. I wanted to find the soldier that walked off so Tasha wouldn't be left alone."

"Uh-huh," Klast said slowly. "I suppose Volt might care about his sibling. Alright, but you must have done something—"

"No."

"—something to raise the hair on a guard dog's back. Whatever you did, don't do it again. You're surrounded by a bunch of over-jumpy trapped heroes. Do use your head."

"It's pounding," Peyton answered. He was right, though. No sparkle hunting inside the arena. These dogs trained to stop that sort of thing. She *had* been stupid.

Peyton got her eyes open only to find that Klast was twenty feet away following the lead of his rushing dog, Volt. Well, not his dog much longer. That put the man and his over-jumpy guard dog much closer to her than Klast. She'd take Klast and his version of guarding over any of these other guys. Lawrence was right. There was no backup plan. It was Klast and the demon dog or no one. She had to get back on his good side. She had to find that soldier! Only now she was out of easy ways to do it. With a glance at the jumpy breeder, she took a step away, only to be stopped by an arena guard.

"Empty your pockets. Security here. Drop all your stuff."

Oh no. The guy had a long gun pointed at her. Might as well get started. She pulled out the hotel key first and let it fall to the floor. Some idiot whistled at her. Next came the rental car key. Then the ticket to get in showing her early pass. There was the lip balm and the pack of Kleenex in case her nose started bleeding. It was impressive that she'd not had to use it yet. Next came the hair tie, the paperclip, and the bracelet. She'd bought it last night for its charm, saying "faith." Last out of her pocket came the medicine, but she didn't drop it and shatter the glass bottle. She held it out, dreading the inevitable reveal.

"What's that?"

"Medication. You can scan my prints for authorization if you need to."

She held out her other hand to be scanned and waited. The man with the gun looked between the glass vial and her. He shook his head as if he knew exactly what it was without needing to prove it. Who didn't know what it was? The liquid inside swirled pink and green, looking like puke if it got shook up as it was right now. It separated fast, though, going back to the swirl. Only the dying got this. Only those who had sold their souls to stay alive walked around with this nasty substance.

"Carry on." He took a step away from her.

She heard the breeder commend his dog for finding medication. Nothing to the animal about acting out of bounds. Peyton slowly got her things and walked off feeling like a loser. Her supernatural hunting skills were out, and so were her options for getting Klast to change his mind.

"Go to the gate, stupid."

"You say something?" Peyton asked a stranger next to her. There were too many guys here. Way too many. Walking through them was like trying to dig out a skittle in a bag of M&M's. The soldier was long lost.

"What?" the guy asked.

Never mind. She gave him a brief smile and walked past him. Klast had told her to use her head. So, if she was a soldier who was racing away from a dog before he had to pay for it, where would she go? The gate.

Just as that comment had said. She felt stupid for not having gone there right away. The soldier would grab his friend, or ditch him, and try to get out of there before the dog or Klast came to hunt him down. That's where she came in. She was going to do that for them. Then they would both be grateful, even if Klast had to save her hide.

Destination in mind, she shoved toward the gate. At one point, she heard a dog fight break out. People screamed. Dogs barked in crazy succession. She struggled to turn out the sound and reach the exit.

The gate! The soldier really was here. Her heart leapt to her throat when she saw him standing beside a group of security officers. It hurt her head to rush forward, but when she drew in closer, it hurt her pride. The soldier *couldn't* get out. He had his arms crossed, his face a hard line. There was a large scanner that everyone had to walk through to exit and enter. Peyton obtained an early pass to avoid holding up the line when the scanner located her medicine. She should have guessed that the scanner would pick up such a thing as an imprinted runaway.

"One more time. Where did you leave your imprinted dog? You can't leave without paying. We will find out if it takes all day. The cost for your silence won't be worth it."

The injustice of the man's actions rose inside her making her want to shout out the answers. He'd left the dog in the middle of the aisle illegally! Peyton nearly started talking but held back. He'd run for a reason, and his imprinted dog had let him go knowing he wouldn't be able to get away. This man couldn't pay for the dog. Perhaps he thought he was going to end up dead, and he didn't want to push that fate on anything else. He wanted to save the dog from his fate. Unlike her. She'd take the risk. Maybe this guy was far nicer than she was. If that was the case, who was she to tattle on him and make him pay a fine on top of the dog fee? She stepped up, earning a glare from the guards keeping him inside the compound.

"His dog is named Tasha, and he left her in her cage beside Klast."

"What do you know about it? Stay out of this," the scared soldier ordered.

She wasn't about to. She stepped closer, determined to uphold her half-truth.

"Klast said that he waved the start-up fee and sent me to tell you. Did you know that his imprinted dog died, and he carries on simply to make the lives of other people better than his? He wants you to have that dog. Honest. He will work with whatever you have going on."

"Klast Burma?" one of the security men asked. "You got a Burma dog!? Blimey. People would kill for those dogs. We put snipers on the roof by his dogs to keep the loonies away. Hold on. I can double-check this."

Out came a phone, and a text went through. The man's eyebrows shot up, and Peyton was certain he read that Tasha got left in the middle of the hallway. However, the guard held his silence. Now there were more of them breaking the rules for the scaredy pants that didn't want to look his dog in the face.

"Back you go," the officer pointed. "No, wait." His phone rang. A moment later, he looked more surprised than ever. "Okay. Only for a Burma dog. I wouldn't let this be alright for anyone else."

"What?" one of the other security officers asked.

"Billy says that Mr. Burma says the dog is paid in full. He can call his dog and go."

"What?!" Peyton didn't care that she was screaming or that the officer had started to cry as he whispered the dog's name. That wasn't fair! *She* couldn't stand by the gate and cry and get a dog only because she wanted one and couldn't pay. This wasn't fair at all!

"He can't do that!"

"Miss. You will maintain order in the arena for the safety of everyone here."

"This is stupid."

Rage flared again and her head pounded even harder. She had to sit down or fall. Her fingers tightened around the medicine in her pocket. She couldn't throw it away because she needed it, but she would have chucked it if she could. She couldn't use it. Her diffuser was the item she'd dropped in the doomscape. As an expensive one-of-a-kind tool created just for her and her weird condition, the company who gave it to her had told her to get it back. They would rather she die instead of costing them thousands more. That's what she amounted to—an expensive dying loser.

Sometimes her heart would stop. Sometimes she wouldn't breathe for hours, but she could still walk around. She'd bleed from her pores or itch all over. She didn't have ribs but steel because they had taken her ribs for bone cancer. Her left knee had a pin in it. One of her kidneys was gone. Once she'd had boils that oozed blue puss. No one could guess what that one was. It all sucked. She already used her dying wish to say goodbye to her family. They'd taken her on a cruise where she'd spent the whole time in the room comatose, her heart not pumping, but her body refusing to let go. She was that way for ten days and had woken up in a casket. At least they had buried her with her phone. She called her brother to let her out. He had left her there another two days scared it was a hoax and she a zombie. They didn't talk anymore. She should be dead. Sometimes the thought of it was easier than all of this.

"Tasha!"

She hated the name suddenly. Hated how she watched the soldier embrace the unaccompanied dog who ran toward him carrying a sack on its back. The brown animal greeted him with sloppy kisses. He reached to open the sack, but Tasha jumped back and pulled a cord to knock it off herself. She pulled out a paper first and nudged it over to her new friend.

"The adoption paper," he said in awe as if he couldn't believe he was getting a Burma dog for free. Next came a fat book. It had to be an instruction manual for how to care for his new dog. There was a smaller handwritten note and then Tasha dragged the empty bag away from the soldier and over to her.

Plop. That's all Peyton got for her effort. The empty bag seemed to laugh at her. Tasha got to leave happy, while Peyton became the animal who played fetch. Angry, Peyton clutched the fabric between her fingers. Uh oh. Her stomach churned. She was going to hurl! She couldn't return a vomit sack, but she didn't want to puke all over the floor. Sack it was. A nasty liquid oozed out of her. She hated checking, but she had to know, so she peeked inside. Green slime today. No blood. The goop sat on top of a black cord.

With an inhale that left her coughing, Peyton sputtered. Not a cord. Tasha had brought her a hidden leash! Peyton *had* signed the paper saying she wouldn't put down a dog leash. She could claim that Klast gave it to her. She could get a dog! However, she was going to need some time. She held up her medicine and groaned when Lawrence was called.

# 4

Klast walked past the empty cages like they didn't exist. Volt, the creamy dog with the one painted paw, was gone. Tasha had left him without so much as a thank-you and cost him a great deal. Then there was Luke. Klast had heard the comments about the pup looking like a red panda all day long and had wanted to wallop everyone for them. He was so strung up! So tense that it took him a while to realize that Luke was the dog calling out into the void for his special someone. Deek had to bark for Klast to listen before Klast was able to muster himself together to praise the teammate. By the time he got the congratulations out, the man Luke wanted was already standing by the cage chatting to him like they were best pals. He'd paid at least. Luke and Volt and Tasha had a new bestie. He only had the one-year-old dogs left apart from Deek.

The money from two dogs was enough to hold him over for now. Tomorrow he'd give it another go for the other dogs. One more day to decide if he needed to change his stickers, even if more names were scrawled beneath Lawrence's rudeness. Klast had had offers ringing through his ears all day long. The higher prices were rather tempting. Thing was, he couldn't get himself to accept them until he let the dogs give it all they had. It didn't feel fair to the new pups to demand they imprint on their very first day. It wasn't like everyone in the world was here, even if it felt like it. He'd been spotting foreigners all day, straining to pick up their words for good-sounding phrases he might use in the future.

Klast walked up to Zen's cage and leaned his head against it, hoping for some peace of mind. Zen was his good luck charm. Red and brown, he'd never once barked in anger. No. He strategized. Perhaps he could tell Klast through osmosis how to handle another day of this. The crowds had finally left. The building was locked, and extra guards prowled in case the desperate tried to break in to steal a dog.

"You were perfect today," Klast heard himself tell the dog.

Zen snorted at him and Klast looked up with a nod of his head. There was no fooling an IB dog about his mental state. Klast was strung out, and they all could hear his insincerity. He looked over at Hero: gray with white-tipped ears. The dog was zonked from trying to sort through thousands of people in one day. Weston was in the cage beside him, looking like a scientist. He was brown with gray-goggled eyes. Like Hero, Weston left most of his food untouched in favor of sleeping. Phantom was next. Red with white spots it was crazy how that dog popped out of hiding when he shouldn't be camouflaged. He was barely staying awake.

"Tent," Klast sighed as he trudged back toward Deek and sat down beside the cage. Deek had been barking most of the day but didn't look the least bit tired. He should be, considering how he refused to finish his dinner. He only ate one-third. A perfect third, as if he was going to put himself on the same strict diet that Klast was holding. It hurt to see that.

"We can live in a tent. How about that, pal?"

Klast didn't care anymore if everyone heard that he was homeless and struggling. Word must have gotten out already anyway, or he'd not have had so many sneaky offers. Klast needed money. Klast was desperate. Get his dogs now before someone else bids higher on a bidding list that wasn't even supposed to be there.

"Question," Deek posed for the hundredth time.

"Nooo." He couldn't. He couldn't figure out what the dog was trying to ask.

"Outside. Go outside. Take me outside."

"No."

"Question."

"Please stop."

"Feeling. Pretty. Outside."

"Stop!" Klast was on his feet, screaming as the tension got the better of him. "You're not going outside! I spent all day long listening to you whine and moan like a sissy that got his head on backward. Shut up, dog! I can't take it anymore! You be quiet tonight or I swear I'll shoot you myself before everyone else gets around to it!"

He pulled out his gun and aimed it at the dog. Deek turned still and then lay down on his belly, not saying a word. Just as Klast thought. Deek would do nothing if Klast shot him. He'd sit there and take it. No fight at all. He'd simply give up if that was Klast's will.

Klast's hand shook. He lowered the gun as tears rolled from his eyes. He couldn't do it.

All day long he'd seen black dogs in the corner of his vision making his heart skip as it foolishly thought that Shadow was there with him, helping him get through the ache of giving up something he loved over and over again. He hated these arenas, but it was the best place to go to find dedicated people who would love the dogs. The dogs needed this place even if he didn't.

"Hey," Mike said behind him. "You need some sleep. I have a pair of earplugs you can use. Come on. Get some rest. I bought everyone burgers tonight to celeb—"

"I don't want your charity."

"Eat the burger and then go to bed. That's an order," Mike said. "You did good today, Klast. I'd have lost it way before now if I were you. Dogs in the hallway. Men running off. Pests left and right, scribbling names and bids. The demon not shutting up and you feeling responsible. It's alright to take a break."

"I don't want your burger."

He couldn't stay in the arena tonight. He simply couldn't. Another night feeling like he had to sit beside Deek wondering constantly what the dog was trying to tell him, was going to turn him mad. Too many black dogs today looked like Shadow already. There was only so much he could take. He looked Mike over and then looked at Deek, who wasn't taking his eyes off him still. The stalker.

"I'm going outside. Don't call me if Deek breaks out and I have to pay for the damages."

Mike shoved money at him insisting he take it. Klast hadn't the heart to refuse. He crammed the money into his pocket, groaning when he felt his mother's letter in there too. Might as well read it and get it over with. He yanked it out and flipped open the envelope, feeling horrible for walking away on Deek. Whatever he needed to say had to be important or he wouldn't be so insistent. There wouldn't be any sleeping without a sedative. Klast would stay up all night worrying about that question.

Pretty. He'd been saying the word all day long. A pretty feeling. A question that he couldn't express. Klast groaned over how he couldn't put it together and pulled out his mother's letter.

He couldn't move. The letter fell to the floor as the rest of the world crashed down around his head. The letter wasn't from his mother. It was in an envelope addressed to him in her writing, but the text wasn't hers. He'd had that feeling of something big coming and this was it.

*"Klast Burma,*

*We had no way to reach you except to trust that your mother's crafty envelope would find its way. We regret to inform you that your parents were on a train going to Brickshaw. The train flipped off the rails. They are both at Valley View Hospital in a coma. At the time of their admittance, they were in the process of changing insurance. Their new insurance will kick in on the 26th of June and cover for most of their latter expenses. Please call us to discuss how we can cover the previously occurred fees of ..."*

"Bronze, what kind of sleeping pill knocks a man right out?" Klast asked, as he stepped over the paper and walked toward the exit. Mike would pick it up for him. Or Imar. He was nosy like that. With extra debts piling up, his dogs were done for. They didn't have time to imprint anymore. The realization made it hard for him to breathe. There had to be something else he could do!

"Think Deek!" he screamed, turning around, letting the tears tumble down. "How do I get out of this? How!?"

What good was the dog if he couldn't use that brainpower when it mattered? They were littermates, even if Deek didn't see him as anything else. There had to be something the dog could do to save him. Deek stood up and licked his lips.

"Question. Outside. I love you."

"You don't love me," Klast hissed back, hating the way the dog could play with him when he was lower than he'd been in a while. Maybe Klast was getting depression again. He'd done just fine after going off the meds, but maybe he should reconsider. He needed to stop seeing Shadow's shadow in the corner of his vision.

"I love you," Deek said again with trembling legs. He couldn't be scared. What was this? "Outside. I love you."

"What are you...?" It finally clicked.

A shot exploded in his gut. He'd lost Deek! That's what had made Klast so upset all day long! It wasn't that he was getting depressed about losing Shadow all over again. It was because he'd just asked Deek to speak to his soul, and he'd lost the connection to the dog when Deek gave it up. Internally, it felt like another one of his imprinted dogs had died. Klast should have known better. He should have kept Deek far away from everyone else and selfishly kept him to himself. He didn't want to lose Deek! Not really. Losing him tore open the hole where Shadow had been.

Klast sank to his knees, unable to do anything else but cry. Everything felt shattered. He watched as Mike picked up the hospital bill. He watched as he showed it to Bronze and Imar. Sahafi had already gone out partying with the people who had bought his dogs for the day. The other breeders in the nearby rows had a clear view of the four of them but they did nothing. Good thing too. The pain was too much. His whole body shook. Deek shook. That was never a good sign.

"You imprinted. Why didn't you *tell* me?"

Deek looked at him like he was stupid. Klast cried harder. His best friend was *gone*. His parents were in a coma. His brother and sister hadn't called him to tell him anything. He checked his phone. Nope. They'd not said a thing. Did they not want him to know, or was it to shield him from the thought of owing more money? If he was lucky, they'd paid those bills to leave him out of it. Yeah. His parents had saved income. They had a house they could mortgage if it came down to that. They'd be fine. He needn't worry about them. He had to worry about Deek.

"Why didn't you tell me?! You know how to tell me. You wail like a love-struck fool. That's what you dogs do. You're such an oddball." He sounded far more accusatory than helpful, and he hated himself for it. He'd managed to cheer all the other dogs on, but for the one he didn't want to lose, he scolded. Pathetic.

"I'm sorry. You don't deserve that. I'm just…"

"Can we help you yet?" Bronze asked. "What can we do to help you?"

"Call my brother and sister and find out what they've done about those hospital charges," Klast mumbled. "Call the gate to see who's still left in the building for Deek. He couldn't have gotten far. Another case of running away from me and my dogs like we're diseased or something," Klast spat.

"Outside," Deek said again.

"He couldn't have gotten outside if he imprinted," Klast reminded.

"She. Outside."

"She. Right well… Oh."

He'd totally missed it! It had been staring at him all day long. Peyton. Klast had been extremely confused when Volt suddenly rushed to help her. The reason was because Deek had ordered him to since Volt had been out of the cages. Peyton was adopted into the pack. She was one of their own now forever, and he'd missed it. If she ever came across one of these other dogs, they would forever add her to their protection detail when she was in their sight.

"Why are her hands cold?" Klast asked, wiping at his eyes and forcing himself to his feet to help Deek. He thought about that mark on her arm, the one that he hoped wasn't the marking he thought it was, and sighed. Speak of the devil. Deek had turned against him to join the devils. All the same, Klast owed it to the dog. Deek had gotten him through so much. It was Klast's turn to get him through this, no matter how much it hurt.

Deek trembled again. "Question."

"What's the question, Deek? You can do it. Form it so I can understand. I know you can do it," Klast said around the lump in his throat.

Deek growled like he'd been trying to figure it out all day long and couldn't. "Dead," he finally got out. "Feeling. Pretty girl. Dead. Outside."

Klast had gotten to his feet, but he sank right down again.

"As in, she just died or she's dying?"

She couldn't have just died or Deek wouldn't be alive still. The sorrow would have already taken him out, so she was still alive. Still not good. Deek wasn't telling him that he had imprinted, because he had to say goodbye. Really say it. He had to tell Klast that he was going to head after a strange girl and die. No wonder the poor dog was scared silly and crying. Klast was crying again, too. He couldn't help himself.

"I'm such a baby," he sobbed as Bronze sat down beside him and hugged him.

"Yeah, because you love that dog. We all know it. He knows it. That's going to be a hard one."

"I'm not a wimp," Klast retorted. He struggled to get up again, but Bronze grabbed his arm.

"Stop. You're overly emotional. What are you doing?"

"Finding Peyton whats-her-name and getting Deek to her before I explode," Klast answered like it was the obvious answer.

"I meant after that."

"Explode. Take sleeping drugs. I don't know. Go back on anti-depressants. I'll figure that out later. Let me go."

Bronze gripped him hard. His tan dog, Cedar, stepped closer. Stupid beast.

"I have to help my dog. If that means taking him to die with somebody else, then that's what I'm going..." Nope, he couldn't finish that sentence. He was crying all over again, waking up dogs that had been sleeping before. Deek whined.

"He doesn't have to die with anyone else," Bronze said rather carefully. "He could stay here with you for that. It's going to come anyway."

He could shoot his dog and end the connection that Peyton had created. He could do that. He could be selfish and take the dog back.

"No. It's her dog. She needs to be happy in the end. I'm going to find her. Get your leash, Deek. Let's go."

He shoved Bronze off him and wiped his eyes dry, squaring his shoulders, forcing himself to keep going. He'd done this before. It wasn't so bad. On the day that Shadow had died, he'd had puppies to feed and appointments to keep. He'd had friends to meet for dinner. He'd canceled those plans, but he had managed to keep going. He'd broken. He had exploded once before and it hadn't stopped him.

"We'll go down fighting. I won't rob you of that. You'll go down the best you ever were," Klast told Deek. "You were never one to take a fight lying down. Leash. Let's go. You know what to do to cheer her up. You know it."

"I really think that's a bad idea," Mike told him.

"You really shouldn't take him out," Imar agreed. "Not in the state you're in. Not in the state he's in. The girl will come back tomorrow."

"You don't know that. She might have only had a single day pass. Wait."

He could call Lawrence to find out! He pulled out his phone and dialed the number, rolling his eyes when it went to voicemail. He left a message asking the guy to have Peyton call him back. Then he stared at his phone like the man would call him back in the next two minutes. When that didn't happen, he sighed and plopped over onto the floor.

He called his brother and then his sister. They at least answered and made his scary news about his parents not as horrible. His parents had woken up and were out of the hospital and all the bills were being taken care of. Klast's siblings had tried to call him but knew he was out traipsing the woods with the dogs and they couldn't get through due to bad reception. When he finished talking with them, he tried calling Lawrence again. No answer. If he didn't get through the bandage ripping fast, he never would peel it off. He had to do this now.

"Please bring the leash, Deek," Klast tried again, worrying about how well the dog would listen to him outside when he refused to do that much. He could be looking at a scheming killer right here. Deek could have already puzzled it out. The easiest path to take was to kill Klast to put him out of his misery and then let himself die after that. They'd all die together. Dogs had done such a thing before when faced with the choice of where they wanted to die.

"Klast, please," Mike begged. "Don't open the cage!"

"I have to trust him if he's going to trust me," Klast replied, but he found his legs shaking as he crawled to the cage and looked into Deek's eyes, trying to determine which way this was going to go. They could all be a tragic headline this time tomorrow. Mike backed away from him. His dog, Cali, was breathing fast, getting ready to tear into Deek when the door opened. Klast looked by the cage wall where he'd put the leash. The whole cage had narrow holes too small for a pen to slip through. Klast could see every part of the cage, but no leash.

"You sitting on it?"

Deek scooted over to prove he wasn't.

"So, where's your leash?"

The answer Deek gave him was so astonishing that he found himself laughing as if the answer could purge him of all his tension and provide comic relief. Bronze looked at him like he'd lost his mind.

"What the devil?" Klast laughed. "How did your leash get outside with the pretty dying girl? What sort of schemes did you pull off today?"

There was no way. The cage didn't have room for things like that to slip through. If it did, people would try to slip drugs to the dogs to claim that the pets were in love with them so they could take them away. Even with the narrow spaces, people had put odd items into cages before. Klast trained all his animals right from the beginning to not eat anything weird. There was no way a leash could have slipped out of that cage, and yet somehow it had. Peyton had the leash and hadn't brought it back. She'd taken it with her knowingly or unknowingly, he wasn't sure, but it was remarkable all the same.

"You still want to go outside and find her?"

"Yes!"

The candor to Deek's spark tumbled back as if his earlier fear was because he thought Klast would shoot him for leaving. Deek wasn't scared to run after a dying woman. He was scared of Klast, and that hurt Klast's heart all over again. Deek worried that his trainer wasn't strong enough for him to break away. Klast stamped down his feelings yet again.

"Klast," Mike tried again.

"If I don't do it now, I won't have the guts for it tomorrow," he answered truthfully. "Please don't follow me. I have to do this."

That was how he left Mike, Bronze, and Imar on his way out the door with an extra leash. Deek was at his side walking like he was the most royal animal in the world. Nothing to worry about. Klast knew this dog. He knew his heart. Deek would never betray his pack, which meant that he wouldn't betray Klast even if it hurt him. He was patient. He was clever. Klast did his best to not think of the word "gone" as he walked through the security monitor. It beeped at him. It always did. He was imprinted without his dog. It left a mark. Now there were two invisible marks. One where Shadow had been and one where Deek had been. Both dogs he loved most were destined to die. At least in the arenas, all the guards knew to expect his alarm going off. They didn't stop him, but they made calls behind him, asking what was going on and where he was going with the dog.

"You're something special, you know that?" Klast told Deek as they reached the refreshing night air. Both of them raised their heads to breathe it in. Outside for two weeks and the arena felt stifling after a single day. Klast shook his head as a black dog rushed behind a bush out of the corner of his eye. He had to stop losing it!

"The bravest of them all. Don't tell the other dogs I said that. None of them would be able to do what you can do. You've got it all, pal. You're the greatest imprinted guard dog there ever was."

Deek smiled at him. A genuine smile that Klast wished he could feel. He smiled back, perfect at hiding the stabbing beneath. For once, he didn't think Deek noticed.

# 5

Peyton would have constructed wings from the hospital bed sheets and flown out the window if only she could stop throwing up. Hospitals! Who needed them? She'd been to too many, and the doctors never did anything to help. She was soul-bound to death, even if Sysmat had promised to keep her alive. They had given her the ability to "sparkle hunt" as she called it, claiming that in order to heal her body, she needed to be able to split her soul. Peyton found the reasoning a load of rubbish, but she couldn't change what they had already done. It was how her life was now. After meeting a person, she could track down their soul by casting out part of her own. Basically, she was a glorified spy apart from the fact that she wasn't cured, and spent most of her time in a state of continuous dying so she wasn't much use to Sysmat. Or to herself. Or to anybody.

Going to Sysmat had been her parent's choice. It had also been their wish that she'd live a normal life up to that point too, which was why she had found herself engaged to a stranger who had brought her all sorts of gifts and held her hand before she was taken away. Roman. She thought that was his name.

It was hard to pay attention to her lover when she felt so crummy. He was nice, and no doubt hired, but he had been hers. For a while. Her mother kept saying that they were soulmates. Peyton didn't believe in human soulmates, but dog ones were special. Too bad she still didn't have the dog. The soul couldn't communicate with the physical world without a body, and the body was useless without a soul. She was rubbish and detached in both categories no matter how hard she tried to be whole.

Her fingers ran over the cold bathroom white laminate tile now turning gray with age. She had avoided looking in the mirror above the sink when she stumbled in. All of her was one disgusting blob. Like the underpart of a slug, she practically oozed mucus. If only her vomit was hygroscopic and absorbed the water she was spewing before it rushed out, she wouldn't need to be so close to this nasty toilet seat. She'd simply burp out gumball blobs and be done with it.

Her eyes strayed to the backpack by her leg. It had taken a hefty amount of prying to get Klast's bag away from her fingers. One of the hospital workers said they would wash it. She'd passed out a few times in her effort to chase the dude to get it back, so they had washed it in the bathroom sink right next to her all the while talking to her like everything was going to be fine and she didn't need to stress because they would take care of her. They had left her in the bathroom. Lawrence had disappeared. Outside, the wind shook the window panes in a continuous rush that sounded like waves lapsing against a rocky beach. Her ears strained for the sound of the demon dog, even if she knew it was hopeless.

Blurph. She'd thrown up again. That would give her at least two minutes to do something productive. Peyton tugged the washed leash and bag closer to her and then pulled out her phone to resume her search. It was rather difficult to find anything about Klast Burma and his dogs online, but once she searched for unusual training techniques, he popped up. Some man named "FightForIt" had a fetish for hunting down clips about Klast. She had watched Klast get his imprinted dog through the footage.

Klast had been playing basketball in a park when a black dog named Shadow showed up. The recording must have been taken by Shadow's breeder because the camera had been hiding in a bush. Klast had smiled when he saw the dog and then he looked around, searching for an owner.

"Hello there, IB friend," he'd said to the young black puppy. "Not from around here or I'd know it. Got a couple like you at home. You bumming time or you need help with something? Pick a language and bark it. Your pal need help?"

Shadow had barked.

"No? What you here for?"

Bark.

"Play. You want to play ball. Alright. Maybe you can teach me some moves. Let's see what you got."

They had played basketball for at least five minutes before Klast realized the questions the dog answered were spoken into his soul instead of out loud. Peyton had no idea how that worked exactly. She was an expert (or so she thought) on soul work, but some people claimed that soul speech was like talking to a ghost beside you. Why would the dog detach part of his soul to communicate when it was right there and could bark instead? Other people claimed that the limited human mind interpreted the soul mutterings as a telepathic link. There had to be some sort of sound for Klast to think the dog was still barking, unless everyone was right that being imprinted to an IB dog warped the human brain. Once connected, the brain could never reverse and repair.

Peyton rubbed her tongue across her teeth to clear them and went back to her phone. She'd left off at a compilation of anonymous videos advising against performing the training techniques at home. Time for the next one. Click.

"Better go get that hat that's blowing away!" Klast called out to a dog that was sitting on the sidewalk across the road from him. He pointed. Peyton couldn't see a hat, because the footage looked to be taken out of a bedroom window and secretly uploaded. The dog in training wasn't her dog, but she knew it by sight. This was the red panda dog. The camera moved swiftly down the road to show two cars traveling side-by-side, heading between Klast and his separated pup.

"That poor hat. Blowing away all on its own with no one to save it," Klast said again.

The dog bolted right into the line of traffic. Klast screamed.

"Go back! What are you doing? You don't chase after a hat. It's not alive. It's not important. You don't go against what you think is right because I have a lapse in judgment. You do what you know is right. Always do what you know is right!"

Klast's dog rushed with the energy of an unstoppable cyclone. Peyton held her breath as the cars tried to screech to a halt. For a split second, she thought she was going to watch the dog die, only she knew it was still living.

"On three, jump! One… three!"

The dog jumped as high as it could go. It got above the front of the first car, landing on its hood and scraping across the windshield where it rolled, scrambling to gain its footing. It slipped over the back of the car and then crashed onto the road. The cars jerked to a stop and the drivers rushed to the dog yelling apologies to Klast, who waved them off.

Klast reached the dog first. He looked over the paws and then the legs and head and body. His words were muffled, so the recording person cracked the window open further and turned up the volume on the clip. She caught the tail end of his words.

"... again."

With a growl, the panda dog returned to the sidewalk. Oh gosh! Peyton was so glad that she wasn't one of his dogs. She'd never do that once let alone again. Klast soothed the emotions of the scared drivers, and he resumed his place across the street. Only this time, he didn't say anything about a hat. He went into a series of convulsions and fell to the ground right as a stream of cars rushed by. Peyton felt rather bad for his pup. It wailed, rushing forward toward the line of cars and then rushing down the sidewalk looking for a break in them to reach Klast. It ran back to the spot he had told it to be and started screaming.

That's when her dog showed up. Silvery and full of glory, with its black ears perked upward and brown paws a blur of color, it appeared from behind a group of traveling cars with the hat in its mouth. It muzzled the pup on the nose so it stopped crying, and disappeared again. When the car line ended, the panda pup rushed across the gap to check on Klast, who sat up with hearty congratulations.

"Look at you for not being fooled by me being stupid. You used your ears on that one, huh? Heard me still breathing and alive and knew that I was leading you on. You were brilliant. Not fooled for more than a second."

He went on like that for a while as the dog blinked at him, taking it all in. It looked back across the street where her dog had vanished. The dog that had told it Klast was making everything up. Then it looked back up at him and grinned. Panda pup had a secret to keep. He'd been tipped off. Klast was going on about how this dog wasn't ever going to be taken down by a car and how most falling over wasn't a cause to get oneself hit by one as the clip ended.

Peyton took in a few quick breaths to calm her breathing before the next clip hit her carrying her off-center yet again. Sirens. The sounds of an irreparably injured human. Peyton wanted to turn them off but her eyes were morbidly stuck on the screen. A guy was being loaded onto a stretcher with a blood-stained light-brown IB dog limping at his side.

"Wait, say that one more time," a paramedic asked as the camera moved with the injured man. He looked rather bad, especially around his head, and his eyes couldn't focus.

"He took him from me."

"The dog?" the medic clarified.

"The dog. When I told him what I do for a living, he took the dog."

"Your dog is right here, sir. Say hello doggy."

The camera moved to the dog, who didn't make a single noise.

"No," the injured man moaned.

"When we imprinted, (beep) took him from me and said he'd bring him back in three months. I was so blazing mad, but he put it in the agreement. I couldn't get the dog until he stayed with (beep) for another three months. When he brought the dog back, he only said one thing. 'We talked about planes.' I'm telling you; the dog landed the plane. I couldn't.... I can't see."

"That's all the blood in the way," the medic assured. "We'll get that looked at right away."

The camera moved away from the man on the stretcher to the crash sight. Boy, it looked bad! No wings. Front end smashed down. The plane was a heap of smoking metal. It was a miracle it had landed. Even stranger, when the camera swept back and forth, there was no sign of scratched ground where the plane would have skid to a grinding halt. It was as if someone had landed the wreckage like a helicopter on a launch pad. Only it was smoking.

"Dog lands airplane, compliments of (beep)."

"You can't put his name in the papers!" insisted the man on the stretcher. Text scrolled across the screen as the image started to fade out, offering up an apology for cutting out the breeder's name. Contract and all. The video faded to black. While Klast's name wasn't listed anywhere, Peyton knew that if one could identify the dog, they could still figure out where it had come from. IB dogs had to be registered. It made Peyton wonder how long "FightForIt" had taken to identify this dog as one of Klast's puppies or if the man stalked all of Klast's animals and stole video clips.

The next location on the clips was a bombed site. This time there was a guy in military uniform holding a camera aiming it at a hole in the ground. Peyton could make out the man's thick boots and the cuffs of his camo army pants. He didn't sound happy.

"We all know who I got this impossible dog from. I'm not saying it, but we all know it. What sort of stupid training did it get?! I've been standing here for half an hour with the dog in the hole, refusing to let me walk off or call for help. Every time I get started, it growls at me like it's going to tear my leg off. If it would let me get help, we'd be able to move already!"

The image turned dark before coming back. The same man was talking. "Might be making some progress here. That same dog just asked for a rope, but the problem is that the rope isn't long enough, and it's not like the dog can tie it around itself and climb out. It's a dog." Another cut scene and suddenly the man was walking beside the dog in a completely different location. Peyton heard a seagull caw in the distance.

"Alright, so I just wanted to report that my dog can tie a rope. You'd not believe it. I know. But it created a harness with a net and a hook and I guess jumped into it while tossing up the hook so I could pull him out. I don't know. All I know is that it brought up a hidden transmitter. If I had called for help, we'd have been located and shot down. We'd be dead. So yeah. Crazy breeder does it again. I didn't teach my dog to tie a rope."

Peyton had to pause the incredible footage to throw up. This whole thing made her want her dog more than ever. If it could pull off some miraculous things like that, she wanted it. She needed a miracle. One large miracle. Stomach ready for another round, she went back to her phone to watch some more.

"George here," a new person scanned his face across the screen before panning toward a hobbling man at his side. "Trevor got in a bit of an accident. It was a large mess and let's just say that his imprinted bodyguard dog got left alone in the apartment for a week. Now obviously we know that the dog isn't dead or Trevor would feel it, but for the sake of evidence to show what a bored dog does alone for a week, I thought we'd record the entrance."

"She's a good dog. It won't be that bad," Trevor grumbled. "A few broken dishes. Look, I can handle it."

"Sure you can. I want to see for myself."

Peyton was shaking her head through the rest of the scene. They walked into what looked like an empty apartment. Trevor called the dog, but it didn't come and he started to worry that it was too sick to move until they entered the kitchen. It wasn't there, but the dog food had been ripped open and left all over the floor. Someone had arranged kernels into words. Bored, come, and sorry were the most distinguishable ones.

"I think your dog can read," George offered as they stared at the mess.

"I think my dog can write," Trevor amended. "Where are you?!"

They moved farther down, pausing at a humming closet. Trevor opened the door to reveal a loaded dryer. His dog had been doing his laundry. Both men laughed about that for a while until they reached Trevor's room. Standing on a shredded bed was the creamy dog holding a sign in its mouth. The text was rather sloppy and looked to be written in split pea soup but it was legible.

"What's your excuse?" it asked.

Trevor was laughing so hard that he hardly cared that his bed was torn to shreds. Fluff and chewed-off springs were all over the floor, making it hard for him to stumble forward to reach his pet. The footage ended before the two reunited, but the dog dropped the sign and gave a hearty bark as the screen went black. White letters advised to never leave a dog alone for a week.

Peyton stared at the dark screen. Nothing about trigonometry was mentioned in there, but she could see Klast at work. She could hear his words. He would instruct his dogs to find a better constructive way to express anger. The dog had tried. It had played with food, apologized, and did laundry along with the bed ripping. She saw his words with the soldier when the dog had warned him to not call for help. She saw what the people at the arena had been talking about. Little human dogs. How did he breed little human dogs?

Peyton's hands closed up into a fist. None of this told her how she was going to convince Klast to give her the dog she wanted. Some miracles were simply out of scope, even if she had been handed a leash. It felt too late to give it back now. It was past midnight. Really? The sight of the clock made her eyes snap shut. She heard herself falling rather than felt it, and then she was out again with the simple hope that her soul would stay *in* her body so she wouldn't be asleep for ten days. The dog show only lasted for three. Klast would be gone by then.

"...know what I mean?" Klast's voice asked rousing her back to consciousness. Bummer. He was still talking so she'd probably forgotten to turn her phone off and the battery would be mostly dead.

"Obviously, use your best judgment, but for the most part, you don't mess with that. Now if you get deathly bored, the bed is something you can play with. See this button right here? It moves the bed up and down like so."

The sound of the bed moving and Klast laughing wafted through the hospital room toward the bathroom. She *couldn't* be making that up. He was here! Peyton struggled to move so she could beg her case. Nothing. Not even her eyes would open yet.

"It's like a rollercoaster. Remember when I took you on a rollercoaster and everyone was freaking out, but you loved the whole thing? Oh, man. That was something. We should do that again... You hear something, Deek?"

A name! She had a name for another one of his dogs. Dog claws and footsteps moved to the bathroom. A cold nose sniffed her.

"Don't look at me like that. I'm not a doctor. I can't give you any feedback unless you let me touch her and you won't."

Peyton wanted to smile at the sound of the growl that followed that sentence. *Her* dog. She'd heard that growl so much yesterday that she had it memorized. How had Klast known where she was? Suddenly she wanted to grab the leash and refuse to let go, but she couldn't move.

"Okay. I've gone over everything I know. If you need to learn anything else, you'll have to pick that up from someone else. I'm heading out."

Bark! The loud sound was a command, one that she understood. Deek was telling Klast to stay. She wanted him to stay, too. As much as she liked the idea of him leaving his dog to sit beside her, she had no idea how the dog worked. Not really. What commands did she need to use? What did it eat and how often? How was she supposed to take care of it if she found herself unable to move for ten days?

One video she had watched showed two of Klast's former dogs meeting each other so their owners could compare them. The dogs didn't use the same commands. As far as they could tell, Klast changed how he talked with his dogs so that no one else could guess how to control them. Without a rundown on the dog, she had no clue where to start. She doubted Klast was going to leave her with an instruction manual.

"I can't," Klast's voice broke. "I don't know what's wrong with her. I did my best to give you a good life. I can't give you a good death. Don't ask that of me. I have to go."

Yup. No instruction manual, because he thought she was going to die. Deek growled at him, telling him to wait. Question. Question. Question. He begged.

"I don't know!" Klast shouted back. "Let me out the door, Deek. I did my part. I got you in here. We both knew that I was going to leave and you weren't. Ask Peyton your question. She can understand you."

His voice was cracking. It sounded so sad to hear it and confirm her fears that he hadn't wanted to give her the dog. If he didn't want to do it, then why was Deek here? She didn't understand. Maybe Lawrence had offered him a lot of money.

Deek insisted again that Klast answer his question. She could feel the resistance rising in the room as if her soul was hearing whispers from Klast and knew what he was thinking. Shoot the dog and get it over with. Shoot her too. That would end the suffering. Jail wouldn't be worth it, however. Only shoot the dog and not her. They'd not signed a contract. It was still *his* dog. He could give Deek a quicker death.

"Question!"

"What?" Klast gasped. "You're killing me here. You've got to let me go, just as I have to let you go. We're not mates anymore."

"Sparkle hunt," Deek said as if he was suddenly using words instead of barking.

Peyton panicked. He couldn't talk about that! She needed him to protect her secrets! Not give them away! She'd promised not to say anything. Sysmat would know it was her leaking information and they could harm her family. Turn them all sick. Make them all think they were dying so that they had to give their lives over to become scientific experiments as she had. Deek had to keep it a secret!

"Sparkle hunt through the air," Deek continued. "What is it?"

"Where'd you hear about that?" Klast asked slowly as if he understood the question on a level far greater than he should.

"Pretty dying girl."

No!

"You know you need to give her a name. Being called dead is offensive. If you let me touch her, I'll tell you."

The tension in the room shifted once again. Nerves. A will of power and trust clashing against each other, waiting for one or the other to bend. So confusing. She didn't feel all of this from other people. It was the strangest thing to be able to sense so much from Klast and Deek. She could understand picking up the dog's emotions if they imprinted, but that had nothing to do with Klast. There was simply something so special about him, that her soul reacted. It had to be that. Without knowing how she heard his thoughts, they were there. A list of times when Deek fibbed. Hard training sessions. Disagreements over how to teach a principal to a pup. Doubt that Klast had the answer to Deek's question, and fear that Deek was using a trick on him.

"We both get what we want out of it. You can't complain. You're the one asking and not letting me leave."

"Fine," Deek barked.

Klast's hands were on her before the dog had even finished agreeing. The first thing he did was pry up her sleeve to get a look at the mark on her arm. The Sysmat mark. Two dots of power stood above and below the swirl for soul. All of that was inside a diamond representing a mortal body. Those images sat on top of the squished triangle of death. It told everyone that her entire life was forfeited. Yet another thing that no one wanted to turn a guard dog over to. There was nothing to keep the scientists from conducting experiments on the dog next, and nothing that was going to make sure the experiments were gentle.

Klast's words continued to unsettle her. She was not breathing. She had fortified ribs, and had been marked in the doomscape. Peyton had no idea how he knew *that*. He also knew that she was currently aware of her surroundings. Then came the worst part. She had a split soul that left traces of itself with other people so she could hunt them down. She was a sniper. A killer. The sparkles were only something she could see, and they floated in the air toward her target. Peyton wanted to scream at him that she had never killed anything. Klast kept going.

She had an invasive alien bug that was highly mutable inside the host, changing how it reacted to evade drugs and breed within her. The bacteria made her look dead when she was still alive. She had to be drawing in air through her skin or something.

"Help," Deek begged.

"I'm not a doctor," Klast said again as he emptied her pockets and noted that she didn't have a way to take her medicine that held back that bug. "You need to find a way to destroy this. Keep in mind that it's illegal for

Peyton to destroy it so she can't do it and she'll fight you on that. It will be her word against mine."

No! Klast wanted Deek to destroy her medicine. He wanted her to die! He shouldn't have known all that other stuff about her, anyway. He didn't work for Sysmat. This man was seriously freaky. It had to all be a dream. One long, never-ending nightmare. Klast couldn't bring himself to kill the dog, so he was going to make her die instead. She wanted to scream for help, too. There was no way she could kill the dog before it killed her and her medicine.

"I can save her, Deek, but you're going to have to trust me. That's going to be hard. I can bring back the thing to save her so you both can live. Will you trust me?"

"Yes. Hurry," her traitorous dog answered.

It wasn't even her dog! She had to wake up! She had to chase after them. Peyton could hear Klast leave the dog with a hug before he rushed from the room. The dog's paws pattered out after him toward the door before coming back. A moment later, the hospital bed moved up and down. Peyton fought with herself. Wake up! Get up! The harder she struggled, the worse it felt until her head was pounding and her body ached like she'd been swimming too long. An undeterminable time later, she got her eyes open.

The first thing she did was pry herself up to her elbows, determined to find Deek and scream at him for killing her. The bed wasn't moving anymore, and from where she was, she couldn't see him there. She crawled to the door, bonking into a rounded object as she went. The medicine vial! Phew! She sagged to floor as she clutched it to her chest. Deek hadn't destroyed it. He'd lied to Klast and left it beside her.

Klast was still on her enemy list, unless she took into account that he'd just said he could save her. Deek could still be on her enemy list even if he left the medicine alone. Maybe he was waiting until the right moment to smash her apart. He was capable of lying to the man who raised him. He could lie to her too. Everyone said that if you couldn't trust your imprinted dog, you couldn't trust anyone. She was supposed to trust this animal with everything, and here she was doubting all of his motives. Another curse instead of a miracle. If she got lucky, then perhaps a twisted miracle.

"Deek?" Peyton asked, trying out his name for the first time. She sighed. He wasn't there. She crawled out the bathroom door into the room just to make sure. The bed was ruffled like the dog had played on it for a while and possibly taken a nap.

"You're funny," the dog said from behind her.

Peyton fell over with a gasp as she turned around. Behind her! The killing machine was behind her! Not close, thank goodness. He was sitting in the corner of the bathroom staring at her the same way he had stared at Klast when he didn't want the man to move out of his sight. He'd even talked when he wanted to stall her in the same way too.

Courage, Peyton. She had to take advantage of this.

"Hi…" She waited. Nothing. Not a very good start to a long-term relationship. She hoped that with all the marvelous things she had seen from Klast's dogs that Deek would not die in the doomscape when she took him there to get her medical diffuser.

"You won't go with me. Problem solved," Deek answered as if he heard the thoughts she didn't voice. Peyton rubbed her ears. Then she glanced down at her chest. She hadn't seen the dog open his mouth. That had to be soul talking even if it sounded like regular speech to her ears. Weird!

"But…"

He had a point. Deek hadn't been there yet. He could rush in and out without too much trouble.

"Promise that you'll bring it back?"

Deek nodded. Peyton squinted. Was he telling the truth? What had Klast bred into the dog? Had he really gone to fetch her help? Peyton bit her lip and gave into temptation, clenching her hands into fists and willing herself to locate Klast through the secret hunting technique she had. A trail of golden sparkles only she could see filtered through the wall, heading out toward the arena. She doubted her cure would be found there. The only thing she had left was to trust the dog.

# 6

Boom, boom, boom, boom. Klast slammed the bidding stickers up on the dog's cages, covering up all the writing from the annoying people the day before. He rushed into the sleeping rig and clicked on the light, much to the annoyance of the sleeping breeders. He grabbed his bag.

"You made it back. How you doing?" Mike asked him, the first to shield the light and sit up.

"I'm leaving," Klast answered. "Sell my dogs for me. All of them. If they imprint, great. If not, they need to sell."

"Klast," Bronze groaned as he watched him slap the cage key down on the table in the middle of the room. Sahafi was still out, and Imar covered his head with the blanket.

The thing was, it didn't hurt anymore. It didn't slice to think of selling the dogs when he'd already lost Deek. What mattered was not *fully* losing Deek. The dog could sit around with whoever he fancied. He was still titled to Klast, and that's where he was going to stay. Anything otherwise, and Klast would end up in jail. He'd find himself tearing through Sysmat to get his dog back. They already owned Peyton. They were *not* getting Deek. Never.

He'd had too close of a call with Sysmat already. On the day Shadow died, Klast involuntarily shifted between worlds landing in Lexia. He thought that he'd died at first, but it was neither heaven nor purgatory. Shifting was explained to him, and he returned to Hyphas only to find the pain of his broken soul to be too strong. Klast woke in the hospital, dragged there by some dog or other after he'd thrown himself off a bridge.

Sysmat surrounded him. They gave him the heebie jeebies with their promises to cure anything that ailed him. No way. They were not going to control *his* soul. He hated that company. He worked against that company. They flaunted miracle cures for diseases, but rumor had it that they put the diseases into the public in the first place. The rational part of his brain told him he couldn't blame Sysmat for his loss, but the emotional part of him couldn't get over the grudge and pain that they'd not saved his dog.

If it wasn't for Clark Manford scooping Klast up, shifting him back into the freezing darkness between worlds, and then running him to a safety station on Lexia, Klast would have succumbed to the life-threat of Sysmat policies. They'd have found a way to claim his free will. Luckily, Clark recognized Klast by knowing his father who was famous on Lexia and grabbed him first.

"I know it was a stressful day…" Mike started.

Klast was already back out the door running for the exit before the guys could muster up their dogs to chase after him. He had to clear the security gate again and let it ring like "normal" before he could shift out of this realm and back into the one that could help him save his dog.

"Get back here!" Bronze screamed at him. "We can't sell your dogs for you!"

"Sure you can. You're very good at selling dogs."

"They won't listen to us!"

"Better hope they imprint then, so they listen to somebody!" Klast yelled back.

Four more steps. The security guards were eyeing each other, wondering if they should stop him from bailing. There was no rule against leaving dogs in the compound. They couldn't fine him for it, but they could get in his way long enough for some IB dog to tackle him.

"Klast! Deek was only a dog. A dog, man! I know it doesn't feel like it, but you have to let him go. You need to take care of the others."

Imar was chasing after him too. Too bad for him. Klast had reached the gate. He rushed through the security monitors, listening to the alarm chime at him and then get turned off. Sometimes he felt like his entire life was one big lie. He bred IB dogs which was the reason why the alarms sounded on him. That was the lie. He'd picked up the dogs *because* the alarms rang at him for his heritage and he needed an easy excuse to get through security checkpoints. What had started as a hobby turned into his life.

Klast dodged around the edge of a tree and shifted.

The air changed. The night faded away to a warm afternoon that was only going to lead to a sunset so cold one inhale killed. He'd shifted in holding his breath just in case, but he released the hold when he found the sun on his skin. This was a place he had never taken his dogs to, although his older ones had smelled the truth before.

It had been exactly two hundred days since he had last been to Lexia. The previous two-hundred moons he'd spent on Hyphas raising a litter of dogs. He left Lexia to escape a woman. Now he was running to save a lady. His feet materialized on the barren ground similar to the wasteland of the doomscape. Instead of being infested by demons that marked you for food, the air itself marked you. He coughed on the dryness as he glanced around in search of the runner's safety station.

It was a requirement to work as a runner to contribute to the safety of Lexia, so Klast was rather familiar with the small huts that blocked out the elements. He'd spent hours and hours in them over the course of five years. On days when he couldn't take the loneliness of being without Shadow, he'd come here to stare into nothingness surrounded by people who didn't believe in soul dogs. Nighttime was when the safety stations were most stocked. People stared out the window searching for shifters who might die from the cold air. One breath in, and lungs started to freeze. A runner would rush into the cold, scoop up the visitor, and carry or drag them to safety.

Klast dashed toward the nearby building. The door of it opened as he turned to it and a friendly wave welcomed him back. Not a bad return at all.

"Where 've you been stranger?" Hank howled at him.

The thing about Hank was that he was easy to spot outside. He always wore his black stretchy hat. The one with the gray stripe circling the middle. It flattened his otherwise uncontrollable dark hair. Nothing could be done about his bushy eyebrows, but he'd grown into them.

"Breeding dogs," Klast answered as he ran. He jumped inside the door smiling back at Hank who laughed at his eagerness.

"You're out of shape."

"I could still pass you in a footrace in the dead of night," Klast replied.

He took in a grateful lungful of the humidified air in the station and sighed in satisfaction. Now *that* was a smell that he missed! If he was a dog and imprinted with smells, it would be this one. The musty smell was similar to that of old books, which made no sense because those were dry and brittle and this was moist. An anomaly. It made him smile.

The only person in the room that he recognized was Hank. Not too surprising, since Klast typically worked the night shifts and these guys were the day crew. Klast gave them all a nod while they eyed each other wondering who Klast was. Klast moved directly to the hazmat reader and unlocked the box with the deftness of refined practice. Let that tell these blokes that he belonged here.

"So, how are the dogs?"

Klast shrugged. He tried not to give himself away over here. The dark empty space he crossed through was the edge of Lexia. Some said that the divide held the difference between a man with a soul and a man without. He was past that boundary most of the time and didn't want people to think he had a damaged essence. Contrary to his birth beliefs, soulless people could exist. Shooting them did next to nothing. One had to pull in the divide's force to crumble a soulless body into dust.

"Ah come on. Last I heard, you had told Isabelle that you wouldn't marry her, and then you vanished over the divide and haven't returned until now."

At least Hank hadn't mentioned the blown-up building. Hopefully everyone had forgotten how Klast ran away from the repercussions of that at the same time. There were ten in the station with them, but Hank was not introducing the day shift, and Klast was on a time crunch, so he decided to ignore the men as well. If he was lucky, none of them would pick up who he was.

"As if everything you did over here was a bad dream," Hank continued. "Your dad was starting to think that you'd forgotten about all of this." Hank swept his hand around the room.

"When did you see him last?" Klast asked, turning to look at Hank for the answer.

"Four days ago."

Klast rolled his eyes and went back to the opened hazmat station. He took out a wadded-up food wrapper from his pocket, which earned a lot of interested looks from the day runners as they tried to guess its origin. Inside the wrapper, he had a saturated business card that he didn't care for (it wasn't the one from Lawrence), that contained the scentless green goop that Peyton had been throwing up. He placed the specimen into the reader and clicked on the machine. A few minutes and he would know if his guess was correct about what ailed Peyton.

"I take it you're not thrilled with your dad's timing?" Hank pried coming to stand beside him with a short glance out the window first.

The window. It was a habit to always glance out the window. Every time Klast got back from one of these gigs, he had to remind himself to not look out every window as if he'd find someone to save. People could breathe just fine where he grew up, and his frequent glances made his dogs jumpy.

"Just wondering." Klast offered a tight smile.

It was his dad who had given him the shifting genes. His mother remained clueless. Once she suspected Klast's dad was having an affair for being gone so long, but his dad was a smooth talker, and she soon stopped bringing it up. The part about his father's timing was that his dad had come here rather than call Klast. No one told him about the hospital visit or the release from it. There *was* cell service in the woods during the hike. His siblings were liars. Klast had no missed call notifications from them because they had not bothered to call. He'd been so distraught about magically making money for his parents that he'd ignored the obvious. All lying jerks. What was this scheme about?

"Your dad thought that you'd not return unless it was a life-or-death situation. He was under the impression that your mind had placed a large fog over the memory of Lexia, and only torment would reopen the wound and send you back into the darkness."

"Mind your own business, Hank," Klast bristled.

"It *is* my business. I'm stuck here sitting around waiting for *you* to show up."

"He's the one?" one of the day runners asked. The man glanced out the window as if there would be someone else other than Klast. Klast almost laughed.

"My dad hired you to spy on me?" Klast guessed.

"He's paying me to tell him if pretending to die was enough to send you back here. He told me everything. You were born across the divide and only when you experienced the loss of a most tragic death did you fade between realms drifting in and out of Lexia. Some snipper organization almost snagged you to turn you against the lot of us, but some old-timer named Clark Manford recognized you for what you were and shifted you over to here where you stabilized. Then he contacted your dad."

"Are you telling me," Klast nearly shouted as he spun around, "that my dad faked being in the hospital so I'd shift? That's super low. I *cried* when I found out. I was already having a bad day, and no, it wasn't him being a jerk that brought me back. Okay? I need to analyze this."

"What is it?" Hank asked, scanning Klast to see how threatening he looked.

"It's none of your business, and if you make it your business, you'll wish that you hadn't."

"Why?"

"It has to do what that snipper organization. Don't ask too many questions."

"You came back because you turned on us?" Hank asked.

"Blooming no!" Now he was shouting. "I hate those guys. I was busy with the dogs."

"Because you know," Hank kept going, "you're one of the natural born. You don't need a gadget to shift. You tell your body to comply, and it moves across matter and essence. The rest of us have to pay for our shifting devices and spend hours and hours working these running shifts to prove that we're worthy to have it. You'd be frightening if you turned into a snipper to kill us off."

Klast opened his mouth to say that the last person he had ever killed had been over here. There had been a soulless man who started sucking on his soul. Now the soulless demon was blasted into particles. Best not tell Hank that he *only* killed men in Lexia.

"I'm going to take that as a compliment that you find me intimidating," Klast said instead.

"What are you doing, Klast Burma," Hank insisted.

Aaannnd there went his hopes that none of the other men in the room would figure out who he was. Klast quickly scanned the men's faces looking for signs that he was in trouble for that broken building, or running away from his "duty" to marry Isabelle, or for simply being the child of a famous man like Jethro Burma. Those in the room remained curious and not hostile, so he went back to his task.

"You know that stuff Matt was talking about that one night?" Hank raised an incredulous eyebrow. "The bacteria from Merlow."

"*Mervolk*," Hank corrected.

"Yes, that. I think I found some."

"That stuff? You found it where?"

"In a toilet. One way to find out if I'm correct."

"You shifted because you saw green slop in a toilet?"

Klast shook his head and turned back to look at the reading. Halfway done with the analysis.

"I don't believe you."

"What's the cure for that stuff, anyway?" Klast wondered.

Matt, who had worked with both Klast and Hank for months on end, had said how horrible it was if ingested. He hadn't said what would happen if one got close to it as Klast had done, but Klast had weighed the risk. It was either sample the stuff and potentially save his dog, or forever feel like he hadn't tried his hardest. He could be dying now too, but that was the risk he took to help a pack member. He was the one jumping out into the rushing traffic to get that hat. Deek was the only one to ever pass his hat test. He wasn't leaving his dog.

When Klast told Deek to go back to the sidewalk, he hadn't done it. That was the real test. Who would carry out the first order and save the hat when his gut told him it needed saving? Klast always placed a mouse in the hat. Many of them had died as the dog valued Klast's words over instinct. It was still a wonderful skill to have, to listen to his leader, but Deek was never fooled by human pecking order. He'd saved the mouse. That was the moment Klast knew he was looking at something extraordinary. Deek was one of the best, and Klast wasn't going to lose him to this *Mervolk* stuff.

"You don't need to be worried about it if you caught *Mervolk*," Hank answered.

"Yes, I do."

"No, you don't. The cure is simple. Jump across the divide. You just did that. It kills the *Mervolk* bacteria instantly. That's why Matt was talking about it. The only way to kill that stuff is to shift. Some people pay handsomely for one shift. Matt was looking for an easy money venture, so he was contemplating signing up for a *Mervolk* shift. You're safe. At least from that," Hank said.

Klast didn't like the way Hank was looking at him still. Now that Klast wasn't being all emotional, he looked back toward the sample he'd brought, his dead sample, and wished that he had shot his dog. Peyton could sparkle hunt. She'd spent a full day staring at Klast. He had to be marked, and now she would know the path to get to Lexia because he had taken that path. She wouldn't be able to shift without first gaining access to a device to do so, but meeting her suddenly looked like an elaborate trap.

Someone guessed or faked or influenced, the connection of Deek to Peyton. Whatever it was, she was there because Sysmat knew Klast could shift and they wanted to follow him. If he took the easy route and jumped her across the divide to kill the *Mervolk*, Sysmat would track her changes in an instant and invade this planet. As it was, he had not taken her with him, but they would hound her for the answer. Lexia was one of the last locations that hadn't been invaded by Sysmat. Klast had just opened up the way for them to get in. They had appealed to his nature to save those in his team and tricked him.

Klast inhaled deeply. He'd already failed. He had joined in the fight to save Peyton against the uppity dog. That had to be part of the trap too. He had just proved twice over that Peyton was part of his family unit and that he'd come to her aid. He'd just joined with Sysmat while attempting to do the opposite. Why had Deek let him do that? Why let him be so stupid?!

"How do you plan on contacting my dad?" Klast asked. "I suggest you do it. I'm going to need his input on this."

The sample finished analysis. Dead *Mervolk* as expected. This bacteria was dead, but the struggle to live wasn't over.

Klast's phone ringing distracted him from making other hasty conclusions. It sounded impossible that the phone would work worlds apart, but it did. The connection was another thing Klast had not questioned for long. There was never enough time to worry about small things like that. He assumed it was something his father had done so he could remain in contact with the family when he was out of the world leaving them none the wiser.

"Hello," Klast answered.

"I'm sorry I missed your call. I would love to buy the dogs from you." Lawrence. Of course, it was him.

"Give me Peyton's number first," Klast bartered.

He got it and then hung up on Lawrence letting the man's frustrated calls go to voicemail. That only reminded him of his sibling's missing phone calls making him irritated. Why go along with the trick? Too many problems at once. He had to warn Deek that Peyton was a trap. Odds were that Lawrence was working directly with Sysmat, and had instigated this whole thing. The instant Peyton picked up the phone, he started rambling.

"Deek. Black box, blue button, trap. Sparkle, sky, box, trap. Work, wolf. Peyt cage, work, out, live. Soul, find, live. Black box, death. Do you understand?"

The line was quiet as Deek digested the words. He had to get it because Klast couldn't say it any other way. If he saw a shifting box it was going to lead to a lot of people dying and was the trap they had walked into. If Peyton tried to find Klast through a sparkle hunt, they would be in danger too. The people she worked for were wolves. The only way to survive this was for Peyton to find a way to connect herself again, get her soul back, and escape Sysmat.

"Question," Deek barked at him.

"Go ahead."

"Green bathroom," Deek barked.

Not the best of sentences, but he knew what it meant. "Yeah, I found the cure, but you have to get out of the cage to get it. Okay."

"Yes," Deek answered.

"You found my cure?!" Peyton cried.

Klast ended the call. Then he tossed the device beneath the hazmat ray where he fried it. He couldn't do anything to get Peyton away from Sysmat. If she was still affiliated with them then he had to turn his back on her and stay far, far away. It was up to Deek now. Up to him to do the impossible. Klast hoped that he had trained him well enough for that. No one had been able to escape Sysmat.

# 7

"He found my cure!" Peyton screamed.

She clapped her hands together before putting them back on the steering wheel of the rental car. Lawrence hadn't been answering her calls, so she had left him behind. She needed to reach the teleporter to get Deek to the doomscape while she still had time left. It didn't matter how hesitant she had felt about Klast before. Just the thought that he was still there with her, that he hadn't walked out and left her when he knew exactly what she was, made a warmth fill her heart. Whoever he was, the dog breeder knew what he was talking about. Suddenly her miracle felt at her fidgety fingertips. She could stop dying!

"So what was the part about how to get it? What cage?" Peyton asked as she slowed down at a red light. "That was strange about that box thing too. What was that?" She looked over at Deek who kept his eyes on the road studying the cars around them. Maybe he was getting driving tips. Who knew? If Klast's dogs could fly planes, hers could probably drive a car.

"You know how to drive?" she asked.

"Yes," Deek answered. "Turn left."

They weren't in the left turn lane. They needed to go straight. The light changed and she gave the dog a hesitant glance before she continued forward. To distract him about how she didn't turn, she kept talking.

"Odd that he called me Peyt. I've never had anyone call me that before. It was almost like he likes me or something."

"He likes you. Turn left."

She hadn't gotten used to this soul talking thing yet. Peyton rubbed at her ears as if they were the things deceiving her when it was her insides that interpreted impressions into words back into her brain.

"You were smart to read that phone number."

She hadn't known who was calling her and assumed it was spam so set the phone down in the cupholder. Deek had taken one glance at the number and used his nose, or maybe his tongue, to answer it. Whatever it was, her phone was now wet. The instant Klast started talking, she was impressed by how he had reached her. He never asked for her number, and all his orders were cryptic. Peyton glanced at Deek again and tried to hide her worry.

"Alright what was that part he said about souls? Find a soul and live. What soul?"

"Yours," Deek replied. "Soul lost."

"I have my soul."

He shook his head no. It appeared that a head shake was an irrefutable answer.

"I do have my soul or I wouldn't be alive. A body needs a soul. It's a little split perhaps, but I still have it."

The dog shook his head again. She glared at him, not about to argue her point with a dog even if he felt like a new human friend. She'd been chattering to him the entire way to the rental car to calm her nerves about what she was leading. She never did put on Deek's leash. It didn't feel right. There was still some underlying scheme about that leash that made her hesitate, and he was perfect at "heel."

"Why did Tasha bring me your leash?" she asked.

"Good dog," Deek answered.

She laughed. "And you're not a dog?" she teased him.

Deek had insisted on sitting in the front seat. She had placed him in the back and told him to stay there so he wouldn't distract her while she was driving. He had refused her order to sit in the front even when she grabbed his collar and put him in the back four times to get her point across. He had willingly moved and then jumped into the front each time. That was another feature that made him not feel like her dog. He didn't listen to simple commands, but then she thought about that soldier and the hole and how the dog had been saving him.

"Why won't you sit in the back?"

"Gut," Deek answered, causing Peyton to swallow.

"You think I'll pass out while driving and you'll have to save me?" She tried to ask that causally like it didn't bother her. At least Deek didn't know that her driving privileges had been revoked for that very reason.

"No. Car chase," Deek replied.

"What car chase?"

Peyton scanned the road looking behind her trying to see if any of the cars were following her. No one was behind her. The only thing she spotted was a running black dog. It made her shiver, so she looked away. The traffic was rather light at the moment. Most people would be in the arena walking around and around.

"I don't see it."

"Turn left."

"Why...?" There wasn't even a left turn right here. To the left was a bunch of fencing.

"Car chase," Deek insisted again.

"Are you lying to me?"

He laughed at her. This was where having Klast in the car would have been helpful. He would be able to tell her what a laughing, devil dog meant. Deek was either making it all up to see if she would listen to him when he had already proved that he wouldn't listen to her, *or* he had spotted a car chase.

"Are you my dog?" Peyton asked, berating herself for pulling over into the next left turn lane.

*"You can hear me."*

Ahh! She rubbed at her ears again. That time it sounded like a whisper in her head instead of audible syllables. True, she could hear him. It was hard to decide if the dog was barking his words or saying them. Sometimes it sounded like both. Sometimes neither.

"That doesn't prove anything. Klast could hear you and you're not imprinted to him. That doesn't mean anything. Are you my dog?"

*"Peyton dog. Klast dog."*

"You can't imprint two people."

"Why?" Deek asked her.

He still wasn't looking at her whenever she glanced at him. He watched the road and his dog mouth wasn't moving as if she was making this whole conversation up in her head. What a nut case she was. First, she lost her soul. Now she lost her mind.

"Because you can't. You're not mine."

She hated saying that, but it felt truer than claiming that he was. Deek hadn't imprinted her in the traditional sense. He had done the same thing to her that he'd learned to do to Klast. Whatever it was, this dog had figured out how to crack the code on imprinting. Clever indeed.

"If we didn't imprint, then why did you have Tasha bring me your leash? What are you here for?"

"Help pretty dying girl. Help family."

"I don't see how helping me helps Klast any. Which one of us are you lying to?"

Deek laughed at her again. Then he gave her a glance that made it look like he found her amusing for figuring out something that Klast hadn't. That meant both, didn't it? He refused to imprint fully so he could lie to whoever he wanted. Hopefully, she could get that medicine diffuser before Deek ran back to his former best friend.

"I want to trust you, Deek, but I can't. What is happening? Please tell me." She started to turn the car back around in the direction of Sysmat so they could reach the teleporter and the doomscape. He growled at her but she turned the wheel anyway. Back to the right.

"Question," Deek barked.

Peyton sighed almost in the same way that she'd heard Klast sigh many times for this one sound already. "Question" meant that the dog didn't know how to put his thoughts into a human language. "Question" meant that she wasn't going to get a clear answer, and she wasn't Klast to pick out what blotched words might mean.

"Wind soul. Darkness soul. Smell. Feeling. Help. Question."

Nope. She had no idea what that meant.

"What is a wind soul?" No answer. "What is a darkness soul? Are they the same soul? Can you smell souls or are you smelling a feeling? Does help mean you want help or you're going to help? I don't understand."

He didn't answer, only turned stiff in his seat and stared at a car as it drove beside them on the right. Peyton glanced at the driver and shivered. There was something wrong with that driver. She had no idea what, but there was something.

"No soul," Deek told her. "Car chase."

Peyton looked again. The driver was pretending to ignore them by keeping her head forward, but her eyes were glancing over. They were icy blue—freezing like a glacier ready to tip over and sink every ship nearby. A person couldn't be driving around without a soul. Not without part of a soul in any case. Peyton was a prime example of having a very small soul at times, but to have none at all felt terrifying. Is that what she was going to become once Sysmat was done experimenting on her? It might be better to die than turn into something that chilled from the inside out with a single look. Peyton tried to cast a part of herself at the person to keep track of the driver's sparkle trail and found that she couldn't. There wasn't a soul to follow. No soul. Deek was right.

"Where did her soul go?" Peyton whispered.

"Darkness," Deek answered. "Car chase."

"Yah. That's not a bad idea."

One more glance to the side and Peyton shot the car forward desperate to get away from the creepy person she couldn't track. How she wanted Klast to show up to punch the driver in the head and save her! She clenched a fist together over her uselessness and watched the sparkles leading to Klast vanish into a point in the air. Not possible. He couldn't be in the clouds. Klast's words to his dog rang through her mind. He'd warned about sparkles in the air being a trap. She was being blocked. That had to be it. Her ability was blocked when she was this close to a person who had lost her soul. It was a good thing she had met Deek and Klast because they were the only ones that could save her.

"What is the black box with the blue button?" Peyton asked. "That was a trap too as I recall."

She swerved around a few other cars watching the back mirror as the soulless woman followed, grinning. Peyton shivered. Then she glanced at the gas and groaned. They were almost empty because she'd not thought to fill up. She wasn't going to win a car chase. She was going to putter out in the middle of the road and that creepy woman was going to reach her. Then something bad would happen.

"Help! Help! Help!" Deek barked.

"You're supposed to be the help!" She reminded him.

"Help. Soul. Help!" He kept barking as she swerved again ignoring the honks.

Unconstructive dog! She didn't know what to do. It wasn't like she could sparkle the creepy woman away. Here was yet more proof that she wasn't a sniper. A sniper would be able to save herself! The only idea she had was to reverse the rental and ram the car behind her hoping that the impact would hurt the woman more than herself. It was not a brilliant move.

Bark, bark, bark, went the dog. Sputter went the car. Peyton screamed when they were rear-ended. Her head jerked forward crashing into the steering wheel instead of an airbag. The bumper crunched. There went the warranty on the rental car. She glanced around for a weapon as the cold-eyed lady jumped out of her car and rushed forward.

"Do something helpful!" Peyton screamed. What good was a bodyguard-dog if it didn't do anything?! She locked the car doors but the chill kept getting stronger.

"Cold soul. Help!"

She was going to start screaming that too. Everything got icier. Her hands took on a blue color turning her fingers numb. The woman outside banged the car window screaming about Peyton's driving skills. Darkness started to creep across Peyton's vision. Not now! Peyton whispered Deek's name in a frantic plea as the ice invaded her brain.

# 8

Smack! Everyone in the safety station jumped except for the kid by the back wall who had been knocked right over. Klast cast a nervous glance out the window (he wasn't the only one to put the outside first), before turning his attention toward the commotion.

"Dad!" Klast cried out.

It was reckless to shift into a full room. There was no way to know where everyone was unless you were like Peyton and could soul lock, but even she had limits. Jethro Burma should have shifted into the wide-open outside like everyone else. Born on Lexia, he knew the rules better than anyone. He was the man in charge of enforcing the shifting rules for crying out loud! There had to be someone to hold him to the same standards as everyone else. Klast increased his glare.

Mr. Burma genetically matched Klast with the same dark hair and the wider tip nose, but the rest of him was distinctly Jethro. Where Klast favored functional clothes that could withstand recreational abuse, Jethro favored the well-tailored suit. Today his chosen color was dark gray with a white pinstripe. If he had looked even remotely tired or ill, Klast would have handled seeing his father better, but the man was in perfect health. Klast was about to punch him. He was not okay with what had happened.

"Everything good with your dogs?" Mr. Burma casually asked.

Jethro's brows furrowed together as if the only reason Klast would be over here was to escape his canine issues. That was typically the case. However, Klast didn't discuss dog breeding with his father. Not since the one incident where Mr. Burma tried to tell Klast how to train the creatures. Klast was going to do it his way. His way was fabulous. Everyone said so.

"You lied," Klast accused.

"Did you leave them all?"

"Dad!"

"The dogs! Did you leave all your dogs by themselves?"

"Of course not. Three of them sold. The others are close to being rehomed and don't go treating me like I'm irresponsible. I left them with other breeders who'd rather lose a leg than lose my dogs. It's not like they're going anywhere. You, on the other hand, have gone to the loonies. How did you talk my siblings into enforcing your lie?"

"You have siblings?" Hank asked him.

Darn. Klast couldn't carry out a screaming match with his father among these witnesses. None of them had the first idea Mr. Burma had other children. As far as they knew, Klast was the only other Burma with natural-born shifting abilities. That was the truth as far as Klast knew, too.

"Half-siblings," Klast lied to Hank. "You still lied about being in the hospital," he directed back to his dad.

"I was in the hospital," his father insisted.

"For yourself?" Klast huffed. "Wait. Why were you in the hospital?"

"You're missing the point," Mr. Burma deflected.

Jethro helped to pick up the fallen runner that he'd knocked over upon entry, and then came over to where Klast was at the hazmat scanner. Klast shut off the screen and removed his sample before his father could see what he had been researching. The scanners were supposed to be used for shifting incidents only. Not for people lightyears away under the care of Sysmat.

"The issue at hand was that you were breaking the law. You had not shifted in over three-hundred—"

"Two hundred," Klast corrected.

"You were well over the number of days for a required check-in."

"I have never heard of a time limit for forcing a person to shift. I thought limits were set in place so people *didn't* shift as much." Klast crossed his arms, still wanting to get at his father for the whole ailment thing. It took a lot to drop Klast to his knees. His father had dropped him.

"Then you're hearing about it now. Things change when you're gone. You could come back and find out that a new political party has overtaken the entire planet."

"No." Klast swallowed. "Me coming back paved the way for exactly that to happen. I should have stayed away. We've got an issue at hand here."

"The issue being that you could have forgotten all about Lexia and no amount of me mentioning the name would have changed that."

"I do not have amnesia. Focus for a second, will you? I met a soul hunter that works for Sysmat. If that person tracks me over here, then Sysmat finally gets what it wants. It gets access to Lexia. We have to do something about safeguarding the borders."

"You met..." Mr. Burma trailed off, eyeing the wadded wrapper that was still in Klast's hand.

Klast shoved his evidence into his pocket. He wasn't going to tell his father about Peyton's *Mervolk* problem. That was a separate issue as far as Klast was concerned. It brought up all sorts of questions about how she had gotten the ailment in the first place when it wasn't native to Hyphas where she lived. Klast wondered if *Mervolk* was native to anything at all. He'd have to do more research about it before he opened that particular bag.

"A Sysmat sniper can track me into Lexia," Klast repeated. "We need a plan to stop Sysmat from invading."

"You are jumping to conclusions. What are the facts, not the story that you fabricated?"

Ugh. His father was good at his job, but part of that required him to be cynical. The longer Klast stayed where he was, the longer Peyton had time to question his location and find him. He needed to get off this planet.

"Fact. Sysmat sent two agents to buy up every single one of my dogs. Fact. The death of one of my dogs led me to reach Lexia for the first time. Fact. One of the dog-buying agents can soul hunt. Speculation that should be fact," Klast stressed. "If Sysmat is after every single one of my dogs with a soul hunter in tow, then they have plans to use the dogs to send me to Lexia so they can find the place. I never should have come back. They're tracking me. I knew it."

"I can see how that would be problematic," Mr. Burma agreed.

Finally. Klast let out an aggravated sigh for being the weak idiot that he was. At least he hadn't brought Peyton. As a soul hunter, she'd be rather fascinated by the soul technology these people lived with. It was something he could never let her know.

"They use a box with a blue button to shift," Klast continued. "If we could figure out how to block their frequencies—"

"Shifting doesn't use frequencies like you're thinking, Klast. It's not some radio that you can jam. Shifting requires a connection between body and soul, and those devices have to be built with a sliver of The Between to work. As far as I'm aware, there is nothing that can block the force that lives between states."

"Nothing stops the voided darkness?" Klast asked.

"Is it dark when you go through it?" his father questioned as if that was the more interesting part of his question.

Klast rolled his eyes. "So what can we do? If they follow me over here, it's not like we'll be able to pick out who is Sysmat versus a traveler from someplace else. Not until it's too late, anyway. The only thing was can do is pull everyone to safety, then check to see if they carry the blue mark on their arm. By that point, they could have launched biochemicals into the air."

"Sysmat is a medical company that protects—"

"That invades other planets to steal their research so they can boast glorious cures for the agents they detain," Klast cut off. "They don't have me fooled. I thought you didn't like them either."

"I don't!" Mr. Burma replied. He put his back to the wall and eyed all the men in the safety station as if one word about this to anyone would get them fired. Most men dropped their gaze rather quickly in favor of looking back out the window. All except for Hank, who stared right back. The daring, gutsy Hank. Klast quite liked him.

"The thing is, Klast, that I shouldn't put out a planet-wide alert based on speculation that a medical company will invade."

"Based on previous facts about what they have done to other planets they located," Klast retorted. "I can't believe that I'm arguing with you about this."

"We are not arguing. You are being jumpy. I said that I *shouldn't*. Not that I wasn't going to. I have nothing except your word on this, but I agree it could pose a threat, so here's the plan. I will put out an alert to forbid any shifting into and out of Lexia for the next five days. If anyone shifts into the area, we will shoot them on sight. No questions asked. If Sysmat is trying to get in, then we'll catch them."

"Five days!" Hank burst.

"They move fast," Mr. Burma told him.

"That's forever! Five days without work is going to put me behind on my bills."

"You will have work to do. You'll have extra work to do. We'll need everyone possible on the posts in case invaders get inside. If their goal is to track Klast to Lexia instead of buying a couple of dogs, then we're looking at a brutal war. Let's hope that Klast is wrong and they only want to buy dogs."

"What would they want my dogs for?" Klast waved his hands through the air. "There are plenty of other ones. This is a direct attack!"

"I find it amusing how you feel under attack from dog buyers."

Oh, there were so many things Klast wanted to say back to that! Dog selling didn't attack him. He knew he was right on this. Sysmat was up to something more than simply looking for a guard puppy. They were targeting him directly, most likely to get into Lexia. Once the first wave of Sysmat agents shifted over, they'd see. Klast wasn't making things up. His instincts had kept him out of plenty of holes before. They were going to see him to the other side of this one.

*"Cold!"*

"It's not the regular buyers that have me worried. It's the soul hunter," Klast insisted.

He didn't like the dog buyers either, though. He preferred letting his dogs imprint, but he couldn't bring that point up over here. That had been one of the first things he learned upon reaching Lexia. The planet saw IB dogs as a myth. They were steeped in legends as soul dogs: magical creatures who bonded to the soul and made a man invincible. It wasn't actually like that. Sometimes Klast wondered if his father had put down roots on Hyphas because it intrigued him that IB dogs truly existed, and of course, because he had fallen in love with Runette.

"And how do you know it was a soul hunter you were looking at?"

"I touched her," Klast answered, narrowing his eyes in case his father thought deeper on that.

Klast wasn't supposed to attempt soul searching on a person. It was a technique that he'd only ever heard about while sitting around in one of these safety stations with nothing better to do. It sounded like a myth to him—to touch a person and have their soul sputter back. Klast was looking for a pulse on Peyton, but when he'd placed his hand on her arm, whispers rushed through him like a sixth sense. There was no other way to explain how he knew what he did. She could track souls. She had *Mervolk*. They were in trouble.

"She was cold, and she left with one of my dogs that told me she was a soul hunter."

*"Really cold!"*

"You hear that?" Klast asked, cutting off whatever his dad was going to say. This was the second time he'd heard something about the cold. It was burning outside. It wasn't going to get cold until the sun went down. Everyone in the running station rushed to the window and looked out except for him.

"What?" Klast's father asked, not seeing anything special outside.

"It was… I heard… It sounded like…" Like Deek talking into his head, which wasn't possible because the dog had left him.

*"Help!"*

There it was again! It *was* Deek! Remarkable. Klast pulled out his gun and looked around to find his dog, only to roll his eyes at himself. He was with Peyton, and she wanted to take Deek to the doomscape. They couldn't have reached it yet, but something was scaring his dog. Something that over-challenged Deek's training.

"I'll come back and help later," Klast told the group.

Then, without bothering to step outside to shift since he expected the runners to tell him he couldn't abandon them, Klast shot across the divide, doing his best to trace the feeling of Deek's call. He couldn't hunt a soul. The only thing he could do was guess. So much for staying far away from Sysmat and Peyton and letting Deek handle everything.

Klast landed in the middle of the road amid a long hooonk! Lucky for him, it was a tall truck. He rolled between the wheels and let it go over the top of him. Swearing offended the air as the truck window rolled down. Klast jumped to his feet and waved the driver off. Where was Deek?

"Deek!" Klast called.

It was nice to have his dog's imprint so he could use their real names in social situations. If Deek was nearby, the dog would do his best to be heard. Klast couldn't make out a dog barking, but the sound of metal crunching into metal and a woman shouting sprang down a nearby road. Might as well start there. It didn't sound like Peyton, but crash sites needed help. Klast dashed off to the left, jumping over a few hedges to reach the other street.

He saw the line of stalled cars called first. Ten of them piled up behind each other with people inside shivering and craning their necks about trying to see what was out there without wanting to go look for themselves. At the front of the line were two cars. One blue, the other black. Both were dented up rather badly.

He couldn't see Peyton, but he could see Deek inside the blue car, baring his teeth and growling at an eerie woman as the chill of her hands slivered the car window, cracking it apart. A few more seconds of that and the soulless was going to get into the car and freeze everything. Soulless?! How had a soulless woman gotten this far into the city without Sysmat stopping her? Or the police? Or some detective?

Klast raised his gun, careful to make sure no one else was in the way, and shot. The impact distracted her from the glass but didn't kill her. It never was enough. She had to be taken out with a different sort of force. Only the pressure of the abyss could swallow up an animated body that had no soul. The first time Klast faced a soul sucker, he had been terrified. The creature had rushed at him empty, dead, and starving to devour him. Soulless people made no sense. It should be dead, not moving.

He rushed to the car. The soul devil screamed at him once before it went back to cracking the glass fixated on the desire to devour his dog. No, she didn't! Deek glanced at Klast. Watching the dog's transformation from snarling to happy was most amusing. Deek barked, trying to tell Klast everything in his head all at once while he bounced in his chair. It made Klast smile way too much. He shouldn't be that happy to see a dog that wasn't his, but he was. Klast was going to smother the dog in praises and hugs the instant he could get into that car. Then he would figure out where Peyton had gone. How dare she leave his dog locked up with a soulless woman nearby! First though, the zombie. His legs pumped faster.

"Be gone soul devil!"

A little bit closer. Klast jumped at the insane woman as the glass of the car shattered. Strands of red-brown hair rose into the air at the change in pressure. Aha! That's where Peyton was. She had fallen over in the front seat. Her entire face was blue, a feature of being eaten alive. Klast shivered as he collided with the zombie. Wham! He yanked in the soul-matter power. Whether it was called the power of the abyss, the void, the darkness, or The Between, it still slammed into the zombie in the same way.

Soulless hadn't the time to scream. She crumbled to dust in Klast's arms, sending him crashing down to the road on top of broken glass. Cuts appeared on his hands and arms, but he hadn't the time to yank out slivers. They had to get off the road! There were too many people watching. He didn't need fifteen witnesses claiming he had turned a screaming banshee into powder. Klast yanked on the car door.

"Locks!" he shouted.

Deek pawed the locks, and they clicked open. He scrambled into the car, pushing Peyton out of the way, but the motor wouldn't turn over.

"Gas," Deek informed.

No gas. Well, there was the other car behind them.

"Come on."

Klast grabbed Peyton as people swarmed toward him asking him why everything had felt so cold. They told him that help was on the way, and he shouldn't move the blue woman. He had to answer questions, and explain where the other woman went. One person blatantly stated that he'd shot her. Yup. Time to run. Klast shoved Peyton in the other car as Deek scrambled over the top of his arms. A turn of the engine and they slowly backed up among shouts and people snapping his picture.

"Horrible publicity," Klast mumbled.

"Question," Deek barked, causing Klast to smile. How he hated that word this week and loved it at the same time.

"Peyton will be fine. She has to warm back up, but I don't dare turn on the heater in this busted thing. We'll ditch it in a minute. That ice woman was soulless. She was eating what was left of Peyton's soul. Looks like she had a fetish for it. Maybe she got a sample of Peyton before and wanted the rest. Freaky. You know, it sounded like you were calling me, Deek," Klast told him. "I wasn't even on this planet. That was very strange."

"Darkness," Deek answered.

"That's right. I went through the darkness to visit some friends. Very astute of you."

"Bronze," Deek voiced next.

"What?" Klast asked, but he chuckled right after.

It *was* the best call to make, given that Klast didn't have any other means of support around here, and his other dogs were in the arena with Bronze. Klast swerved the car out of sight, and made a quick trip into a nearby store to buy a giant bag. He parked the car in a crowd of other tightly placed vehicles, and then casually walked past the arena line to use the breeder entrance. His large bag was now slung over his shoulder.

"They're going to be so thrilled to see me with the way I stormed out," Klast mumbled at the security guard as he strode right through the gateway flashing his badge and acting like he was coming inside alone. He didn't let the man have a second to think about checking his bag. There was a slight protest behind him, but Klast got away with his move miraculously enough.

He wore a long face as he reached the rig and carefully placed the bag inside. Bronze, Imar, and Mike gave him disheartened glances as he trudged back past them. They thought Deek had died, and he had carried his dead dog back home. They sighed at him when he opened the cages of his other dogs and had them follow him into the rig next. Zen, Hero, and Phantom rambled after him not scared in the least. Klast assumed that Weston had imprinted by the way the paperwork was stacked up on his bed for him to sign. Weston's new owner had signed his portion. Klast moved the papers to the table, quickly signing where he needed to without really paying attention to where Weston was. He had no idea what his friends had said to cover for his absence, but he didn't care right now.

He unzipped the bag and grinned as Deek popped out and started wrestling with Phantom, probably teasing him about his clever hiding place since Phantom prided himself on being the best sneak. Phantom howled back about how he could smell Deek the whole time.

Klast placed Peyton carefully on his bed. She was still blue and felt more lifeless than the time he'd seen her not breathing in the hospital. As much as he didn't want her to take that Sysmat medicine, he had to admit that she was going to need it, because he couldn't reverse what Sysmat had done to her soul. It wasn't like he could walk into Sysmat and ask. They'd jump him.

"Zen, Hero, come over here and warm her up. She's freezing."

The two dogs who had been egging on the wrestling match with Deek and Phantom abruptly jumped into work mode. They leaped onto the bed and lay on Peyton, shivering when their fur connected with her frozen skin.

"Now when you see something like this color blue," Klast instructed, "it's because a soulless demon that looks like a person was freezing the soul from the inside out. That's what happened. A soulless woman was sucking Peyton's soul. You can't take down a soulless without pulling in forces of the divide. Deek likes to call this force The Darkness. My dad calls it The Between. I call it a mixture of things, I guess."

"Smell darkness," Zen agreed as if Deek had told him all about the smell. The pup was too young to have ever smelt it on Klast. Klast had not traveled in Zen's lifetime yet.

"Nice inside." Hero grinned as he looked around the rig and then out toward where all the walking people kept going, heedless to the schemes of Klast and his dogs not a few feet away from them.

"I need to figure out a couple of things. We need to get Peyton's medicine diffuser from the doomscape. I can drop Deek in there and pick him up again when he howls. Oddly enough, I can still hear him even through the divide. Care to explain that?" he asked, causing Deek to lose his focus and Phantom to pin him down with a celebratory woof!

"I may have been super distracted, Deek, but not so much that I haven't picked up on what you're doing. You lied to me. You couldn't have imprinted Peyton if I can still hear you. I don't know what you're planning, but sharing that with the rest of us would be nice so we can help you."

"Question," Deek said as he blinked.

"The other thing we need to figure out is how to undo what Sysmat did to Peyton and reclaim her soul. It doesn't make sense that—"

Klast cut off as the rig door opened and Mike slipped in. He shut the door quietly as if he expected to find Klast bawling his eyes out in here. His mouth dropped open on what he saw instead. Klast had to grin when he saw Mike's mind turning, juggling the truth about what Klast had dragged through security unnoticed.

"What doesn't make sense is that the soulless woman who was eating Peyton," Klast continued, "was so set on devouring her. She should have tried to eat me when a stronger target approached. She should have tried to eat

Page | 94

any number of those gawking drivers. She didn't. To me, that looks like this person had been following Peyton around cleaning up all the soul pieces Peyton releases when she's using her Sysmat sniper ability. It's as if…"

As if what?

"Stalker woman," Deek barked, dislodging Phantom from on top of him and jumping onto the bed to help warm Peyton. "Stalker yesterday here. Eat wind soul."

Not understanding what Deek had said, Mike cleared his throat. "I don't think I should be in here," he noted, but he sat down at the table instead of walking back out. Klast smiled at him again. Nothing got a bodyguard breeder more interested than a new puzzle, and this one was looking like a doozy.

"You smelled the soulless person yesterday. Very good, Deek," Klast praised. "Who's a smart dog? We still have to figure out how to unbind Peyton from Sysmat though to keep you out of their clutches, and that's practically impossible. I can't see why they would send a soulless person to eat her if they wanted to use Peyton as…"

Maybe he had gotten it wrong. They didn't want Peyton alive. Sysmat wasn't using Peyton to stalk him through the divide to invade Lexia. They were *trying* to kill her off and make it look like she died of natural causes. Something about her was something they couldn't control or contain, so they had tried to separate her soul and steal it, but she refused to die. She sat around dead and refused to leave. There was no way Klast could call her alive right now, but he could feel a tiny shred of soul clinging to her, keeping her together. She'd start feeling better once she warmed back up and could get back inside herself. From his limited understanding, he could quantify Peyton as a soul repairman. Those on Lexia had a myth about such people. They called them Blazen. She fixed broken pieces of souls. Very powerful. Probably scared the daylights out of Sysmat. A person like her shouldn't exist, but neither should soulless people.

"You know it's not that bad. We have eyewitnesses that Sysmat is trying to kill off one of their agents. They are breaking their contact against the whole keeping-her-alive thing. Bronze knows a good lawyer, right? He can help us spin this to get her out of that."

Deek grinned as if that had been his thought exactly. He barked, asking Bronze to come over by sending for his dog. Mike rubbed at his face, and then looked over at Peyton, questioning if she was even still alive and worth saving. Alive, yes. Worth saving, maybe.

Klast rubbed his face brushing up against the two-week stubble. If the soulless woman had finished eating Peyton in the arena yesterday, her next target would have been Klast since he'd smell more like the divide than anyone. He had been standing rather close to Peyton. Deek had been saving him from a threat that Klast had not seen at all. No wonder the dog couldn't stop barking. There was danger and Deek was trapped in a cage. He'd had to get creative with his rescue mission.

"You're never going to guess what Deek just did," Klast said as Bronze entered the room, guard dog in toe.

"Try me," Bronze said, not looking the least bit surprised that Peyton was in the room more hued than Blue Moon ice cream.

"He pretended to imprint to save my life."

# 9

There were several good smells that Peyton didn't mind waking up to. Freshly baked bread, bacon, or streusel were the top three. There was no bacon, bread, or streusel. What she was smelling was very, very dirty dog. It nearly made her laugh. She wasn't dead, and Deek hadn't left her, but she could tell that she wasn't in the rental car anymore. Peyton shivered, feeling the chill from the cold that had invaded her, claiming every warm cell in her body and stealing it all away. Empty, creepy, woman with no soul.

"It's annoying me to no end," an unfamiliar male voice said.

She had to be in a hospital. Beneath her was a bed mattress, and it was wide enough to fit the fluffy, smelly animals beside her. Wait. More than one!?

"There goes another one imprinting. That leaves only two dogs out of the eight that Klast brought with him," the voice continued to complain. "Eight! I was rather excited when Klast said we'd get to sell his dogs for him."

"Yeah, because you intended to buy one before anyone else realized it was for sale."

"Darn right I was going to! I liked the one that just walked out the door. What did he call it?"

"Hero," the other voice chuckled.

"Well, I liked that one. He had darling white-tipped ears."

"Still two more. You take one, I'll take the other. Who's to know when Klast has pulled them from the cages?"

"The dogs will know," Peyton said as she sat up and shivered.

Not the hospital. She was back in the arena somehow. There were three dogs beside her. One was the familiar Deek. The second was red and brown, and the third was red with white patches. Klast's dogs. The sound outside was muffled by the walls of the sleeping rig that gave the breeders an escape from the chaos. This is what she got for trusting Deek. He pretended to help fetch her medical diffuser, only to drag her right back here, where they couldn't reach it. She was going to die this time for sure.

Peyton looked at her skin, which was a strange shade of ugly gray. Best not to look at all. No one was going to find her beautiful and enlivening when she looked so sickly all the time. She wanted to toss on a sweater and a balaclava. Shoving the ugly thoughts aside and pressing her hands beneath her, she looked at Deek ready to glare at him. He was too smelly to drag back toward Sysmat.

"You should take a bath." She nudged Deek.

*"I'm not a cat."* The words were still in her head. Strangest dog ever.

"Well, yes, the dogs will know we want to buy them," the speaker continued.

*"That's Mike and the other one is Bronze,"* Deek prompted.

Right. She knew that. Bronze was broad-shouldered with a square face and wide eyebrows which gave him a classic tough-guy look. Mike was a hotty. The narrow bone structure of his face was offset by the muscle on his arms. Crisp blue eyes shone beneath black locks. A closer inspection revealed a few strands of white hair, but it only made him shine more. Yikes! Peyton tried to avoid the obvious heartbreakers, and she was going to avoid this one.

"I know the dog will leave the instant he finds someone more amusing, but until that point, the dog would be well taken care of," Mike said.

"And we'd have a good long look at some of Klast's training techniques." Bronze copied Mike's broad grin.

"And the dog would keep up his exercise routines," Mike added, trying to not to sound like a sneak.

"It makes no sense," Peyton complained.

"We have lots of dogs to keep his dog company so they can play—" Mike justified his desire to snatch a Burma dog.

"No. Not that. If the dogs won't listen to anyone that they're not imprinted to, then how do you train them?"

Mike smiled. Bronze opened his mouth to answer.

"They train very well when they are puppies. It's after they hit the age of one that you need to be concerned. Before that, you've got a pretty normal dog. Some trainers refuse to keep IB dogs around past the one-year mark. They sell them off, because after that mark, all loyalties shift. Then there are people like Klast who keep dogs for two to four years. I believe Deek is almost five. Apart from his breed dogs, that's the longest Klast has ever kept one. Sometimes I think he purposely doesn't take extra steps to match Deek with another human."

Bronze looked at the door to make sure that Klast wasn't coming back in. "There's footage of him teaching Deek a really strange alphabet. No one has figured out what it is yet apart from the people who claim to know but will never tell. You can't trust those comments. It's all a bunch of lies so the random dude feels smart."

"You found footage?" Peyton jumped at the bait. She was going to add that to her list of things about Klast. He spoke at least one different language. "I was trying to find information about him too. His name is nowhere. How does he *do* that? I eventually found a few videos of him posted by 'FightForIt' online. Most videos have identities cut out except for some soldiers' names."

"Those soldiers died, so it doesn't matter anymore," Bronze told her.

"You've seen them too?"

He nodded. "Have to stay up to date on the competition somehow. Might as well utilize the anonymous Klast fan club.

"He's not competition," Mike chided. "He's a struggling dog breeder that just so happens to have a few unique quirks."

"Like his ability to make every other dog look subpar," Bronze added. "No offense," Bronze added to the tan dog sitting at his feet. "I didn't mean you. It's a human notion that his dogs are smarter than normal. Doesn't mean that they are."

Bronze's dog yawned. If he thought a comment back, Peyton didn't hear it. She looked at the other two dogs beside her.

*"Phantom is the red one with white stars. Zen is brown and red. Don't let his name fool you. He's not the calmest creature I've ever met."*

And now she knew the other dogs' names, which gave her an added ability to tell them what to do. Maybe she could get Zen or Phantom to fetch her medical diffuser. It hooked into the receptacle tube on her hip where it administered her life-saving liquid at a constant rate. All the other devices like inhalers or patches or syringes gave her the liquid too fast. They made her pass out before she got the full dose. Losing the diffuser had given her severe anxiety.

It had been such a clumsy drop too. She and Sikh were collecting a rare flower for a much-needed medicine. Looking back on the day, she couldn't remember much about Sikh apart from the fact that he was faster than her at everything and not nervous when he stepped through the transporter to reach the doomscape. One minute she was at Sysmat, and the next she was rooted in place disorientated. Peyton had pictured the doomscape being a viny jungle with ravenous animals lurking every few feet. It was actually a long and flat grassland with small carnivorous creatures that scent-locked people when they passed their turf. Pass once and you were fine. Pass twice and it was dinner time.

Sikh had scooped her up after grabbing the flower. She had just pulled out the diffuser to take her medicine to prevent a nose bleed, and it slipped out of her hands as he dragged her away. It was all downhill from there. She couldn't hold back the sickness, and Sysmat wouldn't replace the diffuser.

"You know how you think to yourself that you will never be happy again, and then you see something like Hero falling in love with the most unlikely person ever?" Klast asked as he burst into the room full of smiles. The din from the arena followed him until he shut the door. It was surprising how much sound this rig could block out even if it didn't block everything.

Klast still looked the same. He wore thick black pants with zippered pockets left open. His light blue shirt was slightly loose on him. Around his neck was a brown cord, but Peyton couldn't see what object it held. Klast's stubble was quickly blooming into a beard. Deek placed his head down on the bed as if sad for Klast's excitement.

*"The necklace holds an information tag,"* Deek told her. *"In case he dies, so he doesn't go unidentified."*

"A boy. A little boy! Well, he was about ten, but that's an awfully young age to need a bodyguard. That's going to be a long-lived match right there. Love to watch that unfold. I had to settle everything in the actual office because we had to get parental permission. A pain that. His parents are divorced, but we got through to them both eventually. The woman on the phone wasn't amused that her son was following his dad around a dog arena. What a lucky kid!"

That didn't sound lucky to her. It sounded scary. There was no telling why a child so young would need a guard dog, but it wouldn't be for anything easy. He was going to have one hard life. Peyton thought of the worst possible scenario. The kid might need to run away soon, and all he was going to have was that dog. Hero.

Yeah. Lucky for him to get a constant best friend. She still didn't have that. Her best friend would answer her phone calls and they would talk, but it wasn't the same as it used to be. Peyton couldn't see Cindy anymore. They weren't even supposed to be talking. Once taken by Sysmat, forever taken. Life could never go back to the way it was. Peyton was supposed to make friends within the organization, if she lived, and turn into the person they wanted her to be. Never herself. Never her choice. She was grateful for a second chance, but Sysmat rules didn't sit well with her.

Klast plopped a few papers down on the desk beside the others. He rifled the pages and then shoved them into a bag on the floor. Peyton felt similar to how Deek looked. She wanted to force Klast's dog into the doomscape so she could stop feeling sick. She wanted to ask Klast if he was being sarcastic about the lucky kid. Had he made progress on her cure? All her questions felt heavy in her mouth and too loose in her brain. The question that came out wasn't planned but felt anchored to her survival.

"If the boy is ten, how long will the dog live before they both die? Will he die at twenty? Do IB dogs live ten years?"

"You can get a good forty to sixty years out of an IB dog. However, they do start to slow down with age like the rest of us. The boy will live a good life," Bronze answered her.

"So imprinting an IB dog can shorten a mortal lifespan?" Peyton asked. Forty years was still far below normal life expectancy around here.

"That depends on how you view it," Mike answered. "People end up imprinting because they need something to save them. Without the dog, they'd have a much shorter lifespan. The longest living IB dog reached seventy-two. He wasn't out walking by then, but treat the dog right, and the odds are they will outlive you."

"What were you doing with your life before turning slave?" Bronze asked her revealing what he thought about Sysmat. He had to be one of the people who refused Sysmat aid in his will.

Peyton frowned at his question and looked over at Klast as if he'd bail her out. He was staring at a blank phone that he'd picked up from a chair. There was no point in looking at it except to escape eye contact with everyone else. It made her jaw twitch. Some random kid got all his praise. She got ignored. She wanted his words aimed at her like a bad crush gone wrong.

Even worse, Bronze had asked her to reveal how unspectacular she was. These guys were all super accomplished. Famous dog breeders. Klast could do things like fly planes and spot spyware and understand alien sicknesses. The other guys probably had talents just as special such as deep-sea diving, gem mining, and firefighting.

"Nothing special," Peyton sighed, as if a bad swimming partner was pulling her down.

"You were a movie hostess?" Bronze asked.

That would have been nice. It would have sounded flashy at least. Peyton shook her head. Her life had been worse than that. Boring rather. So dull that at times she contemplated running away and living on the streets just for the adventure of it.

"I was a bagger. For groceries."

She winced and avoided gazes too. Nothing exciting came from putting the dairy together in a bag and the cans at the bottom even if she tried to converse with patrons and coworkers. She tried to make it work. Honestly, but it wasn't for her. Sometimes she had rather vivid dreams about being someone else. Someone who tested chemicals in strange substances looking for impurities. Someone who had discovered that toxins were being administered illegally to people. She was someone who came down with a strange illness so she couldn't speak out against it. But that was all dreams.

"That," Klast snapped his fingers, "was the best job in the world for you to have. I've been trying to figure out why you cling so hard to life and that has to be it. You've not done anything. Yours is the desire to live for living's sake, and that is not anything anyone can take away from you. People can take a purpose away from you. They can take family and friends and career options and goodwill away, but they can't take away the desire to use time."

Had he just...? A thrill bubbled up, starting at her core and rushing through her arms and hands, stealing the remaining chill in her body. Klast had said something nice to her! Granted, he was still calling her boring, but the way he said it felt like a trickle of light. One small trickle. She wanted to be as amazing as he was. She would look into the sky and predict if it was going to rain or snow. She would know if a bird laid five eggs or two. She would pick up a leaf and be able to tell who had stepped on it and how long ago, like in detective novels. She wanted to be somebody special! Nearly dying all the time wasn't special.

*"But surviving impossible death is special,"* Deek noted.

"In any case, it's best to separate our past from our future and use our future to improve our present," Klast spoke as if he was thinking multiple ideas at once and wasn't sure which one he was voicing.

Peyton wondered if that was a quote from somewhere or if he had made it up. She couldn't take her past out of her future very well. It was all lumped together. It wasn't like she could change anything that had happened. Her entire future pinged on what the people at Sysmat told her to do, and that made the future look gloomy. Her parents signing her over to Sysmat wasn't the blessing it was supposed to be. She was supposed to be cured and live a normal non-sick life after that. She was still alive, but the sick part hadn't changed.

"I've heard it all before. You can be anybody you want to be if you try hard enough, but I'll never be a rocket scientist and travel to the moon," Peyton complained.

"Reaching the moon isn't as hard as you think. It's just not as safe as you want it to be," Klast answered.

Ugh. He hadn't let her finish. For the brilliant man Klast was supposed to be, he looked so very normal with his eyes glazing over. There wasn't anything about him that would tell an observer that he was famous.

"I can't make my own decisions as you do. There is no happy future for me, only one that hurts. Do you ever go get the hat that you toss onto the road during your training sessions?" she asked straining for a topic that would make him look at her. His visual distance made her feel discarded. He had the dog back. He had no more need for the sickly girl that had tried and failed to take that dog away.

"The hat?" Klast looked up at her, surprised. He glanced around at all of them before rolling his eyes. "Deek gets the hat. How you feeling?"

Peyton shrugged. Needy and greedy. Scared. She'd almost died again. There wasn't a medicine she could take to save her from those freezing fingers. Her own hands clenched together as she tried to make sense of everything that had just happened. The soul hunting didn't work on the cold devil. Discovering how to use her ability had happened by chance. No one had taken her into a sniping class for training. What they had told her was that she was going to be remarkable. She could find anyone she was looking for. They hadn't told her how. She got sick again before she could take the class.

She endured countless more weeks fighting her own body feeling like she was losing herself. Not her physical self, but her sense of who she was as if the doctors were trying to brainwash her and rewrite memories so she'd stop remembering her family and how to bag groceries. She'd not remember how she wanted to be an elementary school teacher if only she could get enough money to pay for college. She'd not remember that she had a best friend that would answer her calls even if Cindy had signed a contract to distance Peyton from her life forever.

Sysmat had tried to destroy her. That's what made Peyton wonder if those dreams of her being someone else were not as fake as she thought them to be. She clung to the dreams, refusing to forget them the same way she refused to forget about her family and best friend. If she *had* discovered that Sysmat infected people illegally, she could oust the company. They were trying to destroy her without leaving a messy trail behind them by "saving" her.

"You're looking better. That's good," Klast said, offering up a short smile before he turned back to the phone.

He tossed it back on the chair and then glanced up at the top corner of the ceiling. Peyton glanced at Deek to tell her what was going on over there. The dog lightly nipped her hand in rebuke. She wanted to know! What exactly was that cold woman who had tried to kill her? If she couldn't get her medicine how much longer did she have to live?

Her eyes flicked over to Bronze and Mike. They were mouthing things to each other, watched by Phantom and Zen. Maybe they were trying to decide which dog they were going to claim while Klast was distracted. It was odd how everything in the room hinged on Klast. Even worse, Deek slipped off the bed to sit by Klast's feet. Peyton forced the tears to stay away. The dog was leaving her. All chance of further survival was gone, and she had nothing to show for it.

# 10

The demons were coming to get Klast. Deek couldn't take away his pain, but he was doing his best to offer support and prove that he wasn't always a devil in arenas. The dog sat on the top of Klast's feet as if he could somehow ease the trouble of Klast's tornado inside.

Sure, Klast could stand around and smile and talk about lawyers and taking on Sysmat. On the inside, he was terrified. He had just killed off a soulless woman to save Peyton. Even if he saved Peyton, no one was going to come around to save *him*. He was done for if he stayed here. There was no way to spin this. Not with all the eyewitnesses. He had shot a woman who hadn't died. Then he had touched her and turned her to dust. Who did that?! Sysmat already suspected him enough. This was the last straw. He couldn't take on an entire organization on his own. Even if he teamed up with those against Sysmat, they'd still give him the same advice that he was on the verge of making.

Run.

He had to hide. He had to get someplace where Sysmat couldn't reach and burn all his bridges on the way. That meant no more breed dogs. Tuff and Morgal would have to go. If he was any other breeder, those dogs would have already gone a long, long time ago, the same day that they had killed Shadow. No one kept around dogs that murdered half a man's soul. No one but him, because he needed the excuse to stay alive. Needed to have a reason why scanners beeped at him apart from admitting that he could shift through dimensions. Few people here would believe he could do that, and those who could were the people he needed to stay away from. He'd been so low that his entire body had shifted searching for the missing half. Clark Manford got the credit for taking him to Lexia, but Klast had arrived in Lexia once before that all on his own.

He'd nearly taken in a breath of air and died on his first unwanted shift, but he'd been plowed into, right in the stomach, and hoisted over a shoulder. All the air was shoved out of him so he couldn't breathe even if he had wanted to. Boy, had he wanted to! When he was plopped down in the warm runner's station with that humid air, it felt like he'd gotten a second chance. Just one. He'd done the very best with it. Tried extra hard to keep everything together and help others. Still, there were times he stared down into dark water, wondering if Shadow was down there, looking for the reflection of the dog in the dark corners of his irises.

"Klast you crying?"

"Nope. Carry on," he answered automatically as he wiped the tears off his face.

He had no idea what he was even looking at. The wall, probably. He couldn't decide who had just spoken to him. It didn't matter. None of them were Shadow. Whenever he thought about ending his career as a breeder, it brought Shadow up to the forefront of his mind and he couldn't shake it. It was a dumb name for a dog. Shadow. The thing that would never leave, no matter where one went. When the sun shone, the shadow was always there. The darkness that had held his light. The other half of him he could never, ever get back.

"Pretty girl fix soul," Deek barked.

"Not this time," Klast answered.

"No!" Deek barked. He growled at him. "Fix. No. Eat souls. No. Find. Pretty girl finds souls."

"Not mine," Klast replied.

He ignored Deek's sigh and growl. The dog couldn't understand. Klast blamed himself. He had put Shadow in the same pen as the breed dogs. He'd not thought too much about it. They'd had a great day training the pups. The sun had been wonderful, the air crisp and enlivening. He had a future and friends and family in a beautiful world. He felt the tug on his heart the instant it happened. The pain lanced through him along with an instant realization of what had happened.

He'd not thought it through! He'd been careless with half his heart and it was gone now. He should have known better. He should have paid more attention to the signs. Morgal and Tuff did not greet Shadow in the morning. They watched him like he was a threat. Klast had thought they were slow to learning Shadow's mannerism. He should have known better. He should have known!

"I love you," Deek said.

"Honestly!" Klast ground his teeth together as he looked down at the dog. "I don't want your psychology right now. I have to make a very big decision!"

*"I'll do it."* Deek volunteered.

"You will not," Klast told him.

He turned his back on the dog. Not that it would matter. He couldn't keep Deek out of his head, no matter what he did. Not that he'd tried too hard. Most of the time, he welcomed the connection. Any connection. He was so starved for that piece he had lost that he'd not thought hard enough about what he was doing to Deek. The dog was never going to be his. He had to give him up. Over and over and over again, because the dumb animal wouldn't leave him alone. He was going to imprint someday and the connection would be strong and beautiful and real.

*"So strong that I can talk with other people who have broken souls too because you try to find the broken ones so hard."*

Klast shook his head and wiped at his eyes again. He was imagining things. That was not how imprinting dogs worked.

*"Souls have ways to talk to each other. You simply refuse to listen."*

"Shut up, Deek."

"He didn't say anything," Bronze spoke against the sharp rebuke. "You alright over there?"

"Do I look alright?! I have to shoot my breed dogs!"

*"I'll do it."*

"You can't hold a gun!" Klast screamed at Deek. "I have to do it."

"You what?"

Peyton. He'd forgotten that she was in the room for a minute. He didn't want to explain it to her. Klast sighed before bolstering his inner courage.

"My breed dogs. I got into training IB dogs out of necessity. I was born here on Hyphas, but one of my parents was not. My parent and I have a genetic connection with our home planet that allows us to reach it whenever we so desire. That connection makes security monitors ring every time we walk beneath them. So, to get around Sysmat taking interest in me for scientific research, I got a couple of IB dogs to explain away why the alarms went off. It worked well enough. Worked better when I got my own dog. Felt worse too though."

"You said that as if you don't expect me to believe that people exist on other planets." Peyton crossed her arms. "I'm not an idiot. I know they are there."

"Sorry. I should have assumed that you'd heard things. All Sysmat does is lie to natives to steal resources, so I suppose you understand the notion of living on other planets, but most people—"

"You're from Lexia," Imar stated.

Klast's head jerked over to the door. How did *he* get in here? When rather? The blondy was leaning up against the doorway as if he'd been there a while. The stalker.

"You know about my house and now this? You following me?"

"Someone has to look out for you. How do security monitors have anything to do with shooting the breed dogs? You need them gone; I'll do it for you."

Klast rolled his eyes.

"You see that?" He waved at Imar. "That is exactly what I'm trying to prevent. I have to do it myself. Breed dogs, good ones, are highly sought after among those who understand them. I can't sell them. I can't trade them away. If I'm not the one with them, I have to finish them off. I can't have my secrets getting into other hands. They know them all. Can't trust even my best friends with my breed dogs. They might not kill them but save them and use them themselves. Not that I don't trust any of you, but you know the temptation would be there."

If he got the chance to get close to any of these men's breed dogs, he'd use all the time with those dogs he could get. He expected the same from them, no matter how good their intentions were.

"Okay, but..." Peyton scrunched her nose up. Cute. Klast tried to ignore the thought as he kept going.

"I killed the soulless woman that was eating your soul, Peyton. You can't kill a soulless anything without drawing in the forces of the void through which one has to travel when he shifts from this planet to another one. Shooting her in the heart did absolutely nothing. She was already dead. I had to summon external forces, shove them at her, and turn her to dust. There were a lot of witnesses. It was in the middle of the day on a busy street. Only a natural-born shifter can kill a soulless body. Sysmat will know it's me. I have to go. I have to leave without traces. That means giving up the breed dogs. We can fight Sysmat, but not before they chop my head off or suck out the remaining part of my soul. They have a monopoly on interworld travel around here, and they don't like anybody like me who defies that."

"Where are you going to go?" Peyton asked, jumping off the bed and wringing her hands together.

"I can't say that out loud." He wanted to add "particularly not to you," but he refrained himself just in time.

"You actually believe this?" Mike asked, looking at Imar.

Imar nodded. Klast hoped Imar wasn't secretly working for Sysmat or something. The things that guy knew. Gee. It was making Klast rather uncomfortable that Imar knew what planet he was from.

"Are you..." Peyton sucked in her cheeks as she twisted her hands around again and then balled them into fists. Her eyes turned red, which was a lovely shade after the blue she had been earlier and the gray she was trying to escape.

"Are you leaving Deek?" she asked with a slight twitch in her eye.

"No."

The answer was out before he'd even thought about it. Even if Peyton claimed Deek had gone with her, Klast couldn't leave the dog with her again. He kept trying to tell himself that he had to give up the dog, but he couldn't. His heart couldn't. Maybe the dog was right. Maybe Deek and Klast had imprinted and Deek was too polite to be forceful about it when Klast was still grieving for Shadow. He couldn't give Deek up. Not for anything. Not even if it meant taking him through the darkness to hide on another planet. Even if that risk meant Deek dying on the way or the instant he arrived, he had to try.

"You kill off the murderers, you will stop grieving for Shadow. Your soul needs to be avenged!" Deek growled.

It was such a strong sentence that even if the others couldn't understand the words, they felt the intent. They all backed up. Peyton scrambled onto the bed and smashed herself up against the wall like she might be the one Deek was heading after.

"That is very rude," Klast told Deek as calmly as he could. "Those dogs are your parents."

*"Murderers. They tried to kill you. They killed Shadow and tried to kill you. They keep trying to kill you. I save you."*

"What are you talking about?" Klast asked, taking a step back himself.

How was he missing this!? Sure, Deek had growled at his parents, but he growled at all of them. It was his nature to demand order, but what if Deek was only that way because he fought to hold back every single threat Klast failed to notice?

Klast trusted his dogs. He didn't expect them, any of them, to kill him except for Deek. Which was strange because Deek was the one who was saving him. Then again, assuming they imprinted, Deek would want to be the one to kill Klast if he felt like there was nothing else he could do to save him. He'd want to be the one pulling the gun. Let someone who loved Klast hold his last thoughts instead of a traitor. It wasn't any different from the way Klast felt about Deek, really. If anyone was going to kill that dog, it was going to be him. Otherwise, he was going to do his best to save him over and over again.

"Bad Dogs." Deek growled. "Smart, bad dogs. They took your soul. Peyton will help you get it back."

Deek looked at Peyton who squealed and tried to hide by grabbing at Klast's sleeping bag and pulling it up in front of her face. She changed her mind when she realized how much it stunk. Dropping the sleeping bag with a disgusted face, she opted for rushing behind Mike. Klast did his best to hold back a smile, but he simply couldn't. Deek seemed to catch his mood, thankfully, and he started laughing first, which set Klast off next.

"That's two weeks of dirt and sweat on that. Hope you enjoyed it!"

"You smell just as bad as your dogs!"

"I know," Klast laughed again. "Haven't gotten a minute to wash up. Still don't have a minute. I have to take down the dogs that killed my soul and then run away."

"They what?" Bronze asked, catching the hidden meaning of those words. Klast winced. He'd never wanted anyone to know. He'd kept it a secret for so long. Lied about all of it.

"My breed dogs killed Shadow, but I needed them, so I kept them alive. Now you know. There. I said it, alright. I live with dogs who are constantly trying to kill me. I live with creatures who cut me apart from the inside out."

"Oh my…" Imar trailed off as if he'd not picked up *that* secret.

"I'm going to kill them myself!" Mike shouted. "How dare they?! How could you live like that, Klast? Every day struggling to get up and feed the things that destroyed you? I'd have gone mad so long ago. I'd have… If my dogs ever did that to me…"

"That's how he raises such good dogs," Bronze mused. "One of the ways, anyway. The pups see how to brave torment for the entire first year of their lives. They see a man laughing in the face of death. Smiling and standing with a broken soul. They see what a traitorous dog looks like and what a very good dog looks like." Bronze gave Deek a tip of his head. Deek smiled back.

"Peyton get soul back." Deek barked.

"I'm getting to that." Klast gave Deek a look to be patient.

Deek grinned up at him, amused. Klast liked that smile. It was the smile of understanding, the smile that Klast was finally getting around to comprehending what the dog had been trying to tell him for years. If only he would listen. He wasn't trusting his guard dog. Trusting your dog was the first rule written in large bold letters in every guidebook. If you didn't have the first rule down, none of the other ones mattered.

The worst part was that he was an IB dog breeder. He was supposed to recognize the signs of an imprinted dog. It had been there for quite some time. Not in the first year of Deek's life surely, but in the second year, the dog had a couple of "strange months" where he wouldn't do anything but sit by Klast's feet and stare at things. He refused to talk. He hardly ate. Klast had taken him to the doctors for a check-up, but he wasn't sick. The consensus was that the dog had matured from the pup stage to the adult stage and was adjusting. They were right. They were also wrong.

Deek had imprinted him, and that brought the dog a whole new level of problems that he'd not had before. If Deek let his parents know he was now Klast's dog, there was a large possibility that his parents would gang up on him, perhaps get the other pups to do so too, and take him down. To stay where he was, Deek had to hide what had happened. He had to be the unruly one for his own protection. He had to growl, bare fangs, and be obnoxious toward Klast to save them both. He had to treat the man he loved the exact opposite of the way he wanted to treat him. That was a lot of growing up on a dog all at once. But Deek was smart. He was patient. He had waited this long to get what he most wanted, and he was still waiting.

What Klast should have done was not look for signs of an imprinted dog since Deek hid all the usual emotions. He should have been looking for signs of an imprinted person. Granted, Deek had kept his thoughts to himself because if Klast started answering phrases that no one else had heard, it would give the whole gimmick away, but there were other things, too. That spurge in confidence. The way he had stopped waking up at night in fits of fear worried that something was lurking. That had all changed when he had relented to Deek's nighttime yowling.

At night, Klast allowed Deek to roam free. If he didn't, no one would sleep. Ever. Period. No number of earplugs could save one from an imprinted dog wanting to guard. Four months of sleeplessness from Deek screaming, and Klast had not noticed how the nightmares stopped coming once he let Deek out. Klast was simply too grateful to be getting any sleep at all. The thing was, Deek was probably saving his life. Asleep was when Klast was most vulnerable. That was when his breed dogs would have tried to strike if they were still planning things against him. There had been several cases when Deek was so tired after a long night that he had slept most of the day away. Instead of being worried that the dog was sick, Klast had found himself sneaking extra treats into the dog's food as if the subconscious part of his mind knew all along that he had a wonderful, life-saving dog.

The thought of the breed dogs' continual betrayal still sounded absurd in his head. He'd given those two dogs everything. He'd kept them alive, sheltered them from storms, let them in on his techniques, and they still were after him. Was it because they didn't like their pups being sold away? No dog got to keep all their children. That would be way too many mouths to feed. Was it because they wanted to go out on missions or imprint someone and staying with Klast made it so they couldn't do that? They should have simply told him. If they wanted out, he'd have done his best to let them out. Pretended they weren't his breeders and dragged them to a show or something. He wouldn't have killed them for wanting what he preached.

He'd done his best to make them happy. They did their best to make him miserable on the inside, where no one could see. It'd happened so slowly; he'd not even noticed since he was still reeling from Shadow's death and blaming himself for the whole thing. Stupid of him to put them to bed in the same place. Stupid, stupid, stupid. Shadow should have protested. Then again, Shadow wasn't Deek. He'd not seen it coming either. Deek had to see things coming before they happened. He had to always be on alert. The poor dog. No wonder his favorite place was the vet. It was just him and Klast at the vet. He loved it there.

"I'm sorry. I was being stupid. I was hurt. I didn't want to hear you even if I did. I'm sorry it took me so long, Deek."

"Finally!" Mike cheered. "I knew it was that dog. No one keeps around a pup for four years without a reason. He's been going crazy trying to tell you to let him out of that cage on onto the leash beside your feet. You're brilliant and all, but I agree that you've been a tad stupid."

"Mike." Klast shook his head at the guy. If he had seen the obvious, he should have said something about it long ago. Klast didn't believe that Mike knew Deek was trying to tell him anything at all, other than that he hated being around all the people in these arenas.

"Anyway, Peyton," Klast said, watching her shut her eyes as if she was steeling herself for the worst blow of her life. He wasn't sure what it was going to be. Silly girl. He was only going to hit her with words.

"Anyone who goes against Sysmat is going to need to do some serious hiding along the way. It's not my place to decide for you, but I have a question. Would hide with m—"

"Yes!" Peyton shouted as she shoved her way past Mike.

Before he knew it, she had flung her arms around him, coughed on how smelly he was, which made him grin, and lifted her legs off the floor in her haste. "I thought you were going to leave me behind. I don't have... You're the only one that... in a long time..." she stuttered. "You don't see me as dead and..."

"You are not dead," Klast assured her.

He reached up to take her arms off so his sore shoulder could get a break from the neck hugging. He still needed to ice that thing. He also needed to check his brain before his mouth started talking. What was he thinking? Inviting some Sysmat agent to run away with him. He was insane! Cozying up with the enemy. Peyton was the last person he should hide with. Then again, there were a lot of selfish reasons for the way his mouth was moving. If Deek wanted a girl—that one—the dog would have to stay with Klast to get her. Not to mention that if Klast knew where Peyton was, he wouldn't have to worry that she was spilling his secrets. This way he could further work out a plan about Peyton's *Mervolk* problem. Perhaps she could give him some insider secrets about Sysmat. He could turn her into a double agent. Get back at Sysmat for being so greedy.

"Don't be hasty," Klast prompted. "We're enemies even if we're together in this. You probably should glare at me and tell me you'd rather die."

"Me?" Peyton laughed at him.

"Well, yeah. I hate the people you work for."

"Me too."

"Right."

Klast nodded at her as he scanned her over. This could work. Both of them defied Sysmat. Something about that thought felt powerful. However, they were taking in the enemy completely unprepared. They had better figure out what Sysmat was after before it hit them again.

"Want to know why I named him Deek?" Klast asked as he took a step back.

Deek jerked to his feet as if sensing what was in Klast's mind, even if Klast hadn't let the thoughts surface yet. Deek knew him too well. Klast didn't need to think through every plan to carry it out with exactness. The dog wasn't coming. Not this time. Klast had to be fast. He had to do this on his own. He had to burn the first bridge. Quickly!

"We play this game called duck and seek. The dogs scatter into the woods and hunker down when the whistle blows and I try to find them. Deek loves that game."

"Come!" Deek begged.

"He would stop being a pain whenever that game was mentioned. Duck and seek. It's all a matter of duck and seek."

Klast pulled out his gun, and he was gone.

# 11

The room was laughably silent. One minute, Klast was standing there talking about dog names while his three companions were notably ogling the information of a doggy game to play. The next, he was giving Deek a silent command of wait. Then he was gone. Just like that. He vanished into thin air, and they all knew where he had gone. He'd gone to pick up his breed dogs and smile at them. He'd gone to lie. Peyton swallowed.

"Is he... Will he come back crying, you think?" she asked Deek.

The dog was running himself in circles, too anxious to talk to anybody else when the human he loved was off on a dangerous mission without him. In contrast to him, the other dogs in the room were sitting there not doing much. They offered soft snort sounds as if to comfort their pal, who was going crazy.

"Klast is an alien?" Mike asked, now that he was out of the room.

"Half," Imar answered with a nod. "I've known for a long time. He connects with the souls of his dogs in a way that we can't. That's why they train so darn well. I first came across that idea when..."

Peyton stopped listening. As interesting as it was, she couldn't focus on them either. She watched Deek because she wanted to run herself in circles just like that. A million emotions had rushed her body all in the last few minutes. Adoration was the first one for the rescue against the soulless woman. Then there was gratitude for trying to ease her sense of hopelessness. That brought up a sense of loyalty and devotion only to hurt again right away.

Klast said he was leaving.

There came the terror that she was done for. The despair swallowed her up, an unsatiable tasty treat. She'd never make if she ran across another soulless person. She would die without her medicine or Klast's mysterious cure. Doomed. But then he offered that everlasting protection again. Her boomeranging emotions could make her choke.

"So how did he vanish like that?" Mike asked, intruding into her thoughts once more.

"Teleportation," Peyton informed. "It's frequently used between other planets. This planet hides the information about teleporting, but I believe it involves plunging oneself into the spirit realm and then recombining your form on the other side. You need a box to make it work. I've moved between worlds before. Not supposed to tell anyone, though."

Black box with a blue button! That's what Klast had told Deek over the phone. She should have caught the reference sooner. Klast was telling Deek to watch out for teleporters, which sounded unfair since she had to take Deek through one to reach her diffuser. It sounded like Klast had changed his mind about wanting to watch her die, but she was distrusting enough to question him around her current enthralled emotions.

"He doesn't carry a box. We all have to empty our pockets when we first check-in," Mike told her.

Peyton shrugged. Sysmat must have copied the teleportation technology from somewhere. They may have even gotten it from the planet Klast was from so he probably understood how to teleport better than they did. Asking Deek wouldn't do anyone good. He was still running in circles, flinching every few steps as if the thoughts in Klast's head were things he never wanted coming toward him. The dog froze, and Peyton had just enough time to suck in a breath before she smelled Klast tumble into her, smashing her down to the ground in a swirl of sparkles.

It all happened so fast! Colors burst around her in a sea of endless black. Purple trails rushed around green streaks followed by yellow and red. Orange merged into gray. Blue morphed into white. It was like flashing her way through a sea of sitting soul matter. Something large and warm and ethereal crashed into her. It infused through her skin as if she had inhaled to fill her lungs. Bam! Peyton blinked as she fell onto a hardened patch of gray, dusty ground. Klast fell on top of her.

Apart from the ground, the first thing she noticed was that the sound was different. The muffled voices of the arena vanished making room for clear, distinct, nearby screeches. She flinched. They had teleported somewhere and scared people by doing so. Peyton wasn't sure if Klast had meant to grab her or Deek, but she was here now. The gray dirt was too packed to launch into her nose and make her sneeze, but it was arid enough to bring the nose bleed back.

"Bleeding. Move, please," Peyton told Klast as she shoved at him.

He didn't budge, and the liquid was never a gentle trickle. The blood was gushing out of her, so she shoved and squirmed until she could roll over and hold herself up on her hands and knees. She pinched her nose and looked over at Klast. She gasped, which sucked the blood down her throat making her cough. There was something wrong with him. She wasn't sure what, but it was something. He lay on his face, still unmoving and so still that he could have been dead. Her brain panicked and lay still for twenty seconds like an admonished dog before crying injustice to it all.

"Don't be dead!" She screamed, shoving on his shoulder, trying to turn him over so she could check on his face. He wasn't blue, and he wasn't gray, but he honestly didn't look alive either.

"Klast!"

She had to get help! Peyton pushed to her feet to look around, searching for the people who had stopped screaming after one voice began issuing commands. The oddly motionless people became a blur in her vision as her eyes lit upon the buildings instead. They were gorgeous! White stucco with a blue and green glass pressed into the mortar made one building shimmer in the warm rays of the sun. Another one had mosaic tiles moving like waves upward. There was a tower with a spiraling staircase twisting around it. There was a building with metal vines climbing the walls, and large, colorful metal flowers blooming in the crevices. Peyton had never seen anything like it before. Each building was a work of art, an object to be stared at and studied for hours on end. Only she couldn't do that!

"Help!" She screamed, tearing her eyes off the architecture to find sympathetic faces.

Oh gosh. The people stared at her like she was an invasive monster. Lexia. Klast had taken her to his planet without using a device. Remarkable. He traveled directly through soul matter.

There was one person that dared to move, and that man was rushing between everyone, scanning them over with a flashing device, and then shoving them into the nearest available building to get away from *her*. Peyton took a step back, stumbling on the lack of reception and the weight of suspicion. She would have to save Klast herself.

Fine.

She had been in and out of hundreds of hospitals. There had to be something that she could do, even if she had no idea what was wrong with him. He'd gone to kill off his breed dogs. Deek had flinched and turned still, and then they were crashing here.

Peyton dropped back down beside Klast, reaching out with her least bloody hand to check for a pulse. Nothing, but that didn't mean he wasn't still there. She clenched her hand into a fist, feeling guilty for using her soul-hunting power in plain sight when it could be illegal. Oh well. She had to know. Where was Klast's soul? Deek had said that his breed dogs were trying to kill him and take his soul away. It sounded freaky that a dog could do that, but Klast's dogs were creepy smart. The sparkles didn't move very far when she searched. They converged around her and then lit her up.

"No!" Peyton screamed, falling backward as she stared at her hand and then her arm. That warmth that she had felt in the darkness had to be Klast's soul converging into *her*. She'd stolen it from him somehow, just like that soulless lady who had been sucking everything. She wasn't a killer! She had to put his soul back in!

But how?!

"Klast!"

A woman's wail turned Peyton's head in surprise. The stranger looked like an angel with long, blond, flowing hair down to her waist. A flowered headband matched the color of her rosy cheeks. She was dashing out of a building instead of back in.

Klast had been recognized, so, yes, Peyton must be correct to her location. This could be the place that had her cure. Hope entwined with despair and rushed into her system like adding carbonation to a drink. Too much would leave her coughing from the tingles. Peyton didn't want the cure if it meant Klast never moved again. She *needed* him.

"Isabelle!" The man who was scanning the stalled bystanders screamed at the lady. "Don't!"

"It's Klast!" she cried out again.

"Exactly! He could be here with a Sysmat agent trained to kill us! Didn't you hear the announcement? We shoot on sight."

"You shoot that?" Isabelle had reached Peyton and Klast now. She pointed at Peyton, and then dropped down beside Klast. The rushing man gave up on the other people who fidgeted as if they wished they had been cleared to run away too.

"You can tell by checking for the blue mark on the agent's arm," the savior of these people claimed.

Peyton scooted away from him. Not her people. Not her savior. He was going to kill her, and Klast was down on the ground, unable to defend her. She scooted farther back as the runner drew in closer.

"She's bleeding, Tim," Isabelle said as she poked Klast with a finger on the forehead. "She was screaming for help."

"How do you know that?" Tim asked, swapping his scanner for a different device that Peyton assumed was a gun. The trigger looked to be pulled instead of pushed like the way one would pry apart a confetti popper. She hoped it was single-use, but even then, it could still finish her off for good.

"It sounded like a cry for help. Just look at her face."

"I did," Tim replied. "She could be with Sysmat."

"Well, if you ask me, she looks like—"

Isabelle looked over at Peyton and turned ridged. Peyton sighed. No one was supposed to be able to identify her. She couldn't distinguish between a Sysmat manager or a Sysmat field agent even if she got a look at the mark. Her symbol was a compilation of parts similar to how Peyton viewed herself these days. Body, power, soul, and conquering death. She was told that the picture was comforting, but staring at it too long made her think of hypnosis.

"Save him, please," she whispered as she pointed at Klast.

"What do you think she said that time?" Tim asked, taking a step closer to her.

"Don't you dare shoot that! That woman is holding Klast's soul!"

"She ate him?" Tim shivered as beads of sweat broke out across his face.

He had a nice face. Rounded with a pointed chin, Tim wore a thin mustache that matched the obvious trimming of his thin eyebrows. His hair color was a few shades lighter than Peyton's cinnamon concoction, making Tim look brassy instead of red. Peyton tried to come up with something bad about him, but she couldn't. He was doing his job. It wasn't his fault that he was told to shoot her.

"No, I... She couldn't have eaten him. Her eyes are not lost. I think Klast's soul was jostled loose somehow and... I don't know. You can't kill her, Tim! It could kill Klast, and I won't let you do that. Put the weapon down before I attack you."

"Izzy, you wouldn't—" Tim glanced at Isabelle and then dropped his weapon to the ground.

She was holding out a different gun popper. Maybe it was a better, strong one. Peyton didn't know. All she knew was that this woman was saving her life and had to see souls too. She'd never met another person who could do that.

Peyton pointed to Klast. "How do I help him?"

"I don't understand your question," Isabelle said.

Peyton frowned at her. Why not? She could understand everything that Isabelle and Tim were saying.

"Say something else," Peyton asked.

"You should grab her. We need to separate the souls," Isabelle decided.

"I can't separate souls," Tim huffed. "That's not my department at all. Furthermore, I don't trust your intuition about this."

Peyton watched the way their mouths moved. Okay. So they were not speaking in words that Peyton should recognize. The only explanation she had was that if she had Klast's soul inside of her, he was translating. Nothing else made sense, and she could understand Deek by listening to his soul talk.

"Dog," Peyton pointed to Klast again as Tim slowly moved toward her. He picked his gun up off the ground as he went, glancing at Isabelle to judge if she would pull her trigger. "Klast was fighting soul-stealing dogs. We don't need to separate any souls. I simply have to put his back."

Hopefully the solution was simple even if sounded dreadfully hard. When Peyton used her soul to mark others, it wasn't the same as cutting herself apart and leaving herself there. It was more like putting a sticker on them, one that glowed in the dark when she turned on the black light.

"He's dead, isn't he?" Peyton trembled as she looked at the unmoving Klast. Having seen him always in motion before, the stillness of his prone body felt eerie. She half expected his eyes to turn black as some other essence took him over from the inside out.

"I don't know how much time he has, so hurry up!" Isabelle fretted to Tim.

"Who put you in charge?" Tim grumbled as he held his weapon out toward Peyton, looking as intimidating as possible. Her nerves rang with warnings to stay perfectly still.

"On your feet," Tim commanded. "Don't you dare try anything."

"She can't understand you," Isabelle told him. "Hurry up."

Tim reached out, and even though Peyton had told herself she was going to stay right where she was, her instincts took over. She scrambled to her feet and ran. If he wasn't going to shoot her, running could give her a few extra minutes to come up with a solution for Klast. She had to try escaping, even if she didn't think it would work. The landscape and roadways were a mystery to her. No matter where she turned, Tim was going to corner her and cut her off. Peyton clenched one hand together as she ran, still trying to stop the bleeding with the other hand, and tried to push Klast's soul out. Nothing happened. Nothing good anyway.

Tim appeared in front of her as if he could shift his way through the world at will. Peyton couldn't stop in time. She crashed into him and he grabbed her arm, twisting it behind her and forcing her to bend over at the waist. She wailed.

"We're going to help Klast," Tim told her, trying to sound kinder than he was. "You know Klast. You said his name. It won't be but a moment. I'll take you to the soul doctors and get it all sorted out."

"Let me go!" Peyton screamed at him. She tried to find the words inside of her that would be the correct ones so these people could understand them, but the only thing coming up was what she knew. It was a pity that understanding only went one way. If she could change who was the one understanding, she would have picked them.

"You're doing great with the language barrier," Isabelle snorted as she rushed up beside them. "I know a few words. Let me try. Klast okay. We help you."

"How do you expect to do that? Get off me!" Peyton answered.

"She sounded happy about your limited vocabulary," Tim offered.

"At least I'm trying!"

"What do you think you are doing?" Tim demanded as Isabelle grabbed his arm.

"Going with you."

"No. This girl is under arrest. You're not coming."

"You need me!"

"Don't think so."

There was a thud as Isabelle was dislodged followed by a pop and a blur of black. Peyton stumbled forward, not through a patch of dirt but across a light-blue tiled floor into a small metal cage. They had shifted again. That was what she was used to when teleporting between areas. The sudden jolt and arrival were normal. Teleporting didn't include sparkles and colors in a sea of black soul matter. It didn't involve souls ramming into her and out of anyone else. Klast must have done it wrong, and now they were separated. Him on the dirt and her in a cage. Trapped! Peyton screamed to be let out even if it amounted to nothing. She glared as she sat cross-legged in the small cage and looked around.

A hospital. One where the beds were cages. The instruments were full of strange lights and colorful cogs. There were three other people in cages staring blankly as if they couldn't express thoughts. She had better not end up like that! Tim was shaking out his right hand as if he'd received a jolt. The doctor in the room, dressed in black pants and a utility belt that held strange instruments, was walking over to him.

"What's with her?" the doctor asked, pointing as he took Tim's hand and scanned it over with one of his tools. He frowned. "A bad mix of currents. I'll have to give you a shot for that. What's your name? You're a runner, no?"

"Normally, but I'm off duty. That girl appeared in the middle of Parton Street, and Isabelle claims she has an extra soul adhered to her. We need to get it out, so I jumped in to help."

"Perhaps," the doctor said as he glanced at her and frowned.

He walked over to a wall that didn't have cages in front of it and picked up a round disk. This he took back to Tim and quickly jabbed it onto his hand while Tim winced.

"Can you feel your hand yet?"

Tim shook his head.

"Hmm. Give it a few minutes. Let me know if it changes. In the meantime, Isabelle Laundy said that girl has a double soul?"

"She said that the soul bounced into..." Tim pointed at Peyton inhaling deeply as he did so as if he couldn't contemplate such a thing happening. "Izzy didn't think that girl devoured it on purpose. I can't get the specifics because the traveler was speaking gibberish."

"Oh, naturally," the doctor snorted. "You expect me to figure this out with only Isabelle's words that some soul is sticking to another living person." The doctor pulled out a magnifying glass to look at Peyton and turned silent.

"What?" Tim asked, now massaging his hand. "What is it?"

"Blazen," the doctor whispered.

"Honestly?" Tim seemed to perk up at the word as if "blazen" wasn't an expression but some fascinating find. "That's fantastic! She never was dying then!"

What did he know? Peyton glanced between Tim and the doctor. The doctor wasn't looking as thrilled.

"Where did she come from?" he asked Tim with hands on his hips.

"I can't tell you for certain where she got off to, but Klast was the one to bring her—"

"You don't say?!" the doctor exclaimed. He shook his head at Tim and stormed back to the wall to pick up a multifaceted mirror.

"Wait! You can't. They'll kill her for shifting in with him! Can't we solve this without telling anyone else? She's not harmful!"

"Tim was it? Anything relating to Klast Burma has to be reported immediately."

He pushed a button on the mirror thing.

"You're making the wrong call," Tim insisted. "All we need to do is put Klast back together and he can tell us what is going on."

"You know nothing about Sysmat, do you?" The doctor asked. "They are never a simple fix. It's always complicated."

"KNW. State the emergency." A voice came through the bumpy mirror thing. Phone. That was a strange-looking phone, but at least Peyton could put a name to it. Tim was making angry faces behind the doctor.

"I need a full medical team, toxic team, and squadron, please."

"She's not toxic!" Tim insisted. "The squadron will kill her, and the medics won't know a twit!"

"I need someone to remove Tim, the off-duty runner, too."

"Of all the stupid—!"

Peyton sighed and tested her nose by slowly taking her hand down. Clotted and uncomfortable. She was used to being on her own, but this was something else. Hospitals had felt like cages but hadn't actually been one before. Using both her hands, she pressed against the coldness of the cage searching for an opening. She knew which way she had entered the cage, but as Tim had stepped back, it had somehow sealed shut, hiding all evidence of seams. There were five forearm lengths in all directions, giving her enough room to turn, but not any room to stand. Drawing her feet up to her chest, she kicked the exit, hearing the cage rattle even if she couldn't see a gap. She kicked again.

"She speaks the Burma language. If we called Jethro Burma, he could translate."

"Don't you think he'd shoot her?!" Tim squawked, stealing the mirror phone and shoving it back on the shelf. "He's the one telling everyone to shoot people. I know he's supposed to be this great military mind—"

"He's the interplanetary general."

"—but I'd much prefer Klast over him any night."

"Well, you'd better not let them hear such treason."

"It's not treason. Klast thinks things through. His dad is into advancing first and—"

"He's into defending the borders."

"The borders *he* crosses," Tim pointed.

Peyton rolled her eyes and kept kicking. Nothing was happening! The two arguing men weren't even looking at her. It was almost like they couldn't hear her. Peyton yelled at the top of her lungs. Either they were fantastic at ignoring things, or they honestly couldn't hear her in here. Fine then. There were other things she could try. She pulled out her phone and eyed it suspiciously when it still received a signal. It shouldn't *do* that.

*"I don't have a phone,"* Deek's voice found her thoughts.

"Do you need one?" Peyton asked him. "I need to reach Klast. Perhaps if I call him, he might hear it and decide to grab his soul back so he can answer his phone."

*"Klast's phone is broken. Bad dogs took his soul,"* Deek told her. *"Klast killed the bad dogs and then fell to the darkness."*

That would be a horrible thing for anyone to see. Peyton pictured Klast yelping in pain and then vanishing into complete silence. How could he have ended up on top of her to drag her along with him if he wasn't controlling himself?

*"Happened when Shadow died too. Klast falls into darkness, searching for his missing soul, but he can't pick it up."*

"Well, I don't think the bad dogs kept it. It's on me, and some lady named Isabelle saw it too. How else can I understand what everyone is saying?"

*"You hear through your soul,"* Deek confirmed. *"Bad dogs destroyed Klast's soul. You found his missing half that Shadow launched away before he died. Shadow gave Klast up to save him and then died for it."*

"So Shadow wasn't killed by the other dogs?" Peyton asked trying to decide how a soul could have sat around in that sparkling dark place for so long only to bump into her at the right moment. Uncanny.

She looked at the useless phone that couldn't call Klast's broken one and shut it off. It was rather interesting to hear about this from a dog's perspective. Klast had made it sound like the breed dogs had torn Shadow up or something.

*"Bad dogs try to take Klast's soul from Shadow. He gave it away. Breaking the connection killed the dog. I don't know how else to say it."*

"Were you alive then?" Peyton asked. Did Shadow turn into a dust cloud? Did he simply fall over as if he'd had a heart attack, only it was a soul attack?

*"Not there."*

She laughed. "Then how do you know?!"

*"I asked the other dogs!"*

"Any idea how to give him back the soul?"

*"No."*

"I don't know either. It doesn't sound possible," Peyton told Deek, but it proved Klast was still alive. Deek was still talking to her so he had to be.

*"Not if you have his soul. I told you. Klast dog. Peyton dog. Peyton can find souls. You feel like Klast and think like you."*

Yuck. Klast was great and all, but she didn't want to be him at all. It was tough enough being herself without adding another personality into the mix.

"Do you know what blazen means?" Peyton asked Deek right as the squadron of soldiers rushed into the room. None of them had weapons drawn, but they all wore gray pants with a black stripe that matched their black shirts and the painted black line on the left side of their faces. Twenty of them crowded and spotted her out right away.

*"I think the Blazen are... question."*

No! She needed him to find the right words!

*"Not there,"* Deek tried.

Peyton sighed. Nope. That wasn't going to help. She was perfectly here to watch as one of the soldiers picked up a different sort of magnifying glass to spy on her.

"You called because of that one?" the man asked the doctor.

"I called because that one came in with Klast."

"So where's Klast?"

The doctor looked at Tim. Tim crossed his arms. No one had tried to remove him yet, and it looked like he was going to keep his silence so that they wouldn't. A new soldier walked up to the cage and flicked the top of it whelping as if in pain. Peyton tried kicking out again to no avail. Drat.

"She's in an isolation cage and remains active," the soldier gawked. "This thing is on. What is going on, soul doctor?"

"Oh yes, it's working. She remains unaffected by the components of the rays like she's blazen," the doctor agreed.

"That's a myth."

"Explain the phenomenon to me then," the doctor said. "Ah. Here we go."

Myth! That had to be the word that Deek was trying to get across to her. He had said that she wasn't there like a myth. Now it made more sense. Blazen was a myth only she didn't know the myth.

Another group of people came scurrying into the room wearing facial coverings. That had to be the toxicity crew. They looked at everyone who wasn't wearing a mask and started to pass them out. Tim refused to put on one, claiming that she wasn't toxic. Then the last group arrived. Not in any sort of uniform, the doctors rushed in with a tray of instruments, demanding to know where the patient was.

"Right there," the masked soul doctor pointed to her. Peyton was certain she was looking as annoyed as she felt. All these people staring at her and no one helping her save Klast!

"Will you let me out?!" she screamed at them. "I have to figure out how to transfer a soul!"

"Did any of you catch that?" one soldier asked.

"She speaks the Burma language," the doctor answered. "If you'll all pay attention to the screen, the isolation cage has done a full body scan, both body and soul, and I'd like your input on how to proceed."

"Like not killing her," Tim stated.

"Can we please help Klast?!" Peyton shouted.

She tried to pry a finger through the narrow grid of the cage, but it was too small. She peeled off a fingernail and shoved it at a gap, watching as it bent on an invisible force and didn't escape. Not good.

"We have in our presence a modified Sysmat agent without avid memory loss. Take a look at the brain readings."

A picture of her brain flashed onto the floor. The interested people formed a circle around the area, preventing her from seeing a blooming thing. She gave up on the nail idea and tried clenching her fist to see if she could tag anyone in the room to spot them down later.

"Fully active brain. Here you can see the area that is usually the most affected by Sysmat. On this woman, it is only slightly dampened."

"We know what a Sysmat brain looks like?" a soldier asked.

"As a soul doctor I have seen such acquired information," the talking doctor informed. "I do believe most of that information was stolen, so whatever I say can't leave this room. It's highly confidential. She's got metal ribs and a pin in her left knee. One missing kidney. Now, here you will see an area of additional oddity. On her right hip, there is a tube. Its purpose is unknown to the scans. It doesn't seem to be doing anything helpful. Would one of you be able to remove it?"

"No!" Peyton screamed as she banged her hands on the cage. Soldiers who were still watching her noticed, but they said nothing. They couldn't take her medicine tube out! She needed it!

"We need more information first. I wouldn't want to take it out if it's a shunt," one of the doctors answered. "It could be vital."

"Or a torture method," the soul doctor shrugged. "Like this right here. In both of her wrists is a device that seems to alter her ability to connect with souls."

"Stop trying to tear me apart!" Peyton screamed at them.

Those were what made it so she could see the sparkle trails. She'd gotten used to using it now. Having it gone was going to be strange, but not the worst that could happen. Either way, she had to do something. She had to! Clenching her fists wasn't helping. No sparkles appeared, as if the cage blocked all such connections. It was probably supposed to turn her into a comatose patient too like the other people locked up, but she wasn't about to have *that*. She turned her attention to the other side of the cage and tried kicking again.

"The wrist things alter her soul connections in what way?"

"Judging from the readings, I believe it's range intensive. It stops her from looking too far."

"Looking?" one of the poison control agents questioned.

"Oh yes. Haven't you heard the rumors about Sysmat agents? Some of them can peg you from miles away if they see you, and then they can hunt you down and steal your soul or any other manner of horrific violence. That's the case with this agent right here. She pegs people. It comes from the blue mark on her arm, you know. That's not repairable or reversible. Taking that away would be a death sentence, which, as Tim here likes to point out, is not an option today due to this reading right here."

"And that reading is..." a soldier wondered.

"The yellow represents the woman's soul."

"It looks translucent."

"It is. The blue represents the soul of Klast Burma, so I've been told. Tim here wants Klast removed. Now I can kick the blue soul out and feed it back into him, assuming we find him, but it won't be possible to remove it with that other Sysmat gadgetry in the way. The tube and the wrist devices need to come out."

"What's that?" a doctor asked. "It looks like *Mervolk*."

"That's what it is," the soul doctor agreed. "Our woman here is dying from *Mervolk* which has only one known cure. Since she is here, we can agree that she's been cured. Klast yanked her through the rift, annihilating that dreadful bacterial infection. In other aspects, she's perfectly healthy, which is why I don't think that tube, shunt or otherwise, is needed any longer."

"Hold on. This is a Sysmat agent," the first soldier stated, moving out of the huddle to look at her.

Peyton stopped kicking to watch him. She couldn't get anything out of the cage, but that didn't mean nothing could get in. If something was coming, she wanted to see it so she could try to break it.

"We're supposed to kill her."

"That is where you're wrong!" Tim yelled.

"That is why you soldiers are here," the soul doctor said, putting Tim behind him. "To watch the Sysmat agent while the doctors operate, and the toxicity crew can verify that she's not dishing out any diseases to the lot of us."

"Why are we trying to save her?"

"Is there anything else we can do when she has the soul of a Burma?"

"Where's the proof?" one soldier asked. "You can't prove that she has swallowed Klast Burma."

"One doesn't swallow a soul."

"Let me out!" Peyton screamed at them again.

"I've had enough of this," the lead soldier said.

He pulled out a device from the soul doctor's tool belt, aimed it at her, and flashed her with a blue light. Several people gasped. Others screamed like Tim. The soul doctor shook his head and took the device back.

"Okay. Who's up to doing this my way? We need to first remove the Sysmat gadgetry."

"That's not..." the soldier trailed off as if something should have happened.

He pulled out a popper gun and shot it in her direction. That was nice of him. Now she could see how those operated and what they were. The guns did not contain bullets. Peyton crossed her arms at him and watched as a yellow flash of light hit the cage. It rattled the metal and did absolutely nothing to her.

"Are you ready to do this my way?" the soul doctor asked again.

The soldier shot her cage several more times. Shucks. It wasn't a one-use device. He did have to reload the shot each time by pushing in the popper stick before he pulled it back out again. It was fascinating that he was able to aim the thing when he had to pull out a stick. If she did that, she would no doubt jiggle the entire thing and get her shot wrong.

"I think we should start with the tube on her side. Thoughts? I'm not one to perform surgery like that."

"Can we sedate her?" one doctor asked slowly, as he looked at his friends.

"If we were capable of that, we'd have already sedated her with the confinement cage," another doctor pointed out.

"I can't perform surgery on a person who is wide awake and kicking!"

"Not to mention bleeding. She still bleeds, I presume. She has blood on her hands and face."

Yes, about that. These people claimed the *Mervolk* was gone. She could only assume that was the name of the bacteria that had been taking her over. If she was completely healthy, she shouldn't have gotten a bloody nose. Klast had supposedly saved her, but he hadn't been able to save himself. She had to get out of here to figure out how to do that! Peyton shook the cage, pressing her hands to the sides and ramming it with all her weight.

"Yes, she will bleed. Maybe a local anesthetic would hold her for a time?"

"That creature is wrong!" the lead soldier pointed at her.

"She is a modified Sysmat agent. All of them are wrong. Are you going to help, or do I need to kick you out?"

Peyton rolled her eyes. The doctor hadn't kicked out Tim. His threats looked empty. All the same, she fully believed that he was going to get the medical tube out of her hip and the sparkle finder out of her wrists. How was she going to stop them from doing that? She would have to come out of the cage for the procedure, but the soldiers would hold her down the entire time. She wasn't much of a match for the fifty or so people in the room. She kicked the cage again.

"Are we soul locked?" one of the poison control people wavered.

"That I don't know. Hopefully, we can do this without her thinking we're trying to harm her. We'll need to show her a few before and after pictures to prove our good intent."

"Taking out a medical tube on a strange planet will make a Sysmat agent think we have *good* intent?" a different doctor huffed. "This is a disaster. What is your explanation for why she didn't die?"

The soul doctor opened his mouth to answer, but the door burst open and the sound of wailing filled the room. More people came in, one of them dragging something heavy. Peyton strained to get a look at who it was, although she guessed by the pitch. When the wailing turned into tearful begging, Peyton bonked her head against the side of the cage. One of the soldiers winced.

"I won't let go! I won't!" Isabelle screamed. Isabelle and Klast were here. That meant that Klast would be subject to the doctors next. She was even farther away from helping him now.

"Why did no one inform me of this immediately?!" an angry voice shouted.

There was pushing and the angry man came to crouch before her. Dressed in a gray suit, one look at him pushed Peyton's heart into overdrive. Something about him got her hammering. Perhaps it was the way he looked so intelligent. Maybe it was his clear resemblance to Klast with his dark hair and all-seeing eyes. He would be able to understand her. He had to be Klast's father: the interplanetary general. Jethro Burma. That was it.

"What happened to Klast?" he demanded.

"His dogs tore him apart," Peyton said.

"You turned the sound off?" Klast's dad asked as he stood back up and shoved through the people again.

"She was screaming," the soul doctor informed.

"It was quite loud," Tim agreed.

Peyton missed the button or whatever that affected the sound of her cage. She didn't miss the way the doctors took the opportunity to huddle together and converse on the best way to take her apart. She had always put up with doctors out of necessity, but she seriously hated the lot of them.

"Let's do this again. What happened to Klast?"

Jethro was back. He once again crouched at eye level, which wasn't anything anyone else had done. His movement felt oddly out of place as if he was both her friend and not at the same time.

"Sir," the head soldier said. "She's moving around while the cage is active and the SD's don't kill her."

"I was trying to tell you that she's blazen!" the soul doctor interrupted. "She can't be killed by the disconnection of her soul or anyone else's soul. Your SD soul destroyer gun won't work."

"Actually, that's not true. I've died quite a few times," Peyton corrected with a sigh. She had felt disconnected from her body more than twenty times. She'd lost count after that point. It didn't seem to matter anymore.

"Can you understand them?" the crouching man asked, moving backward a little.

Peyton nodded. "But they can't understand me."

"Remarkable. You were with Klast before he ended up like this?"

"To an extent," Peyton replied.

She craned her head, trying to get a glimpse of Klast and the crying Isabelle. To her surprise, Jethro shoved back through the crowd and dragged

Klast by his shoes over to her. Klast wasn't in reach, but he was close enough that she could see him. Isabelle was lying on top of him, a scandalous gesture from the looks on people's faces, while she wailed about him being dead and smelling bad. Peyton couldn't help but chuckle.

"He stinks from two weeks of hiking and not taking a bath. His dogs smell just as bad," Peyton said, even if Isabelle couldn't understand her. Jethro didn't translate.

"What happened to my son?" the guy asked again.

Son! She guessed it right. Peyton launched right into it. Klast's breed dogs had been trying to steal his soul away. He went to kill his breed dogs so other people wouldn't get his training secrets and he'd fallen on top of her and crashed her into this planet when he came back.

"That doesn't explain—"

"Something warm crashed into me between the worlds," Peyton continued. "Isabelle said that it's Klast's soul. I agree with that. I'm hearing his imprinted dog talk to me, and the dog thinks that the theory is correct."

"Wait," his father cut off as he gave an annoyed look to Isabelle. "Klast has an imprinted dog? Since when? I believed you up till that part."

"It happened a few years ago. I believe the dog imprinted him, and Klast refused to reciprocate since he was still mourning Shadow. Must be a hard thing for the dog to love someone who does his best to not love back. Do you know the names of his dogs? I can tell you which one."

"You know his dog's *names*?" his father asked her, impressed. "All of them?"

Peyton nodded. He sat down cross-legged before her.

"Don't sit down! We have to get his soul back into him. I don't know how!"

"You know the dog names. He trusted you with the dog names. What does his imprinted dog look like?"

"He looks like the silver of the moon with brown boots and black-tipped ears."

"The devil dog?!"

He'd heard *that* name at least. Peyton didn't like it. It didn't describe Deek at all.

"He's not a devil," Peyton answered. "He's misunderstood, although he is a liar. He totally was lying to everyone to achieve his overall purpose of saving lives. Are you going to let me out of here?"

"Not yet. Where can I find the devil dog?"

She leaned up against the cage in frustration. Klast was right there! She had to save him! Jethro Burma was not helping her much. He wasn't translating, and he wasn't releasing her. Maybe he couldn't, and if he had no power in this room, she was done telling him everything. Besides, she refused to say anything to betray Deek. That was her dog. Well, not hers, but it still felt like hers sometimes. Nothing Jethro could do would make her oust the dog.

Klast's father stood up as if her expression revealed that to him. He glanced at the available people and then started pointing out a few of them. "You're coming with me. We're getting Klast's imprinted dog. He had a misfortune with soul dogs. What we need to piece him back together is his soul dog."

"Aren't those a myth?" one of the doctors asked, looking up from their procedure notes.

"You all think the blazen are a myth, but here sits Peyton. Do try not to kill her." Mr. Burma laughed.

He'd called her Peyton! She hadn't told him her name. Fear clawed at her throat. Klast said they needed to hide, but she had not expected the news back home to air that fast. How long until Sysmat found her in Lexia? Everyone on Hyphas had to know about her already.

"Soul dogs exist too. Klast trains them. Now come on. We need to pick one of them up, and I don't know if it will be easy or hard since he trains them as guard dogs. The one we need to find is the most ornery of them all."

"While you're at it, perhaps you can locate something to sedate the patient so we can remove the Sysmat technology," the soul doctor hinted.

"Absolutely not!" Peyton shot back. There were a lot of things back home that could knock her out and sedate her for a good long while.

"Which Sysmat gadgets?" Klast's dad asked. He stepped away from her and over his dead-looking son to join the huddle of scientific hooligans.

"I don't want my sparkle trail taken away!" Peyton shot at him over the tones of talking.

"That is a strange tube," Jethro agreed as he looked at the scan.

"Leave it alone!" Peyton growled, hating the thought that she had no control over herself ever.

"Doesn't look like you need it," Jethro said, walking back over to her. He didn't match her eye level this time. His taller hovering made him look sinister.

"Let me out so I can save Klast!"

"Oh lovely," his father snorted. "Klast not only has a system in place to prevent his death from a soul-stealing by having an imprinted soul dog, but he also has a blazen feeling indebted to him. The guy won't die unless it outright suits him."

"You want your son dead?" Peyton gasped.

"Of course not. I was simply remarking how unstoppable he has become."

Oh sure. Peyton narrowed her eyes at Jethro. There was a lot of that statement that didn't sit right with her. All of it, in fact. Her parents had done everything they could to save her, and when they had failed, they had done the only thing left they could think of. They handed her over to the enemy of souls in a desperate attempt to keep her body alive, knowing that they could never talk to her again. They let her die from their presence for the assurance that she was still alive somewhere else. Klast's father wouldn't make the same decision. It was oddly disturbing. She wanted to ask Klast about his relationship with his dad, but she couldn't. He still couldn't move. The longer she looked at Klast as if he was an empty shell, the harder it was to hold back the water in her eyes.

"Klast is not a tyrant," Peyton heard herself defend. "It doesn't matter if he is unstoppable. He is a loving person. He's the kind of person you want to have around a long time. He was living with backstabbing animals for years. He kept them alive. All the guys at the dog fair were astonished."

"Dog fair! That's where we can find the devil. Darn. I have to go alone. I can't have you all coming back with soul dogs. I'll be back in a bit," his father claimed and then vanished into the air.

His disappearance brought about a lot of talking. People were gawking over the topics of blazen and soul dogs and how to take her apart. Peyton balled her hands into fists and slammed them into the cage.

*"Deek,"* she tried to think to the dog, not knowing exactly how the connection worked or when it did, or if it ever turned off. *"Klast's dad is coming to fetch you. Can you hear me?"*

There was nothing, and there was no way for her to know any of the details of what was happening to the dog otherwise. Peyton kicked at the cage again and then slumped against it to watch Isabelle cuddling. It wasn't as if the woman was holding onto Klast sideways the way Peyton would have done if they had traded places. Isabelle was curled up on top of him, arms around his neck, her head tucked to his shoulder.

A blast of jealousy rushed over Peyton so strongly that she forced herself to back away from them. That was weird. It had been a long time since she'd been jealous of someone on this level. She'd been jealous of the people that got to walk around outside and not worry about dying all the time. That was a familiar jealously, but this was something else. This was the type of jealousy that made the inside of her hurt with secret fears she didn't know she was harboring.

Klast could like this other woman better than her. He could have a relationship with the lady and probably did since everyone had left her where she was. It made Peyton feel rather inadequate. She didn't have the same godlike qualities as the gorgeous Isabelle. She didn't even have a fancy name to hold up to the woman. Everything about her felt below praise. The notion made her slightly mad, but it wasn't the type of anger that would make her lash out at anyone but herself. Insecure. The word blasted through her brain and she shut her eyes to block out the sounds.

Honestly, couldn't the lady stop crying yet?! It wasn't like Klast was dead. He was simply sitting around in darkness, unaware of anything at all. She should know. She'd been there before. It wasn't the worst of places to be, but it produced a burst of anxiety when she got back into herself. She'd grown accustomed to the sudden feelings of mistrusting everyone and everything around her when she came to. The world always looked darker, full of people who would harm her and chop her head off while she couldn't do anything about it. Not that she'd be able to do anything about a head-chopping person in the first place, but still.

Peyton pried her eyes back open and studied Isabelle some more. The woman had better not be trying to strangle him. The neck was the worst place to find anyone when you woke up from being outside of yourself. Peyton shut her eyes tight against the memories.

Someone checked her pulse once when she awoke from a soul splicing. She'd never thought of herself as a violent person, but boy, had she gone at it, fighting and punching and grabbing at sharp objects. She'd caused quite a few injuries to the person helping the fallen girl beside the road. She felt bad about it all. The way she'd gone crazy and chased the person as if they were the cause of her sudden disconnection. Give that experience to a man like Klast and he was going to kill Isabelle.

"Isabelle, get off," Peyton said firmly.

She had to get the woman off before Deek showed up and patched Klast back together! She had to remove the temptation to kill anything that was touching him.

"Isabelle!" Peyton screamed at her, hoping that her sound wasn't turned off. By the way the doctors all looked over at her, she knew they could hear her. The lady was simply refusing to listen.

"Tim," she tried next.

He, at least, was reasonable. Even better, he took a few steps closer to her and gave her a nod. Peyton pointed and mimed her request. Get Isabelle off. He didn't look very enthusiastic about the request, but she needed him to be.

"You have to get her off!" Peyton begged. That was step one. Then there was the second part of distancing weapons. Oh, gee. Peyton eyed Klast's gun. It was still on his side.

"The gun next," Peyton pointed and mimed taking the gun away from Klast. They had to get the gun!

"Um… We don't touch each other's weapons here," Tim told her, shifting on his feet nervously.

"Take the gun!" Peyton screamed. She didn't know how else to say it, so she mimed the whole thing. She waved her arms, pretending that a soul was coming into her, and pointed to Klast. She shut her eyes and then pretended to wake up and then she pulled out a finger gun and started shooting everyone in the room.

"Take the gun!"

"I'll do it."

Since she'd been on her back, she had to scramble over to see who had said that. The head soldier. Of course. He carefully took Klast's gun away and then searched him over for other weapons. He yanked Isabelle off the man next.

"There has been a concern that since Klast was probably fighting before he lost himself, he will continue with the fight when he wakes up," the soldier told Isabelle as she stretched out her arms and tried to get back to the guy on the floor. "You are at risk of dismemberment if you stay there."

"He needs me," Isabelle wailed.

Oh, bother. For some reason, those three words took away the jealousy that Peyton felt. If Klast fell in love with a whiny thing like that, she'd eat a hat. Then again, maybe that was the kind of thing he was into. He loved Deek, and the dog was often rather loud. However, it also stressed him out.

Peyton sighed and collapsed back against the edge of the cage again, drawing more winces from the soldiers who thought touching the metal should hurt her. The doctors were still talking going into technical words and terms that they probably thought no one else understood. She'd heard all the words before. This was going to be one painful surgery if they had their way. Far too invasive. If they simply yanked out the tube at her hip, that'd be less painful than all their theories of chopping into her hipbone to slice it out.

Peyton looked at her right side and fingered the tube. She didn't need it anymore if Klast cured her. There was no sense in keeping around the medicine either. She pulled it from her pocket and placed it on the floor of the cage. They could have that if they wanted something from her. They were *not* going to cut into her and then replace the bone. She already had no ribs. What were these people? Honestly, she could do a better job at this herself.

She reached beneath her pants line, glad that she always wore stretchy waistbands to keep the tube from jamming into her. She was tired of people doing everything for her and telling her what she had to do. If anyone was going to pull this tube out, it was going to be her.

# 12

Bark! Bark! Bark!

Those stupid backstabbing dogs! At least Klast had gotten them out of Sue's line of sight before they decided he looked like breakfast. He had done his best to make sure they did not know what he was thinking, although coming to pick them up early was probably the only giveaway they needed. What did he need them for? He'd gone to a dog fair. He could have bought new breeders and accepted Deek. There was no reason to pick them up early unless he was planning something.

They'd jumped at him instead of getting into the car. He had shot. Sue had screamed. He couldn't let the dogs turn feral and go after her next. Tuff and Morgal were on their last night. He would see to that.

Bark! Bark!

They'd had their chance to change their ways, and they hadn't. He blamed them for all sorts of things. Deek needing to slip out of his cage to trail Klast, who pretended he didn't know the dog had escaped so he wouldn't have to figure out how. The need to take pups out one-on-one to train the most basic of tricks. His inability to rest well for years.

Deek had probably been retraining the pups. Klast had noticed at the arena how the dogs listened to his instructions at a moment's notice. Volt had saved Peyton against the overpowering emotions to find a human to imprint. That was some strong loyalty. Tasha had helped move Deek's leash likewise not chasing down her imprinted human in favor of staying by Deek. They honored his wishes, because when they did, Klast praised them for lessons well learned. They had all learned the subterfuge.

Too bad they hadn't learned how to appear out of nowhere as Deek had. If Deek was here barking his head off in a deadly rage, Klast had to get up and do something. He must have missed the shots. The breed dogs were still out there. Deek had come to kill the dogs Klast failed to stop. He couldn't fail! He couldn't put that sort of pressure on his dog to do the dirty work.

Wait. Get up? He was on the ground.

Get up! He had to get up! Klast reached for his gun. Gone. He yelled as he forced himself up off the floor, smashing into someone who was either trying to help him up or shove him back down. The lines were a little blurred right now. Deek's voice vanished into silence as other sounds pummeled Klast's ears.

His eyes refused to open. That made things harder, but he trained to do things the hard way. Sue must have called for help. These voices came to cut him down for shooting the dogs. They would want him dead for destroying a soulless.

Voices yelled about blood and cages and constraints. Klast punched whoever it was behind him as he struggled to get his eyes to work. He must have hit his head when the dogs jumped on him. He'd worry about that later. In the meantime, he had to help Deek. Klast punched down someone else and tried to clear his eyesight again.

"His eyes are black!" a voice screamed. He headed for that sound next. "Your genius plan isn't working!"

"Because you're not listening to me! We needed to have that girl workable before he showed up!" some other person shouted. "It's not the dog with his soul. It's her!"

"All we need is the dog!"

His dad! His dad had brought in a team of people to stop him. The fury that rushed through him had him turn away from his first target to find his dad.

"How dare you!" Klast screamed. "You leave my dog out of this!"

"Didn't even know you had imprinted one again. What are you going to... Stand down!" His father yelled as Klast shoved through people he couldn't see.

Frightened people scrambled away from him. Other bodies rushed toward him. Klast tried to make sense of what was happening. Deek had stopped barking. Two people were crying. Women. Did Sue have someone with her?

"The aggression is part of having your soul knocked out!" Peyton yelled over the din. She sounded hurt. Like… like, really hurt this time. Her voice was strained. Gasping.

"Where are you?!" Klast screamed, as his fury changed from anger to indignation.

She'd been through enough! Everyone always tried to kill her. He wasn't about to let that happen again. He had no idea how she had ended up next to him, but he was going to blame his dad. The man had probably hunted her down to kill her off before she ever reached safety. Klast was going to stop him. The stupid man. Klast didn't care if that made him a criminal in every place he had ever lived. He had to do something!

Klast started punching everything in his path, left and right. Whoever he was facing was strong, but he was better. He could sense a restraint on them as if they feared touching him when his eyes were black. He felt no such emotion. Klast plowed through the men like dummies in a training course.

"Hold him down!"

"Let her out!"

"I think my arm busted!"

"Ow…" That was from Peyton, struggling with something he couldn't see.

"Where are you, dumb dog?" Klast snarled.

He knew he'd heard Deek. The dog was close. The animal should do something unless one of the guys had knocked Deek down or tied him up. In that case, Klast was unsure who he should rescue first. Deek or Peyton. The urge to save them both was too hard to sort through.

"Wait," Deek barked at him.

"It's not time to wait. Do something!"

"No." Deek defied him.

"Don't you dare betray me next! There are some kinds of betrayal that I won't forgive."

"He's a good dog," Peyton whimpered. "Breathe, Klast. The aggression will tamper down if you do something stupid like stand on your head. You need to clear that. Also, has anyone asked you to take a shower?"

"Shut up. Why are you hurt?"

"You're contradicting yourself. Telling me to be quiet and talk at the same time. Stop punching people. You'll regret it."

"I won't," Klast insisted.

She was still wheezing! Forget Deek. He had to reach Peyton. He punched someone that was trying to sneak up on him. The man screamed and then all commotion broke out.

"The dog!" someone yelled.

"The cage!" another person screamed. There was mad scrambling and shoving, all of which avoided bumping him.

"Forward!" Deek barked at him.

Good dog. Klast rushed forward, tripping over someone that was in his way. He heard a yelp somewhere between the sound of relief and mortal pain.

"Peyton!"

"I think I know what to do," she trembled as he tumbled down on top of her. "Enjoy your life."

"What do you mean by—"

He tried to figure out what was happening, but he couldn't talk. The next thing he knew, Peyton's mouth was on his. Warmth rushed into him from all over the place. He'd been kissed before, but this was something else. This was like placing a heated blanket on the inside of his body on a chilly day and warming him just so. It was like finally accomplishing a task after a long struggle. The relief and calm that washed through him were amazing. Peyton was amazing.

Klast grabbed her back, not caring that other people were watching, gathering ideas about their non-existent relationship. He should ask her out. It would be rather interesting to date a person like this. Klast smiled at the thought. He could live with Peyton. She was sensible and understood a lot about life. Plus, his dog liked her. He wouldn't have to explain anything to Deek and she was super cute. She was brave, too. Standing up to Sysmat wasn't easy for anyone, and here she was holding out against them over and over again. That was admirable.

The warmth was cozy and all, but he'd never been one to be taken off course for long. There was still fighting to do. He still had to figure out what was happening, and the longer Peyton stayed on him, the longer he realized that there was a different warmth flooding his shirt. Warm and sticky and smelling like iron. Something was bleeding into his clothes, and he was fairly certain it was Peyton. Enjoy your life, she'd said. Not their life. Not life *with* her.

"No!" Klast screamed as he tried to shove her off. Already he could feel his vision clearing while she slipped from his arms. Peyton had given him back his life, but he didn't want to lose her! Klast shook his head with his eyes pinched shut, desperately trying to get his sight back. He peeked and tried it all again. Come on! He'd not hit his head that hard. His head didn't hurt at all. He had to see!

"What do we do?" some guy asked.

"Based on the readings of the soulometer, we don't need to do anything more than wait. She got the soul back into him."

Soulometer. He wasn't by Sue's house at all. They didn't have soul measuring instruments there. He had to be in Lexia right where everyone was told to shoot Sysmat agents on sight.

"No!" Klast screamed again.

He pulled his eyes open, relieved when he could see again. However, what he saw made him tremble. The blood was Peyton's. She was covered in it, and so was he. The pool was coming out of her side. He'd seen her blue and lifeless before, but that wasn't anything compared to her looking alive and nearly dead. Alive and bleeding was so much scarier. She was losing too much blood!

Klast shoved her over to find the source of the bleeding and tried applying pressure to make it stop. The hole was too big. What kind of bullet had done that?!

"I'm going to kill whoever did this," he growled as the sounds turned to whispers around him instead of screams. Those were mixed with moans from the people he had snapped at. He didn't feel bad about it. None of them were on the floor nearly dying. Right? He glanced around, unstable about everything.

Lexia. That was his location for sure. More precisely, he was in a soul hospital with Dr. Luke Browning in attendance. Why was the better question regardless of the fact that Klast had picked up on the answer. He had lost his soul and Peyton and found it just as Deek had predicted. That meant that Klast had failed to keep the Sysmat sniper out of this place. Who knew what technological advances she'd picked up on, but he couldn't do anything about it now. They had come here to put him back together so he wouldn't end up a soulless feeder. There was Deek, standing with feet wide and teeth bared toward a few soldiers who were bleeding from bites. Deek was at the controls for the confinement cages. Brilliant dog to have figured out the control slides on the floor.

Who had been in the cage? Him? Klast glanced around for the cage, only to tremble again. There was one open cage. Blood was in there, along with a metal tube and something that looked like intestines. Then there was the medicine vial that Peyton had been carrying around. The one his dog hadn't destroyed, apparently.

"You put her in a cage?!" Klast screamed the words looking for his dad. He spotted Tim first. Odd to see him here, but okay. Klast nodded back to Tim, having spent countless nights with him in the runner's station, and then glared at his father.

"Explain!"

"Peyton made herself bleed."

"Oh, there had to be a reason." He hated the way his voice both trembled and cut at the same time. "I don't have the time for this. You can explain later. I have to help Peyton. Geez, why does everyone have to die this week?! First you and mom, then *all* the dogs, then him," Klast nodded toward Deek refusing to say his name before this crowd, "and now Peyton. Second time! It's like everyone's trying to kill me off."

He was exaggerating a little, but it felt like everyone was dying on him. Leaving him behind. Distancing themselves from him when his heart needed them around. He was emotionally bleeding out, just watching the pain on Peyton's face. She was part of their group and he had failed to protect her. The week couldn't end fast enough.

"You did die," a chilling female voice said from behind him. Isabelle. If Tim being here was a surprise, she was worse. Way, way worse.

"You touch me and you'll be next," he snapped at her without bothering to glance in her direction.

That would be the other woman that he'd heard crying. The woman who couldn't stay away from him. When he said that there were some betrayals he couldn't stand, hers was the betrayal he was talking about.

"Klast, there's a team full of doctors here," his father told him as if he could guess just as fast as Deek what he was going to do.

"Not my doctor," Klast replied as he peeled away, shifting through the dark to reach the one hope he had. He didn't know how they had gotten here, but he was going to Peyton her out of it. Poor Deek. He was leaving the dog behind in one of the absolute worst places with people he didn't know or trust.

*"I'll stand by Tim and be a good boy,"* Deek told him.

*"Thanks,"* Klast answered.

What a "good boy" meant to Deek was questionable at times, but he'd been there through quite a lot and done his doggy best.

Klast crashed down in the middle of a front room, scattering school books all over the place. They probably got blood on a fair number of them as he went since Peyton was still bleeding out. She needed to be sown up. Now! Several squeals followed his arrival, and he looked up to see three children with wide eyes.

"I need Clark!"

"Dad!" one of them yelled.

"Doctor, doctor!" another screamed.

"My homework!" the third complained.

They were still on Lexia, so Klast wasn't too concerned about the homework problem. The kids could copy another homework page. These people printed their course material themselves in their own homes.

Clark scrambled into the front room, holding a saucy spoon in one hand. His mouth flew open, and then he rushed back to the kitchen to shut off whatever he had started. It smelled good.

"Sorry to ruin dinner," Klast said as the guy rushed back carrying a bunch of tools in his arms.

"No matter. That looks bad."

"I have no idea…" Klast cried, and he couldn't wipe at his eyes because his hands were covered in blood. "I can't get it to stop. Please…"

Oh, this was a bad week. Clark ordered him to get Peyton's shirt off. He ordered his kids out of the room, but they were stuck there staring in morbid fascination. Klast yanked off the shirt, clenching his teeth as he did so. Undergarments were not the same where he grew up as what they had in Lexia. Peyton was rather conservative, but it was still highly noticeable. So was the blue power-over-death mark on her arm, claiming her life belonged to Sysmat.

"You sure about this?" Clark asked him, noticing the symbol.

"Yes. Please. She's my friend. I know what she is. It's not *who* she is."

"Hold this." Clark passed him a sharp tool and got right to it.

Most doctors in Lexia were not like Clark. Klast learned he was a rather compassionate person, honoring the wishes of his patients over his better judgment. He was the exact opposite of what Sysmat was in that regard. He got his doctorate on the Moon of Endet, and then came back here where he opened a private practice so he could function by his own rules.

"She may have lost some wall lining," Klast managed to get out. His eyes were still blurry. The back of his mind told him to be worried about Deek. "If you sew it…"

"There's some serious damage here. I'm going to need a blood transfusion, and sorry to tell you this, but she might not make it. Sysmat isn't very kind to their people."

"I know…"

He had to save her. Clark had to! Klast swallowed, unable to shut his eyes even if he was suddenly super tired. It was that fighting. He was too tired to pull off something like that when he'd not slept well in a few days. Then all that worry. That took it out of a man really good.

"I was going to save her," Klast heard himself say. "They were abusing her over there. They sent a soulless at her. Had her stuck on their ridiculously addictive medication. Told her they wouldn't try to keep her alive if she couldn't save herself from *Mervolk*. She's been dying for years, so if she has to go… make it painless," Klast whimpered.

It was surprising how much this hurt! Like part of him was being tortured because Peyton was dying. He didn't even know her. Not really. He knew her first name. That's as far as any of this went. He had no idea if she liked classical or alternative better. He had no idea if she preferred snow or rain. He didn't know what would make her laugh. He hated knowing what made her cry.

"Kevin, call Jean and Tosh," Clark ordered his child. "Tell them I need help. Then get Lula over here to finish dinner for you all and keep you out of the way."

"Uh… kay," stammered Kevin. The child had to be close to nine, and his eyes were still bugging out of his head, but he dashed off to do as he was told.

"When they come, Klast, you are going to get washed, fed, and put to bed in that order."

"I won't be able to sleep," Klast claimed. "Not like this."

"You're going to fall over. I know a wasted man when I see one."

"It's been a long week, but I'm fine," Klast lied.

Clark didn't reply. Klast shook his head to keep his eyes from drooping. So tired! There was nothing he could do to help Peyton any longer, and nothing he could do for Deek. He was too exhausted to shift to fetch the dog. Why did it feel like he'd been shifting for seven hours straight?

The front door burst open, followed by Lula. Klast had never met her, but the middle-aged woman looked kind. She was also very good at ushering him away from Peyton's side with a lot of reassurances once she saw the problem. All Klast could think about was Peyton dying. He had failed a mission. Him. He didn't get too many missions that he couldn't handle, but this was the one. The one where he broke to pieces.

*"Tim is great. Treats me like I'm smart. He's playing a game called guess where Klast just went. Should I tell him where you are?"*

"I have no idea," Klast mumbled right as Lula said something to him.

"Eat while you're in the shower, then. I'll get a bed ready while you do."

Lula shoved a protein bar into his hands and then shoved him into the washroom along with some of Clark's clothes. The clothes were not the greatest fit, but they'd do. Klast wanted to protest to stay near Peyton, but he knew he'd only be in the way, and he honestly couldn't think. He ate the food, wondering when he had eaten last. He washed up as fast as he could, and then stumbled into whatever room the nearby babysitter had made for him. Despite his claim that he wasn't tired, he found himself falling asleep right as the door burst open again and worried voices entered.

"What can we do?!" a woman asked. That had to be either Jean or Tosh, two assistants or nurses or something.

"Is that a…"

"We're going to save her if we can."

"But isn't that dangerous? I mean… She's the enemy."

"Looks that way. Looks can be deceiving. Now pass the suture staple. We need to get this bleeding under control."

"Who is she?"

The door banged open again as if the next intruder thought knocking would keep the door barred. That was hardly the case in Lexia. Everyone knew how quickly the night could set in. It wasn't uncommon to welcome in guests who hadn't made it home before the freeze took over. Everyone had a guest room or closet or trundle bed for such occasions.

"Good night!" a dog barked through the house. The kids clambered about at the sudden sound. Klast smiled. Deek was here! He'd watch over them all while Klast got some rest, and then the poor dog would probably sleep until late noon the next day because of it.

"That's Peyton. She's with the Burmas. Very confidential at the moment," Tim said as he shoved closed the door. "I'm Tim, and this is Klast's soul dog. Thought I'd bring it by. I won't be in the way. Will she make it? She's a blazen. Dr. Browning just proved it, but surviving a lost soul isn't the same as surviving tearing out guts…"

Blazen. He'd suspected before, but those weren't real. Klast's mind shut down so he could rest. He welcomed the darkness to hold the pain for a while. It was going to be horrible when he woke up. If Tim could find him, his father and all those other people could too.

# 13

There was white noise. There was also a mat on the floor beneath her, as if Peyton wasn't in a hospital bed. Peyton fingered the edges of it, not willing to open her eyes and sort through her current physical limitations. She might not be able to walk with the way she'd yanked the tube from her hip. There was a large chance she had lost her ability to do a sparkle search. If Sysmat wasn't out to kill her, they would be now. She'd fallen prey to an alien species taking their technology. They weren't too kind about things like that. Klast had come back to himself just in time to get her out of the next hot mess she had found herself in, but she couldn't hear him. She could smell his dog, however.

"You are going to take a bath."

Deek nuzzled her with his nose as if he knew the comment was for him and didn't want to bark to answer.

"Awake?" a kind voice asked her.

A hand checked a large bracelet placed on her arm. There would be new tubes in her. She'd heard the word blood transfusion, but alien blood wasn't her blood. What did that make her now?

"Clark!" The voice called.

"A minute!"

Peyton took in a deep breath, expecting to find areas in her body that were tight and hurting. She felt surprisingly nimble, given everything that happened. Her hip was sore, but apart from that, she wasn't aching. Her right arm felt a bit hot, and when she curled her wrists, she whimpered. This doctor had done it too. He'd taken away the sparkle finders.

"She's awake!"

"I'm coming. I was checking on Klast. Never seen that guy so skinny. He's been running himself down lately. What's got me interested is that his dog is more concerned with sitting over here than in the room with him. Soul dogs are very loyal companions."

"That particular one is a monster in disguise," came the sound of Klast's father.

Okay, that was it! Peyton woke herself up fully and turned to find Jethro. He didn't make it too hard. He was staring at the dog and therefore her.

"Either you talk nice about the dog or get out," she demanded. "You have no idea what this creature went through to keep your son alive. No idea at all."

"He bit me," Klast's father told her.

"I'd consider biting you too."

"Okay, okay." Dr. Clark came into the room. "Mr. Burma is only here to ask you a few questions regarding your current mental health levels and then he will be on his way. He understands that the patient needs rest. Lots and lots of rest. I'm Clark Manford. These are my assistants, Jean and Tosh. We are all glad that you have survived the night."

Clark waved to two women who curtsied at her like old-fashioned ladies' maids. Neither was older than their thirties and both had blond hair held back by matching blue headbands.

"Very glad," one lady smiled at her.

"You'll be moving around in no time," the other replied.

Peyton blinked at them, trying to sort through why those sentences sounded so strange. It took her a moment to get it. They were speaking her native language without any hint of an accent at all! So was Clark.

"You speak Muthreny?" Peyton asked.

"Yes. We were born and raised here in Lexia, but have been over to your world many times," Doctor Clark Manford answered. "I maintain a great number of contacts over there in the medical world. It was me who first brought Klast here before Sysmat could snatch him when his Shadow died. A tragic day for them. A lucky day for us."

Klast was almost a Sysmat agent? He'd never mentioned his close call to death.

"If you want, I will explain to you the procedures that we completed."

"Uh…" Peyton reached over to pet Deek's fur. Her fingers entwined into the hair and then she froze. She was touching him! She'd wanted to pet that silky smooth fur ever since she saw it and hadn't dared attempt until right now. She met Deek's gaze and then grinned. He was soft. His fur came out a good four inches, so he probably needed a bit of a haircut. At the moment that would have to wait. She was touching an IB dog! Deek yawned at her.

"That tube was strange. It looked like it was missing a connecting piece," Clark continued.

"Yeah, it filtered my medicine," Peyton answered. She had to turn her head to the other side to see Clark. That meant she wasn't looking at Deek and Mr. Burma, but that was alright. Deek wasn't going to hurt her any, and he'd fend off everything else. She ran her fingers around the top of his head and he moved his face to lick her hand. Like a dog.

"Has the dog gotten anything to eat?"

"We tried, but he won't eat and Klast is still sleeping. The poor man looked like he'd not slept in a week."

"Or eaten in three," his father added as if she was supposed to explain that.

"He's out of money," Peyton responded. "He was paying for the dogs to eat and starving himself. I heard the mention of a blood transfusion. Am I alien now?"

"No. No need to worry about that. I fetched what you needed."

"Why is he out of money?" Mr. Burma asked her.

"I don't know. It's not like we're best friends or anything. I was only interested in his dog. Klast keeps saving me though, so I'm rather appreciative. You took away the sparkle trail stuff?"

Peyton glanced at her wrists, which meant that she had to stop petting Deek. Near the edge of her wrists by the bones were incision marks and stitches. She clenched her fists together, trying to use what wasn't there anymore. That other doctor had said it limited her range, but without it, there was nothing to see. It had given her the range in the first place. Okay. No matter. She would learn to live without it.

"Anything that Sysmat could use to track you over here had to go, I'm afraid. I did run it all past the dog since he seemed intent on watching over you," Clark answered. "The blue Sysmat mark on your arm is gone."

"I thought that was impossible."

"You died a few times," Clark answered, looking apologetic, "but we found a way to remove it and make great headway for the future if we ever need to do something like that again. You had devices in both wrists and feet."

What? Peyton tried to reach her feet, only to be stopped by a sharp pain in her hip as she bent.

"Careful. There was a great deal of internal damage. Not all of it done by you yanking the tube. It takes time to heal."

"I've been sick a long time."

"Do you remember how long?" Mr. Burma wondered.

She looked over at him, trying to remember the year. It was after or before or during her school studies. She had graduated, not graduated, not even started college. She'd worked with chemical reactions in her dreams, making her think she was a chemist. It was either that, or she'd worked bagging groceries. For years. All of her earlier memories were inconsistent and jumbled.

"No," she answered. "I don't know that."

"Who do you work for?" Mr. Burma asked her next.

He stepped around Deek so that he could see her better. Deek tensed. Peyton wanted to reach out and reassure the animal that the movement was fine, but she refrained. Deek would know this man better than she did. He would make the better decisions here. She hoped.

"I don't have a job. I'm not certain that my memories of my past job were everything they claim to be. I'm well aware that Sysmat messes with memory functions, Mr. Burma. I tried to hold onto what I could."

"What would you think if I told you that you had been with Sysmat for only sixteen months?"

"Not possible." It had been way longer. She'd been sick for ages.

"What would you think if I told you that your friend Cindy isn't a real person, but a group of people designed to answer your questions?"

"No," Peyton said firmly feeling nervous that he had learned about Cindy in the first place. "I kept in contact with Cindy. Sysmat wouldn't have suggested I look into IB dogs to save myself. The recommendation came from my friend."

"Why not? There is evidence suggesting that a soulless woman with black hair tried to devour your soul right after Sysmat thought you had imprinted a dog. They had already done a lot of research on your ability to not die. It was only another experiment, one trying to determine the impact a soul dog could have on a person like you. They sent you over there."

"Cindy is my friend!" She knew she was! She had to be! Cindy was the only friend she had left.

"You never had a friend named Cindy," Mr. Burma told her.

Peyton wanted to call him heartless. She expected this military man to ask her tough questions about Sysmat. Not take away the one connection that had made her feel normal. She should have guessed differently. Sysmat was all about physical torture. These people were all about the emotional sort.

"Can you go away?" Peyton asked him.

"Do you know your age?"

"Go away."

"Do you recall your last name? Your parents' names? Family?"

She looked up at the ceiling and refused to answer. She had thought she knew her family until he asked that question. She had parents and a brother. She could see fuzzy faces, but their names refused to come to her as if Sysmat had tried hard to take them out of her soul.

"What can you tell me about yourself, Peyton Finch?"

Was that her name?! It sounded windy, like a bird in flight running away from the storms that just kept coming. It didn't sound familiar at all. That would make her a P.F. Her first thought about that was that she sounded like perfume. Here. Try the amazing Persimmon Floral scent that will whisk you away to the tropics during the cold season.

"Okay," Mr. Burma said after she'd continued to stare away from him for a few uncomfortable seconds. "Tell me what this is."

She glanced down to see a test strip. "It's a PH level checker."

"And how do you know that?"

She shrugged.

"And this?"

"A fold out chart of elements."

"What can you tell me about *Mervolk*?"

"It's an alien bacterium that feeds on the host in cycles…" No. That's what she had been told. That's not what it was. "It's a biochemical weapon that attaches to the soul and is only transmittable by injection," she modified. "That is why it dies when taken through a shift," she guessed. "There is so much other soul matter out there that it scatters and attaches to everything else, leaving the weakened host alone because it's not as enticing anymore. It disconnects the soul from the host in pieces so that the body attacks the cells in rounds, messing up various bodily systems to give the sufferer a most unpleasant form of death."

She launched into the itching and bleeding and barfing. She talked about the aching and dying. She explained about the medicine that would put the disease to sleep for a while, and how when it wore off, everything came back. She talked about the many nose bleeds. The different ways that she had tried to take the medicine to hold *Mervolk* back. She mentioned the diffuser that gave her a full dose before she passed out.

"And what was it that you saw Sysmat doing that dragged you into all of this?"

"It was only a dream." Peyton shivered reflexively.

She'd been sick. That's all there was to it. Sick with something that doctors couldn't cure so her parents had made the decision to hand her over to Sysmat. That's all that happened. She had not seen Sysmat do anything that would make them take out revenge. Jethro shouldn't even know about this dream. Had she talked about it in her sleep? Had she talked about Cindy?

"Then I'd like to hear the dream."

She shook her head.

"In your opinion, you think that curing a person from *Mervolk* spreads the disease into the area between planets?"

"Uh... yes?"

"So we have only expanded the problem instead of getting rid of it," Mr. Burma grieved. "In saving one person, we are passing it off to another. Did you pass that onto Klast? Is he going to suffer from *Mervolk* now?"

"I..." Peyton stammered. She wasn't an expert on this. Everything about *Mervolk* bounced around in her head the same way ideas about her previous life did. Grasping the truth was complicated.

"I don't think so. It would have gone toward a stronger form. Klast's soul broke apart a few times. He wouldn't be that desirable to a soul weapon. Listen, Mr. Burma. I have no scientific proof for any of this. I can't back up these claims. I hardly know what I'm talking about."

"But you can stay alive to figure it out. Thanks for your time." He backed up a few steps before clasping his hands together and bringing them to his chin. "Actually, I have a few more questions if you don't find it too intrusive. Do you think you already had the ability to be blazen, or was it something that Sysmat gave you as a byproduct to their poking?"

"I still don't understand what blazen is."

"A person who can repair their broken soul. Typically it's thought to only be your own, but we've seen you carry Klast's, so we have to take that into consideration."

"I had Klast's soul because of his dog," Peyton answered.

His dad looked confused by that. She looked over at Deek, trying to figure out how to explain it. Deek blinked at her without giving her any ideas on how to form such a thought when it was more of a feeling than anything else.

"Um… Okay. I don't know how to explain it. I saw this dog and really wanted it. I looked at him and knew that he could save me. The goal at the time was to retrieve my lost medical diffuser. Anyway, when I met Klast and his dog, they had already imprinted, but somehow the dog started talking to me too because his grip on Klast isn't that strong. Klast still feels this large loyalty to his first dog Shadow, who is dead. So, the dog talked to me and Klast in an attempt to…"

*"Stop the soulless woman who was chasing you down before she could harm Klast,"* Deek provided.

"Right. That," Peyton nodded. "He wanted to head off the soulless woman that was following me before the thing reached Klast."

Is that what the dog had been doing?! It was nice that he finally told her.

"To do that, the dog forged a connection to me, but since he also had a connection with Klast, Klast's missing soul recognized the link when I entered the area between planets as you called it. It tried to patch itself back together. The soul pieces didn't know how to join through Klast so I guess it picked me….? I don't know!" Peyton wailed.

"You patch souls back together," Mr. Burma told her again. "You called out to the missing pieces. Do you think you could do that with anyone you latch onto, or only if there is an IB dog involved?"

How should she know?! Her devices to latch onto anyone were gone. She shrugged, which reminded her that her arm was still hot where the blue Sysmat mark had been. She pulled up her sleeve to look at the location. She had a large sunburnt rectangle instead of the power-over-death mark.

"If you could summon *Mervolk* and destroy it, that would be something."

That sounded hard, actually. It wasn't like rushing through a shift would bring every single speck of *Mervolk* clambering toward her. She wasn't sparkly enough for that. She was breezy and translucent, a thin screen that things rushed through. Peyton could keep the bugs out of the house, but she wasn't solid enough to block the wind.

"You said it attaches to frayed souls."

"*Mervolk* gets injected," Peyton repeated. "Drinking it will give a person the runs for a day. Maybe it really does get destroyed in the shift. I don't know."

Ouch. Her head. She was going into a tailspin over a past nightmare. She had not been trying to figure out what made Michael sick. She didn't even know a Michael! She had not met him at a party. He'd not taken her to get fabulous dinner and then ended up sick with "food poisoning" that came out green. She'd not offered to look into it and... then what? She always woke from the dream after that.

"I can't destroy that stuff. You're asking the wrong person."

"Maybe," Mr. Burma said as a way of an answer. "See you all later. Let me know when my son gets up."

Clark nodded but then shook his head when Mr. Burma vanished from sight as if he wouldn't contact Jethro. Peyton wiped a few stray tears that leaked from her tired, weary eyes. Her version of friendly Cindy was gone. She'd lost all her friends and family. The only thing she could blame it on was Sysmat. She'd been healthy before that. Not perfectly, but healthy all the same. Sixteen months. She'd been there sixteen months when it felt like five years or more.

"You just take it easy," Clark told her. "You've been a bigger help than you know. Don't worry about all that other stuff right now. Focus on a good recovery."

"How long?" Peyton asked.

She'd had trouble walking when the tube first went in. It had hurt like crazy to pull it out. She should have been more patient and just left it alone, but there was no changing her decision now. The strange part was that if she'd only been at Sysmat for sixteen months, that wasn't enough time to go through a full hip recovery. It didn't add up.

"I've got some rather good restorative technology to work with. Let's give it a few more days and see."

"Days? Not months? Not years?" If these people could fix things so fast, why couldn't they come up with a better cure for this *Mervolk* stuff on their own? It didn't make much sense.

Clark smiled. "One day at a time. Now if everyone is in agreeance, I would love to help you with something else. All in favor of me getting this dog a bath?"

Peyton chuckled, which hurt her side so much that she had to hold it. She looked at Deek, who yawned at her and then stood up to follow Clark.

"And eat something too!" she wheezed after the dog. "Also, use the bathroom. You can use bathrooms, right?"

She heard Deek grunt at her. Hopefully, that would mean yes. The dog needed to take care of himself, particularly when they were in a location where that was possible. Deek had been having a rough week, and no one was out and about pampering him. He deserved a dog treat or two.

Water turned on and she heard Deek yelp in surprise and Clark laugh. She worried that Deek would do something dreadful, like shoot acid from being startled, but the fear left when Clark laughed again and his low tones explained how the water system worked. She had to hand it to Deek. He was one well-educated dog. The two nurses walked out next, telling Peyton they'd be back with something easy to eat now that she was awake.

With the room quieter, Peyton focused on her breathing. In and out. She was going to be better much faster than anticipated. She would get to start over. The thought had her crying all over again. She didn't exactly want to start over. She wanted to remember who she was!

"Would it scare you if I...?"

Peyton jolted. She'd thought she was alone to cry in peace for a while, but no. The movement made her gasp and then grab at her side as Klast gave an embarrassed chuckle. He'd been asleep! The doctor had just checked on him! Then again, maybe he had been hiding in the room until his father had left.

"Sorry," Klast said, walking silently to where he could see her better. "I guess I did scare you. Would it scare you even more if I helped you sit up some?"

"Yes. No. I mean, I want to sit up to see my feet, but no, it wouldn't scare me if you helped. I don't think I can move..."

She tried it only to gasp. With a wince, she fell backward, having not moved more than an inch off the floor. Klast caught her. His movements were rather slow, tilting her by degrees, stopping whenever she looked the least bit uncomfortable. It didn't hurt, though. She did none of the work and allowed herself to rest against his broad chest as he held her shoulders. When she gave a nod that it was enough, he stopped. From where she sat, she could see that she wasn't alone in the room at all. There were two other people in there with her. One was Tim. The other was a man with incredibly thick eyebrows. A black cap with a gray band hid his wild dark hair. From the collared green and white checkered shirt he wore, Peyton gathered that he was a hipster. He certainly looked confident about his cool nature at first glance. The man and Tim felt more like a protection squad than anything, so she allowed herself to not fret about them watching her cry.

Peyton closed her eyes. She wasn't ready to see her feet. There would be a scar there related to who knew what. She wasn't ready to face everything that came next. At the moment, she felt completely friendless, even if she had Klast right there behind her. Sysmat had taken everything away. It brought to mind something that Klast had told her. They could take away her memories and connections, but they couldn't take away her will to live. That felt like the only thing she had left, and it didn't feel so large right now when she suddenly had the future back to consider and nothing to attack it with.

"I don't know who I am," she whispered. "I have nothing and nobody."

"Ouch," Klast said so suddenly that she jerked her head around to look at him. It wasn't the best of angles. She could see the hair on his face and right up his nose, so she stopped looking.

"Double ouch. Sorry about the face. Mike told me I was scary enough to frighten any woman away. Normally I shave at least. I do apologize. I've been rather busy."

"I'm not scared away," Peyton told him. "And Mike is wrong."

"Well, you also can't move," Klast reminded. He lightly squeezed her shoulders and then let his hands fall to the floor.

"No, I meant... You don't scare me, Klast. Not at all. You're kind and patient and compassionate. You'd rather suffer yourself than put suffering onto others. It makes you remarkable. You have a way of offering praise that reaches into the soul and spreads joy. Around you, people feel safe. Dogs feel secure. You're a pillar of strength. Not scary."

"I failed," he grunted. "I was going to save you. Instead, I lost myself again and when that happens, I slip through the air without knowing what I'm doing. I never should have brought you here. I can't believe I failed so horribly."

Silence hung heavy in the air. Peyton didn't know what to say to that. Klast had lost his soul, so he'd gone looking for it. He'd rushed toward the one point where it had been—with Deek. Then he had crashed into her and flung both of them here. It was his fault for going up against the breed dogs without understanding how to protect his soul from their stealing first, but how *did* one protect from that? She stayed quiet.

"Alright. I was hoping for a better reaction than that."

"Yeah, me too," she agreed.

Peyton shifted a little so she could angle her feet and look at the bottom of them. The cut line was at her heel, and she had no idea what had been there. She'd never even noticed.

"Right," Klast sighed again. "I'll do better. I'm sorry that you don't remember who you *were*, but that doesn't change who you *are*, and that is an incredibly brave, beautiful woman that I owe the world to. You saved me, Peyton. You saved Deek. I can't thank you enough for that. It hurt when you said you have nobody because you do. You've got me and Deek. You've got every IB dog I've ever trained and their trainers and their trainer's friends. Once part of the pack, always part of the pack, no matter where our paths go or how far away. We'll see them again someday and then you'll know. You have a large family out there. It loves you. It's always going to love you."

She shrugged.

"You're deciding not to believe me, huh?" Klast asked. "One day you'll see it, Peyt. I can't believe that you…" He choked. "You gave me back my soul, sounding like you were going to die. Like you'd die for me. I've never had that before."

"Well, I was going to die. I did," she told him. "Clark said I did."

"A spiritual death, though. You die physically and you really die."

She nodded. She knew that, and she *had* thought it was the end for her. The least she could do was see that Klast got his soul back before her own stupidity took her down.

"It's what you do all the time! You give away all those dogs to be happy and it hurts you. I know it does."

"Nothing more than waving the kids off to college to start their own lives," he replied modestly.

"But you do it over and over again and none of them stick around for *you*," Peyton persisted. Klast shrugged behind her. "I'm going to stick around for you."

"Pardon?" he asked as if he'd not heard her right. "Don't let me cramp your style. You're free, Peyt. Go live! Go on fabulous adventures. See the world. Become extraordinary!"

She couldn't help but smile. He was doing it again, trying to give another living thing a better life without any thought to himself. Why would she want to leave that? She didn't need to be extraordinary when it was going to find her if she stayed near Klast. Not to mention that she was on an alien planet and no one but him could understand her.

"I like it when you call me Peyt," she answered.

"I think we should decide to be friends then," Klast said.

Peyton chuckled as she craned her head to look up. This time, Klast was looking down at her, so she didn't have to see up his nostrils. It was much better. His gray-blue eyes held a light sheen to them like he was about to cry, but his mouth contained a soft smile. Peyton shifted so that she could reach backward and place one of her hands over his.

"I would love to be your friend. I really would."

"Glad we got that settled," he grinned. "Imagine me sitting right here with an enemy."

"You'd do it," she blurted. "You'd say pretty things and smile at the person."

"Yeah, but I wouldn't dare admit that they were beautiful."

Peyton blushed and looked away from him. Truly? She'd thought of herself as fairly average for such a long time that the smallest compliment got her face all red. She rolled her eyes at herself, but couldn't stop the smile. *The Klast Burma* thought she was pretty.

"You tell people that all the time, don't you?"

"No!" Klast laughed. "I haven't found anyone to be pretty since..."

Peyton looked back at him. He was gazing at the wall now instead of at her, angled so that her face was more in line with his stubble than his mouth, which was crooked in a frown.

"That's okay. You don't have to tell me."

"Not since Isabelle."

She knew it! There was something between the two of them. How could there not be with the woman crying about him forever? Peyton rolled her head back around so she wouldn't have to look at Klast. The frown was probably guilt. He felt guilty for calling a girl like Peyton beautiful when there were women out there with angelic hair like Isabelle.

"I don't want to talk about it."

"Okay," Peyton answered as she swallowed. They were still friends. She didn't need to feel so disappointed about this. It wasn't like she wanted to date Klast or anything. She'd only just met the man.

"There are some types of backstabbing that even I can't overlook," Klast sighed.

"You don't have to tell me."

"She was nice at first," Klast plowed on.

Peyton glanced over at Tim and his friend who were watching them. They couldn't understand the conversation, but they'd have caught the name. It made her wonder what they were thinking. Klast was talking even if he said he didn't want to. Maybe he didn't have anyone to share this with, so it was bleeding out of him. Well, she could handle it. She'd be the listening friend he needed, even if it was making her doubt herself.

"One day Isabelle walked over to me and put her hand on my knee," Klast spoke as if he was far away. He mimicked the interaction by shifting his free hand to her left knee. The one with the pin in it.

Peyton blinked at him, confused. Tim's friend whispered.

"That's what I thought," Klast said, as he looked back at her. "It was a bit forward, but not overly so. Only I was wrong about that. Over here the action is akin to saying that you'll marry someone. She purposely tried to pull me into a marriage relationship without explaining it to me. People kept congratulating me and I was clueless."

"Uh," Peyton said as she pushed his hand off with another glance at Tim. Hopefully, he didn't have any ideas that Klast was proposing when he couldn't understand them.

"I avoid Isabelle now. It's wrong to steal your way into another's life like that. Honestly, she knows nothing about me. I'm not marrying some lady who could never hold her own among the dogs."

That statement sounded like Klast was trying to talk himself into the idea. Peyton smirked.

"I don't know about that. She was pretty good at hanging onto your neck when you were out."

"She what?" Klast coughed.

Peyton found herself explaining how Isabelle had stood up for her. Klast only rolled his eyes and then looked at Tim to ask him to explain what had happened. His version of events was quite a bit different from how Peyton saw them. Tim had shot Peyton when she and Klast had crashed in the street because of the shoot-on-sight orders. Peyton had not noticed at all since she'd been flattened by Klast. When she had moved and Klast hadn't, Tim worried that he had missed and harmed one of his best friends. That's when Isabelle showed up, claiming that Klast's soul had moved. Tim was determined to fix his mistake. Not by trying to kill her again, because by that point, he believed that Klast had brought Peyton there for some military strategy. She was going to point out all the Sysmat agents as they arrived so they could shoot the correct ones. He felt like he'd blundered up the whole thing.

So he took her to Dr. Browning hoping to explain the situation and get it resolved before anyone started pointing fingers at him, and it all exploded from there with Isabelle still wailing and guards and doctors and Klast's dad and his dog. All the while, Klast was on the ground unmoving while Tim watched each of his actions lead to worse consequences.

"I'm so sorry," Tim told him. "That's about the time that I called Hank because if there was anyone who was going to piece together what you might think, it was going to be him. You talked to him more than the rest of us."

That's who hipster man was. Hank. He sounded even more important now. A friend of Klast's. Klast had told Peyton that they shared friends, but she wasn't so sure about this guy. He stood so confidently that it made her question how she looked when she stood in place as if beside him other people didn't compare. There was a certain vibe about him too, a mix between trust-me and back-off that was both amusing and alarming at the same time. There had to be hidden secrets behind a face like that. Peyton closed her eyes just to hold the feeling. It was impossible to link onto anyone now that she'd lost the sparkle finders, but she wanted to. She wanted to find Hank again as if helping Klast locate his friends at a moment's notice was important.

"I'm not mad at all," Klast assured Tim. "I think we all made a few mistakes lately that we're not proud of. Let's leave them where they belong and move onward."

Lights danced beneath her eyelids and Peyton jerked backward, moaning on the movement to her side.

"You alright?" Klast asked her. "What was that?"

"Falling asleep sitting up?" she guessed.

She had just woken up, but talking about sleep made her feel instantly groggy. Klast slid his hand out from under hers and then slowly lowered her back down, telling her to get all the rest she needed. He needed to check up on his wet dog, after all.

Peyton nodded and let herself relax against the mat. The lights beneath her eyes came back. Sparkles danced. They seemed to lead her right to Hank without her clenching her fists at all. Could it be?! There was only one way to tell. Peyton picked another target. Klast's dad. She'd not knowingly tagged him with any invisible stickers, but he'd be a person to keep track of too, even if she still didn't understand his relationship with his son.

A line appeared, and it was as if she was flying across the ground outside, straight to where Mr. Burma was. There were more brightly colored buildings that she wished to stop and look at, but she couldn't slow down. Windows and fake windows brushed past her. She zoomed past doors of all sizes and pillars and balustrades. She rushed through an office building wall in what had to be a vision. As if knowing he was being gazed at, Mr. Burma spun to look back at her.

"Back at it, are you?"

Frightened, Peyton gasped and shot her eyes open, only to find the nurses there with some soup for her to eat. She thanked them and ate it as best as she could. That tiredness was coming back on strong. She finished half the soup before she was asleep once more. Healing at a record pace was exhausting.

# 14

Klast stood in the hallway, looking at the door that separated him from Deek. He didn't need to see the dog. Deek was always good at getting cleaned up, but Klast needed to think and give himself a good shake. He'd just had Peyton in his arms. He'd enjoyed it even if there were some clear issues standing in the way. She couldn't remember who she was. Her personality was in flux, and yet, he felt like he still knew her when he knew nothing at all. He'd still save her, no question about that, but maybe he needed to tone down the heart-to-heart stuff. Talking about Isabelle wasn't anything he had planned on doing. There he was, sharing yet another part of his soul with Peyton. He had to stop doing that. The stranger had enough of him as it was.

"What's the deal with the girl?" Hank asked him, slipping into the hallway after him.

Klast shrugged and then rubbed the back of his neck before leaning up against the wall. It was true that he'd talked with Hank the most out of anyone in the runner's station, but he hadn't shared important details about his life. He'd mostly asked questions and learned about *them*. All the same, he'd built up a comradery that he hadn't expected with Hank and Tim. It was enough to make them go out of their way to watch out for him. Hank had waited around for him to show up when his father was getting worried, and Tim had been trying to save him in the only way he knew how.

"I honestly don't know. I just met her."

"Must have been one good first impression," Hank commented.

"No, it wasn't," Klast answered, remembering the way her hands had been cold, and he'd been irritated that she and Lawrence wanted to buy his dogs. Speaking of dogs, he reached for his phone to call Mike to find out about Zen and Phantom, only to remember that he'd destroyed it so Sysmat couldn't track him. Maybe Peyton still had... no. All technology near her was gone too. She'd lost one link to Sysmat, but that didn't change the feeling that she couldn't escape.

"When I first met her, she was freezing. Then she was trying to help one of my dogs that'd just imprinted. Then she was gone and Deek was a mess. We found her dead, and she pulled herself back together. She died again from a soulless woman getting to her. After that, she died several more times while over here. She's got to be tired of dying all the time."

She'd touched his hand today without being cold. That had made him happy, but also a little scared. He emotionally liked Peyton more than he mentally should.

"Deek?" Hank asked.

"The dog," Klast pointed toward the closed door. "He's been marvelous trying to head off this threat I hadn't seen coming, but his response was to join the opposition to keep me from doing that. I guess I'm still on edge. Sysmat already knew about me. So perhaps they expected Peyton to die in my presence so I could show them how to kill off *Mervolk* bacteria. Perhaps they expected me to defend the world from the soulless that they sent to her so they could analyze how to destroy one of those. I can't decide if the attack is directly related to Peyton due to a vendetta against her, or more related to me. Maybe they expected the soulless to be the end of me.

"Then there's still the whole part about soul tracking. If Peyton had reached Sysmat again after connecting with Deek, would they have used her to get into Lexia? Are they still trying to reach this planet? Is there an impending war that I've been the start of, or is the threat to all of you over if Peyton is disconnected from their grid? I don't have any of the answers, and it's not like Peyton does either. She works her hardest to avoid being brainwashed, but it's impossible to not carry scars.

"If I look deeper into the whole mess, it only brings up more questions. I had breed dogs that were trying to claim my soul. Why? Were they a part of Sysmat somehow and I missed it? It could be that Peyton is a byproduct of Sysmat getting annoyed that they hadn't killed me off yet. Most of the time, they couldn't. I keep company with at least one bodyguard dog at all times. I have a team of five to eight with me most days. You can't just get around that without infiltrating into it."

"Wow." Hank shook his head. "You live like that? Why did you stay over there if you had people trying to destroy your soul?"

"I can take walks at night," Klast answered, causing Hank to laugh at him. Everyone here had a strict curfew to avoid death in the dark. "My family's there and so are my friends. It's my home. I had no reason to leave it when I couldn't see all the threats."

"You've decided to leave it now?"

Klast shrugged. "I've decided that I need to stay out of Sysmat's sight for a while. I'm not ready to leave my home forever."

Scratching came from the other side of the washroom door, so Klast turned the handle and let Deek out. He looked all fluffy from being dried off. Klast grinned at him and started patting down his fur before he could burst into laughter.

"That's a soul dog? He's both bigger and smaller than I expected," Hank gawked.

For an IB dog, Deek was average, reaching to Klast's lower waist. He stared at Hank like he was going to eat him for lunch. Klast rolled his eyes. He needed to get the dog fed soon. He'd been overworking lately.

"Peyton said the dog needs to eat," Clark agreed with Klast's thoughts as he stepped out of the room covered in water and dog fur. "He wouldn't eat anything we gave him. Maybe I was guessing wrong about what he eats."

"Probably not. He won't take food from strangers, no matter how well-intentioned," Klast answered. "What you got?"

They migrated over to the kitchen, followed by Tim, where Klast picked over grains and meats to feed the dog. It made him wonder if Deek would eat food if Peyton fed him. Klast was still a bit upset that Deek had chosen to run off with her. Now that her imminent death had come and gone and everyone had survived it, it didn't seem necessary for Deek to continue to harbor feelings for Peyton. Klast was never going to sign the paperwork to give him up. However, he was adopting Peyton on his own, so he wasn't sure where that put him with the dog.

Deek stopped chomping mid-bite and sat down to stare at him. Klast looked away.

"She needs me," Deek barked at him.

Not so great. Deek still wanted a lasting connection with some other human, because Klast wasn't good enough for him. *He* was the one that could hear Deek's thoughts. The dog should be his.

"You like her," Deek prompted. "She can hear me."

Klast stomped over to the open cupboard and pulled out a cup to get some water. Peyton was in the same situation as him right now, but she would not stay that way. Not her. She had too much fight in her soul. Too much desire to explore and learn. There was going to come a day where she would part ways with Klast, and then he'd be losing Deek all over again. She had no right to hear his dog in her head. None at all.

"I need you too!" Klast stormed, banging the cup down on the counter without filling it. "You're all I have left. The only thing! I don't have a home, a job, money, or IB dogs. I gave all of it up to be with *you*, and this is how you repay me by treating me as if everything I did is worthless!"

If he didn't know any better, he'd wager a guess that Deek was working with Sysmat too. Heck, he *didn't* know any better. His dog could be the mastermind behind everything that had gone wrong. The blown-up house, the loss of home and property and money and everything. Deek had known all along that Peyton was going to show up. He'd been trying to get Klast to be a wreck. Their story could still turn out to be tragic.

Klast could go shoot Peyton right now. If she died, then there was no one else left to appeal to his dog. Deek would stay with him. If Deek wasn't fully attached to the woman, he'd refuse to talk to Klast for a month. If he was attached, he'd kill Klast off, and then once both his people were dead, he'd die next, and they all could die together. Sysmat would win, and Klast wouldn't have to worry about any of it anymore.

Klast moved his hand down to his gun holder, clenching his fists together to find it missing. He'd lost the weapon somewhere between his fight with the breed dogs and the soul doctor's office. To have it gone made him feel weak. He couldn't shoot Peyton. Not that he actually would, he sighed. The most he'd do is stomp over there and glare at her, but he was mad enough to do more.

"Now is probably a bad time to tell you that I think I can still sparkle hunt people," Peyton's voice said, small and breezy from the edge of the kitchen.

Klast spun around to find her down on the floor by the door. It looked like she had army crawled her way over here with one arm. Her other arm was holding herself around the waist as if that would stop the pain. This completely proved his point! She wasn't about to give up soon. She'd keep fighting to get what she wanted.

"What are you doing?" Klast berated as he stormed around Deek, pointing down at the food so he'd finish it off. Deek watched him reach for Peyton to help prop her up. Then he turned himself so he could both eat and stare at the same time. Peyton shouldn't be crawling around yet. She wasn't better. She needed to rest.

"You were screaming," Peyton remarked. "And I had that dream again. The one where I'm not a grocery store bagger, but a chemist studying what was making people vomit out all that green goop. Normally I wake up in the middle of the dream, but I finished it this time. I think your dad is right, Klast. I know how to stop *Mervolk* and so does Sysmat."

His emotions were so wobbly, that the only thing he did about that comment was grunt. Peyton ignored his bad mood. It was almost like she expected it, which made him feel both better and worse at the same time. He had to pull himself together. Yes, it was a very stressful week, but he was better than this. He'd hardly praised Deek at all, even when the dog was saving his life. The only thing Klast had done was whine at him. It was shameful. He felt bad about it, but he couldn't make his hurt emotions go away. There was one thing he didn't want to lose, and it kept trying to escape him.

"So, in the dream," Peyton continued as she leaned into him, heedless of his treacherous thoughts to shift her to a cliff and toss her over, "I discover that a certain acid can disrupt the format of *Mervolk*. The type of acid is biologically located in only one known species carrying the common name of Imprinting Bodyguard dogs."

"Wait." Klast took a step back, which off-balanced Peyton. He had to steady her out again when she stumbled and inhaled sharply. Clark showed up in the kitchen, listening rather carefully. Deek stopped eating again. Shifting stopped the disease. What was this?

"When Deek shot that acid," Peyton mused, ignoring her physical discomfort, "I had a short flashback of myself scooping some up to examine its properties. It's not every day you get your hands on that stuff. For one, IB dogs refuse to shoot it out on command no matter who is asking it of them. Then there's the problem that they don't listen to most people in the first place.

"I think Sysmat wants the acid. Deek must know that instinctively, but he can't say why without me to connect the dots. He has so many questions lately that he can't form and I can't remember. You sounded like Deek is leaving you, but he's not. He's trying to help find the answers."

"They want the dogs," Klast whispered.

Suddenly, all of his bad vibes toward Peyton were gone again. It helped that she implied leaving Deek to him, but the greater reassurance came from this insight about how Sysmat thought. Assuming they didn't know the shifting cure, they had found a formula for another one. One that involved IB dogs, the very things they were trying to buy from him.

It was highly possible that neither Klast nor Peyton were the main goal for the company. Sysmat wanted the dogs as first suspected, and now Klast had a reason why. It wasn't only him that had suffered strange attacks lately. There had been a lot of IB losses in the last few months. Sysmat was trying to gather acid from the dogs! He had to warn his buddies. Everyone with a dog was in danger. Klast reached for his phone again only to groan. Deek chomped down the rest of his food as fast as he could go.

"You don't have a hidden phone?" he questioned Peyton.

"No, but your dad probably has one. He's down the road in the building with blue glass and silver pillars on the third floor by the window with the red pots."

"Uh-huh," Klast nodded at her, remembering that she had just told him she could hunt for people still. Interesting that the first person she hunted down was Jethro Burma.

"I'm not sure about him, Klast. He bothers me. Sometimes it sounds like he's disappointed that you're still around and I can't figure out why."

That was good to know. Klast was just about to leave, but with an odd warning like that, he waited. He'd held an unwarranted grudge against Sysmat since Shadow died, but the grudge didn't apply to Peyton. If she was worried, he should exercise caution. Did he need to be more concerned about his dad?

Klast looked at Deek for the answer. Deek stood there silently, going over everything that he had seen about Klast's father lately. He licked his lips to clear off the food and then shook his head.

"Aha!" Peyton pointed at him. "A head shake! I've been meaning to ask you if that means he's telling the truth or if he's lying about his answer."

"Shaking his head?"

"Yes. Is there a difference between him barking yes and shaking his head? Your dog lies to me."

*His* dog. He would never get over hearing that, even if Deek wasn't the one to affirm it to him. It made him smile all the same and then groan because he was being horrible to Peyton. Horrible to everyone really. If he could simply get out of his head and distance himself from his fears, he might be doing better.

"Sorry," he mumbled.

"Well, I figure he lies to a lot of people, so it makes all of us even."

"No. Not that. I'm being horribly mean to you inside of my head."

Instead of stepping away from him, Peyton only laughed. She leaned into him even more. What was it with this girl? She was strange.

"Sort of like I'm the worst enemy you've ever faced and I'm going to lie to you about everything and you can't trust me?"

"No. More along the lines of you're going to take away everything I care about and I want to kill you."

"Riiight..."

She tipped her head to look at him and study the lines around his eyes. Klast couldn't believe he had even told her that. Get her by his arms and he was admitting all of his faults to her. It made him mad. He didn't want to like her. He needed to stop telling her this stuff!

"And when did this all start?"

"I have never liked you," Klast told her.

That only made her laugh harder. He glared at Deek as if the dog was telling her jokes, but Deek was super focused on Klast's face as if scared Klast would to carry through with the thoughts in his head.

"Why are you laughing? Did you not hear me? I feel like killing you. Death is not funny."

"No?"

She smacked the back of his head. It was hard enough to make him protest, so he did. This woman was crazy!

"I have no cure for your moodiness. You'll have to work that out on your own. The first time I lost my soul, it took me like a month to feel better, except that your father just told me I've only been with Sysmat for sixteen months instead of five years, so I can't give you any clear dates. Time has been stripped away from me. You'll start feeling better soon."

"You repair souls. I don't," Klast reminded.

"You're going to be fine. Honestly. Nothing here wants to strip you away. You'll stop feeling like you need to defend yourself in a moment. For the record, I would never hurt you, Klast. You saved my life. I owe it to you. I'd give you anything."

"Even my dog? You take him out of your soul and you'll—"

"Die?" Peyton cut in. "Be as grumpy as you? I'll manage."

Gee, she had him thinking that he was overreacting. She was very effective at that. What a little soul spy. The worst kind of soul spy. He both loved her and hated her at the same time. She still held a link to Deek that she wasn't giving up despite her talk.

"I need some space from you."

Peyton waved around at the world at large as if he had all the space he needed. It wasn't enough.

"The admin building you said?"

"Third floor," Peyton agreed, reaching out for Clark to prop her up so that Klast could step away. Klast did so, eyeing her the entire time like she'd fall over without him. Then he moved to the front door, happy to have Deek following at his heels.

The dry air blasted his skin and parched his mouth right away, but he talked to Deek on his walk over. He felt like a nutcase. He liked her and didn't. He wanted to help her and hurt her. She was insane yet strategically on point. If she had screamed about his words, who knew what Hank and Tim would have thought and done? Gotten jumpy. Dr. Manford and his nurses understood the words and had to think he was crazy. Klast didn't betray people. Certainly, he never turned against his team.

Deek licked his hand as he jabbered away. His mood was probably exactly what Peyton said it was. He got grumpier when his soul left him. He distanced himself from the very people who could help him and took it out on the people he most trusted because he felt safe that they wouldn't turn on him for his wayward emotions. There had been lots of days when he'd turned down offers to spend time with friends because of his moods. Now that he'd distanced himself from the breed dogs that were the problem, he could turn back into the person he wanted to be. He didn't want to be the cynical psycho that failed to spot everything around him because he was too stuck inside his pain to notice. On that note, he glanced down at Deek walking at his side and smiled. The faithful animal was back on duty, eyeing the area for potential problems.

"You get any sleep yet?" Klast asked him.

Deek shook his head no. Right after he talked with his dad, Klast needed to let his dog sleep. Deek would start to get as grumpy as him if he didn't get rest. The both of them not having clear heads was a bad combination. He'd talk with his dad, and then go sit by Peyton, who would laugh away his bad moods to save him. Deek could rest through that. Peyton would know what to do. She'd been through it all before and it didn't scare her one bit. It was calming to tell that to Deek. The dog could get some rest knowing that Klast was beside the soul repair expert. Nothing to worry about.

Deek didn't respond to him. He stayed focused on watching people. He caught every scent he could and heard every snippet of conversation that reached him. He understood it all, too. Klast had taught Deek the language, although not told him where it came from.

They reached the third floor inside Peyton's described building without incident. His father was in a meeting, but he stepped out into the hall the moment Klast's escort knocked and announced who was there. It was strange, but it felt like Klast hadn't seen his father at all since the scare of his hospitalization. He stood there looking at his dad, feeling like he'd been missing him for a long, long time. They didn't have a relationship where they embraced, but Klast wanted to change that.

"My emotions are a mess. Peyton says it's a symptom of losing my soul, but since I've not sorted it out yet, can I…"

"What?" Mr. Burma asked.

Klast didn't bother to ask. He rushed forward and hugged his dad. "You're okay. You and mom are okay. I've been so worried about everything. Literally everything. It's been hard to process each emotion as it comes up because there are too many. That was really… mean. To pretend to be hurt."

And he was back to balling. Some emotional control he had. He was upset with his dad, but he also had the best father in the world. The man hugged him back fiercely, which surprised Klast even more.

"I didn't know what else to do. You were so distant and closed off," Jethro Burma voiced. "There were no answers given back to your mother's letters. You hid away with those dogs and no one could approach you."

Klast didn't miss the nasty glance Mr. Burma gave to Deek, but Deek was too tired to do anything about it. He sat down on the floor and waited.

"It wasn't his fault. He's been fighting my battle for years without me realizing it. If I had realized it, the real devil dogs would have cut me down before I withstood them. When Deek saw Peyton, he realized it was now or never. He made his move to save us."

"About her," his father said, taking a step back. Klast didn't feel like letting go, but he did so. He respected his father too much to cling to him too hard. He wiped his eyes and offered a comforting smile, even if he still felt wobbly tobbly. "Please tell me if she was soul hunting me, because if it wasn't her..."

"Yeah, it was. She told me where you had gone."

"Okay," his father let out a sigh. "It was rather freaky. It felt like a ghost standing behind me. It's dangerous in my line of work to have that sort of thing happen. The information a spy like her could pick up could destroy everything."

Dangerous. Klast nodded as he understood why Peyton felt put off by his dad. It was because he was scared of *her*.

"I'll talk to her about it. Put on some limits and such. She'd said she'd do anything for me, so it shouldn't be too hard. In any case, I need to borrow a phone. I was looking at everything wrong. It's not me or Peyton that Sysmat wants. It's the dogs. They were using us to reach the dogs because IB dog acid is another cure to *Mervolk*. Peyton remembered it."

"And you need my phone for that?" His father asked carefully.

Klast nodded. "If I alert the breeders that Sysmat is after the dogs' deaths so they can collect the acid, they'll all gang up against the company and help stop them from being tyrants. Sysmat makes great medical advances and all, but the way they go about it just curls my hair. Right now, the best breeders are all under one roof. It's the perfect opportunity."

"Yeah," his father agreed. "There might be a massive explosion about to happen. You make those phone calls. I'll pick up where you left off."

Klast grabbed at the offered phone and started dialing. He paced the floor as he did so. Deek didn't pace with him as he normally would. He was already asleep in the hallway, having given everything he had for the last few days. By the time Klast had finished, there were plans to evacuate the arena to better safeguard the dogs.

"Great," his father nodded.

Jethro put an arm around Klast's shoulders and walked him down the hallway as he took back his phone. The physical contact felt strange even after Klast giving his dad that earlier hug. They simply didn't touch much in their family.

"That will protect the dogs from Sysmat. Assuming Peyton is correct that IB acid is the cure, have you any ideas on how to get some?"

"They don't shoot it out often," Klast agreed. "It's considered rude to use it around friends. They rarely use it around enemies either since it exposes their belly."

"Klast, how do we get this cure?" Jethro asked again.

Klast looked behind him where Deek was still sleeping and shook his head. Even with a dog like him that acted rude more often than not, he didn't avidly shoot acid. Klast could recall only two times that Deek had ever shot it.

"I don't know. I'll think about it. Deek's too tired right now to give me any ideas."

His father opened a side door. It was probably alright to leave Deek sleeping where he was. He could hear through the doors to find Klast when he woke up. It still made Klast feel a little hesitant to enter the room without the dog, but his father guided him inside, still holding his shoulders.

"What makes them shoot acid is a mad dog that wants to escape something," his father said as if he was the expert on IB dog behavior. It was comments like this that got Klast annoyed. His dad didn't breed the animals. He couldn't know this stuff.

Jethro let go of Klast's shoulders and kept walking. Klast rolled his eyes and followed him, only to step on a latch on the floor that dropped a cage down around his head. Oh great. He'd walked right into one of those confinement cages like a moron.

"Can you hit the release switch?" Klast asked.

"As far as I'm aware, the acid is rather effective against wooden structures. It's useable against metal too, but it takes longer for that to break apart. The more impressive part is how the dogs can still claw at places they have put the acid on."

"Dad!" Klast screamed.

The sound shouldn't be off. His father should be able to hear him, and yet he was still walking away and talking, oblivious to the confinement cage. Surely, Jethro would have heard the walls activate and shoot up from the floor.

"Hey!" Klast reached his hands forward, scared to touch the walls. If he did, they would burn him. Not a physical burn, but a hot sting to his soul. It was a weird sensation to feel. He'd felt it only once before when he had touched a cage to see what it did, and that was only the outside of it. The inside hurt worse. If his father couldn't hear him, the cage had to be on.

"If they think that's the only way to break open a cage, they will use the acid. That's what I'm thinking," his father nodded without turning around.

He walked out the other door of the room without holding open the door for Klast to follow him. That right there made Klast's jaw pop open. No way! His father had *not* walked him into a cage hoping that Deek would shoot acid at it when he woke up. That was dumb! First, his father had faked an illness that the rest of his family went along with to scare Klast into shifting, and now Jethro had locked him in a cage! Klast should have listened better to Peyton. She'd told him that his father was being weird.

"Hey! Anybody! Deek!" Klast yelled. What was he yelling for? His sound was muffled. Deek wasn't going to hear him.

*"Can you hear me?!"* Klast tried to send the words to Deek, but if the dog was too tired to listen, that wouldn't work, either. Perfect. He was stuck, and he still didn't know why his father had wanted him to shift in the first place. Not really. His excuse about him being gone too long didn't add up. This cage thing was a bit more telling. He wanted Deek anxious enough to give him a sample of acid. The guess didn't justify why that had to happen in Lexia instead of back home on Hyphas. Klast was missing something. Something very important. Maybe he'd be able to figure it out while he stood inside this skinny cage.

# 15

Peyton had just made it back to the front room after learning how to use a bathroom on the alien planet when Mr. Burma appeared. She wasn't thrilled to see him. He was Klast's father and all, but she agreed with Tim that in a choice between Jethro Burma or his son, she'd take the son.

"Klast is making calls to warn the other doggies about Sysmat wanting their acid. When he's done with that, he'll go to his place. I told him we'd meet him there for lunch."

She didn't want lunch. She'd eaten soup already and didn't feel the least bit hungry.

"No thanks. You go on ahead. I'm going to stay here," Peyton answered, bending at her knees so she could slowly lower herself down the mat in the front room.

"In the middle of this man's home? This is not a hospital. Clark will come to visit you if you have the need, but it's rude to stay where you are."

Peyton glanced at Tim and then Clark. Mr. Burma was speaking so that both men could understand him. It was still remarkable to her that her "soul" could translate the words. If she didn't know any better, she'd have guessed that she had learned this language before and then conveniently "forgotten" it, just like her chemistry dreams.

"No. I'm going to stay here," Peyton insisted.

"You will not. You'll like Klast's place. Come on."

Mr. Burma gripped her elbow and pulled so that she stood back up. She hadn't the ability to fight him off.

"Don't let him take me!" she begged Clark, but it was already too late.

He shifted. Jethro Burma was like his son in that he didn't need to use any filters to move him through space. The darkness rushed up around her, causing her to stiffen in the event that she contacted *Mervolk* by moving back through the empty matter. She didn't want it again! She'd done her part to sort out what it would do to a person. She'd suffered enough.

The ground rushed up toward her feet. Landing hurt. Mr. Burma steadied her enough so that she didn't fall over, but that was about it. Nothing he did helped her to breathe again. Each inhale was torture. Her hands were on her hip, trying to lessen the pain.

"Remember this place?" Mr. Burma asked her as he left her standing and gasping.

This was *not* real. He had no reason to ask her that. None at all. Peyton was standing in a room composed of blue and purple shifting metal. The walls, the floor, the table, and three chairs all matched. Spanning one wall was a cage holding a lazy black dog whose eyes were half slits with boredom.

"I've never been here before."

"You hear that, Shadow?" Mr. Burma asked her. "Peyton Finch has never been here before. They wiped her brain. Took out all her memories and turned her crazy. How's that for infiltrating an organization and coming out the better for it? She's also got holes in her hips, no ribs, and a pin in her left knee."

The dog growled.

Peyton stopped trying to breathe.

"They ripped her soul out again and again."

The dog barred his teeth. She wanted to shrink backward, but the best she could do was slowly lower to her knees to catch herself before she fell over.

What was happening?!

Mr. Burma had called the dog Shadow. The black dog couldn't be *Klast's* Shadow. That dog had *died*.

"Guess what she learned from it all? Absolutely nothing."

"What was I trying to learn?" Peyton asked, ignoring the dog.

She couldn't do this if she focused on the dog. That dog shouldn't be here. She didn't want to believe that it was Klast's imprinted dog, but who else could it be? His father had his dog. The one ripping out Klast's soul wasn't the breed dogs. Klast's soul was being torn because somebody else had Shadow. No. That couldn't be right!

"What indeed?" Mr. Burma asked. He moved to the table, where he pulled open a drawer from beneath it and placed a book on the top. "Be right back. Oh, and in case you forgot, you can only get in and out of here by shifting."

He vanished.

"Klast!" Peyton screamed as if he'd hear her.

Shadow jumped to his feet and stared at her. She couldn't make herself look back. He was still snarling as if she was the one tearing Klast apart. As if all of this was somehow her fault when she couldn't remember any of it.

"I didn't do it!" She screamed. "What is happening?"

There were no doors. The only door was the one on the dog cage. The book on the table had to be important, but she was too sore to move toward it. Her blood pressure was rushing again. It made her fear another nose bleed. She tried to make sense of everything she could remember. Sysmat was trying to cure her of *Mervolk*. She had no proof that they were the ones to have started the soul-latching disease, even if she wanted to blame them for things she didn't like. Rationally, if there was anyone that would know how to destroy a person by using the soul to harm the body, they would be here in Lexia. They were the people with the soul cages.

"Did I have *Mervolk* so I turned myself over to Sysmat for a cure?" Peyton asked.

That didn't sound right, either. She had to shift to reach Hyphas. She'd have lost the disease simply by trying to reach Sysmat in the first place. Maybe the disease was given to her as a method to sneak her into the organization assuming that Mr. Burma was correct that she was a spy for *him* and not *them*. He knew weird things about her like that whole comment about Cindy being a group instead of one person. What could she have learned from dying over and over again?

"I don't remember!" Peyton screamed, lowering to the floor.

A thunk in the cage turned her head upward. It wasn't Shadow, but Mr. Burma landing. He set down another dog beside Shadow and told the dogs to play nice. He left again.

"Deek," Peyton whispered.

He raised his silvery head to regard Shadow who had turned his snarled rage onto him. It didn't look like Deek was going to do anything to defend himself against the other dog's rage. He yawned and closed his eyes.

"No!" Peyton screamed, not stifling her pain as she flattened to the floor so she could crawl over. "Don't hurt each other! Don't do it!"

Shadow was all snarls and growls, but he didn't attack. Yet. It scared Peyton to get closer to where acid could launch at her, but she moved anyway.

"Deek, do something! Mr. Burma said this dog's name is Shadow. He's a black dog. He can't be Klast's dog."

Deek opened one eye to look at her. He continued to ignore the snarling dog.

"Klast dog," he barked at her.

"But he can't be! Did you know he was alive?"

"Yes," Deek answered.

"What is happening? Why are we here?"

"Shadow is Klast's dog and Peyton's dog."

Huh? "Then whose dog are you?"

"Peyton's dog and Klast's dog," Deek answered. "Sleep."

"No! Don't go to sleep. I don't understand. Have I been here before?"

"Question," Deek barked, which was oddly the sound that made Shadow stop snarling as if no other beast could use that exact bark apart from something Klast had touched.

"What is the question? I don't have any answers. I can't even remember who *I* am. Mr. Burma was acting like I'd been here before. That would mean that I knew about Shadow. It makes no sense."

"Question," Deek barked again. "Peyton soul. Shadow soul. Deek soul."

"You make no sense." It hurt to hold her head up, so Peyton let it collapse onto the floor. She was tired again. So, so tired.

"Klast soul here."

"Klast has his soul with him."

"Peyton fix Klast's soul."

"Deek please!"

The words trembled out of her like a leaky balloon. She pinched her eyes shut and searched for Klast. The sparkle hunt stuff would have been the new feature that she got from Sysmat. As far as she could tell, the people here couldn't do things like that. They could shift and they could lock up souls, but they couldn't hunt souls through broken connections or reflections or stickers or whatever it was she was going to call it. The closest they got was seeing another soul where it didn't belong like Isabelle spotting Klast's essence. At least that's as far as Peyton could tell.

She couldn't reach Klast, but Peyton could see him. Klast was in the building where his father had been, but he was now stuck inside one of those cages that had no way out.

"Klast is trapped," Peyton groaned. "We're all stuck. Why are we all stuck?"

"Hi," Shadow barked.

Peyton lifted her head to peek at him. He was looking at Deek, not her, so she groaned and let herself feel a long moment of self-pity.

"Question," Deek barked. "You talk to Peyton?"

"No," Shadow answered.

"Talk to Klast?"

"No. Klast sick."

"You die?"

"Yes."

Shadow had died. Klast hadn't specified that his dog had physically died. Maybe only his soul had left him.

"Peyton work here?"

"Yes."

No, she did not!

"Peyton fix you?"

"No."

"Peyton fix me?" Deek asked.

"No."

Deek felt sick? That could explain his ability to bond with multiple people. It could be the reason why he didn't fully imprint Klast. The same with Shadow. Klast was the one with the harmed soul. He could have a strain of *Mervolk*, only his dogs kept eating it from his soul so he didn't get the nosebleeds and all the rest.

"Hold on. I was hired by Mr. Burma to infiltrate Sysmat to learn a cure to *Mervolk* so I could heal Klast's soul?"

Neither dog answered her, so she strained her neck to look up at them again. Both of them were staring at her without blinking, similar to the way they treated Klast when they didn't want him out of their sight.

"You're not... peering into my soul, are you?"

"Yes," they both answered.

Was that a yes that they were or weren't? Creepy.

"Was I trying to learn a cure for *Mervolk*?" Peyton repeated.

"I guess," Deek yawned at her. "Peyton soul like Shadow soul."

With that, he closed his eyes and went back to sleep. Her mouth dropped open as her brain struggled to catch up. Sysmat had sent her directly to Klast as if there was something they needed from his particular dogs that they couldn't find from other ones. She should have paid better attention to what that breeder Imar was saying. He mentioned that Klast connected with his IB's on a stronger level because he came from Lexia. That's what made his dogs "little humans."

If she ran with that theory then she didn't get *Mervolk* as a way to find a cure and repair Klast, she got it so she could fake a need to earn one of his dogs, and she had done a swell job at sneaking her way in. Deek was hardly four feet away from her.

That didn't explain Mr. Burma, though. He sent her down there to learn something. Most people on Hyphas didn't have access to shifting to cure them of *Mervolk* so they needed a different cure for the soul infection. Sending her wouldn't have been all that scary knowing that once she learned a different method, she could simply shift back and be cured of the torment in an instant.

However, she had shifted before when going to the doomscape and she had still felt sick right after the shift proving that *Mervolk* wasn't her only problem. Her nosebleeds continued, and she still needed her medication. When she got back from losing her diffuser, all the symptoms came back, also proving that Sysmat had injected her with *Mervolk* all over again. Jerks. If both Sysmat and Lexia knew the shifting cure, really, what cause did they have for the IB dog acid? To hide from the rest of Hyphas that shifting was possible?

"I can see how Sysmat would want a different cure to *Mervolk* apart from shifting, but I don't see why Mr. Burma would want the same thing," Peyton voiced. "What are we here for? What was I supposed to learn?"

Jethro's part in all of this was confusing the dickens out of her.

"Don't eat my soul," Peyton demanded as she glanced at the dogs again. "There's not much of it left."

Deek gave off a rather long yawn and then closed his eyes to sleep. Not a bad idea. She was exhausted simply trying to make sense of who she used to be. Mr. Burma had them all locked up. He separated Klast from the people and creatures who held parts of his soul. Peyton was certain she wouldn't like the answer to why.

# 16

Nobody was coming. Klast's feet were sore and crouching made nothing better. There wasn't enough space for him to rest his legs or his knees. He took light steps back and forth, trying to ease the strain. The sun had set through the glaze of the window, proving that he had been here alone for nearly nine hours. There was no sound, and he was at the point where he might start reciting alphabets to simulate company. It had been nearly eight years since he had this much time by himself. He didn't like it.

What got him the most was worrying about Deek. The dog hadn't barked or come to find him. He couldn't still be in the hallway. There were two scenarios that Klast could come up with. One, his dad took Deek to make the dog anxious enough to spray acid. Two, Deek was causing problems around the town, trying to find someone who would help Klast escape. Of the two options, the first one was more likely.

"You could have asked, Dad. Come on!" Klast yelled into the silence. Not that it did any good. His words only reverberated back through his ears. What was the point of his father wanting acid? It didn't help to protect the borders of Lexia. This wasn't right.

"You said you'd do anything for me! Where are you, Peyton?" Klast tried next. That was an even worse question. She could hardly stand up on her own. Not a lot of use she was going to be.

"Please let me out!"

Klast held his hand out to the wall of the cage. Nine hours and he hadn't bothered to check to see if the cage was active. There was a chance that he was standing here for no good reason even if the chance was marginal. His father would have come back for him if that was the case. He wouldn't have left him in anything unsecured. Still... Klast changed to his elbow at the last minute. No sense in burning his fingers when his elbow could have the blast. He let it touch the side and gasped.

"Ow! Ow, ow!"

Fire seared into him at the slight contact, turning everything on the inside that resembled a soul hot and bothered. His right side hurt where the contact had been. Only his right. Weird. Klast looked down at himself as if he could see his soul through the physical constraints. The last time he had touched one of these cages, he felt singed from head to toe for three excruciating minutes. This time, there was less of him to torch, and already the heat was escaping away. Broken. He hated thinking of himself as broken.

*"Are you bleeding from anywhere?"*

"Deek!" Klast cheered. "About time. Where are you? I'm stuck in a cage."

*"Me too. Peyton tried to reach us, but she can't get me or Shadow out. Come help me."*

Shadow? If Klast wasn't warm from touching the cage, a chill would have overtaken him. His brain felt frozen. There was nothing to prepare him for this. Something was horribly wrong. Deek was talking about a different Shadow. Not his dog. A man couldn't be imprinted to two soul dogs at the same time.

*"Shadow can't talk to you. Come help."*

"Stay away from him, Deek!" Klast yelled.

Shadow was dead. He'd buried the dog himself in the backyard and then refused to venture to that spot ever since. The grave was at the very edge of his property line and unmarked. It had to be overgrown after all these years unless his neighbor plucked weeds over there.

*"We are in the same cage,"* Deek told him. *"Shadow remembers dying and then waking up here. He is crabby and mean, but I'm teaching him things, and that calms him. Gives him a focus. Come get us out. Mr. Burma sounded like Peyton had been in the room with Shadow before."*

"Where are you?"

*"I don't know. I would ask Peyton to tell me through a soul hunt, but she's not stirred since falling over on the floor. No heartbeat that I can hear. I thought we cured her of the disease, so maybe she's dead this time. Or maybe*

not. Shadow and I are confused. We know that Shadow lost his soul and died. The shock took his pulse away. You buried him. Your father must have dug him out and revived him somehow. He must have found a way to put a soul back into him."

The only person Klast knew that could put a soul back into things was Peyton. There weren't instruments that channeled that unless he'd simply not heard about them yet.

"Peyton is very confused about why she has been with Sysmat and why your father seems to know her, but Shadow claims that she was working with your dad before she got stuck over there. If she's from here, that explains why she understands the language."

Peyton born on Lexia? That was a new development.

"Question," Deek wavered with the word as if it wasn't the one he really wanted to use. Klast waited for him to form his ideas into words. "Worried Deek bad dog."

"You are not a bad dog," Klast assured him.

"Bad dog," Deek insisted. "Shadow says your soul is sick. Tuff and Morgal could have been taking it to purge you of the illness."

"But I don't have…"

Klast trailed off. He might not need to have *Mervolk* for his breed dogs to believe that he did if they had come in contact with Sysmat as he suspected. Peyton couldn't remember vital information. They may have been brainwashed too.

Klast swallowed, pinching his eyes shut. He could still hear the shots from his gun. He could still see their faces before him and the way they had stared at him and pulled out everything he had left. They knew he'd come to kill them, and they had tried to kill him first.

"Peyton is certain that she's still sick with something and it's not Mervolk," Deek continued.

That didn't sound ominous at all. Klast sighed and shifted again on his toes. How he wanted to sit down! But he couldn't, so he might as well make the most of it. He'd not made progress on his father's motives, but if he assumed Jethro had figured out Tuff and Morgal were taking Klast's soul away, Jethro could have been trying to get Klast to shift away from them to save what was left. That could explain the fake hospital visit. Then Klast had mentioned IB acid as an alternate cure. Maybe his dad was trying to obtain some to bargain with Sysmat to not track them down anymore. If he gave them what they wanted, they could remain under the radar of more headlines.

"Can we back up?" Klast asked, searching around the now dark room for signs of life even if there weren't any. "You are in a cage where?"

"Someplace your dad put us. He said the only way in and out was to shift."

"Oh perfect," Klast grunted.

"You can shift out of your cage and save us."

No, he couldn't. He was in a soul-trapping cage! He couldn't shift without separating from the half soul he had. Losing his soul would leave him an empty shell, and he did not want to be that again. Everything had been very, very murky.

"Shadow can't dent our cage. He's tried everything."

"He could also be lying to you."

"Want me to try acid?" Deek asked him.

"No."

Shadow. Klast was scared to think about Shadow. Deek had heard Klast's thoughts about the dog before, but this time, it was going to end up differently. Klast couldn't have two dogs. He'd given Shadow a place in his heart for the last seven years, refusing to acknowledge Deek. Shadow haunted dreams and appeared out of the corner of his eye. Now when Klast had set his heart on keeping Deek for himself, Deek had even more competition. Klast couldn't choose between Deek or Shadow. He loved them both.

To have them back in his life was unfathomable. Shadow would scheme to take down Deek. Deek would scheme to take Shadow. Klast would be unable to shoot either one and saddened if they died. They carried him through so much. How could he choose? He refused to give Deek up to Peyton even if that was the simplest answer. He could have Shadow take his natural place at his side, and Deek would shift over. Only he couldn't do that. He wanted Deek for himself. He wanted Shadow for himself. Perhaps he *was* sick. Sick with a greedy soul that clasped onto everything around him and didn't let anything go. Perhaps his breed dogs were right to stop him. He didn't train exceptional dogs. He stole parts of their souls.

*"No. Tuff and Morgal were taking your soul out. Imprinting pups share part of their soul with you. They don't take yours away."*

"What made you share with Peyton?" Klast asked. He didn't want to hear the answer, but he needed the facts to line up.

*"She felt like you. She felt like darkness and broken aches, like hope and grief. She felt scared and tired and determined. She already had a piece of you before she showed up. When I talk to her, it's like talking to you."*

"Say that again," Klast said, shifting to his heels to change the ache in his feet.

*"Peyton already had part of your soul."*

Remarkable. "How did she get it?"

*"By being Blazen?"* Deek guessed.

Being blazen was a myth. One could claim many things about a myth, but at some point, they had to look the facts in the face. Blazen implied that she could repair a broken soul, making it harder to kill her by disconnecting her soul with those Soul Destroyer guns. That part she had proved correct, but she couldn't also already have part of Klast's soul without ever meeting him. Klast had not met her before the arena. It was possible that she'd spotted him somewhere long ago and locked onto him, but that didn't solve everything either.

*"Come help me. Make Peyton wake up,"* Deek begged.

"You know what makes people wake up," Klast laughed.

It was nice to laugh again. Everything else felt too scary. What was he going to do if Shadow was still alive? He knew Deek wouldn't lie about this, but his brain and heart were in heavy denial.

# 17

Bark! Bark! Bark! Awooo! Bark! Bark! Bark!

Woof!

Ugh. They wouldn't stop being loud. Peyton shuddered against the sounds. It was Deek doing most of the barking. Shadow was doing the growling probably hoping that the younger animal would stop being so loud! They were in a very small room. The sound bounced off of everything turning the confines into a drum belly.

"Deek be quiet!" Peyton snapped.

"No!"

Honestly! "Why not?"

"Wake up. Out. Want out."

"Did you happen to see a key?" she sassed.

It wasn't like she knew how to open the cage to let him out. Not to mention that she didn't want to open the door. Shadow was in there, and he had growled at her. She trusted Deek to a point. She didn't trust Shadow.

"Out!"

"Not happening."

With a grunt that wasn't hearable, she shoved herself over onto her back. Eh. Her neck felt stiff. She'd been sleeping on her belly too long.

"Dead," Deek barked.

"Who is dead?"

"You."

Nice. She was never going to get better, was she? She was always going to be dead. For someone who was supposed to bring others back to life, she was horrible at keeping herself that way. She'd had no dreams explaining to her things she wanted to remember. There was nothing new to go off of to help her sort out what she was supposed to do now. Sitting around in a locked room for the rest of eternity wasn't something she aspired to.

Peyton gazed up at the roof which was still the same color as everything else: metallic purple and blue. Well, Mr. Burma had left the book on the table. That could be something important. She rotated slightly forgetting that her midsection aggressively hurt and gasped. Drat! She couldn't get herself up off the floor. It was going to be hard to reach the book on the table when it was above her. If she could let a dog out, the animal could help, but glancing at the cage revealed nothing important. No locks. No keys. There was a seam on the door though, so that was something. If she was lucky, it pushed inward to open outward. Worth a test in any case.

There was no way to get onto her stomach to hoist her way up, so she had to figure this out from the position of her back. Peyton pulled her knees upward testing out how much it might hurt. Not too painful. She planted her feet and scooted herself across the floor on her back by pushing. Great. She was now a floor mop. It was slow going, but she made her way to the cage and gave the door a few good kicks. Then she laughed at herself while the dogs silently watched her. A door kick? As if Shadow hadn't already shoved himself against the walls before. If the cage was going to break from pressure, it would have. He was stronger than she was.

She scooted her way over to the table and gave it a nudge as well. Bolted. The chairs were not though. It was a strain to pick up a chair and try to angle it so that she could knock the book off the table. The first chair banged to the ground out of reach. The second one got stuck on the table with the feet too high for her to reach when she tried chucking it. The third one knocked into the second one and bonked the book down. Success! Now to reach the book.

"Question!" Shadow barked.

"What?"

"Walk."

"As in why can't I stand up and walk? Sysmat put a device in my hip that filtered in medicine to neutralize, not kill, the *Mervolk*. When I got here, the doctors were talking about cutting it out of me, so instead of letting them drill into more of my bones, I yanked the tube out. Nearly bled to death," she answered the black beast. He made her shiver. Something about him just gave her the creeps.

Okay. There was the book. She scooted herself over to it wondering if it was something she would be able to read if she had forgotten Lexian text composition. Propping the book up on her chest, she glanced at the cover and flipped open a page.

"You have got to be kidding me!" Peyton groaned.

She could read it. Every alien word.

# 18

"There you are!"

Klast squinted into the bright light as it turned on in the room. A man stood there with flattened hair creeping out beneath a cap. The checkered shirt made Klast grin. The bushy eyebrows had his hope flaring back up. Saved! Klast had never in his life been so happy to see Hank. He had been debating splitting his soul to find Deek even if he'd be left worse than dead if he did that. He was very close to giving it a go anyway, but here was Hank!

"Help me out!" Klast screamed as he pointed to the floor switch that would give him his desired outcome. Hank didn't need any extra help. He was on the button, shoving it around until the cage around Klast melted from view.

"Bless you!" Klast cried as he dropped to his knees. His legs! They were not happy with him. Walking for two weeks and then standing without a break for nearly a full day was not recommended. He rubbed the muscles eagerly.

"Tim and I were worried about what happened to you. You never came back and your dad took Peyton away to your house. No one is at your house."

"I know," Klast nodded. He'd not been to his place for nearly two hundred days. He wouldn't be surprised if he got a host of squatters hanging out there from time to time. "My dog told me. Peyton and Deek are locked away in some strange bunker, and my dad stuffed me into here. He walked me right over the button and then he left me. I am so mad at him! What is going through his head?!"

"Uh…" Hank shrugged. "Does anyone ever know? You said that your *dog* told you he's in a bunker?" Hank looked around to find the dog.

"Through a psychic soul link, yes," Klast nodded. "From an outside perspective, what reasoning could my dad have to lock me up?"

"You shifted into Lexia during the week no one is allowed to come in?" Hank guessed.

Ugh. "Besides that?"

Klast had told the runners' station that he was going to come back to help. There was no reason to lock him away for shifting after his father's border control declaration.

"You brought with you a Sysmat agent?"

"He didn't explain his thinking at all or even cite me for abusing any laws. He can't just lock me away!"

"Maybe where you're from." Hank rolled his eyes. "In Lexia, your dad can do what he pleases. He's got a bunch of people upset with him for it. They think he bends rules too, but if he can claim that it protects the planetary border in any way, he gets away with it."

"Rubbish," Klast gripped. There was more to it than Klast shifting in on a restricted week. If that was his dad's call about the matter, Klast was going to seriously punch him. Klast was the one who had asked for the restrictions against Sysmat agents. They weren't supposed to apply to *him*.

"Anyway, I can't change what happened, and I'm not about to go head-to-head with your dad, but I can spring you out. Look what I have."

Hank reached behind his back to pull out a gun that he had wedged into the waistband. Not just any gun. It was Klast's gun!

"My hero!" Klast cheered as he snatched it back up and put it in the holster. He was going to treat Hank to a five-course meal the next chance he got.

"You need to see something. Doctor Clark Manford recorded it from Hyphas, which he says, is the planet where you live."

Hank pulled out a portable video player from his pocket. It looked like a flat crystal with slots to attach other crystal balls. Right now, the movie crystal was pink and the player green. The object was set down by Klast's feet as Klast continued to cater to his sore legs.

"I must say that I found it all more fascinating than I should. Every time it showed what your planet looks like, especially at night, I was captivated," Hank gushed. He tapped play.

The first thing that popped up was an image of Klast's face. Klast groaned at the words that scrolled beneath it. He was wanted for questioning to explain recent strange events. The news anchor stood on the street where Peyton had been attacked by the soulless woman.

"Earlier today West Avenue experienced a large delay following a car crash. Witnesses claim that it involved two women and an IB dog identified as belonging to Klast Burma. One of the women was shattering a car window with ice and then was later destroyed when Klast appeared on the scene. This footage was turned into the station, but if you have any evidence relating to these events, please contact the local police who are in touch with special investigators."

Klast had been recorded. He stopped rubbing his legs to glance over at Hank who was more interested in watching the recording over again than claiming Klast was a murderer. In Lexia, Klast hadn't done anything wrong to destroy a soulless soul sucker, but in Hyphas he was in hot water.

"You see that?" a male voice asked pointing the camera out of a frosty car window.

"No. My eyeballs are frozen. Even your camera is frozen over," came an answered reply. The sound of a gunshot rippled through the air, followed by a nearby scream beside the camera.

"That man shot the freezer woman, and she's not even scratched. Not even bleeding. What is that monster?!"

It wasn't the best footage, but the camera caught Klast's back and zoomed in on the pile of dust where the woman used to be. The clip ended as Klast was pulling Peyton from the car and people started yelling at him to leave her for the medics.

"Klast later canceled the IB arena event with a phone call," the news reporter came back on. "He claimed that Sysmat was trying to steal the dogs to harvest acid for a medical cure to a rare disease. Rumors have it that Klast had come in contact with this disease when one of his dogs imprinted a Sysmat agent earlier that day. There has been no contact made with Klast regarding the incidents with his dogs. His father, Jethro Burma, was taken in for questioning regarding his son's location after agents in the field discovered that Klast's notorious breed dogs were dead."

So that's where his dad was! He was being stared at by police and questioned. He probably wouldn't get out of there until all his alibies had been checked to prove that he'd not seen Klast recently. Not on that planet anyway.

"The woman who had been watching the breed dogs claims that Klast killed them himself and then died right beside them. His body was not located, and his keys were left in the car. While Klast is not thought to be dangerous, this is now a matter of national security. Any sightings of Klast Burma need to be reported immediately. He may be traveling with this Sysmat agent."

Peyton's image was flashed onto the screen. "Do not approach either individual. Contact the police. We turn the time over for an exclusive interview with the men who saw Klast last.

This was where Hank scooted closer to the images so he could see them. A different reporter was standing next to Mike. He had all his dogs hooked to a shared rope and they were lounging on a patch of grass beneath a streetlamp waiting for Mike to be done with the pests. Hank indeed looked interested in the notion that so many people could enjoy the nightlife. Behind Hank were a lot of other breeders, dogs, and buyers still trying to make the best of a canceled event.

"What are your thoughts on Klast's claim that Sysmat had plans to disrupt the arena?"

"If you've not met Klast Burma, you're missing out," Mike answered. "I'd trust that man's gut over my own any day. If he says that Sysmat was going to do something to take the dogs, then Sysmat was going to try to take the dogs. They've been coming after him for years. He was in a very vulnerable place. They saw a weakness to attack."

"What do you mean by vulnerable?"

"No comment."

"Have you a—"

"They blew his house up!" Imar cut into the camera feed as he poked his blond head into the frame. "They were trying to kill him. He keeps himself off social media as best he can. Keeps to himself making a living by helping other people stay alive. Some people get scared by that and tear a man down. Sysmat cut down all his assets. He experienced a series of hard losses. House blown up. Overcharged rent. Overcharged housing payments. High medical bills for 'accidental' injuries he got on the job. That's what Mike means by vulnerable. They were forcing him under. They were trying to take all his dogs. He was starving himself to feed the dogs as it was because they ran him out of money."

"Sir, there is no evidence that anyone blew up—"

"Yes, there is!" Imar grinned. "We have our proof and I'm going to share it with the world."

"Please come talk with our detective team..." Imar was dragged off the camera. He looked perfectly smug with himself even if Klast was shaking his head. Even if Sysmat was not the cause of the house fire, they were going to go after Imar next.

"Did Klast talk to you about his fears regarding Sysmat?" the reporter asked.

"Nah," Mike shrugged. "He talked it over with his dogs. I simply overheard. Sysmat was trying to obtain all his dogs. They'd given him a death threat."

"That wasn't mentioned before."

"They sent a dog stealer! They were trying to take his imprinted dog away, only the smart animal faked a connection and saved Klast and the Sysmat agent. That's a death threat. You take away an imprinted dog and a man feels like dying."

"He was talking about going on antidepressants if they succeeded," Bronze added. The camera panned to the other side of Mike where Bronze stood. "He saw the threat."

"What do you think about the news that Klast killed off his breed dogs? Will we not see any more remarkable dogs from Klast Burma? His animals have turned into a legend."

"We knew he was going to take down the breed dogs," Bronze agreed. "He came rushing back to the arena saying that Sysmat would intervene because he saved their agent from the zombie. He couldn't go into hiding with his breed dogs, so he had to put them down. No man leaves his breed dogs in another's hands. Klast was no different."

"But at the time, the dogs were staying with a sitter," the reporter pointed out. "That was hundreds of miles away."

Bronze ignored the time frame. "Having dogs stay with a sitter is not the same thing as leaving the dogs with people who know how to use them," Bronze replied.

Sue. She knew enough commands to get the dogs to cooperate while she watched them. She could have let a Sysmat agent into the house one time. That's how they got brainwashed. Maybe Sue was screwy too.

"Sources say that Klast took one of his dogs with him. Do you think he will continue his legacy and return stronger than ever with that dog as his next breed dog?"

"He took his imprinted dog, and he's finally facing his foe instead of hiding from it. Of course, he will come back stronger than ever. If you don't know that, then you've never met a Burma and his dog," Bronze claimed. "They pull off miracles."

"Thank you." The news reporter decided he was done asking questions and turned back to the main screen. "As you can see, there have been rather hefty claims made by Klast Burma about Sysmat. Detectives are investigating the situation. Please contact the police if you have any evidence or saw anything relating to the incidents. We turn the time over to our weather forecast..."

Hank turned off the recording as it flatlined. That was all the doctor had recorded for Klast to see. It was enough of a headache as it was. Klast couldn't escape his problems anywhere he went. There was always something getting in his way, and now he had to decide if he was being too hasty in his claims. He couldn't prove any of it. Standing before a team of detectives wasn't going to help anyone.

"They're treating you like a criminal," Hank pointed out.

"To them, I might be one," Klast agreed. "I can't kill a soulless woman around spectators and get away with it. We don't get soulless people on Hyphas. Not any that the government or Sysmat will release to the public in any case. Furthermore, without proof that Sysmat is attacking, nothing will be done to them."

"Nothing? They used your dogs to cut up your soul!"

Interesting how Hank was making such a bold claim without Klast telling him everything he had been going through. If Klast took out all the conflicting information strewn about to put him off track, it would look very much like Sysmat had used the breed dogs to take Klast's soul out. But why would they want that?

"I can't prove anything using the instruments on Hyphas," Klast sighed. "I've had hours to think about this, and still, I can't seem to make things right!"

Everything he did to save people only got him into more trouble. His first thought was that Sysmat was using Peyton to reach Lexia. That invasion could still come, but they would slow it down with the sudden investigation. Going with this theory, Sysmat had tried to gain entrance to Lexia from his father for years, only he wouldn't say, so Sysmat had turned toward hunting Klast instead through Peyton.

Assuming that his father didn't know that Tuff and Morgal were latching onto his soul, Jethro could have gotten worried that Sysmat had brainwashed Klast into forgetting Lexia so they could force Klast to shift once they got hold of his next imprinted dog. Jethro *had* mentioned a fear that Klast forgot the planet. Killing Deek would make him shift. However, killing off

Tuff and Morgal had done the same thing. Make Klast scared enough, and he gave Sysmat what they wanted—a way to track him directly into Lexia.

He still couldn't prove any of that either. It wasn't like one snipper from Sysmat coming to look at his dogs, and not buying any of them, could prove everything he felt. Then there was still that soulless woman to fret over.

He couldn't believe that Sysmat would shove a soulless lady onto the street in the middle of the day. It couldn't have been them, and if it wasn't, the only other possibility was that the lady came from Lexia. The only person Klast knew that moved between the two planets regularly who could have brought a soulless monster was his father.

Klast's dad, then, sent the soulless. Klast could only justify that thought by claiming Jethro wanted Peyton stopped before she started an invasion, but had he truly seen an invasion coming before Klast had? His father had looked like the notion of an invasion was new when Klast brought it up.

What use was taking out Peyton's soul if she could repair it? If Jethro had been working with her previously, he could have known that about her already. Send a soulless at a person like Peyton, and she would look dead only to revive a few hours later. Jethro could have sent the soulless woman to fake Peyton's death so he could take her back, away from Sysmat!

There. That was another possible explanation. Jethro wanted Peyton back because she repaired broken souls, like the soul of Shadow. Klast shifted about uncomfortably on the thought of the dog yet again. Sysmat had found Klast after the dog had died. If Mr. Burma had brought back a dead dog to save Klast from the anguish of losing his friend, Sysmat would have grown even more suspicious of them. They would have known the Burma's were hiding a planet and technology to revive the dead. That was the sort of thing they would kill for. Jethro couldn't bring Shadow back after that.

Klast couldn't picture Shadow being happy with a caged life. He'd have tried to escape it the only way he could, and that may have resulted in him giving up his soul for a second time.

Jethro had never been satisfied with failing. If he came in and found Shadow gone, he'd have asked Peyton to revive him all over again. Off she had gone, to collect more fragments of souls to feed into the dying dog. And where would she find them, but beside Tuff and Morgal who kept casting Klast out? The cycle would continue until Shadow gave in and accepted his lonely life or Klast had no soul left to give. That had to be how Peyton had gotten part of Klast's soul without them ever meeting. She got it through his breed dogs.

*"Peyton does not like the book on the table. She wanted it to be information about who she is. Instead, the book is a menu to order food when we get hungry."*

"Fabulous. Have her order some food and then track the delivery backward so I can find you."

*"You can already find us. Peyton knows where we are. She's searched around enough to pinpoint a location. 150 N 32 E. She claims that we're underground. I think that some of her memory is coming back unless I'm only hoping that it is because she hopes it is."*

"I'm still missing a major part of this puzzle," Klast expressed.

"Have her order some food?" Hank eyed him like he was going crazy.

Klast chuckled. "Sorry. I was talking to Deek. He just started talking to my soul. I'm not as good at responding silently. The food comment was for Peyton. Know anything about her? Recent information leads us to believe that she was born on Lexia."

"You don't know, do you?"

Hank rubbed the back of his head with both his hands before he placed his movie player in his pocket.

"Lots of us know Peyton Finch. People would talk about her all the time because she was always missing from school. Her family refused to say what the illness was, but it had Tim crying in class a lot."

"Tim?" Klast asked, flabbergasted. He stopped rubbing his legs so he could cross them instead. The stretch was incredible.

"Yup. Tim's her brother. You should have seen his face when you touched her knee the other day. He went all rigid, but then he remembered that your social rules are different and Peyton didn't look like she was trying to gain affection and you were talking about Isabelle, so he let it slide."

"Tim is her brother?" Klast asked again. "So he can tell her who she is and how she ended up on Hyphas! We're thinking maybe my dad hired her for a job. Peyton thinks it was to stop *Mervolk*, but I'm thinking it was so she could find my missing soul since I kept losing it. She can't remember the facts, and I don't know them."

"Tim doesn't know what happened to his sister," Hank told him. "I already asked. He could only tell me that one day she vanished and now she doesn't remember him. She looks at him like a stranger. She's not how she was before."

"How was she before?"

Hank shrugged. "Tim won't talk to me about it. All I know is that she was rather smart, albeit reclusive. Peyton discovered a subspecies of a toxic weed down in the forest biome. She gave some presentation about the side effects if one devoured the plant and then she vanished."

"So she was a scientist?" Klast asked, interested.

"Biologist," Hank replied. "Or a chemist? I'm not sure. As I said, no one saw her too much, and there was something about her that her family refused to talk about. Don't think you'll get it out of any doctor, either. They sign patient confidentiality clauses."

Klast rolled his eyes. "But Peyton doesn't remember things herself. Someone has to know how to help her."

"And that person wouldn't be you, would it? It would be her parents."

*"Are you coming?"* Deek whined.

"My dog needs me to rescue him. I fully appreciate your help, Hank. I honestly do, but I'm going to shift now."

"I'll tell Tim. We were both trying to find you. Oh, and Klast?" Hank asked as he stood up. "If you do have intentions toward Peyton, can you please take it slow with her family? All of them are overprotective."

Because they knew she could repair souls! That knowledge in the hands of someone like his father already had devastating consequences on Peyton. She'd forgotten her life while she searched for another's. She was a slave. Klast had to set her free. He gave Hank an approving nod and then shifted. 150 N 32 E a little underground.

Toppled chairs, the heavy smell of metal, and psychedelic blue and purple blasted his senses as his feet touched down. A book was bent up against one wall as if it had been chucked. There was a large pull on his core as if something was sucking on it the instant he arrived. It couldn't be Peyton. He saw her lying on the floor with one knee bent up and one foot tapping the floor impatiently. She looked too bored to be the cause of the sudden strain. It had to come from one of the dogs. Funny that in a setting like this, he could feel it. Also funny was the way his head refused to turn to see it. Once he looked, he'd have to face the answers. The real ones. The ones that probably pointed to him burying his best friend alive.

The room was a seven-foot square with one full wall taking up space as the cage. That's where Deek and Shadow had to be. Peyton was unaware of his arrival, but the dogs didn't miss it for a second. His dogs. The corner of his mouth tugged upward. Shadow. All this time and Shadow was alive! Preparing himself for the worst tongue lashing he'd ever gotten, Klast slowly turned his head.

Shadow was grinning at him, his tail wagging as fast as it could go to see the man he loved. Happy days of playing basketball and scouting through brush filled Klast's mind. The birthday party where Shadow ran off with the steak. The time he invented bubble brush warrior to escape a bath. How he used to always sing when Klast took a shower, even if Klast wasn't singing a thing.

The dog was meant to be free to run and explore and protect. He'd aged well, although standing around in a cage had made him noticeably weaker than Deek beside him. Where Deek was muscled and proud, Shadow looked like a wisp of his former self. Hair cut short, skinny to the point of ribs being noticeable, it hurt to see the dog locked up. However, it also made Klast thrilled to find the animal breathing. Shadow!

Deek contrasted with the happy nature of the older dog. The front half of him was down, and he wasn't looking at Klast at all. He stared at Shadow, ready to pounce on him should the dog do or say anything that Deek didn't like. Deek had offered to take out the breed dogs for him. He'd go after Shadow too, and he wouldn't stop at taking out a soul. He'd tear the dog limb from limb to make sure he never came back. That hurt too. Deek had always been the law and order. Always the one at the top of the list when it came to Klast's life. It was going to be strange to see how this all panned out because Klast couldn't let them kill each other.

Klast pictured himself getting Shadow into his arms and hugging his friend to the end of the century. He pictured Deek whining at his side and then tumbling into Shadow on accident coming up with some version of king of the mountain that Klast would allow where Deek playfully demanded to be the top dog even if he was deadly serious. The thing was, Shadow would allow it. He didn't mind not looking the part of the leader as long as he thought he had a firm grip on how to keep Klast safe. He'd bend anything to achieve his objective. That's the kind of dog he had been trained to be as a puppy before Klast got him. Deek, on the other hand, had so many side objectives it was impressive the dog could keep them all straight.

A thousand orders rushed through Klast's mind to tell them. No imprinting him due to his unstability. No fighting with each other. They had to work together as a team. They had to listen to him. All of those thoughts and demands to be the alpha in the room never made it out of his mouth simply for the reason that when he opened his mouth, the only thing that came out was, "Let's stop those guys."

Peyton jerked and tried to sit up, only to groan and clutch at her side as she grumbled to herself. She turned her head to see Klast instead of rolling over. Klast wanted to know her thoughts because her expression made him take a step back. Smiling. He'd never encountered such an electric smile. There was trust behind that look and deep devotion. It was both inspiring and terrifying at the same time. Dogs he could do. People were a lot more complicated. It was strange to feel responsible for another person, one that could both drag him down and hold him up.

"I know how to stop Sysmat," Peyton told him.

This was his team. A fondness for all of them rose in his chest. Standing here made him feel more whole than he'd felt in the longest time. It felt like coming home instead of stepping into a cage. It felt like sundrops and first snowflakes, like rainbows through a crystal dancing on the wall.

Klast made eye contact with Shadow. Even if the dog couldn't hear his thoughts, he could read his expressions. Shadow looked toward Peyton and snorted as if he wanted to roll his eyes about following her. He returned a head nod of approval though, and Deek stopped staring him down. Deek squared his feet and looked at Klast as if to say, "What are we waiting for?"

"That's it?" Peyton asked as she rotated herself on the floor so that her head was toward Klast. She started to plant her feet and push herself toward him like a swimming torpedo. "No outburst like 'Shadow I love you, you silly, scary black thing!'"

"The love is in the work," Klast told her. "He knows."

Yes. It had been a long time, but that's exactly where it was with Shadow. The dog felt best when he was included in plans. When he had a mission to fulfill. The largest show of love Klast could give that dog wasn't praise. It was a job. Deek, on the other hand, would have gotten a smashing hug, his ears flattened, his tail pulled a little, and his fur rubbed the wrong way. Deek snorted next reading behind the teasing smile that crept onto Klast's face. It was a different sort of relationship. Both strong and both beautiful. It was going to be a grand adventure to see what sort of relationship he had with Peyton.

# 19

Klast was so strange. If Peyton had been the one with the lost dog, she'd have cheered and hollered until her lungs couldn't hold breath anymore. Not Klast. He stood there as if his instincts told him everything he needed to know, even if he couldn't understand them. It had all made sense after Peyton had thrown the book and Deek had told her she died again. The feeling of death was so commonplace to her now that it wasn't anything she focused on. Normally it was a pain that she tried to avoid due to how unpleasant it all was. Most of the time, she took hours and hours to come back to life after dying. Not this time. She had come back to barking and that's when it all clicked.

Shadow was still dead. He had no soul of his own because Peyton had it. Klast wasn't rushing to Shadow because, deep down, he realized Shadow wasn't his dog. Deek had said Peyton's soul was like Shadows. It had taken her a while to figure out what he meant, and she only grasped the concept when she did a hunt for his soul only to find it on her similar to the way she'd found Klast embedded into her cells. That was Deek's feeling question. He couldn't place her soul until he met the actual dog. Shadow's soul was the reason Peyton hadn't died fully while infiltrating Sysmat.

When she lost herself, the soul she was using returned to Shadow because the larger part of soul she carried was his, and when she came back to life, it was Shadow giving her back his soul once he got the courage to part with it all over again. It was the dog's fault she was blazen, which meant that Klast was blazen too. He simply didn't realize it.

Shadow was a starving soul dog that wanted a soul to guard. He'd lost his human counterpart so latched onto her. He had growled at her because he didn't want her to reclaim her full soul. If she did, he had no purpose to fill.

That realization had startled her, but not as much as the other memories that blasted at her after such a long time of trying to remember them. One phrase in particular beat through her head on repeat. Save Klast! He kept losing his soul and she was going to repair him. It made sense as she had a large portion of Shadow's soul in her, and that was exactly what he would want to do. She had been actively hunting for Klast's soul!

Her old memories made her wonder if she was "FightForIt" or at least uploaded secrets for the user to find, because some of the clips she had watched of Klast and his previous miracle dogs came back to mind from a whole new perspective. The dog that couldn't get out of a hole for instance. *She'd* brought him a rope and tied him into a harness and helped him out in exchange for his piece of Klast's soul.

The landing of the plane. That dog had told her what buttons to push and which levers to pull. She saved the dog and his human in exchange for a piece of Klast's soul. On and on it went with one disaster after another until she could gather enough parts to patch together the son that was broken.

It had started as a job but turned into an obsession. Finding Klast. The more she had of him that got sent back to Shadow, the more she wanted. The more she needed. His dogs were brilliant. She'd been waiting to meet the actual man for years until Sysmat had gotten to her for questioning their use of *Mervolk*.

Then she had turned sick at their hands as they tried to force the information of their evil practices out of her mind. They could take her thoughts, but not the feelings that went through her soul. Those were safely returned to Shadow every time she died, and she'd died quite a lot. In order to stop Sysmat, the only thing a person needed to do was ask Shadow how it was done. He had all of her information. All of her lost memories. Most of her soul.

"I'm sorry," Klast said, as he took a few simple steps toward her and sat down beside her instead of helping her get up. He grunted like sitting was a chore.

Peyton stopped scooting to look up at him. There wasn't an easy way to tell him what she had discovered. The dog he had been dreaming about finding wasn't his anymore. She had stolen his dog without meaning to. She had revived a dead creature and bound herself to the dog's fate at the same time. When Shadow died again, she'd be the one gasping in pain. Not Klast.

"Your dad hired me to save Shadow," Peyton told him. "He thought that if I could put the dog's soul back in his body that he would be reborn and you wouldn't be in pain."

"I guessed at that. You did too? I figure he couldn't return Shadow once I'd declared him dead because Sysmat would want the power over death and realize that I could naturally shift," Klast added. "When the dog died, that was my gateway to start shifting. I'd never done it before. My siblings don't shift. They've never had a reason to go searching for a soul that hard. Sysmat has been trying to kill off my connected dogs so they could track me to this planet and invade it for its soul technology. They've been trying to force me to shift. We're the reason there's going to be a war. We led everyone right here. We're the traitors to Lexia which is why my dad is locking us up."

"Riiight."

She'd not contemplated any of that. Peyton squeezed Klast's hand. His fingers were much warmer than hers. Hot even, which probably proved that she was freezing again. That was yet another feature about herself that she had learned to ignore. How dead she always was because they split apart her. Shadow needed to feed her more of her soul again. She'd killed herself the first time to bring back to life a dog that was supposed to save the man holding her hand. The dog kept on saving her instead. Until now. Shadow was going to fix this.

She glanced over at him, taking in the splendor of the blue eyes and short fuzzy hide trying to guess what he might tell her about how to stop an invasion. The easiest solution was to destroy the technology Sysmat used to shift in the first place, and hope they couldn't rebuild it all. She wanted to constrain them to one planet so they couldn't figure out how to create blazen people like her and Klast even if they probably had a good idea already. It was the dogs. Those with intelligent IB dogs could withstand a soulful death and be reborn. They must know that she already had an IB dog in hiding, only she couldn't remember that at all after they tampered with her mind. They sent her to Klast as if he would recognize her. As if she had one of *his* dogs because they had traced her link to him. She did have his dog, only he still didn't know it.

"Shadow has my soul and I have his!" Peyton blurted. "That's what makes me blazen. When I die, his soul returns to him until he decides to give it back to me."

Peyton waited for a reaction from Klast, but it didn't look like she was going to get one. He stared straight ahead. She glanced over at Deek to see if Klast was communicating with the dog, but Deek sat down in answer. The silver guardian looked over at Shadow and then back at her. He let out a sigh of relief that Peyton didn't understand, and then barked at Klast. Peyton frowned at how the word escaped her comprehension. It looked like Deek had released her from their soul connection now that he could tell she was linked with Shadow.

"Wow!" Klast exclaimed, making her wince. "Look at you using your skills to save a wonderful person like Peyton. I'm proud of you, Shadow," Klast said, just like he would when he was giving away a dog.

It made her heart hurt and smile at the same time. Now she knew why Klast's words had that effect on her. It was because Shadow loved them. His tail went back to wagging and Peyton felt her fingers grow warmer as if the dog was swapping their souls around so he could enjoy all the happy vibes from Klast's statements himself.

"You've done a great job. Blazing brilliant you are. I'd love to have that sort of genius around me for a good long while to come, so don't go back to being a stranger. Peyton and I were meant to be friends."

"Klast," Peyton whined. "Don't. Don't go sounding all happy. I don't want you to be sad."

"I'm not." He pulled his hand away, making her doubt his words until he leaned over her so she could see his face. "I am relieved. I was rather concerned about Shadow and Deek fighting for dominance, but they don't have to now. There's no competition, thanks to you. You've truly saved us. All three of us."

Peyton wanted to tell him he was wrong and that she'd done nothing noteworthy, but she simply couldn't. Not when he was smiling at her like he was highly contemplating leaning in a bit more to thank her more intimately.

She swallowed. Shadow barked a warning at Klast, who laughed and straightened. He clapped his hands together.

"Right. Not a moment to spare now that we've got that figured out. How are we going to stop Sysmat and clear our names from being traitors to the Lexian empire?"

"Ask the dog," Peyton pointed to Shadow. "Every time I died with new information, he got it all."

"Shadow's not imprinted to me. He may harbor a fondness for my scraggly mug, but he's only ever going to release information to you, Peyton."

"Well, then," Peyton tried to sit up yet again and groaned at her weakness. "Shadow, tell us how we can get out of this mess."

One minute all her hopes for finally rescuing Klast were standing right beside her, the next all those hopes were dashed.

"Memories lost," Shadow barked at her.

The bark hurt. Peyton turned her head to study Deek instead as if he could have found them. He was back to staring at Shadow, but this time, Peyton saw the intensity of his gaze differently. This time the gaze didn't look like anger but something that grated against Deek's senses.

"You don't really think he should be alive, do you?" Peyton asked Deek.

"Out!" Deek whined before he jerked his head away from his doggy companion and rammed into the cage. "Out, out, out!"

"Okay, okay. Hold on," Klast agreed.

He scooted away from her side as Peyton sighed and winced. Pain erupted from her lower back as if she'd burst a kidney or liver or something. It felt familiar—the pain. As if she'd experienced it over and over. Died over and over. Tried to escape herself over and over again. It was nothing new, but it sure hurt!

Her lungs were freezing up again. Ice seemed to crawl through her body. The shivers were so bad that every strand of her hair seemed to wave weak and desolate. A craving for her medicine erupted in her chest. She'd failed to get the diffuser. Then she'd pulled the tube out so that she couldn't take the medicine like an idiot. She'd trusted Klast to save her, but she could feel herself slipping away. He wasn't a doctor. He'd never worked for Sysmat. She was going to die right here on the floor. Die and never come back as her internal organs failed.

She closed her eyes and clenched her fists, trying to locate the pieces of her soul. A lot of it was with her thanks to Deek and Klast and Shadow, but there was a much larger portion trailing out away from her. She followed the sparkle trail backward through the darkness, across roads and rivers and fields. Her mind reached into a building that she knew rather well as Sysmat. This was it. She was going to figure out where they were keeping a part of her soul so that she could reclaim it and escape them for good!

Peyton stopped beside an occupied hospital bed. Tucked under the covers was a body full and warm. A body with cinnamon sideswept hair, a pointed chin, and closed cashew brown eyes. It spoke, and she screamed, but she couldn't bring herself to look away.

"Finally!"

It was her voice talking back to her as if the voice was both inside her head and outside at the same time! Peyton felt her body convulse in fear. Her tremors grew bigger. This was wrong. Something about this was all wrong! It looked like Sysmat had found a way to mimic an IB dog connection and it was between her and this other version of herself.

"You have to tell Klast! From what I can see, if his black-cloned dog keeps escaping Sysmat, then Klast is smart enough to escape them too. You figured it out, right?"

The creepy body shifted beneath the blanket. It shouldn't be alive! She screamed. Nightmare! She had to wake up! Too bad her eyes were refusing to open, but she could make out that Klast had grabbed Deek out of the cage near her because the dog was pressing his nose up to her face. He pulled back and barked out "question!"

"Peyton!" The Peyton in the bed shouted at her. "Tell me you figured it out! I've not been splitting my soul to feed to you for no reason! There were others. Many others. With each whisper, I got closer and closer to escaping, but it's got to end with you. It's creepy, you standing there like a ghost, by the way. I could feel your presence wash into the room. It woke me up in a weird—"

"Who are you?!" Peyton shouted at the body that continued to look like herself. This person had a part of her soul. Not the soul of Shadow. The weirdo had said that Klast's clone dog kept escaping. Like, Shadow was a clone?

No, it couldn't be. Shadow the dog was the one giving her back her life. It wasn't this woman on the bed. It wasn't. She refused to believe it. She refused to believe the thoughts in her mind, or rather, the *lack* of thoughts in her mind.

She wanted to tear down the real traitor inside Sysmat. Wanted to... but she was dying. She needed that special formula of medicine to stay alive, because without it, she wasn't alive. Her *Mervolk* was gone, but that didn't change the fact that *she* was the clone.

Sysmat had taken the medicine away from her because they thought she was getting too close to exposing them. Again. They had every intention of letting her die. They didn't think she would actually succeed in getting back to the doomscape to save herself. Once she died, they would release a new clone version of her so that they could continue to study the actual living Peyton still confined to the hospital bed. There was no way they'd let the real version of a soul hunter loose. All this time...

"Are you at least in a position to tell Klast where the evidence is?"

The evidence. What evidence? She couldn't remember any evidence.

"I don't know where it is!"

She wasn't real!! She had felt so real! She thought herself an actual person. A living, human being, but without the medicine, she was going to resort back to a lifeless shell. She'd not be able to sustain the connection of holding a real soul because her body was fake. That's why she kept putting the pieces of soul she found into Shadow. She cast out herself to stay alive! If she was dying again, that had to mean that not only was she lacking the medicine to keep her clone body upright, but that she was holding too much of Peyton's soul. She had to shove it back out! Being partly soulless was her only way to stay alive, but go too far and she'd be a soulless. She'd be the cold, sucking soul feeder. That's why she froze so much. She *was* the enemy. The very thing that Klast wanted gone. He'd kill her if she messed up how much soul she shoved out of herself and into the Shadow clone. Peyton felt tears leak from her cloned eyes. Done wrong, and the one man that could save her was going to kill her.

"I know you don't know where the information is. We got so close to revealing it once before. We got Klast's dad to dig up Shadow's grave, but he got distracted by the whole dead dog aspect. He'd retrieved one of the Shadow clones and couldn't decide if the dog in the grave was the real one or not. The evidence is buried in the grave. Have Klast dig up the grave. Hopefully, he won't be as distracted. You have to tell him!"

"What are you talking about?" Peyton whispered to herself.

It was really hard to talk to herself. Her back was killing her! She had to release Peyton's soul and soon! She couldn't hold this connection much longer. The longer she used the stolen soul to talk to herself, the quicker she died. Her feet had no feeling. Her legs were next. Her hip finally stopped hurting, but her back was still dying. Spots danced before her eyes. Her lungs burned from the pressure.

"The one thing that will stop Sysmat is evidence that they are releasing the very diseases that they claim to cure. They will shut down once we release what we know. You have to get that."

"How did it get in Shadow's grave?" Peyton asked the other version of herself. It was strange looking at herself like this. So surreal, like she could almost hear the thoughts and memories that she lacked. She wanted to reach out to herself and steal the memories away so that she would be the living one instead of the trapped Peyton. She wanted to claim the full soul. Be alive!

"The Shadow clones were able to communicate with each other after ripping out the Sysmat technology that prevents that. They were really brave at tearing themselves up. Their influence was rubbing off on you this time around. You took out the part that makes you wrong. It's taken years for the Shadow clones to find a way to escape, but it's what they do. They escape.

They protect the one person they love more than anything. Shadow wasn't the first dog that Sysmat went after. They cloned Klast's breed dogs too. They've not managed to escape yet, but the shadow clones have. One of the Shadow clones found me and came up with a plan to help us both destroy this insanity.

"If we could locate the pieces of Klast's soul that were in his other dogs and return them to a Shadow clone to hold, then we could hinder Sysmat's siphoning of Klast's soul so they could not experiment on it."

She knew it! Imar was right that Klast had a special soul. He was probably the naturally blazen one just like he could naturally shift.

"No doubt they thought that knowledge of his soul would grant them access to shifting without the use of devices," the real her said.

"It took months to get Shadow outside to move my backup information into his grave for a Burma to find. The last time we had to do all of that without my clone self being much use at all. This time I strained myself harder, gave you more. You've lost the Sysmat blockers now, so you're able to communicate with me. The other clones never made it to this point, but there won't be much time. Please! I know it's not easy realizing—"

"I'll do it," Peyton said as she unclenched her fists.

She had to. As hard as it was to know what was coming, she was ready for it. She was ready for this version of her to die. She was ready for the pain to go away! But first, she had to get cold again. Just enough to keep herself alive. Just enough so she could tell Klast where to find the evidence to save them all.

# 20

Klast grabbed Deek from the cage and tumbled backward, shifting from instinct more than anything. Wrong! There was something wrong in that cage! Deek barely had time to sink his teeth into Klast's arm to hang on as Klast shifted right back out. He didn't feel like berating his dog at all when they landed in a humph on the other side of the cage, even if his arm was bleeding. There was a strange energy inside there. Cold energy. Creepy energy. Deek licked Klast's face to tell him sorry and then ignored Shadow completely in favor of repeating his downward hunting behavior on Peyton. Nose to nose.

Yeah. Okay. There was something strange going on between the pair. This close, there was no telling what Shadow and Peyton had just done. She was still on the floor, unable to move, so not a threat. Deek seemed to disagree.

Whatever it was, the dog would figure it out. Deek could look between the two souls better. However, he couldn't form his thoughts into words as well, so Klast couldn't give up on searching for the truth. It was on the tip of his mind, refusing to surface. Just as long as he didn't lose Deek, he'd be fine. Just as long as he didn't lose Peyton, things would work out. He needed her inside information. She had to remember something to save them even if Shadow had just said they didn't know.

What was Shadow doing? Klast stared at him. The gauntness to the dog looked more intimidating now that he'd been close enough to feel the lack of heat the animal gave off. His father had made a grave error in reviving his dog. Shadow felt like a zombie. Klast couldn't feel it on this side of the cage, as if the bars were one of those soul-trapping things.

Peyton was mumbling to Deek, but Klast couldn't pay attention to her right now. His skin still felt chilled. It was the same feeling he got when he held Peyton's hand. Cold. The chill. It shouldn't be possible for Shadow to have that same quality, but he did. That was what Kast was overlooking. Shadow had encountered Sysmat. He'd died because he would rather choose that path than having Klast destroyed by them.

"Deek, promise me that you've never been taken by Sysmat," Klast said.

"*Promise,*" Deek answered him, mentally sparing the rest of his attention to stay on Peyton. Klast rubbed at his arms, still feeling the lingering chill in the air. It was coming back as if Shadow was casting the coldness out of the cage over to where Klast was.

"Peyton!" Klast screamed as he jumped to his feet and rushed over to her. "Shadow should be dead. I know he should be dead! He must have encountered Sysmat. Don't let him do anything to you!"

Klast nearly tripped over Deek in his haste to reach her. She'd been through more than enough. He had to stop this cycle of torture. Deek would help him. Klast glanced at Deek, but the dog slunk backward in fear and whimpered. Chills traveled up and down Klast's spine. Nothing scared Deek. Nothing.

"What is it?" Klast asked as he took Peyton's hand and gulped. She was freezing again. So cold. Cold as death. Her eyes pinched shut; her fingers limp.

"She'll make it," Klast told Deek. "She always does."

Deek whimpered again.

"We cured her!" Klast screamed.

He couldn't do this. He'd put too much hope into Peyton having a plan to save him. He'd got his heart tangled up in the idea that he could be whole. She was dying on him again. Dying and there was nothing he could do!

"Do something!" Klast yelled.

"*I can't. You have to kill them.*" Deek whimpered and retreated into a corner as he gave his opinion.

The coward! He had to know that Klast was going to disagree. This woman had held his soul. She'd held Shadow's soul. He wasn't going to let her freeze to death.

"You stupid dog!" Klast shouted at him.

"That is the smartest dog I've ever met," Peyton gasped.

Klast gripped her hand harder. She was so cold! The very air she gave out escaped her lips in a puff of frost. If he didn't like her so much, he'd have found it to be extremely disturbing.

"I'm sorry, Deek. There's something wrong with me," Klast sighed for yelling at him. "It's not you."

Broken. His soul was still broken. Why trust something that was torn asunder?

"I'm a clone." Peyton leaked icy crystals into the air with her breath. "Shadow is a clone. The real me is still in Sysmat. The real him is dead. You need to—"

Peyton sucked in a deep, hungry breath. More coldness seeped between their connected fingers. Ice traveled directly into his soul as if she was feeding off him. Klast tried to yank his hand away.

No.

He didn't want to believe it. He hadn't developed feelings for a clone. Peyton wasn't going to turn soulless in front of him.

"This is your fault!" Klast screamed at Shadow.

He wished he hadn't looked. Shadow didn't look a thing like his former self. The glow behind the dog's eyes was gone. In its place, two dark hungry pits stared out at him, trying to devour his insides and steal his soul. Through Peyton. Klast tried to yank his hand out of hers again, only to find her grip unmovable.

"The grave, Klast!" Peyton screamed in obvious distress.

The room kept getting colder. Soulless. She was turning soulless. Shadow had become soulless. They had given themselves up to patch him together and the only thing he could do was turn numb. He loved them. He had to save them. They couldn't die for him!

"You have to dig up Shadow's entire grave to find it! I'm sorry I can't explain any more. It hurts!"

There was a last shudder through Peyton's body before her eyes snapped open. Klast wanted to weep. She was gone! He'd failed her again! How could he fail her so much?! Pits of empty desire bore into his face from her black eyes. Her mouth opened. If she started sucking his soul, he was going to lose everything she had just sacrificed to keep him alive. However, he couldn't bring himself to face the truth. This darling, adorable woman wasn't what he thought her to be. She wasn't blazen. She wasn't an invincible pillar of hope. She was there to destroy him, just as Deek had guessed. Deek had used her, and when she really needed *them*, he whimpered in a corner.

"Attack!" Deek barked at Klast.

"I can't."

"Attack! Attack! Attack! Peyton in cage. Attack intruder!"

"She can't be a clone!" That was the part he didn't want to believe, because once he started thinking about it, he got scared. If she was a clone, was Deek? Were his breed dogs? How many clones had he let his heart love only to be betrayed by them? Lying to him about who they were gutted him.

She didn't know she was lying.

It wasn't her fault.

"Attack!" Deek ordered him again. "Don't fail!"

Geez! Deek had to say the one thing that was going to make Klast pull in the force of the void. Fail. Klast refused to fail to a demon that had stolen Peyton from him. She'd fought it hard. Fought it with everything she had so she could deliver him a message. Dig up Shadow's grave. The one place he had avoided for years and years.

"Okay," Klast agreed, right as the demon Peyton turned his arm light blue. He pulled in the force of the void and watched her turn to dust in his arms. He wanted to scream. The nightmares this was going to give him would be bad. No time to psych himself up and make that thought true. He turned toward Shadow next. He couldn't let his father return here and get caught by a soul-sucking clone IB dog. Klast shifted into the cage, yelling in pain as the demon Shadow jumped at him and bit into his throat. He yanked in the power and turned his old dog to dust before stumbling out.

"Hard to shift out of that place," Klast noted as Deek remained where he was still flattened to the floor, waiting for more words of treason to come out of Klast's mouth.

"I'm sorry. All those mean things I say to you and you stay with me anyway. Maybe once I'm not broken anymore, I'll get better."

He'd killed Peyton. He'd killed Shadow. They had the true heart of a protector. He could admire something like that, but it had been a very long time since he had proved he had what it took to match their greatness.

"I won't fail you again, Deek."

Deek rolled his eyes as he got to his feet. The dog shook his fur as if shaking off the bad cold vibes. They still lingered, turning the underground prison icy.

*"I knew you could do it,"* Deek told him. *"I knew you could kill your best friend."*

"Don't make it sound like I wanted to!" Klast burst back. "I know I threatened to kill you, but I wouldn't have, really. I can't. It kills me too. Peyton said they were clones. They'd turned soulless to give me back my soul. There was nothing left to them, Deek."

Even to his ears, the justification sounded hollow. He couldn't let loose a soulless IB pair. The horror they could accomplish would be incredible. However, part of him feared that there was a lie to those words. She wasn't a clone. He'd killed her, and he'd never see her again.

*"You have to do it again,"* Deek told him, looking him in the eye. *"I see Shadow often. I chase him away. He's wrong. He's always wrong. I had to build you up so that you could be angry enough to kill off your best friend. I'm sorry too. I didn't know how else to save you from him. What is a clone?"*

Ah. That was why Deek was so impossible at times. He made himself the worst because he loved the greatest. He'd been working toward a point where Klast would tell him the very thing he had—that he'd shoot him. That right there should feel like the largest betrayal of them all, but the only thing Klast could do about it was sink to his knees and start crying. How it must have hurt for Deek to get what he'd been trying to accomplish because he didn't know how to describe Shadow appearing. He didn't know what a clone was. He didn't want to tell Klast that Shadow was there and lose his best friend to an animal that felt wrong. In Deek's mind, he had to force Klast to betray himself. Betray the trust of the IB bond so that Klast could turn against his first IB dog whom he still loved.

"A clone is a copy of a living thing created by copying the cells of the living creature to make another one exactly the same. They're illegal, and in this case, not complete. When they lose the binding soul, they turn into demons."

Here was more proof that Sysmat was creating demons and using illegal methods to do their dirty work. He couldn't prove that Shadow was a clone unless he caught another clone Shadow. Same thing with Peyton. He couldn't prove it unless he could get to her again, but this time, she'd not remember him and she'd have no reason to trust anything he said.

Klast wiped at his eyes. Time to stop moping. He ignored looking at the piles of dust and reached out for Deek. They had a grave to dig. He didn't want to end up doing that alone.

# 21

Digging up dead bodies was not the most pleasant thing Klast had ever done. Shadow was wrapped as Klast had left him, but there was evidence that someone had tampered with him. Klast had sealed the sack shut before he'd buried him. The lock was gone, proving that years back Shadow's DNA was stolen. Holding on to the anger of disrespect for the dead made it easier to lift out the dog. He felt heavier than usual. Klast tried not to dwell on that. Deek was right beside him, not looking at the hole, but on high alert in case anyone was watching them dig up a hole on their own property.

"Don't you think Sysmat is too distracted by the dogs at the arena to know that we're unburying a dog?" Klast asked him. There shouldn't be anything to worry about at the moment, but that didn't stop Klast from scanning the trees himself every time he looked up. It wasn't Sysmat exactly that he was wary about. It was finding another Shadow.

Klast gave Shadow's sack a good pat over. It was unnerving to feel the fur and bones through the covering. However, it felt like a form of release. Shadow was gone and not coming back. He could let the dog's memory rest in peace inside his thoughts, knowing that those glances of seeing Shadow out of the corner of his eye weren't him hallucinating.

"Should have cremated him," Klast mumbled to himself. Next time he had a dog die, that's what he was going to do. Less chance anyone would send him ghosts about the death afterward.

With shadow out of the hole, Klast looked down at the continuous dirt. There had to be something more, so he continued to dig. There was a plastic tube twelve inches down that looked like a time capsule with a taped screw-on lid. Klast glanced around to make sure they were still alone.

The first piece of paper from the tube was something he didn't understand. Charts and technical words filled every inch of space and looked like a report for some sort of substance. He looked at the next page and then the next. More charts. These had dates and people's names listed, revealing when they got sick with a mystery substance and when they were taken by Sysmat. There were more pages documenting how the substance was created by Sysmat in the first place and then the real kicker. Clones. Peyton had learned about the clones and documented it by sightings of herself. She even had the composition written down of the medicine that her clone took to survive. It was a rather impressive composition of evidence for a person that was supposedly still captured by them.

Klast reached into his pocket for his phone to call Bronze for a lawyer recommendation. No phone. He took a few steps toward his house for the landline. Gone. He'd gotten the shovel from the empty dog pens, but he had no way of reaching Bronze right now.

"You wouldn't happen to know who Bronze would recommend going to see about this, would you?" Klast asked Deek, as he carefully replaced the papers in the tube. They bonked something on the bottom so he dumped it out to find a jump drive. He put that into his pocket. That had to have a copy of the papers in case these ones got destroyed.

"Come," Deek barked, already taking off as if time was of the essence. Maybe it was, but not quite yet. Klast couldn't leave Shadow sitting out in the open like this even if he was years dead. Klast carefully lowered the bag back and shoveled again. Deek helped by kicking dirt all over the place. Once Klast had stomped the dirt down with some good jumps, Deek was barking to go again.

They rushed away. Klast was taking down Sysmat. It felt exciting and noteworthy and scary all at once. If they picked a lawyer that was on the wrong side, he could lose his mind. Sysmat had already tried to drag him in before to claim the connection between an IB dog and its human. If he'd not had his other dogs, he would have succumbed. He would have turned into a villain preying on the innocent in the name of science. It was like these people had no conscience. He had to stop it. They were not going to take him, and they were going to release Peyton. He'd see to that.

# 22

Peyton opened her eyes and looked over at the clock. The monitor beeped, cuing her into the fact that she was alert even if she already knew that. Two in the afternoon read the clock. The next thing she looked at was the worse number. It showed the days that she'd been lying here in a vegetable state while her brain and soul traveled around without her. She'd beaten her record. Ninety days. Lifting her arm was a chore. She wanted to tug off the thick bands that wound around her to give her electric shocks so she wouldn't lose too much muscle mass. They didn't do much. Everything about her felt weak. Buzzing muscles weren't the same as moving them herself.

She'd poured herself into the clone this time around. At first, it felt like a betrayal to her real self to give her soul away like that. It felt like she was aiding the demons around her. Helping them to infect others. She had, in fact, infected others. Then she had recorded it to put herself in prison. She was going to burn in a fiery grave and no one would save her from that. The nightmares that came back to her were enough to break her into cold sweats. Even in a coma, she felt those. She struggled to live as two people at once.

Her first two clones had gone down in a few days. She'd refused to let them take the lifesaving medication. They were not her. They had no right to steal her thoughts. Her feelings. Her soul. Sysmat had adapted against her. They invented new ways for the medicine to enter her clone body. They gave her more "freedom" to make her want to be outside in the clone instead of trapped in the hospital room with her real body.

It was much better out there. She knew what was coming now that she was awake and she couldn't stop it.

Peyton wobbled her head from side to side. She could feel the stickered wires stuck to her head and face. Her memories were a couple of buttons away from being wiped again. Every time that happened, she had to start over from scratch. What could she pick up from her soul? Did anyone know her? Did she feel safe around anyone or anything? How could she get out of here?

The door opened. Closing her eyes would do her no good now that the monitor had marked her alertness. If she was lucky, and she hadn't been yet, they hadn't had enough time to create a new clone of her to inhabit. She'd get to stay in her own body for a while longer. Move her real muscles for a change.

"Hello, Peyton," came the doctor's voice. The doctors didn't wear name tags, so she couldn't ever identify people, but she had drawn pictures as best as she could. She'd drawn images of all the Sysmat people she had come across that she could remember. She was so close to taking them down and her along with them. It wasn't like they would let their experiments live. She was going to go up in a ball of flames, but it was a risk she took to prevent anyone else from ever going through this.

"I brought you something to cheer you up," the doctor continued. He pat the bed and stepped over to her monitor to scan it even if there was no need. All the information and more was revealed to him before he entered the room.

She was familiar with this man. He was tall and skinny with thin-framed glasses that barely rested on his nose. The man kept his light-brown hair at a perfect inch tall at all times. A pointed nose extended from his face, but his chin was rather round. Peyton did her best to look into his brown eyes when he was around. To scare him away.

"Come on. Come up." He slapped the bed again looking at the floor.

A dog jumped up. Peyton gave it half a glance as it crawled up toward her face timidly. Silver and fluffy and large. Deek! Sysmat had found a way to get a sample from Deek. Maybe they used dog droppings or blood samples from the vet. Even hair trimming from the groomer could work. Peyton wasn't about to let the creature think she loved him. She didn't. Not this dog. His soul would not be the same as Deek's at all. Last she checked, there was nothing wrong with Deek's soul. He had all of it save the small part that he'd given to her and Klast to communicate out of love.

She had returned Deek's shared soul before she had turned soulless, so he was as good as whole. She had no way of knowing what soul they had shoved into this clone dog, but knowing Sysmat it was going to be something cruel. A human soul in the mind and body of the dog seeing if they could mimic the intelligence of Klast's trained dogs without doing any of his intensive training.

Peyton wiggled her legs. She tested out her lungs. Tight, but she had her real ribs back. Out of habit, she wanted to wipe her nose. This would be the part where her nose started bleeding, only she wasn't her clone, so she didn't have to worry about that. She had other problems.

"What do you think of the dog?" Doctor asked.

"It looks scared," Peyton answered honestly. Her voice came out scratchy and strained, making her miss her ability to sing. But enough about her. She felt bad for the poor creature that had been taken apart and stuffed into here. The dog moved its nose to her face and trailed its wet nose along her cheek.

"It likes you," the doctor decided for the animal.

"It's scared," Peyton repeated.

At least the dog wasn't scared of her. If it was, Deek would have growled and bitten her face off by now. He probably only walked beside the doctor nicely because he was told he got to see her. No. That was dumb. This was a clone. It wasn't going to act anything like the real Deek unless it got the dog's real soul. That was the only way to control a brainless clone so it would do what the soul bearer wanted. Give it more soul. Turn it more alive. Hurt more when it died.

"We have a few routine questions to go over. You have not been awake for the last ninety days. Should I say congratulations or my condolences?"

"You can explain why you're the devil with a different face," Peyton retorted. "Who'd you shove into the dog?"

"What side effects are you currently experiencing?"

"I would love to be able to stand up and use the bathroom on my own."

The Deek clone reached her chin and then moved its nose across her face starting at her cheek. She could feel the wetness where it had just been.

Different soul or not, Shadow had known how to escape. Deek would be no exception. He'd get out soon enough. If killing Shadow wasn't bad enough for Klast, killing Deek off was going to scar his already missing soul.

Peyton strained her head to knock Deek off her. It didn't work. She stared back at the dog as she went over the nose nudgings again. Deek was writing to her! H-E-L-P. Help. This had better not be Klast trapped inside his own dog. The creature wouldn't be able to release that soul on his own. He wouldn't be able to turn demon because Klast was the one person he wanted to protect.

Oh dear. She had to find out. There was a full missing half of Klast. She had used her clone to look high and low. She disobeyed orders to return for the night after infecting people to search for Klast's previously trained dogs. She'd stolen shifting technology a few times to reach them, and Sysmat had let her because when she came back with extra soul traces clinging to her clone, they sucked up as much as they could before she remembered how to shove the sparkles outward into the hiding Shadow.

That dog clone was gone now. She felt him fall. Shadow had given her the courage to let go, and since they had been beside Klast, both soulless bodies would be destroyed.

Peyton clenched her hands into fists trying to soul search. It took more effort than she liked to move her hands and did absolutely nothing. Clone her had gotten the Sysmat tech out of her body. Peyton hadn't. She couldn't use "sparkle trails" or soul hunting or anything of the sort. She had no way of knowing for sure if this Deek held the missing piece she had been trying to find, but it felt like something Sysmat would do. They'd entice Klast to them by dangling his soul before his face. Either that or trick his dog into rushing forward to reach it. Then they'd have the real Deek and Klast would turn himself over to claim the dog. Yup. This was a setup, and it was sitting on her bed asking for help.

"What's the last thing you remember?"

"I think my appendix burst? Who knows? All the pain blurs together after a while."

"Interesting. Do you remember the dog now? What's his name?"

"What?" Peyton asked.

She'd done this every time. At least, she thought she had. The only thing she would answer the doctor was that she experienced a lot of pain and the shock of it all erased everything else from her mind. She refused to tell them how she struggled to take them down. So close! She was counting on Klast to pull through for her. She'd done as much as she could to help him. He had to do the rest now.

"His name is Deek."

It was a shame that the doctor knew the dog's name. It held power. He could convince the dog to walk beside him by knowing that especially if the name sounded familiar to the soul of Klast, which it would.

"Who picked that name?" Peyton asked. She rolled her shoulders and then strained her stomach muscles, trying to sit up. Not even an inch. Dang, she was weak!

"What a silly name. It makes me think of smelly feet."

Deek growled at her. She wanted to wink at him to let him know she was talking smack because the doctor was in there, but the doctor was watching.

"Now, now," the doctor said softly.

Peyton wasn't sure if he was talking to her or Deek, but either way, it didn't make either of them calmer. Peyton felt her heartbeat tick up. Deek's ears picked up the added fear and the fur on his back bristled. Any minute now she was going to forget everything. Any second, the doctor would nod or whatever and the electrodes would activate and wipe her away again while she struggled to keep one thought in her head to hold on to. Klast. Save Klast. If she could remember that, and so far she'd been successful, then she was able to slowly pick up the other missing pieces of what she needed to do. She'd learned so *much* this last time. Tears formed thinking about losing it all. She wanted to shout it all out at Deek so that he could remember it for her, but that would be a disaster. Then Sysmat would know.

She was born in Lexia and hired by Klast's father to fix him. She was locating Klast's soul and trying to patch him back together. At times, she failed at that, because Sysmat grabbed up the pieces. Deek was now a dog clone and could have Klast's soul. For Klast to live, clone Deek had to die. It was a rough thing to accept, but she'd killed her clones before. None of those words could be said.

Her death location was going to be the next question her doctor asked her unless they believed that she couldn't remember anything once she woke up. She did not know if other people could or not, but she guessed they would feel similar to herself. Belligerent.

"Where did your appendix burst?" the doctor asked her on cue.

"Where the appendix is located, of course," Peyton answered not about to tell him about Lexia. "It might not have been that. Other things bring sharp pain to the back. My back killed me from the pressure. I'm no doctor, so I can't say for sure."

"You held on for a long time. That was new for you. In your words, what makes a life worth living?"

Philosophy? Really? Peyton looked away from Deek even if he was still bristly so it was a bad idea. He shifted, letting one of his feet press into her side. It hurt! She tried to not let it show as the claws pricked her.

"When I burn in the depths of darkness, I'm taking you with me," Peyton told her doctor allowing her eyes to bore into his.

For once, he looked intimidated and took a step away. The door opened again, bringing a look of relief to the doctor's face as the nurses came in. Three of them flitted around her, carefully ignoring the dog that growled out warnings. One of them wiped off Peyton's face. Another emptied the bladder bag that prevented her from needing to get up and use a bathroom. It was strange to think that using a bathroom would be the thing she missed the most out of anything, but it was. She supposed she missed the independence. Stuck in bed made her feel like a helpless baby.

Doctor decided to check her temperature even if it was pointless. Wires recorded all of her readings. She was so hooked up that she was never going to get out of here, but it didn't matter anymore. If she could save Klast, if she could save at least one human from the torture, her life was worth living.

"What is the last thing you remember about being here?" the doctor asked her as he made a mental note about her temperature. It was most likely fine. She wasn't a clone. She wasn't freezing. Right?

"What does it say?!" Peyton begged, trying to get a look at the reading. "I'm fine, right? You didn't shove me into another clone of myself instead of back into my own body?"

Deek jerked his head up, startled by the sentence. Peyton paid him no attention. She had to know. She could picture them tricking her into another clone right away so that she never knew where the real version of herself was. She was dependent on them all the time. Her arms and legs crawled with bumps on the thought of never having the means to break free.

"What did you say?" the doctor asked her.

"My temperature. I'm not freezing. Tell me that I'm not freezing."

"Do you remember freezing, Peyton?"

She noted how he avoided any comment about her being shoved into clones. That's what they were doing to her. He had to know it by now.

"Yes. My back hurt and I was freezing."

"Don't do it!" a voice screamed as the door flew open yet again.

Deek stopped growling when he looked at who it was. Peyton wasn't sure if she should be calmed by that or more frightened. Did the dog want to listen to the newcomer or be ready to spring? It was hard to tell with Deek. Klast would know.

"What is the dog doing here?!"

Peyton decided she didn't like the newcomer. She tried to get a good look and ended up straining her neck. It'd been too long since she moved her neck. Ninety days of comatose. There was no need to worry that she was a clone. The lacking mobility should tell her everything she needed to know. She was getting too jumpy.

"The dog needed a walk, and he's always on his best behavior when he passes this room. Dogs have a good sense about nice people, so I let him in to—"

"You can't let *that* dog meet Peyton!"

"When do I get to go home?" Peyton asked, trying to interrupt the tirade before Deek was kicked out. "I'm feeling much better."

"I bet you are!" the newcomer burst.

He was a mad one. He stormed to the other side of the room where he could see her and monitor Deek as if he didn't trust the dog. This man had a bald head with white thin eyebrows. Peyton wished that they were shaggy brows instead. That would have made him look more intimidating instead of sweet.

"What did you tell him?!"

"Who?" Peyton asked.

"Don't give her any ideas," the doctor hissed. "I've worked too hard on this!"

"She knows something!"

"Did you check the wall before walking into the room? She's been unconscious for ninety days. I hope she still knows a few things from before that time or I'd be very concerned."

"Have you seen the news?!" the angry man asked.

Maybe he was a lawyer. Peyton looked over at clone Deek, wondering if *he* had seen the news. He shook his head as if he could guess what her question was. She smiled at him and then looked back at the confrontation.

"Yes. That was why this time around, the medical check was performed before I entered the room. It's written on the wall. There won't be any problems."

The memory sweep. He'd already done it! He'd run the procedure while her clone wasn't dead yet, so there was nothing to erase. Nothing new anyway. Peyton studied her doctor closer. She didn't think he'd be the type to help her out like that, but perhaps he expected the company to fall, and he wanted one sympathetic voice in his favor. Aiding an organization that infected, kidnapped, and tortured humans would not be an easy to escape sentence.

"What?" the bald man looked over at her with his mouth hanging open and then back at the doctor. "I told you not to do that! I need her to tell me what she told him!"

"Told who?" Peyton asked. She hoped she was doing a good job of pulling off the innocent look. In reality, her heart was still hammering. It hurt like she'd run a marathon simply by lying in bed. Gee. She needed to get up more!

"According to section—" Doctor said but never finished.

"I need to talk to you in the hallway," grumpy guy stressed.

Her doctor shrugged and walked through the door leaving Peyton alone with the nurses and Deek. The dog went back to writing on her face. O-u-t-s-i-d-e. It was such a Deek-like comment that it made her smile.

"Don't suppose that there's a window to open for fresh air around here?" Peyton asked.

Deek licked her face for understanding the message. It wasn't going to help him any. Perhaps the message writing could work both ways though. She stroked his fur and then ran her finger in letters along his nose while her other hand pet him. The nurses adjusted her monitors and reset her counters to show how many days and hours she was awake. Less than one so far.

Peyton wrote. This version of Deek was a clone—a copy of himself. He most likely was keeping Klast's soul in his body. Klast was the man who raised him. He would want to thank Deek for keeping his soul safe, but he was going to need it back. He was coming to save them. Deek would know who Klast was the instant he saw him. He'd love Klast and most likely see the real Deek near the man. It was hard being a clone. She had been one several times, and death hurt each time, but it was worth it to save Klast. They were currently trapped by Sysmat. They were destroying it.

Deek was unusually still while she wrote to him. She wasn't sure how much he understood, but he seemed to grasp the major concepts. He stopped bristling at the mention of Klast's name. He removed his claws from her side when she said they were going to save him. It was remarkable that even without meeting him, the Shadow clones and the Deek clone felt this great weight of responsibility to Klast Burma. It was either that, or they calmed down when she told them they had a sense of purpose. There was a point to the madness. A reason to fight. A reason to survive whatever torture Deek had already gone through.

"Okay!" Her doctor came back into the room, stomping his feet as he went. He looked around the room, trying to decide where he had left off. His eyes settled on Deek, at the way that the dog returned the look full of newfound determination. Peyton hoped she wasn't messing things up. She hoped Deek would not be used against Klast now that he knew about him. He had to be smarter than that. He had to be.

"Right. How are you doing without your shadow following you around?"

Peyton felt her heart leap at the question. Deek tensed. He wouldn't know about Shadow, but he could hear her nerves.

"What are you talking about?" Peyton asked.

They knew about the dog! They knew he had died along with her clone. Okay, that was stupid. They might not "know" from reading devices in the Shadow clone since he had torn his Sysmat devices out, but the Peyton clone was dead. They had to guess that her imprinted dog had died along with her. She had died from not getting her medicine, just as she had feared. Her doctor was concerned that she was going to sink into depression without the connection from the dog. If she gave up living in this form out of unexplainable sadness, there went his science experiment.

"I know what I'm doing," Doctor told her with a sad nod, "and I want you to know that if you need to talk about it, I'm here for you. No need for you to suffer alone."

Deek looked at her, trying to figure out what was going on. He stared at her with those intense eyes. Peyton clenched her jaw and then released it when that got too tiring. If it wasn't for the IV giving her food, she'd probably starve. She doubted she could chew effectively. She twitched very slightly to bonk into Deek's paw trying to communicate multiple thoughts into a single touch. No imprinting. Not right now. If they split Klast's soul between them again, it was only going to be that much harder to get it back to him. She'd have to remove it from herself, and if she did that in this weakened state, there was no telling if her real self would survive it. She couldn't hold his soul. The clone dog had to have it.

"If you know what you're doing, then why do you do it?" Her voice was getting even raspier. She wanted to sleep and fix it all. Sleep and escape the moment the doctors and nurses left the room, leaving her with nothing but the time to remind her she was stuck here waiting to die.

"I'm doing my best to cure you of a deadly disease. You are a very sick person, Peyton."

"What's my last name?" Peyton asked.

The doctor shrugged. "That's not in your file. What is in the file leads me to ask you a set of questions when you wake up. The question about your shadow following you was penciled on the page in my handwriting for when you woke up this time. I'm to erase it for next time as I assume it won't apply anymore. Have you anything to say about the question?"

"Do they wipe your memories away all the time, too?" Peyton asked him. "You think I close my eyes and see shadows creeping around the room or something? You're wrong. I don't see anything. I can't. Sysmat broke me."

"Okay. Then I'll assume that the question no longer applies. Anything you want to tell me before I leave?"

She laughed at him. The open-ended question was there so she would spill her guts. The man had to think she used to be hallucinogenic, and he'd cured her of it. The poor doctor didn't know what he was doing. He couldn't remember either. Someone up the command ladder was a very messed up individual. There would be horrible consequences to wiping away memories like this.

"She laughed at you." One of the nurses sounded impressed instead of horrified. "What do you think that means?"

If Peyton was facing herself right now, she'd be disturbed that her head was on backward.

"I have an answer to your question," Peyton told the doctor. "What makes a life worth living is the resolve to save someone. Might be yourself. Might be a friend. Might even be a stranger. You're trapped in the same rut that I'm in. You honestly think that you're saving someone. May one of us be correct."

The room turned still. Not even Deek was blinking as they all digested her words. The nurses looked at each other like Peyton was losing her mind instead of finding it. The doctor eventually gave her a respectful nod as he headed toward the door and held it open for the nurses. He called Deek to join him. The dog nudged her with his nose one more time before jumping off the bed and heading out. Right before the door shut, the doctor said one more thing even if he was wrong.

"I hope we're both correct."

# 23

The room around Klast was stuffed. Not with people or bodies or even dogs, but with silence. Deek had known what he was doing. He'd ran Klast nearly ragged, staying off all the major roads until they reached not the police, but the head of government security. They didn't reach the man's office either. They arrived at his actual house. Klast had no idea who the man was, but the guy took one look at him and knew *him*. That was a bit creepy. Security man had scanned the area as if expecting a horde of cameras or perhaps Sysmat to have tracked them. Then Klast was invited inside.

Klast had apologized for intruding and admitted that he did not know where he was. He blamed the intrusion on the dog. Klast had nearly forgotten the time he answered Deek's question to tell him about Jonas Stilkins. Head of government security. Whoo eee! Klast didn't think that Bronze would give him such a recommendation, but going for the top worked well with him. He could avoid all the intermediaries that would only stall his progress.

The guards around here were in casual dress, but Klast wasn't fooled and neither was Deek. They lounged around the place playing board games, getting drinks of water, and reading books. They were spying.

Klast's meeting with the head of security was taking place in the main room slightly off from the front entryway. They had moved away from the paper documents to the flash drive and that had brought the silence.

"I can upload, but not see what else I put on here due to time constraints. I apologize if anything I say repeats. I need to take these *insert-a-nasty-bad-word-here* people down," Peyton had said. The words felt branded into Klast's brain.

"They deserve to burn. They deserve the agony they give to all of us. Don't tell me I said that. I'm rightly mad right now. I'd be embarrassed if I knew how cruel I could be. Actually, I really am. Cruel. I know what they're making me do and I'm doing it anyway. To fit in. To hide the fact that I found a way to remember what I'm doing after they wipe my memories away. I found a way to hide this from them, too. There's one spot they never check when I return. It will be totally irritating and a reminder to myself to record everything I can. Here it goes. I know this is enough to put me in jail, but there's more than myself at stake here. Humanity is at stake. We're all dead if Sysmat keeps this up. All of us. I have to stop them if I can.

"Today, I dropped a chemical compound known as—"

Peyton went on to detail how she had infected a group of people and how she had comforted them when they got sick. She had called in the report that she'd done it. Her next report was nothing like the first message.

"My gosh! I must be crazy. A drive and a note to record everything I did today? What is this? I can't think that anyone else but myself came up with this idea, so that means that I must be crazy, because I don't remember this at all. Even more surprising is where I found the note, but we'll not get into that. In any case, here is what I did today. I helped to ease the burdens of families who are suffering with nowhere else to turn but to the wonderful Sysmat. We can cure anything! I'm living proof! That's what I told them and out came the people."

Peyton named off nearly half the people she had just said that she had infected. Most of the reports were like that. She'd disgust herself one moment and then praise Sysmat the next. That was until she met Shadow.

"This black dog came up to me today while I was in the women's restroom at the restaurant. I looked at him and started crying. Right out of the blue! It was like I knew him from somewhere, but I couldn't place from where. I can't recall a moment where I questioned my reality more than I did right then. He *felt* familiar. My soul had to know him and yet my mind didn't. Where are my memories? Who am I? What am I doing? He's a black IB dog, and if I knew a black IB dog, that means that either I imprinted one or I know someone else that did. You don't just know IB dogs for nothing. I'm scared. I can't remember my last name. It didn't bother me at all before now. I asked the dog, but he didn't tell me. He told me one thing. 'You forgot him.' That's what he said, and it made me cry even harder. Forgot who? Who did I forget?! Why does my heart know that the dog is one-hundred percent correct?"

"It was an awful day for me today," Peyton whispered from inside a bathroom stall. "Sick again. Dying, they say. I randomly skimmed this drive to find myself saying that Sysmat cures everything. I sounded cured, but that is not the case. Today they tell me I have an incurable illness and I can't forget to take my medication. This is stupid. I've spent all day being surrounded by nurses. You'd think they'd get bored of me by now. One of them whispered I was dying. It felt like it, but I didn't mind so much. When I closed my eyes to give up, a whisper entered my mind instead. Chin up and eyes on the prize. The work wasn't done. I had to find him again. I asked who, of course, expecting that I was making everything up. Then the voice answered.

"Klast Burma. I have to locate the scattered pieces of Klast Burma's soul. That's what I was doing before I forgot. Now I'm thinking that I was trying to save Klast from Sysmat. They're the only ones I can think of that separate souls like that. How I know that I have no idea. I simply do. I argued with the voice for a while. Long enough to realize that it wasn't a voice I could make up. Guess who it was? Shadow an IB dog. I have an IB dog!" Peyton hissed that as she glanced toward the bathroom door.

"We have a plan. He's close by and he's going to help me sneak out tomorrow while everyone thinks I'm asleep because Shadow located a dog nearby that could have part of Klast's soul with her. Sounds good in theory, but that still leaves me with one major problem. I can't remember how to do anything with souls at all. Is that who I am? I find lost souls? Sounds much better than being a sick science experiment. I'm going to believe the dog. Wish me luck in figuring out how to hunt a soul. Oh, and wish me luck that I'll even be able to stand tomorrow. I feel like…"

The scene cut away as Peyton puked into the toilet. Her next reports were better. Full of resolve and names and dogs that she had hunted down with Shadow. Klast knew every single person and dog that she mentioned. It was a haunting thing to watch her talk about them. Then came the last entry. Peyton was hiding under a blanket as she recorded.

"They killed him," she hissed with red eyes. "They killed my dog! The one thing I learned about IB dogs is that when they die, their human dies soon after. I guess my time is up. Odd thing is that I don't feel like dying. It's almost like Shadow was never fully with me. I'm sad, but there's no hole in my soul where his voice used to be. I'm rather concerned about that. Tomorrow I'm going to do what Shadow told me to do if all else failed. I have a number I need to call. I need to get the person who answers the number to dig up Shadow's grave. That's what I'm to tell him. Funny thing about it is that I feel like I should know why.

"Will there be something in the grave? How will I even know where they bury Shadow? As far as I know, Sysmat doesn't bury things. We incinerate them. I think I lost my mind before they killed the dog. A science experiment. If I can't remember that I have a trailing IB dog, will it hurt me when it dies? Sick. It's so sick. Sysmat is going down! In any case, I need a safe place to hide my information. The paper trail is getting too long. Without the dog as back up... wait. The voice is back! But he died. He died! I saw him... Oh... my... gosh."

That's where it ended.

Not even Deek could move when everything ended like that. Klast was waiting for everyone to get over the shock of what Sysmat was doing because he had even more news to spring on them. It was going to be as unpleasant as Peyton's oral testimony. Five minutes. Ten. No one said a thing.

Tired of waiting, Klast broke into the men's stunned thoughts.

"Peyton called my dad." Deek had been able to tell him a little bit more of Peyton's final thoughts on the run over here. There were gaps where Deek failed to catch everything, but it was enough.

"The grave they went to dig up was my first imprinted dog's grave, not the grave of the dog that Peyton saw killed. Shadow was mine, and yet you can hear Peyton claiming that he was up and moving around. That might sound impossible, but I have something to tell you. Both accounts are correct. My imprinted dog died, and Peyton heard him years later. Sysmat cloned him. My father found a Shadow clone, too. He put him in a bunker where the dog resided up until yesterday when I found him.

"The thing you need to know about the Shadow clone my dad had was that it was cold. Freezing cold. The cold of death. The only thing holding that animal together was broken pieces of my soul that first came to him from the betrayal of my breed dogs cutting me apart and handing me over to Sysmat for experiments. After that, the hidden Shadow clone grew stronger from the other clones and the Peyton clone, which sent him the soul pieces that they found since he was tucked far away from Sysmat by my dad. That was why Peyton said she could still hear Shadow talking to her after he died. She started to hear the *other* Shadow clone. The one my dad had.

"Deek," Klast looked at his dog so everyone would know who he was talking about, "reports that my breed dogs had been stealing my soul for years. He did everything he could to protect me until he could come up with a plan to help. He had to first figure out what was happening without being able to talk, so forgive him for not alerting everyone sooner. He did try to bring up Shadow a few times, but the name ravished me. I'd yell at him for the topic and he'd stop. I broke when Shadow died. Shadow was my soul. He was my everything." Klast's voice cracked on his words. He swallowed them and kept going.

"I was broken and cracked and on antidepressants. Before you blame my dad for not bringing up what he found, consider that he couldn't. He found a zombie dog. Sysmat was already breathing down both our necks. They still are. If he showed off what he had found, Sysmat would have cracked down on us worse. For years, I thought I was going crazy seeing my old dog out of the corner of my eye. I wasn't. I was right. Deek kept chasing the clones away because they scared him. He couldn't explain them and my broken heart refused to listen.

"The Peyton in these recordings is not really her, either. It's her clone talking. I was just with the clone Peyton Finch and witnessed her last moments. I didn't record it, sorry. It didn't occur to me that perhaps I should. I didn't realize that she was a clone until she told me on her dying breath. She'd died on me before, you see, and I expected her to revive from it, but she didn't."

"Finch?" Mr. Stilkins spoke interested that I knew her last name when she couldn't remember it.

"Yes, Finch," Klast nodded. "She told me her last name because the trapped Shadow clone told her the name." That was a bit of a stretch, but oh well. He had to leave Lexia out of this. At least for now.

"It was on her dying breath that she told me to go dig up Shadow's grave. That's where I found this information. That's where she put it."

More silence followed this next part of his information dump. It didn't last as long.

"You're saying that clone IB dogs can imprint souls, trade souls, and communicate with their own clones?" one of the guards pretending to read a book asked.

"Not all of them," Klast answered. "Only the ones that are sharing the same pieces of chopped soul."

"That doesn't make sense to me," another guard admitted.

"IB dogs see souls sort of like we might see a shadow or ghost. Imprinting dogs can sense that one soul they fall in love with from miles away. It's in their nature to guard and protect that soul, but to communicate with the soul, they take a part of it for themselves, and share a part of their soul in return, so that the soul parts can talk between each other and share the deepest thoughts and desires. A good IB dog would rather die than harm his life partner by taking more than his fair share of soul. However, in the hands of Sysmat, those IB dogs forget what they have and they take more and more."

"How does Sysmat harvest that and put it into a clone?" Mr. Stilkins asked. "They would have done the same thing to Peyton to clone her. They stole parts of her soul."

Klast nodded. That had to hurt. He'd been so out of it with his soul gone. He felt better with half of himself back, but he still didn't feel like he once did.

"I don't know how they harvest and store souls…" Yes, he did. "The soulless! You saw the news of the soulless woman coming after the Peyton clone trying to suck up her soul? All they need to do is get a soulless person to suck up a soul and then destroy the soulless person close to a new clone so that the soul drifts toward a body that is familiar and gets stuck there. Living clone created!"

It wasn't his dad sending the soulless person after all! It had been Sysmat the whole time. They wanted to take out Peyton's soul fragments from her clone that was getting too smart and transfer it into a different clone version of her to stop her.

"No offense, but this whole thing sounds like fiction," a guard interrupted as he stepped into the room from the direction of the kitchen.

"Crazy, I know, but everyone can have their soul sucked up if Sysmat releases the demons," Klast sighed.

"Shooting the demon did nothing," Mr. Stilkins continued. "How did you crumble it in your hands? How does Sysmat do the same thing?"

And now Klast was out of options for leaving Lexia out of this.

"What I tell you can't leave this room," he started.

He described Lexia, and his alien planet heritage, and their use of soul technology that Sysmat was trying to obtain by tracking Klast and his dad. He described his guesses about Sysmat sending in people to attack, and how Peyton was really from his homeland. That was why she was a soul hunter without needing to encounter Sysmat for their technology. Commander Stilkins nodded and then looked around at his team.

"Normally I wouldn't base such a large decision off only two testimonies, but given the circumstances that everyone else who encounters Sysmat won't remember anything they have done, we don't have much to go on. We've heard the rumors for years that their cures were too remarkable. That those who work for them never quit. No company encounters zero turnover. No one unless the employees are not allowed to quit. I think when we infiltrate that building, we're going to find clone technology and stolen alien technology and some very, very exhausted, uncured people. I believe that we need to stop this. Any objections?"

"I have a cousin that was taken there," the book reading guard said slowly. "They have such harsh rules against never seeing family members again after they are cured. It makes sense now why. They'd not remember you. We've been sending people to a clone factory voluntarily. I'm disgusted. I'm all in with whatever the plan is."

The phone calls started tumbling out. It felt strange to sit there and watch it. Klast wanted to do more to help. He'd ratted out the organization thanks to Peyton and her ability to split and find souls, but it didn't feel finished. He was still missing something. If only he could figure out what.

# 24

Amid the chaos, there are brief moments of respite that can calm the nerves. Peyton found herself waking up in one of those. She could hear nurses scurrying around and snapping at each other, but none of it made her scared or anxious. There was sun on her face. Actual sunlight. They must have found her a window and accidentally left her by it to take care of some other emergency. She kept her eyes closed and breathed in the sensation of light rays touching her skin. She didn't care if she was a clone right now or not. She didn't care if she was being taken to a shredder because she had the sun.

Days spent wandering alone across a dusty environment on another planet peeked up through the back corners of her mind. There were struggling plants, and then there was the jungle. Wrongly pocketed with life on a planet where most other things withered, the jungle had created a system to escape the darkness. It evaded the freezing cold temperatures every night because the perimeter bushes folded up in on themselves and kept the heat in for everything else. Some vines stretched out for thousands of miles below the surface of the ground. The vine flowers leaked water onto everything. Small animals provided scat to enrich the soil, and birds sheltered in tree hearts as they ate bugs who destroyed bark. It was a fabulous ecosystem and a rather good interpretation of the life she wanted to live. She wanted a shelter from the darkness that was warmed and healed by the sun instead of burnt by it. She wanted the darkness to be respected instead of feared. A normal part of life that wouldn't maim her.

Must not be a clone, Peyton decided as she sighed in pleasure at the sun and her past memories. Alright, time to move. She started with her legs. They could lift, but they were strapped down and unable to make it far. They also felt tired and weak. Another point that told her she wasn't a clone. Her arms were next. The last thing she knew, she'd made them achy by repeatedly raising them at a ninety-degree angle and then letting them drop. She could feel the strain of the sore muscles. Her stomach was likewise in need of rest and strapped.

Now to figure out what was going on. Peyton opened her eyes and forced her neck to turn from side to side. She couldn't be waiting in a clone chamber. There were way too many gurneys around her filled with people in random vegetable states. One of them moaned repeatedly like a zombie wanting to feed or perhaps like one of those morning birds that refused to shut up when you wanted to sleep in. There was a woman beside her whose eyes were wide open, staring blankly at the roof. Now and then she would blink to prove she was alive, but the vacant expression on her made Peyton want to pull the covers over her head. There was a smaller figure a little farther off that had to be a child. No movement came from that bed as if the child was dead.

"What's happening?" Peyton asked, causing a nurse to gasp and rush over to her.

"Oh my gosh! This one talks! Why does this one talk? Who put this person in here? There's no room tag. I think she's in the wrong place, Noah. Noah! This one talks! No tag on her bed. I don't have the time to deal with everyone's lack of reasoning right now!"

"It wasn't me!" Noah answered, out of sight. "I haven't moved anyone into the hallway at all."

"Then you're being slovenly!" came the nurse. "Come move this one out!"

"I have to—"

"No excuses. Move it out!"

"Yes, ma'am," came a sassy response. The nurse that had rushed to her rushed away and Peyton found the top of her bed handles grasped by two larger hands.

"Dumb question, but where are you supposed to be?" Noah asked her.

"Outside and free," Peyton answered, causing Noah to laugh at her.

"You're funny. What color were the walls of your room?"

"White," Peyton told him. All the walls here were white. Did he expect a different answer? "My room had a great big window in it to let in the sunlight."

"Why wasn't I assigned to people like you instead of people like them?" Noah mumbled to himself as he tugged her out of the hallway through a door and into a crowded elevator.

"Where you headed?" some doctor asked him.

"I don't know. This person doesn't have a tag on the bed. She tells jokes, though. She doesn't belong down here."

The elevator door closed and moved again.

"I could use a good joke," another doctor grimaced. "I can't believe they expect us to move everybody all on the same day."

"How many fish can you fit into a convertible?" Peyton asked.

"How many?" Noah answered with a hint of relief in his voice that he was talking with a semi-sane person.

"No idea. They can't tell you and they all swim out the top," Peyton answered.

"I think she just made that up." A female doctor's face hovered above Peyton's as she looked into her eyes. "Do you think she's supposed to be on the top floor? That was remarkably put together."

"There's no one on the top floor," some other voice in the back responded. "I was just there. It was evacuated first."

"Evacuated?" Peyton didn't want to get her hopes up, but this was sounding fabulous. They were getting out of here! Everyone was getting out of here! Klast had done it! "We all get to go home now?"

"No honey. This facility is being closed for maintenance and everyone is being moved to the surrounding hospitals. You're going to be just fine."

"Do I get visitors in the other hospital? Can I call home?"

"You know what? I think I prefer the ones that don't talk after all," Noah voiced. He slapped his hand on the elevator buttons and the lift crawled to a stop. He shoved her out of the elevator into another hallway.

"You're leaving her *there*?" came a cry as the door closed.

"I haven't the time to walk her everywhere asking if a doctor recognizes her face!"

"No one is going to recognize—"

The door shut and Peyton found herself in a much darker and quieter hallway. Not good. She should have kept her mouth shut and not told any lame jokes. Now there wasn't a soul around to help her get anywhere at all. The building was not going to be serviced. If anything, it was going to be systematically gutted and destroyed. What if Sysmat planned to "evacuate" everyone, all those who couldn't speak out against them, and the rest of the crowd was going to be gassed to death in some hidden chamber? If she had only pretended to be a blank slate, she may have gotten out of here! She'd have found herself in an actual hospital.

Peyton laughed at herself for wanting to be in a hospital when that was the one place she abhorred. Then she tried to spot something useful. A call button or a light switch would be nice, but there was nothing she could reach.

"Help!" Peyton screamed, crossing her fingers that yelling wasn't a bad idea and that whoever found her wouldn't put her in a shredder for knowing how to talk.

"Deek!" she tried next, even if that was going to give her away.

"Klast! Tim! Mr. Burma! Somebody! Anybody!"

She added in a bunch of other names after that. Any name she could think of she shouted until her throat got too scratchy to talk and her lungs refused to scream anymore. Oh, this was bad. It could be days before anyone found her. Days and days...

Peyton snapped her head to the side as the air turned an uncomfortable degree of cold. No. No! She was left in the clone hall! She was going to encounter a clone, or even worse, a soulless person. Despite the ache of her throat making her want a mint drop, Peyton screamed again.

"How can I asssissst you?" the chilling person asked as it got closer. It extended the "s" quite horribly like she was living in a nightmare. She was supposed to be getting out of the nightmare. Not dying before she had a chance to escape!

"You can hit the elevator button and put me back on the lift," Peyton answered. "I got bonked out."

The cold came closer and closer. Peyton wanted to keep her eyes shut to avoid seeing the face that was going to kill her, but every time she closed her eyes, they sprang back up, terrified. She'd survived this long, and she wasn't going to go down without a fight. There had to be something she could do! Like invade the soulless person with her soul and take it over. Then she could shove her own body in the elevator and destroy the soulless person by drinking some sort of nasty chemical (there had to be that around this place) so that her soul would release. Yes. That was her plan. Soul invasion. She was ready. She refused to die here!

"Gladly," the voice answered.

The person stepped in right next to her. To her surprise, the cold individual was wearing doctor's garb. A loose-fitting flower pattern shirt flowed above black cotton pants. The doctor didn't so much as touch her. He hit the elevator button, and when it opened, the doctor shoved in her gurney with a nudge of his foot, avoiding the protests of the new people in the lift who had to squeeze out of the way.

Not dead! She wasn't dead! Peyton let out a sigh of relief as the new doctors tried to locate her gurney tag and failed. One checked beneath her mattress as if it would have fallen in there, but she was fairly certain that she didn't have one because *her* doctor was trying to save her. The first floor was empty where she'd been. They were probably all dead. Her doctor had saved her by erasing her identity. He saved her and she never even knew his name.

"Thank you," Peyton whispered as drops fell from her eyes. "Thank you, thank you."

"She talks," a nurse pointed out as the woman pushed through the others to hover above Peyton.

The lady didn't look like anything special with curly blond hair turning gray, but she had a kind expression, the kind that could warm an injured soul. "I'll try the fourth floor. I'll take care of it."

It was weird being called an "it" as if Peyton couldn't understand what was happening, but she wasn't about to say more than a few words at a time and give herself away again. They jostled her around as people moved in and out, and then it was her turn to leave. The nurse pushed her out onto the fourth floor. It was even more chaotic here with patients screaming left and right and nurses cursing at the noise. The nurse who had brought her here gave her an apologetic smile.

"You'll be sorted out eventually. For now, I'm going to get you a generic tag so you aren't lost on the mummy floor."

No one stopped the woman from going to the check-in desk and printing off a tag. Peyton wished she could read what it said as the lady popped it onto her bed and then wheeled her into an empty room with the door open. She left her there and rushed off to go take care of moving more people.

Peyton didn't like this place. She couldn't mimic being a screaming lunatic because her voice was already strained in a whisper. The nurses here were not kind. Objects were thrown. Threats were shouted. The word "neutralizer" was the most common phrase around. No one came to check on Peyton for at least two hours.

When a passing doctor spotted her in a room that should have been empty and checked her tag, the doctor swore and shoved her back into the elevator. This was going to be a long day. They checked her tag and those in the elevator huffed about it.

"This is laziness at its finest!" one complained. "Whoever did this should be fired."

"Don't say that. My friend got fired, and she never came back."

"That's what being fired is, brains," came a snappy retort.

This time Peyton got left in the elevator as the people moved in and out around her. No one wanted to deal with her case for another forty minutes until one strained young man couldn't get a different gurney inside with her taking up the room. He pulled Peyton out and left her on another busy floor. She got shifted out of the way over and over again until everyone on the floor was evacuated except for her.

"Your nurse never came back for you?" The doctor that was closing the floor asked. Unwilling to talk still, Peyton shook her head. The hope that she was going to get out of here was hard to keep down. Please! This person had to get her out of here! He looked at her tag and didn't so much as sigh about the lack of instruction it gave. The man shut off the lights and then wheeled her into the elevator with him. Having been here a lot today, it was strange to enter it and find it quiet now. It felt eerie that way.

"I know I'm not supposed to say, but this is not what happens when the maintenance crew comes through. It feels like we're being shut down. I can't afford to lose my job. I have a family depending on me, you know."

Peyton nodded at him and he frowned in reply as the elevator kept dinging the floors.

"You can talk?"

"Yes," she whispered, not wanting to end up someplace worse.

"A bit croaky there," the doctor smiled at her and then yawned. "Sorry. We've not had time to give anyone water or food all day. You must be hungry. I'm starved. I'm looking forward to a calzone. That sounds fabulous right about now."

He rambled about the food he wanted to eat until the elevator stopped. When the door opened, he turned horribly still. Peyton found her breath hitching up. They must have reached something bad. Like a scene where everyone was on the floor dead and there was nothing they could do and they were going to be next.

"Welcome to the rest of your life," came a voice dispelling her thoughts of mass death. "While you have been working for Sysmat a lot of changes have occurred in the world around you. Please give us your legal name and we will check our database to see if we can release you."

"What do you mean by 'release' me? What's with the guns?" the doctor boldly asked.

"The facilities are being shut down due to malpractice," the voice answered. "Memories have been wiped on most everyone to hide the evidence. A lot of people find that they remember rather old data about where they live, and we can't have a storm of doctors knocking on house doors where they don't live causing chaos. Can you remember your legal name?"

"Of course, I can!" the doctor insisted.

"Fabulous. What is it, sir? I'll check the national database and get you the care that you need."

There was a long pause where Peyton wished she could see what floor they had landed on, and then the doctor bolted. He didn't make it far, and he started blabber-crying right after.

"I know my name! I have to know my name!"

He didn't know his name. Peyton knew how that felt. Whoever caught him assured him he was going to be fine. They were going to locate his identity with facial recognition and/or a blood test. If he could calmly follow them, he was going to be taken care of. The doctor screamed and sobbed. A man in a black uniform with a long gun strapped to his back entered the elevator and came to push her out. He shook his head at the lack of identification on her tag.

"Peyton Finch," Peyton croaked. "My name is Peyton Finch."

"Seriously? You made it out alive?" the guard asked as he looked down at her. "This one claims to be Peyton Finch!" the guy hollered.

He probably wished he hadn't been so loud a moment later. There was a massive explosion of dog sounds, followed by human screams and scrambling. Dog claws beat against concrete flooring while people shouted that the animals had gone mad. The soldier raised his gun to defend himself and then decided that getting out of the way was the better option. Peyton's gurney was shoved into the wall and then wheeled away from the elevator. Defensive growls sprang up all around.

"I can't see you!" Peyton croaked, doing her best to be heard over the sounds even if the dogs could pick her out anyway. She could feel them shoving and hear them breathing, but it was unnerving not to know which dogs were moving her away. It could be a massive host of Shadow clones for all she knew. She didn't want Shadow clones to hide her away forever.

"I want to see Klast Burma! You'd better take me to Klast!"

"Yes!" came the bark of a dog she was more intimately familiar with.

Deek. The Deek clone had organized a hostage situation. It couldn't be the real Deek if they were still inside the Sysmat building. The dogs kept moving her. A group of soldiers broke away from the main group to follow along, but none of them wanted to go up against the massive organization of dogs.

Peyton was jostled out a door. She held her breath out of habit. Dark. It was nighttime and if she took in a breath, she'd freeze her lungs from the inside out. That was her first thought anyway until she heard the continued sounds of panting dogs and questioning people. It helped her to remember that she wasn't on her native planet, but where Klast had been born, and she could inhale at night. Peyton took in a deep lungful of air. It was marvelous! Her eyes looked up at the stars. It felt like years since her own eyes had seen stars and even longer since she'd taken in non-sterilized air.

"Bark!" Deek commanded. He might as well have ordered the city to turn on tornado sirens.

# 25

Klast had both won and lost the war. Won in the sense that Sysmat couldn't invade Lexia any longer because even the CEO of the company no longer could remember what he had done or what he was doing and pled insanity. They had tried to keep everything as quiet as possible, but still, the information about the invasion was leaked and memories were stolen away before they could get inside. All the same, the CEO was in prison for life, along with a handful of colleagues. Every clone was destroyed inside a nearby furnace since they couldn't function on their own anyway. The databases had been wiped by some emergency code, proving that Sysmat was suspicious. The worst part was that along with the clones, everyone that had been cloned was killed too. No more Peyton. They hadn't gotten inside fast enough.

Klast sniffled again. She had gone down bravely. She'd given her life to save the world. Two worlds. Hundreds of worlds and no one was going to remember her name.

A buzzing filled the room and Mr. Stilkins pulled out his phone, frowned at it, and answered.

"It's for you," the head of security passed Klast the phone. Klast was hesitant to touch the device. He couldn't think of anyone that would call him on through Jonas Stilkins.

"Hi," Klast answered, not able to muster up a more passable greeting than that. He hoped he didn't have to give any statements to the press. He'd said everything he knew already. They had drilled him for a couple of hours after the invasion plans were finalized.

"Hello, Klast. This is Gallenger leading the shut-down party. We have a situation. We checked for clones extensively. We double-checked for dogs, but then this unidentified gurney came out the elevator, and your dogs, Klast, popped up from everywhere and nowhere all at once!"

Klast laughed, even if Mr. Gallenger sounded stressed by this change of events. Klast expected nothing less from his dogs.

"Which dogs?"

"All of them. I kid you not. All your dogs. Every single one on your breeding records. We've called the owners of the dogs that are still living and they claim to have their IB dogs with them, so we're forced to believe that your clone dogs survived the purge."

Klast dropped his smile and looked at Deek, who was back to staring at him. Deek had claimed that he was never taken by Sysmat, but his other dogs hadn't been either. The company must have gotten DNA in other ways.

"All my dogs?" Klast asked again. "Even Deek?"

"Especially Deek. He barks, and the hoard does everything he says. We can't get close to the person on the gurney, but it's believed to be Peyton. I think the only one who's going to sort this one out is you. You need to come claim order over your dogs."

The tissue in his hand dropped to the floor. Claim order? That's what this man was going to call it? That's not what it was going to be. What Klast was being asked to do was kill off every single dog he had ever loved in his entire life. All at the same time. There's no way he could do that, and yet if he didn't, that left a chunk of clones that were going to fight with their real counterparts to claim the lives they wished they had. Klast stared back at Deek.

"Alone," Deek whimpered at him. "Go alone."

"I need you!" Klast whined. "You think like yourself! You'll know what you're planning! You can't expect me to go through this heartbreak on my own! I can't do it. There's no way!"

Deek shook his head vigorously and then crawled under a chair. It was strange seeing Deek in this cowardly state again, but Klast couldn't blame him. Such a group would destroy Deek in two seconds. He couldn't defend against every dog they had ever known. Not by a long shot. They were clever enough to escape Sysmat and locate Peyton. Thinking of her was enough to fill Klast's stomach with lava. What if she didn't remember him? He'd only met a clone.

Easy, Klast. This was about the dogs. They'd find some way to trick everyone into thinking that they were the real dogs instead of the fake ones, and owners would end up killing parts of their souls for the clones. Klast was going to be killing off his soul again just by seeing them. He sucked in his fear of the torment and nodded.

"Alright, I'm coming. Where are they at and what does it look like? Do we have a good view of Peyton?"

"We had a description from the man she told her name to. She declared her first and last name in a strained whisper. That's more than we've got out of most people today. The guy who wheeled her out said she wasn't looking good. He described her as sickly and emancipated, but her eyes were sharp."

The dogs would know if it was her or not. If they all thought it was her, it was.

"They are currently in the parking lot of Sysmat on the east side, howling up a storm. All the cars from that side evacuated, but we have a few troops surrounding the area to keep out curious onlookers. It's incredibly loud over there."

That made Klast smile. If it was Deek leading the pack, they wouldn't be anything but max volume.

"Can I hear what they are saying?" Klast asked.

"Yeah. I got a recording. Hold on."

Klast waited for Mr. Gallenger to get situated and then looked over at Deek under the chair in bewilderment. They were all repeating one phrase: the jungle bushes!

"That's it?" Klast asked. "That makes no sense."

"Don't ask me. They're your dogs."

Yes. Untrained clone dogs that really shouldn't have the same memories of the exact phrases he had used in teaching any of them. These clones made no sense. He needed a good strategy for taking them down all at once because one-on-one was going to be the end of him. A bomb maybe. He'd get them to hand over Peyton and then he'd bomb them all. Klast glanced around the room and snatched a few bombs from inside a canister. No one stopped him. He checked the bullets in his gun and increased them.

"Need to go run some interference," Klast told everyone, finding the strength to act carefree about it all. He reached over to Deek and hugged the dog. There were some places that Deek refused to let him go alone, most places in fact, but he wasn't about to budge right now.

*"Come back,"* Deek begged.

"See everyone soon," Klast agreed.

He walked toward the door trying to decide how best to get back to Sysmat. Driving felt too slow and he didn't have his car. He wasn't about to ask for an airlift. Might as well prove everything he had told these guys were true. He could shift. Klast decided on a landing spot that was not too close and not too far from the parking lot to avoid crowds. Avoiding eye contact, he shifted himself through the darkness and back out into the darkening light.

Klast landed in a normally empty location. A hill connected to a children's park a couple of blocks away from Sysmat. On top of the hill was an electrical box unit, so most people gave it a wide birth. Today was an exception. Klast tumbled on top of a group of people lounging on a blanket staring toward the Sysmat building. They weren't the only ones either. Crowds had congregated everywhere, staring outward.

"Hey!" the man he flattened screamed as Klast jumped to his feet and dashed away with a mumbled apology. Gee. It looked like the entire town had come out after work due to the invasion. He passed a few stores that normally would be open. The workers were standing around in front of the buildings, chatting and enjoying a brief reprieve.

Woof! The loud bark echoed off of everything. Deek. Klast could place that dog anywhere!

"Here it comes again," someone said as Klast rushed past. "Think it will go on all night?"

Klast laughed. They had no idea. He'd endured many sleepless nights of that sound. A chorus of dogs started chanting. It almost sounded like a song with the way they were going about it. Each one was saying a different line. We hate pickles. Don't chew socks. Ice cream, please. Their messages bounced around each other as if the only thing they were trying to accomplish was to make a ton of noise. It wasn't supposed to make sense, but it had to. Klast strained his ears for Deek's voice. He kept running. Two blocks. One block. He could see the start of the security guards in the way of the parking lot when a ball of fur came charging at him from the side and smashed him to the ground.

Play dead!

The weight of the animal felt like an IB dog, and since he didn't know who it was, he grew still. There had been a lot of IB dogs sold at the arena this week. It could be any one of them defending the borders against a man charging toward the off-limits area.

The animal didn't bite. It licked him and whined, "I hear me."

"Volt!" Klast cheered.

Oh, he was so excited! He didn't get to see the dogs he sold this quickly. Klast shoved upward on the creamy animal, who immediately backed away. If Volt was here, then the woman he imprinted wouldn't be too far behind. Sure enough, he spotted her running at full speed, looking exasperated. Behind her came Tasha and her soldier. From the other side came Weston and Luke, chased by two buff guys. Hero came racing up with a large grin. The kid he protected was struggling to hold on to his back.

"Slow down!" Klast cried out, spinning around to see all of them, but no one wanted to listen. All of them raced up to him regardless.

"Yee-haw!" the child cried out. "I'm so getting grounded for breaking out of the hotel!"

"What is Volt saying?!" the woman begged to know. "He won't stop barking either!"

"What's going on?" Tasha's soldier asked next.

Klast looked over at the man that Luke had imprinted, a runner by the looks of it. He wasn't out of breath at all. Then there was Weston with his new love. Klast had never met this guy since Mike and Bronze had helped to sell Weston.

"Klast Burma," Klast shook the new man's hand, trying to place why he looked familiar. He looked down at Weston for the answer.

"Boxer," Weston answered his unspoken question.

A famous boxer. Well then. That explained why the handshake was rather firm and the man full of muscle. He made a good addition to the spread-out Burma dog family.

"Volt is complaining that he can hear himself barking," Klast told the woman. "He's right. Sysmat cloned my dogs. All my dogs. They were experimenting on bonds and souls and tearing me apart. You can't go over there. This is something that I have to fix on my own. You go over there and you're liable to have your soul ripped up. I don't advise it. It hurts."

"Deek?" Tasha asked him, looking hopefully toward the loud barking tones.

Klast sighed. "That's a clone of him. The real Deek stayed behind."

Woof!

Deek's sharp bark cut off the chant in an instant. The sudden lack of noise sliced through the air with the excitement of carving a birthday cake. Those closest to the cake waited in eager anticipation. Everyone else on the outskirts got a lot louder to drone out the birthday song.

"Stay here," Klast ordered the IB dogs. "Do not go over there for anything. I've already been torn apart. I know how to handle this. I don't want you over there dying for nothing."

He glanced around, expecting to find Phantom and Zen only to remember that they had stayed with Bronze and Mike. Those two wouldn't let the dogs go charging toward a sound that could gut them apart. No Phantom and Zen, but standing even closer to the commotion were a group of his other dogs from previous seasons.

"What are you doing? Don't get close to that!" Klast shouted at the people.

"We're not stupid!" Bullseye answered him. He had a white ring around one eye. The rest of him was a dark chocolate brown. Seeing him had Klast grinning all over again. His dogs!

"You always did have a big mouth," Klast replied as he rushed toward them, groaning when the other dogs behind him ignored his order and came charging after him again. This was what he had talked about when he told Peyton that she had a family to protect her now. It was this right here. This stubborn, wonderful group of brave heroes. He couldn't stay mad at them for more than a moment.

"You always were bossy," Bullseye sassed back, causing not only Klast to laugh, but the older dogs as well. The younger ones didn't fully know what Bullseye was saying. He was speaking his litter vocabulary which wasn't the same as the litter behind him.

"Oh, you guys! I love you guys. I'm so happy to see you all!"

There was no stopping now. Klast dropped to his knees and hugged all the dogs. He'd not seen Bullseye, Vivi, Persimmon, or Porto in ages. He wished he could catch up on how everyone was doing, but there wasn't any time.

A howling rent the air. Normally it was a sound that struck joy through his heart if only for a moment before he started to shower the dog in praises and encourage the joining of a connection. This time it made him feel sick. Imprinting. The clone dogs were starting to imprint.

"Are you listening!" Klast screamed at the dogs at his feet as he jumped back up. "Those dogs over there are clones of *you*! They are going to love the same thing you love. They catch the scent of your human and they'll stop at nothing to get it for themselves. They've already formed a pack to make their demands. You're good and all, but you cannot let them get close to you! It's ridiculously hard to stop soul-stealing from an IB dog. In fact, I'm not sure it's even possible."

"What about you?" the kid asked him. "You said they'd kill us. They'll kill you."

Maybe. This was his pack. He had to rule it.

"I have Peyton," Klast assured the child. "Hero, get that child someplace safer. Please."

He looked Hero in the eye feeling the dog struggle against listening to him. Hero gave off a short growl, but then another howl filled the air. Clone Hero was imprinting to the child he was already imprinted to. This was a disaster! Klast couldn't think of a worse threat than two of the same dog wanting the same imprinting. Another howl. Another.

"Make good choices," Klast said as he rushed around the dogs he loved toward the worst disaster of his life. The bombs were in his pocket, but he couldn't use them. He loved these dogs, clones or not. There were going to be dogs that he'd not seen in five to seven years. He had nine dogs that had died in service or training that he never expected to hear from again. Sysmat was horrible, but it was also amazing. It had revived the dead and restored to him everything he had ever given up. He had no idea how he was going to destroy the very thing that brought him joy. He couldn't.

# 26

Klast was here. There was no other explanation for why Deek ordered everyone to shut up. He'd heard Klast finally. The dogs had bitten the straps off her, but she was still stuck to the bed from her physical weakness. She'd been whispering to the dogs a lot, trying to think what Klast might tell them so that when he appeared, they wouldn't be at each other's throat. Or worse, at his.

The sacrifice of her voice didn't seem to make a dent. She could hardly whisper anymore and she'd not changed Deek's mind. Peyton huffed, struggling to turn herself onto her side so she could see better. She'd made slow progress, but she was almost there. Another inch. Another shove on her shaky arms. Another push of her trembling legs. She refused to let herself rest this time. She had to turn over!

There. On her side. It had only taken her an hour or two to get that far. Dwelling on the thought would make her cry, so she focused on the dogs instead. So many dogs! She could spot thirty-eight dogs from where she was along with armed soldiers pointing guns in her direction. More dogs finished the circle behind her. Peyton scanned them, searching for Shadow. The action felt intuitive like he really should be hers and should be here. He wasn't, but Deek was.

Deek stood there in silver glory, not looking outward toward the scents and sounds of the city, but regarding the pack as a whole. He gave a nod to one of the creatures, and that dog started to imprint howl next. Wait. It was a trap! They weren't imprinting at all! What was the point of that? As if sensing her gaze, Deek turned to look at her and shook the gurney as he jumped up on the top of it. Peyton had no warning before the dog shoved her onto her back.

The demon! He was undoing all her hard work! If only she could link into his mind to shout at him, she would. He continued to shove her, forcing her onto her other side. The only thing she could do was exhale an angry breath. She sucked it back in the next. Klast! He rushed onto the scene from the other side. It was hard to make out what he was thinking, just like his brilliant dog. His mouth looked grim, but his eyes were flashing with excitement. Confusing. If she had stayed as she was, she would have missed him.

He skid to a halt, one hand in a pocket and the other on his gun. His message was coming out loud and clear. A few of his dogs growled. Some whimpered as if the thought of making him angry was too much to handle. Deek remained silent on top of her apart from a snort that cut off the imprinting song.

"What do you want?" Klast called out, squaring his shoulders. "I'll negotiate with you, Deek. I only have one demand which I bet you can guess. Release Peyton. Bring me Peyton."

"No!" Deek answered. "Peyton wind soul."

Not this again!

"Yes, she is. You need to let her go."

"No. Peyton fix you." Deek trembled on top of her and then he looked away from Klast to look at her. "Wind soul. Fix. Now."

What exactly did he want her to do?! She had Sysmat technology stuck in her skin. She wasn't able to see souls. She couldn't fix anything. She also couldn't explain that to Deek because she'd wasted her breath.

"Deek whatever you're planning, it needs to st…" Klast trailed off as he shook his head. "I can't." He said the words so quietly that Peyton couldn't hear them, but she could feel them. Klast was struggling with this.

"I promised you. The real you. I promised you that I'd do a better job of trusting your decisions, but this is rough on me. What was all the howling for and then them going mute? What kind of trick are you pulling here? You can trust me, Deek. Tell me your demands."

Klast set his gun on the ground, followed by a few round objects that had to be bombs. This wasn't good. Even Peyton knew he couldn't let go of all his defenses in a horde of clone dogs. She was right. Deek glanced between her and Klast only once before he turned demon. He shoved his head down to her left wrist and bit. Peyton thought she couldn't talk anymore, but she *could*

Page | 270

scream. Klast was swearing at the dog. Literally swearing. She'd never heard him so mad before. Another dog jumped up next and bit her other side. The gurney shook from the force.

"Ahh!!!"

The IB dogs were attacking her! She couldn't believe it was going to end this way. Both her wrists were ripped apart, followed by her feet and then shoulder. Tears exploded across her face. She wanted to beg them to make the pain end. Dying as a clone wasn't the same as dying as herself. It was much, much worse!

"Open fire!" a guard on the perimeter ordered. Bullets whizzed toward the dogs coming from the left. Dog howls rent the air along with the smell of gunpowder. Klast was forced to drop to the ground, but he kept screaming.

"I trusted you! Leave her alive! Please Deek! Don't do this!"

"Wind soul fix now," Deek ordered as a bullet smashed one of his pupils apart. Peyton couldn't watch any longer. She tried to curl in on herself as she shut her eyelids. Tried and failed as Deek plopped over her and turned very, very cold.

He couldn't do that! He was going to die anyway. He might as well just accept that and die instead of turning into a soulless dog. She couldn't grab at Klast's escaping soul like this!

Wait.

Her wrists. Her feet. Her shoulder. The dogs had torn out her Sysmat marks! They had tortured her to restore Klast. All of them together planned on laying down their lives to save his. And she had first-hand experience that she did not need to die herself to move his soul back into him. If she could get close enough to him, she could push the soul back in, or Deek could slowly siphon it from her and push it into Klast. She had done that before as a clone, right? She vaguely remembered giving him his soul once before through a kiss. A stray bullet hit her leg. Agony! She hadn't the time to dwell on it, though. Her fingers couldn't curl into a fist to help her focus because she couldn't feel anything in her wrists and hands except for pain, but she could still make out the sparkles when she shut her eyes.

There he was. Klast's soul floating in the air all around her, coming up at her from the dogs near her gurney dying in unison. Klast was screaming over the firing squad for them to stop. He pointed out that the dogs were not attacking anymore. He yelled about the soldiers being clueless about what that meant. They had to stop killing the dogs. They had to!

The guns stopped, but Peyton needed them to continue. It wasn't only Deek that had the remaining parts of Klast's soul, but all these dogs. She couldn't get those pieces unless they gave them up. Peyton took a long shuddering breath, the kind that mimicked a soulless inhaling a soul. Deek was still freezing on top of her. Soulless, he still kept himself in place even if the bullets hadn't killed him off. The smart dogs around her got the message. Her bed became an icicle as they gave up the soul. She could hear Klast crying, but she couldn't help him yet.

Peyton pulled. She yanked at the particles, drawing them into herself. It was exhausting, and she must have passed out a few times, but she kept coming back to take in more, pushing her soul to the side so she could hold his. They were going to save Klast. They were going to! That was the only thing she had left to live for. It was better to dwell on that with her adrenaline than the chopped-up places on her body that stung.

Sparkles danced behind her eyes. Pain danced around her body. Ice covered everything else, stealing her breath away.

Force pummeled into it all; a dark, greedy, empty thing that was only familiar to her because she had seen it before. Klast was destroying the soulless dogs. He was turning them to dust. He started with Deek's body on top of her. Powder. The lifted weight felt wrong. Then he rushed at everyone else as the creatures snarled and snapped at him. He yelled from being attacked on all sides. She peeked and wished she hadn't. She had bled from all her pores before as a clone, and that's what Klast looked like right now. One arm was hanging limp. He fought his dying dogs with power.

Anyplace he bumped them, they crumbled apart. Blood oozed from all around him. The soldiers rushed in even if there was nothing they could do against a hungry, soulless IB dog. Klast yelped as two dogs attacked his leg before they crumbled. He struggled under the weight of three more. Peyton closed her eyes again and sucked up the residue until there was only one dog left. It stood above her on the gurney as if waiting for death but too scared to take it. Tasha. This was Deek's favorite sister. Peyton couldn't remember how she knew it, but there the dog was, a bloody mess struggling to stand. All Klast's weight was on one leg. If he didn't get patched up soon, he was going to pass out. His skin was turning white and a puddle of red kept oozing to his feet.

"I love you," Klast told Tasha through half a face.

It looked like it hurt him to talk after being turned into a dog feeding fest. Peyton glared at the dog. She'd wanted to help the dog before, but she only had anger for it now. This wasn't saving Klast. This was killing him. He didn't deserve to be killed by the very dogs he loved. Sysmat was the vilest company she had ever heard of. The Tasha clone had to die to end all of this. Klast couldn't do it, and the soldiers were standing there, unsure of themselves. There was only one last thing she could think of. Peyton pushed the rest of her soul out and inhaled.

Tasha whimpered. Klast screamed upon seeing the dark pits of Peyton's eyes, but still, she pulled until the dog on the top of her turned blue and frozen. Until the soul released. Then she fainted. Darkness swallowed her up as if Klast had burst both her and Tasha apart. A fitting end. His soul had escaped Sysmat. Mr. Burma would hire some other soul finder to fetch it back for him, and Peyton could finally rest in peace. Mission accomplished. She allowed herself a brief smile as she gave in to the dark.

# 27

What a day! As far as missions went, this one had gone from crazy to psycho. Most things around him had lost their souls, or rather, his soul. Klast was hesitant to say anything directly to Peyton in case she didn't remember who he was, but he grunted the lopsided weight of his body onto her gurney to see her. She was exactly as described. Skinny, weak, and drained. No intelligent life gleamed out of her closed eyes. At least they were closed though because he didn't want to see the pain reflected inside of them. His pain was pounding through his skull unable to stop.

With a painful yelp, Klast placed his mouth on hers, hoping that it wasn't too late for Peyton to live. He'd never kissed a nearly soulless person before. It went against everything his mind, heart, body, and soul told him, but he knew Peyton, and he knew his dogs. Once Deek sacrificed himself for the black eyes, he understood what the plan was. They could have done it all in a much gentler fashion, but it was what it was now. Deek had convinced the IB dogs to die for him. The plan was to get Peyton to pick up his soul before it got lost somewhere else. They had torn out the Sysmat devices that stopped her from functioning as a soul hunter and then died.

"Come on," Klast winced, watching as he added to the blood already all over Peyton. His head was swimming, his face was half gone, his neck burned, he'd lost an arm and a leg and everything else was shredded, but he couldn't let her leave his sight until he knew Peyton would recover. She'd come back from worse before! She could do this! She could die and find herself again. That's what she did. She was blazen!

"Live again, Peyt," Klast demanded. "Live again!"

"There's a medic on the way," a soldier informed him.

Klast already knew that. He'd heard the additional running feet with his right ear. Sound was muffled because his left year was bitten off, but even if he didn't hear the shouts for bandages and gauze, he would have guessed that there would be medics on the way.

"Peyton Finch!" he screamed at her as he kissed her again, feeling the warmth rush between them as part of the cold dissipated. There it was! His soul was moving back into him! Once he was out of the way, Peyton would have room for herself.

Strong hands gripped him around the middle, prying him away from the girl. Klast screamed, but it was no use. He hadn't the strength to fight. He hardly had the strength to yell. A needle pricked into the one spot of flesh that wasn't already bloody, at his right elbow, and his vision swam on him. They'd drugged him. He was out of time to save her. At least Deek was still alive. He still had Deek.

# 28

It was the sound of a news anchor that pulled Peyton out of her deep dreams. The name of Klast Burma and Jethro Burma got mentioned again. Peyton stilled her breathing to listen. It was believed that the threat of invasion was over due to their work across the divide. Klast had sustained many injuries from battling clones that had stolen his soul, but he was expected to make a full recovery. Tests indicated that his soul was restored, and inside sources hinted that a new cure to *Mervolk* would be in circulation soon.

Peyton didn't hear her name at all, but it made her smile. She'd done it! She had finished helping Klast. It would be nice to see him again, but now that her job was done, she could move on. What was it going to be this time? Locating lost children from hiking groups? Discovering a technology to help people breathe in the dark so that night shifting wasn't so dangerous? Fixing all the people who *Mervolk* had touched?

"Are you smiling? Are you awake Peyton?"

Tim! She expected to find herself in a hospital if she woke up at all, but she hadn't expected to find Tim. That only went to reassure her that she was no longer on Klast's alien planet, but back home in Lexia. Hopefully, it would feel like home again soon. Peyton nodded and then looked around.

She had to be in a hospital room because she could make out the glowing science fiction monitors. Her bed didn't strap her down, but the bars were made from that soul-locking material so she was probably pinned in again. There was a glowing ball that looked like a stereo system that was dictating the news. Instead of white sterile walls, she was greeted with red brick lines, a window that had a top light blue pane, and a clear white pane beneath. Pictures of children playing on playgrounds hung on the walls. Home. It'd be better if she could remember more about it, but she'd take it any which way she could.

Tim was standing near the edge of her bed. Behind him was an older couple. The man had a narrow face with three lines on his forehead. The woman had dark bags beneath her eyes to match the man's worry. Both had light red-brown hair.

"I'm awake," Peyton agreed. Her throat was still scratchy which only made her jolt. Her wrists! Her feet! Her shoulder! She struggled to look at her arms to see the damage. Gray bandages covered her wrists, preventing inspection, but she could feel her fingers again and they could move. No blanket covered her body, so seeing her wrapped feet was possible. Bandaged up but moveable.

"Clark Manford fixed you again. He wasn't very happy when Klast told him that the you he fixed last time was a clone who died."

"Tim!" the woman admonished. "She won't want to remember that."

"Oh yes, I do!" Peyton declared. "Those are my only memories. I'm keeping them!"

There was a short gasp from the older woman. The older man in the room shivered, and then the lady teared up. Okay... Peyton glanced at Tim, confused, and then back at the couple who continued to be distraught. The woman now clutched the man as if the sight of Peyton was beyond emotional resilience. She started crying, clinging to what had to be her husband for support. His emotions flashed from shock, to sadness, to anger.

"It's not that bad. I've been far worse, believe me," Peyton told them. Whoever they were. Hopefully, Tim would tell her soon.

"We can't understand you," Tim pointed out as the man cautiously took a few steps closer. He dragged his woman with him as he went. Peyton flinched backward, deeper into her bed.

"What did they do to you?!" he demanded.

"I honestly hope I never remember that," Peyton replied with a smile. The day she remembered that was the day she'd never sleep again. It was better not knowing.

The man's mouth hung open as if he couldn't believe anything that he was seeing or hearing. He poked her in the arm, testing to see if she was real. Peyton rolled her eyes at him and looked at Tim. Enough of the confusion. She nodded between the man and woman demanding Tim tell her who they were. He got the silent message, but he only sighed and then pushed a button on the side of the bed, which dropped the soul railing so he could sit on the edge of the bed instead. He put his head in his hands.

"Tim!" Peyton demanded. "What is happening? Who are they?"

"She said your name," the woman nudged Tim.

"Because you said it. She doesn't remember us. She's gone."

"I beg your pardon. I'm right here," Peyton insisted. "Where's Klast?"

He'd tell her what was going on. So much for trying to move on and not invade his life again. She laughed at herself for already resorting back to him, but that's as far as that got. The man's anger grew into a tangible force in the air. It was so impressive that Peyton tried to reach out to touch it. Weird. Super strong emotion against Klast right there.

"I will defeat you," Peyton declared, looking directly at the Klast hater. He had no idea who he was dealing with. Peyton shoved back at the feeling and Tim's head snapped up. He jerked himself between her and the hater severing eye contact.

"Don't! The both of you!" Tim ordered.

"She said Klast! She's talking about that traitor. I won't have that kind of talk around me!"

"Good thing I don't have to be around you all the time then!" Peyton snapped back.

"Stop," Tim tried again. "She can understand everything that you say. It's us that can't understand her. I hoped since learning her clone had died that the strange version of her was gone and the old her would return, but clearly that's not the case."

"The old me?" Peyton questioned.

"Yes, the old you," Tim answered, turning to look at her as if he guessed the question around the words. She smiled at him. "We knew you before you lost your mind. Long before you were taken by the Burmas."

"Klast never took me," Peyton said slowly, trying to piece together missing events.

Tim couldn't know what he was talking about. She had volunteered to save Klast. It was her job. She hoped. All the same, the job was over now, and she had to figure out the rest of her life. She could only think of one reason why Tim of all people would be in the hospital room with her along with an older couple.

"Family?" Peyton asked the word pointing to all of them as best as she could with a completely bandaged hand. It impressed her that she could make her arm move. That was nice. Her muscles still felt extraordinarily tired, but they were there.

"Tim," she whined. "Tim, Tim, Tim."

He shook his head at her, but the faint hint of a sad smile was enough to tell her he'd seen her whine at him before a long time ago.

"Are you my brother? I knew I had a brother! These are my parents, aren't they?"

Peyton tried to look around Tim to see them again. She squinted as she contemplated hair color and facial structure, trying to decide if there was enough resemblance to make her guess correct. It was possible. Not every family looked like clones of each other. Tim's hair was lighter than hers. Her parent's hair had a lot more red. They all had different eye colors. Peyton's eyes were a very light brown if she was remembering correctly. Tim had green eyes. Her mother saw through a dark blue, and her father's vision looked through dark brown irises. They shared a pointed chin, so perhaps that was telling. Both Tim and her father had narrower faces than her and her mother. Still, Peyton struggled to find herself reflected in their features.

"Timmy just tell me!"

"Don't call me that. Whatever that was." He wiped off his arms like she'd covered him in dirt or something.

Peyton huffed and rolled her eyes and tried to sit up. She'd find Klast on her own. He had to be in a nearby hospital room with her. All she had to do was walk, or maybe crawl down the hallway, and he'd tell her what was happening. She made it up half an inch before her body failed her, forcing her to collapse back onto the bed in defeat.

"What is happening?!" she screamed at them.

If they couldn't understand her in words, they had to be able to understand her feelings. She pushed it on them. She wanted answers. Assuming this was her family that she couldn't remember, Peyton tried to find sympathy for what they were going through and fell short. They should love her no matter what. They should be willing to sacrifice for her, even if that meant learning to live with a person who had changed.

The woman sank onto the edge of the bed next and cried into Tim's shoulder. The man stalked over to the window and looked outward. Peyton wanted to go into a long rage. She didn't like the way they sounded against Klast. He'd not done anything but nearly kill himself trying to save her. All he had done before that was survive Sysmat destroying his soul. It wasn't his fault what had happened to her. Klast would never have asked her to do any of it. He wasn't the type of person to ask to be saved. He gave himself to others all the time.

"She doesn't know us," the woman sobbed. "Can you feel that? She doesn't know us."

"That's what Sysmat did to people." Tim's voice wobbled as if he was holding back his tears. "I know you hold what happened to her against the Burmas, but someone had to stop this from happening to all the rest of us."

"They didn't have to steal our daughter for it!" the man at the window bellowed.

Aha! There was the word daughter. Tim must be her brother.

"We don't have all the information," Tim defended. "Even Doctor Manford agreed that she's blazen. Peyton might have been the only one that could have saved us. If given the chance to save an entire world to protect everyone you care about, wouldn't you take that risk?"

"It destroyed her," her mom whimpered.

Poor Mom. Peyton could only offer her a half sympathetic smile. Without knowing anything about the woman, the connection simply wasn't there. There should be a lot of excitement in the room to see each other again. Hugging and laughter and smiles and quick-fire catching up phrases were what she wanted from a family reunion. Instead, she got tears and anger. Welcome back, Peyton. For all she knew, it was always like this.

"It saved a lot of other people."

"That's what the news said, but the news is warped and twisted. It always paints the Burmas to be the glorious ones."

"Be careful what you say about them!" Tim insisted again. "Peyton *likes* them. She and Klast love each other. You don't want to tangle with that. Just look at what happened the last time Klast was in love."

"Did Klast love Isabelle?" Peyton asked.

He hadn't sounded like it, but he could have glossed over a few things or other people saw it all differently. It was strange hearing someone say that *she* loved Klast. In a way, she guessed she did. She wasn't sure if it was more than friendship-type love though. She respected his personality and would help him out in a heartbeat. She'd help him even if she didn't have a heartbeat. He was fair to look at, and he made her want to sink into his praises, but he'd never acted in love with her. He'd held her when her clone was injured, which was what Tim was basing his assessment on. That didn't mean that Klast loved her. He'd told her he was angry with Isabelle, but there had to be more to it.

"See?" Tim pulled slightly away from their mother to look at their dad, who had jumped away from the window like he'd been scorched. "She understands everything that we say. She didn't lose all her memories. Just some major important ones."

"What happened with Isabelle?" Peyton asked again.

"Can you say the word 'yes'?" Tim asked her.

"Yes." Peyton rolled her eyes. She cleared her throat too. It was still scratchy. Some water would be nice, but she had no way of communicating that apart from miming the action. She did so, but no one jumped to her aid.

"Say the word 'no.'"

"No," Peyton answered as she regarded Tim.

He was trying to communicate with her. It was nice to have a supportive brother when she didn't feel the same vibes from her parents. Her mother treated her like she was wasted and gone, and her father was on the verge of casting her away from himself forever because he didn't like the name Burma. She didn't need them. She'd managed to live on her own before. She'd do it again.

"No need getting all defensive," Tim told her as if he too could feel the shift in her emotions. It had to be something in this room that amplified emotional connections. What was it? Peyton scanned the area again. Window. Brick walls. Glowing radio thing. Hospital bed. Three people she should know, but didn't. That made her frown. Her soul at least should recognize her own family. It felt like a betrayal that it wouldn't.

"Do you love Klast?"

"Maybe," Peyton answered.

Tim shook his head at her for not using the two words that he'd just learned from her, but what he was asking wasn't fair. He wanted her to distance herself from either her family or Klast in one fell swoop. She wasn't going to do that.

"What an awful question. Let's not start with that. Do you remember me?" the woman asked.

"No," Peyton answered.

"Mom, don't ask her that!" Tim chided. "I told you. Sysmat is a medical company that erases the memories of its patients. It then uses them as field agents to attack the minds of other people it deems important for future use."

"You heard that on the radio," her father accused.

"Clearly, that's what happened to her!" Tim pointed at Peyton.

"Sysmat was an evil company that I defeated!" Peyton agreed. "Now go away. I'm tired."

Of them. She'd come back to this when she had a better understanding of how to communicate. There was always Klast and Deek to help her out. They knew both languages. They would teach her what words to say and she could tell her family that Klast wasn't some evil liar. As for Mr. Burma, she recognized he was an important figure, but she still had questions about him. His intentions were probably good. His methods might not be the best.

Peyton shut her eyes. One would think that verbal speech and oral understanding would be linked, but her links were broken.

"Honey, don't close your eyes," her mother begged. "Don't go. You're doing it again. You can't do it again!"

Why? All she was doing was hunting for Klast and Deek. They were not as close to her as she would have liked. Not remotely close at all. The meanies. She woke up on Lexia and they were miles and miles away. The sparkles were trailing into the sky again.

"What happened to her blocker?" her mother gushed. "She's going to fade again!"

"It's gone, Mom," Tim answered. "But I think she'll be back. She's blazen. All this time, we've been stopping her from being blazen. Mr. Burma must have figured out what she was long ago."

"She's going away. She's going away! Make her stop!"

Nope. Peyton was going, especially with the strange notion that her own family had been stopping her before. If she had the words, she'd find out why. She couldn't ask them yet, so she had to go.

Peyton pinched her eyes tighter and shoved through the divide down to a more familiar planet where she could be with Klast and Deek. They were in the back seat of a car driving away from her, but it wasn't hard to slam herself through a crack in the open window, causing a tan dog to start barking obscenities at her from the front seat. Next to the dog was Bronze, who was driving. Deek snapped at Bronze's IB and howled with excitement. He was

Page | 283

looking clean and fluffy. Klast had shaved his face, which was a new one for her. His right arm was in a sling, hence Bronze driving, and his left leg was in a large bulky brace.

"Peyton!" Deek cheered.

This was a much better reaction to her arriving. Peyton smiled back, feeling her heart beat faster inside her body in excitement millions of miles away.

"Deek!" She cried back, trying and failing to hug him. Darn. She had no physical form like this, but she had presence. "I love you!"

He barked even louder. Instead of looking sad that she was still connecting to his dog, Klast looked downright smug about it. He must have gotten over the disorientation of losing his soul.

"You say that and you'll get to his head," Klast told her, mimicking giving her a high-five that she tried to feel. Oh, she wanted her body over here to feel this! Oh well. Her body couldn't move much right now. In this form, she was free to fly, regardless.

"Super weird," Bronze said from the front. He looked in the rearview mirror and then glanced over his shoulder. "All three of you can see her when all I can get is her voice if I strain really hard."

"She held my soul for a while," Klast pointed out. "If it weren't for that, I'd not be able to see her either. It should only be the dogs that can see her."

"But hear her?" Bronze asked.

"I think she wants to be heard," Klast replied.

His smile grew larger and larger as if he was battling down his emotions. Peyton tried to hug him. She failed on that, but the sentiment was there. He winked at her in return, which did something weird to her body back home. She was fairly certain that it blushed.

"I need to learn how to talk again!" Peyton cried out. "I think I met my parents and my brother. Is Tim's last name Finch? The Tim that got me off the street? They're in my room arguing and they can't understand a thing I say. I need to learn how to talk again."

"Sure," Klast grinned at her. "Just answer everyone with 'pass the bread, please.'"

Peyton laughed. "You forget that I can understand what you just said. That's not going to work on me. My problem is not being able to disentangle the words. They all get interpreted the same even if the movement of the mouth is different. I have to figure out how to train myself not to say what I hear, but say only what I see."

"A tricky situation," Klast answered. "Totally something I'm up to tackling."

He tapped the fingers on his good hand against the side of his leg. Peyton squealed and pretended to slump into the seat beside him. Deek scooted over for her. He was going to help her! With Klast on her side, she could accomplish anything.

"I missed you," Klast said.

It took Peyton a moment to pick out that he was talking in a language Bronze couldn't interpret. That would be a good phrase to use on her parents. Good thinking, Klast. If she could pretend that she was a part of their family, they might accept her better for the changes. Peyton tried to copy the sounds of what she was seeing. She didn't get it right because Klast laughed at her.

"No. I… missed…you," he said slowly.

Each word shot into her soul like he was uttering a truth, a secret one, that he didn't want anyone else to know yet. Peyton's heart gave a rapid jolt. There was no way she could repeat that phrase right now. What she could do was stay right here forever, basking in the comfort of Klast and Deek and their unfailing bravery and compassion. Perhaps what Klast was saying wasn't that he missed her, but that he loved her. Tim could be right. Given her own body, she might love him too. Startling.

"Was I asleep when you came to visit me? How long was I sleeping?"

"I don't know. I wasn't allowed to visit you," Klast answered.

"Why not?"

Klast shrugged at her and looked away as if he didn't want to tell her. Suspicion floated around her, but he made no mention if he could sense the feeling. Peyton looked at Deek instead. The dog would go against Klast if he thought it for the best, but Deek simply gave her a doggy grin and left it at that.

"So where are you going?" Peyton asked.

# 29

Where was he going indeed? He was running himself in circles. At the moment, he couldn't reach Peyton. Klast had hobbled down to Peyton's room once he got his face reconstructed, and ear replaced, and arm and leg braced up, only to be told to never show his face again. Not only was her family in the way (a large pain that), but the head of Human Rights sat outside of Peyton's door too. That man was even worse. He accused Klast of being a danger to Peyton abusing her goodwill when she needed extra emotional help. At that point, Klast had argued about Peyton's competency, and her family had stepped out of the room.

Since that family included Tim, Klast was shocked when Tim pretended that they were not friends. They were pals! Social rules in Lexia needed some fixing, because if Klast's dad told his friend to jump off a ledge and stay lost, he'd have told his dad to jump first. Not Tim. He stood there looking apologetic, staying super quiet.

From that enlightening conversation, Klast had only learned two things. One, Peyton's father hated him. Two, when Peyton was a small child, she would spend days sleeping, not waking up. They took her to different doctors to assess the condition, only to decide that there was nothing they could do. She laid around looking dead for days until some scientist devised a "blocker" that would keep her from traveling outside of herself. She could remain awake when she wanted to be awake, but she also developed a fetish for germs and refused to go most anywhere.

Klast took all of that to mean that she was soul traveling from a very young age in search of something. Her soul refused to settle, and he wanted to know why. There had to be more to it than simply having a "wind" soul, as Deek called it. The only sure way to know the answer was to get Peyton imprinted. Then the dog could tell him what the matter was.

It was perfect timing that she was hanging around, because Klast was going to visit a person he'd never gone to before. Bronze thought he was insane when he asked to go see the IB dog breeder, but Klast had done the research, and he had his mind set on a certain dog. If it didn't work out for

Peyton, then he wanted the animal as a breed dog to restart his career. He'd mentioned the breed dog part to Bronze and left out Peyton.

"Your silence could split a stone," Peyton claimed.

Hmm. All her words could make him turn giddy no matter what they were. That human rights activist had warned Klast that if Peyton haunted him, he was supposed to report it right away so they could stop her. Peyton didn't haunt people. She found them. She was the best backup one could ask for. Those stuffed necks could go sit in a museum. He was keeping her as long as she wanted to stay. He felt more connected to her than anyone else even though she had given his soul back.

"Your dog's silence is a wedgie," Peyton tried again.

She was so hard to ignore! Klast snickered.

"Bronze, where are we going?"

"Igene Barker's place," Bronze answered. "Klast wants to scout for a new breed dog there. I told him that mine are perfectly acceptable. They are way better than anything that Igene Barker has. Way, way better. You'll see what I mean when we pull up. His things are as wild as a skunk. They smell that way too."

"Oh. So Klast is in good company then." Peyton chuckled, even if he was cleaner than he'd been in weeks. She couldn't tell that, though. A soul didn't smell.

"This is a bad idea. Anything from the arena would be better. The breeders opened up several smaller arena locations after Sysmat closed down and are doing a longer showing. Does he go there? No. It's like he wants to breed demons."

"They are good dogs," Klast finally answered. He ignored the way Deek snorted in disagreement. The videos Klast had perused last night in an endless stream of dog spying kept leading him right back to Igene Barker. Call it intuition, but he had to go there.

"I call it dumb," Deek barked.

"It's not like I'll bring back a dog that I think you'll hate." Klast looked over at Deek, who was too busy staring at Peyton to look at him. He was probably trying to figure out why she strayed from her own body so much.

*"You don't like my answer,"* Klast huffed. *"She's searching for something. Something that her soul craves. It won't settle until she finds it."*

*"Doesn't have to be a dog,"* Deek thought back. *"Could be a person. Could be you."*

*"Really,"* Klast sighed. That would be amazing and all, but highly unlikely. *"She said hi to you first."*

*"It wasn't me she hunted down."*

"I hope you realize that your secret conversation that I'm not supposed to hear is highly hearable while I'm in this state," Peyton informed them.

"Well good," Klast said. "Then maybe you can tell us why you are not staying in your body."

"Because they are arguing over there and I haven't the means to reply. I told you," Peyton pouted. "And Tim mentioned some blocker that didn't sound good. And then there's the problem that I can't even sit up on my own, so what's the point?"

"Don't worry about it." Klast gave her what he hoped was a reassuring smile. "Deek and I will figure out the soul part. You can focus on the sitting up."

"Yeah well, maybe when they don't realize that's what I'm doing so they aren't staring at me fail. Besides, I wanted to see how you were doing. You said you'd teach me to talk."

"Won't happen all at once," Klast answered.

He glanced out the window before Deek could shoot him with a "told you so" look for Peyton being there only for him. He felt the look anyway, and Peyton laughed, but he didn't want to see it. Peyton had not been soul searching for him all these years. If she had, there would have been some large "aha" moment when she realized that she'd found him. Maybe it was simply something that blazen people did as a preliminary exercise to build up traveling strength. He'd never know without an imprinted source to think about it.

"You know what this means?" Peyton asked. "Everyone's acting like I used to do this before I knew what I was doing. So that means that my memories of going to lots of doctor's offices could be true."

"I'd look up your medical record so you can compare names and faces and wall colors," Klast offered, "if only I could."

"Exactly. You'd try to help me with something logical. You'd not start balling all over the floor or screaming at a window."

"I like the window idea," Klast smiled. "They don't scream back."

Peyton tried to shove his arm. Good thing she couldn't, because the pressure would have only reminded him how he was busted. He wouldn't lie to himself. It had been rough on him to ask for help that morning. Mike had shaved Klast's face. Bronze had helped with his pants and shirt. Deek had ordered Klast take-out when he couldn't make a simple sandwich without wanting to swear. He felt like a baby.

"And here we are. Welcome to the jungle. I hope you know what you're doing," Bronze said as he slowed down and turned off the road onto a dirt path.

There wasn't a sign or even a mailbox to show them where to go. Without Bronze, Klast would have passed the exit, especially since he was distracted by Peyton. Klast's father had said that it was creepy when she traveled around like this, but Klast found it comforting. It proved that Peyton was still alive and not blocked.

Deek stared out the windows jumping around the car to scope out the area. Bronze's dog, Cedar, chuckled at Deek like he was silly. Klast felt slightly scared. If Peyton had true memories of doctors in Lexia, what sorts of ideas had Sysmat taken from her? They would have only let her keep the connections so they could see them. They let the doctors they tortured remember all their doctor training after all.

It's over. Sysmat was over.

He so wanted to believe that, but if it was to come back again with information about how to transfer souls around like an IB dog, he needed to be ready to safeguard everyone he most cared about. He needed to understand what had blocked Peyton before and why. He needed to understand how she traveled. How long she could travel. How to tell if someone had invaded a soul.

"I'll help you out," Bronze offered as he stopped the car in front of a post that held a bunch of leashes. Igene Barker had been very specific about where they were to park.

Peyton squeezed out the window somehow and was walking around long before Klast got both his legs out. How far could she travel? Did she have to link onto a person before she could move around? Did she have a certain distance she had to stay to that link? So many questions. Maybe what she had been searching for wasn't one particular person, but a strong enough link. An IB dog could be just the ticket.

"Charming," Bronze grunted when Klast nodded that he was good enough to hobble around on his own.

Before them was a rundown shack with the roof caving in. The scratched-up door was hanging off the hinges. The windows were yellowed and broken. Paint peeled down the walls like melted crayon art drippings. Shingles hung off the room in random spots, and weeds grew between an old cobblestone path. No dogs were in sight, and one look at Deek and Cedar told Klast that he'd be venturing onward on his own. Their ears were back like a shrill sound only they could hear was warning Igene's dogs from running into the road.

"You going to push through it?" Klast asked Deek. Deek shook his head and then rushed back into the car along with Cedar. Klast didn't expect Bronze to leave the two dogs on their own in his fancy car and he was right. He hedged over to it and Klast grabbed at his clutch to lump down the rest of the path alone.

Igene Barker didn't sell his IB dogs in respected pools. He bred them for companies looking for hunter guards. Most of his dogs were stripped of their ability to imprint the instant they were born, but there were a few stragglers. One in particular kept creeping up on videos staring from the background.

For a man who prided himself on security, Klast felt rather insecure to not see a single dog as he walked. He didn't hear them either. One of them should be around here. Klast stumbled on rightly spooked. No dog tracks on the ground. No prints in the mud. No scraps of fur on the bushes or claw marks on the trees.

He had to stop a few times to give his busted leg a break. This was his first public appearance after all the Sysmat news. Igene would have seen it by now. If he hadn't been watching the news, then one of his buddies would have alerted him. It was dangerous for Klast to be here, but when did danger make him stop his plans? Klast's face was now famous for interrupting an IB arena and then getting Sysmat shut down. Hopefully, Igene would not pester him with questions about the event.

"The dude is just around that turn."

Peyton's voice made Klast jump, stumble, and then shake his head at himself. She flashed before him as she shifted in view. Hey! Not a bad thought. Perhaps being blazen was a different type of shifting. She shifted her soul instead of body and soul. He had figured out shifting so he could figure out blazen.

"All the dogs are in cages up there too. All except for a few that are sitting still as statues listening to you walk up."

Klast gave Peyton a thankful nod. This was the sort of information that Deek would have given him if he'd come with his sharper nose. It was nice to have some advanced knowledge since the silence had been getting to him. Now that he thought about it, not even birds were making noise. It was that sort of eerie silence—the silence of walking into a trap wounded and unprepared. Igene probably planned it that way on purpose. Hopefully, his dogs hadn't told him about Klast's informant ghost woman.

Who was he kidding? That would be the first thing the dogs noticed. A disembodied soul was wandering around. It was alarming just thinking about it. Oh well. If he was going to find an IB dog for Peyton, the dog would have to get used to the notion of her soul being gone.

Klast turned the bend, coming to rest on the edge of his crutch to take pressure off his busted leg. He wasn't supposed to be up and walking on it much yet, but he couldn't bring himself to use a wheelchair. Not for a meeting about a dog. He had to appear somewhat capable of caring for it.

Igene had an impressive, as in crowded, display of dogs. Four to a pen, they all stood there staring at him adding to the creepiness of his arrival. A couple of dogs outside of the cages didn't stand but lay there ready to jump at him if he got riled. Igene was in the middle of the display, watching him with eyes that portrayed he was just as trained at determining human traits as dog ones. Those eyes shifted over Klast and then looked directly at Peyton.

"I want you to be aware that I am recording everything and saving it in multiple locations in case there is any later discrepancy against me and my policies or my dogs."

Klast hated cameras. He hated how people saw things and made rash comments about them. When training IB dogs for dangerous situations, it was required to put them in dangerous situations so they could learn how to deal with stress and quick thinking. They needed to learn loyalty. They needed to learn when to listen and when to disobey. Seen through a one-sided lens, a lesson that took months to prepare for could appear cruel and unjust.

"You posting this recording?" Klast asked. He scanned the cages of the dogs carefully, trying to find the one that had been staring at him online.

*"Which dog?"* Deek asked from the safety of the car.

"I'll be posting it wherever I please until you find a way to take it all down," Igene grinned at him.

"Darn right, I'll be taking it down," Klast mumbled.

"For the record, I expected you to look worse," Igene told him.

"For the record, I expected you to look better," Klast replied.

There! Igene didn't flinch, but the light tan dog at the far end did. That would be his own IB dog. It was a one-and-a-half-year-old puppy. Igene noticed Klast's extra focus and frowned. Klast glanced away from the animal, scanning the pens again. Not there. It wasn't here.

"Where's the other dog?" Klast asked, braving to take a few steps closer and then stopping again because his leg was protesting. No sense in making his recovery fifty times worse.

"These are all the dogs."

"No. This one."

Klast carefully put weight on his good leg so he could reach with his good hand into his pocket and pull out his new phone. He flicked to the image he had saved of the dog. There it was. Still crying out to his soul somehow.

"I'd walk it closer to you, but we can both see how well that would go."

He angled the phone as best he could. The dogs' sharper eyes would be able to interpret the image for him, but Igene was nice enough to leave the safety of his overloaded pack of dangerous killers to see it for himself. The animal only showed up a few times in the movie clips. Each time was a few seconds, but the dog would look directly at the camera, saying something with those warm brown eyes. It had a creamy coat the color of aged ivory with one brown ear and one brown back paw. A real sweetheart despite where it was raised.

"I don't have that dog anymore," Igene stated as he recognized the picture.

He didn't get too close because Peyton swooped over to look as well. Klast didn't think Igene could see her, but his dog had to be warning him about some trick that Klast had brought with him. In the very least, it was confusing for a pup to see a wandering soul. Even Deek had trouble putting that thought into words.

Peyton grinned at the image and then eagerly started searching the cages. It wasn't there. Klast could pick out dogs fast. This one was remarkable. One look at it, and something about the animal whispered.

"Is this what you meant by your need to prove your innocence against illegal practices?" Klast asked. Not that it was illegal to not show a dog, but he could make it sound like it was. "You keep this one out in the forest and use it for hunting practice for all these other trained saboteurs?"

"Curse you," Igene spat at him. "I don't have that dog!"

"Where did it go?" Klast demanded.

For that matter, where had Peyton gone? She was no longer beside him or looking at the cages. She had horrible timing. He was upsetting a dog breeder who had the upper hand on him. Even if Deek rushed to his rescue, Klast would not make it out of this in one piece.

"I have honestly not seen it in four days."

"Four days," Klast mused.

That didn't mean that the dog wasn't around. It could have been trying to escape, or perhaps already had done so. Neither of those reflected well on a dog breeder. That was like admitting that you'd let an aggressive wolf out of a zoo.

"Does it come when called?"

Igene shook his head at him like he was stupid. That was the first thing anyone would have tried. The next step was sending out the other dogs to find it. He'd have looked already for the animal the first night it didn't return, but it could be trapped inside of something or using old scents to mask new ones.

"If I find it, can I have it?" Klast asked, instead of asking more questions that would get Igene upset. He had a few choice ones about his lack of finding the lost animal.

"Why?"

"I like it." Klast shrugged.

"You won't once you know what you're getting into. It was born mute. That dog can't bark, Klast. It can't guard if it can't alert anyone that there's an intruder."

A mute dog. That's why it wanted to leave this place. They regarded it as less than every other dog around it for the defect.

"Fifty thousand," Klast said as he glanced around, looking for Peyton. "Where did it go?"

"We looked. Four nights long we've looked," Igene sighed. "Can't you want some other dog? What do you want that dog for anyway? It's broken."

"I'm a little broken too if you've not noticed, and I didn't mean the dog that time. Where did the trailing soul go?"

That got a few reactions from the dogs, most notably Igene's dog who wagged his tail now that he could identify what Peyton was. Igene looked at his imprinted friend and sighed.

"It took one look at that picture and dashed off. You're being followed around by an almost dead person? Tell me honestly, why are you here?"

"I looked at that dog and thought Peyton should have it," Klast whispered, hoping that Igene wasn't miked with his whole recording business.

"*You* looked at the dog… and imprinted it for *someone else*?" Igene questioned. "People say weird junk about you, Klast, but I've never heard that one before."

Klast shrugged.

"Does that trailing soul belong to a person who has been on the news recently? The dog you're after went crazy after watching the news. Just dashed out the door and refused to be found ever since. I figured I'd get a call about her sometime within the next month when some cop found her wandering down a road."

"She?" Klast asked, even more interested. Female dog. Deek couldn't get upset with him for bringing back a girl.

"Yes, she, and I didn't see the person on the news. I had to drill the other dogs to get that information. They didn't know who the woman was. Did you just say Peyton, as in the Peyton who is a Sysmat agent? You're out of your mind. The dog is not for sale."

"It's not like you can stop an imprinting," Klast reminded. "I'll call you when I find her."

With that, Klast put his phone back into his pocket and turned to hobble away. He wasn't shocked when Igene gave his horde a signal to stay put and then slowly stepped out after him followed by his personal canine.

Igene was either going to take the money or he wasn't, but Klast was going to get that dog. It didn't matter to him if it was mute. The dog was perfect as she was and cute as a muffin. There were more ways to communicate apart from barking.

"What's the dog's name?"

"No."

Klast passed some invisible barrier because the caged killers behind him started snarling and making a fuss. After the unnerving silence, the growls rose the hair on his arms.

"Despite what you think about me, I don't sell dogs to half-dead women so they can die within a week."

"I gave a dog to a dying person before and it worked out great."

"Which says what about you?" Igene snapped. "That you're plum crazy. You came out of your encounter with Sysmat looking a quarter dead with your brains scrambled. Your friend has come out another quarter worse."

"She'll be fine. My friend is very good at surviving deadly encounters."

"The dog won't live, Klast. I have to have something that keeps the dogs inside my property. As many as I have, there's no way to constrain them without security measures in place. The dogs know what happens if they go out of bounds. Being half-imprinted makes an animal crazy and rash. She's not here, so she must have risked it and suffered the consequence. Not only can your dog not talk, but she won't be able to hear anymore either. Untreated blasted eardrums don't make for a long-lived dog. Don't go looking for her."

Double dirt potatoes! That's why Deek cowered away from the sound. Igene was bursting dog brains, and the muffin-eyed dog had been wandering half crazy in pain for four days, looking for a person on another planet.

"Klast," Igene tried again when he made no indication to reveal what he was thinking. "Do yourself a favor and let this one go."

"Does the dog handle the vet well?" Klast asked, not about to let it go when he knew Peyton had seen the animal. If she'd not shown up today, he'd let it go, but she had seen it. A girl like that and she'd feel half imprinted forever. She'd always be looking for the missing half! Maybe she'd already been imprinted to something and lost it long ago without realizing it. What though? It wasn't like IB dogs existed on Lexia.

Those evil Burmas. Stole her away…. It was something her father had been screaming about.

"Please drop this."

Klast fumbled with his new phone again and called his dad. Nothing. The man was ignoring him. He tried Tim next. It seemed more likely to him that Tim would ignore him too, but he picked up on the first ring.

"Interpret," Tim demanded first, holding the receiver close to a girl stuck on a hospital bed.

It was awful. Peyton was slurring words together, both from his world and from hers, making no sense about what she was saying at all. Igene's dog at his heels whimpered and hunched downward as if that was a sign that the person it could hear was too unfit to chase any longer. Better to leave that broken person alone.

Igene was right. Half imprints were dangerous. They were the things that could kill people in arenas. They created starving creatures who became consumed with only one desire—locating the missing part. It was a rather powerful connection, one that Klast was glad Sysmat hadn't cracked yet.

"She's starving," Klast answered. "Do you happen to know anything but your dad's accusation that Peyton was stolen when she was younger? Is it possible that she encountered a soul dog years ago?"

Given her age and the dog's age, that half-imprinted dog could have just died, leaving her free to pick another. It was possible. Jethro had found a way to lock up a Shadow clone undetected leaving Klast with a half connection. Sysmat would be his excuse for why he never told Klast what he'd done. Klast hadn't confronted his father about it because this was his dad, and he respected his father for trying to save him. However, the hidden Shadow clone had done more harm than good on Klast's psych. His father should have seen that and put the dog down.

He didn't. For years Jethro kept the creature locked away as if *Jethro* was the one who wanted to study the effects of half connections. If that was true, why not lock away a half-imprinted dog that had seen Peyton's picture? His father could have initiated a half connection long ago with Peyton as his first victim. Her soul kept running off trying to find what was lost.

Klast swallowed. The thing he had been missing! He was overlooking his father's part in all of this because he didn't want to see it. It looked like his father had been the one studying effects of imprinting so that he could control it. And if his father was into that, and *Mervolk* was created to strip souls, and soulless people were wandering Hyphas taken from the void, and Klast had felt it in his best interest to avoid communication with Jethro unless he did something drastic like pretend to die, then Klast could only conclude that it was his father behind everything all this time. The person they put in jail for running Sysmat was a memory lost decoy. Or if the jailed man really was the director, his father knew enough of the ins and outs to use the technology that Sysmat capitalized on. He could revive the entire organization that Klast had tried to shut down. That's who had tipped them off about the invasion. Jethro had gone in, wiped memories, and hidden everything he wanted to use for himself.

This wasn't exactly over.

Klast's breeder dogs wouldn't have stripped away at his soul, clone or otherwise, without great outside pressure. They wouldn't have given in to some stranger from Sysmat. But put Klast's dad in the picture and things changed. Klast trusted his dad. They'd let the man get close to them without suspicion. He'd must have wiped their brains himself.

Then there was the whole thing about Klast's siblings never traveling into the void or even considering it. His siblings had to wear blockers just as Peyton had done. His dad was the one to figure out what could block a shift, and he had used Peyton as his experiment so he could keep his kids where he wanted them. Klast simply found IB dogs before his father could block him.

"I'm going to puke," Klast complained.

"I don't think we've fed her close to a week!" Tim blurted reminding Klast that he was still on the phone with Tim. "I'm sorry! Mom thought that I had taken care of it and Dad thought the doctors had, but there's no record of it anywhere."

"Will you just feed Peyton already?" Klast snapped.

The poor girl was starving, both body and soul. What a horrible way to feel. Peyton wasn't out here searching for the lost dog. She had returned to her body to help her find it, but she couldn't move. Klast shivered. He knew what blazen was. Peyton was a natural shifter, only she still had that blocker somewhere so that her body couldn't travel with her.

After proving that she could soul search without moving her entire body, his father had introduced her to Sysmat to control the direction she went so she could scoop up soul pieces. Sysmat was never going to invade Lexia. His father had simply allowed Klast to run with that theory because he had to do something to keep Klast off track. Plus, it gave him a great excuse to personally invade the organization.

"Yes, of course," Tim answered.

Klast hung up on Tim without telling him any of his thoughts, and found himself calling the head of security again. Jonas Stilkins answered on the second ring.

"I can't prove it, but I have another tip for you," Klast said.

"Hardly a thing a man wants to hear again."

"Yeah, and I can't prove it. Not at all. The guy leading Sysmat might be jail, but I know of another person who has access to all the tech it was using and making. He lives between two different planets and walks around under the name of Jethro Burma."

"Klast is this a joke?" Mr. Stilkins asked sternly. "Don't mess with me."

"He hid away the first clone of my IB dog Shadow for years. It just hit me how he's been controlling Peyton. She's half imprinted. That's why her soul can travel around without her. Sysmat's technology is able to study the effects of cloning and Jethro has been using their tech to study the effects of soul separation."

"Klast."

"If you don't hear from me again, please dig really deep for events around my strange accident. I'm hardly in a state to defend myself right now. This is going to get back around to him. He's going to come for me."

Klast clicked off the phone again and shoved it into his pocket, more anxious than ever to return to Deek. How long did he have? How long did Peyton have? He needed to reach his protection. He needed to get Peyton better protected too. He needed that missing defending killer dog!

# 30

Ow! Everything hurt. Peyton thought she was done with the nosebleeds because she wasn't a clone. She shouldn't have thought that at all. Every time she thought she was cured, it was only to turn around and find herself right back where she had started. The only good thing about the nosebleed was that it got her father to prop her upright so she wasn't forced to swallow draining blood. The rest of her was shaky and utterly exhausted. Not only did her body feel strained this time, but her soul did too. There was no other way to explain it apart from "balloon." She had gotten so used to the feeling of being overly inflated that it was strange to feel flat. Her soul was flat as if it was missing something. What was anyone's guess.

She could remember words fumbling around her head and coming out of her mouth right before she woke up. Her mother had rushed out the door to find a doctor to stop Peyton from "doing that weird talking thing again."

It shouldn't surprise her that she had done this before, but it did. What weird talking thing? All the words made perfect sense to her, even if they were clipped like dog speech. Hunt. Back. Dog. Find. Hurt. Dog. That had to make sense to other people. Those phrases were a sentence.

How she wanted Klast! Like really, really badly. She'd had cravings for medication before, so the only thing she could compare this deep desire to was a craving. Either that or desperation. Klast would save her. All these years of holding onto the thought to save him, and she needed him to reverse it. Perhaps the craving was as strong as it was, because she knew that he had reversed it.

Klast wasn't out looking for a breed dog. He had been searching for a dog for her. It was the sweetest thing ever. Peyton took one look at the picture of the adorable animal and found herself wanting it on a whole new level. This was even worse than wanting to be with Deek. She wanted that dog like her entire body depended on it. The image was burned into her head, embedded in her cells and molecules. The aggravating part was that instead of staying with Klast to find it, she had found herself back in her own weak body. Screaming was the first thing she did. She wanted to go back! She had to go back! The dog was down there!

A cup was shoved up against her lips. Too late for that. She pushed it away. This wasn't the time for water. She needed to reach the dog. Not even closing her eyes let her go where she wanted to go. The sparkle trails refused to materialize as if she was too weak to pull it off right now. The hardest part was knowing that she couldn't find the dog even if she strained herself again. She was limited to searching for souls she had encountered before. That didn't include a picture of a dog housing a special soul, even if the picture was the thing that had awakened this unforeseeable yearning.

"You have to at least drink something!"

Tim. Her brother was annoying. She shoved the cup away again, aware of the way her dad held her, pressing cloth to her nose to keep the blood from getting everywhere. No one could drink with a bloody nose.

"Klast said you need to eat," Tim insisted.

"Find him!" Peyton screamed. That came out in the right language, right? She couldn't tell anymore. She'd not been able to tell the difference for a long time. There was something wrong with her, something that even Klast wouldn't be able to fix.

"We agreed to not talk about Burma's," her father grated.

"You never talk about it. What happened to her, Dad? She was fine when we were really little. I remember playing with Peyton and everything being lovely until all of this started up. You never told me what happened."

"I don't know."

"Then how do you know to blame the Burmas?"

"One has only to look at them and their actions to know they are suspicious."

"Mr. Burma is suspicious. He totally mumbled that Klast would be hard to kill off."

She still felt uncomfortable with that. Why should his father care if his son was hard to kill? He should be happy that Klast was going to live a long life. There were so many things one could learn from Klast about being happy around incredible sadness. Klast was inspiring.

"You heard that, right?" Tim asked.

What? Peyton strained her ears. It could be her dog! Klast could have found it already and was going to bring it to her. He'd find a way. That's what he did. It's who he was. The miracle dog man.

"Mr. Burma is trying to kill his son?" Peyton's dad whispered.

Oh. They hadn't heard her dog. They had understood a sentence for once! Funny that the only sentences she could get herself to say over here were ones that led to suspicion and hatred. Ugh. She was cursed.

"Peyton?" Tim nudged her arm. "You have to eat something. You're too skinny to keep skipping meals. You're going to die."

Death! That had to be what the nosebleed was about again. When she got close to dying, her nose let her know. Fine. She'd drink the water, because if she didn't, then she wouldn't be alive long enough to see her dog. It took nearly two minutes for her to get her arms to obey her wishes. Tim and her father watched her slowly raise trembling limbs. One hand held the cloth over her nose, the other reached for the cup.

"Mr. Burma locked Klast up recently," Tim whispered once he made sure that Peyton had swallowed. "He was in a soul cage in the administration building, standing there stuck for hours. His legs were shaking when he stepped out and that was before they were broken."

"You think his dad was trying to kill him? Why?"

"I didn't say that. If Mr. Burma had wanted Klast dead, it wouldn't have been that hard to finish the job while Klast was trapped. He was in a standing cage. No room to move any direction."

Peyton gripped the cup tighter, trying to decide if she knew about this before or not. It was hard to say. Her entire head was woozy. There was more to this food thing than she was giving credit. She couldn't think without the resources to do so. She took a sip. Okay, her soul felt vastly different. What had just happened? She was missing the larger picture. Her family was understanding her again as if the pressure sitting on her soul that prevented her speech had left.

"You need to think like a criminal if you're going to see a criminal, Tim. Look what happened to Klast after he got out of that cage. How did he get out?"

"Hank let him out," Tim whispered back. "We went looking for him to tell him that Peyton had been taken…"

By Mr. Burma. Peyton snapped her eyes open and looked at Tim.

"That was a clone version of me that I had given my consciousness to. Mr. Burma left me beside a clone of Klast's imprinted dog Shadow."

"Why?" Tim asked. "What happened then?"

They were understanding her! She couldn't talk about other things, but somehow, she could talk about this. Weird.

"I fixed Klast's soul," Peyton answered as she squinted. The lights in here were too bright. Gah. Her chest thumped in her chest and she felt clammy as if she'd said something false. What?

"You fixed part of his soul?" her dad asked, impressed.

"Yeah. I've been doing it for years. Tracking down missing parts of Klast's soul and getting them back to him. I… I came up with some system to defeat Sysmat by restoring Klast, but I can't fully remember what it was."

"And is Klast fully restored?" Tim questioned.

Peyton shrugged. He was mostly better, but he'd never be what he once was. "Sysmat is taken down."

"Klast gets his soul back and ends up nearly dying in a dog attack where you were used as the bait," Tim pointed out. "Could you have died from that encounter?"

"Easily."

"You both could have died before revealing that Mr. Burma had a clone of Klast's soul dog."

"Well sure, but..."

This version of her suspected Mr. Burma of using Klast to mimic connections because he wanted an IB dog of his own and couldn't get one, but Tim's question had her thinking a little deeper about it all. She knew she'd done things she couldn't remember that left her feeling guilty. What if she'd done it again? She hadn't given Klast anything when her clone died, and she would have taken back the sliver of his soul that the Shadow clone had been holding. Where had that gone?

Furthermore, with her ability, Sysmat's rules of where she was allowed to sparkle hunt didn't make sense. Why would one city be illegal while another one safe unless she was forbidden from using the power in places that Klast himself would be at? It wasn't like walking into a new city changed much of the sparkle trail. It stretched onward regardless of city boundaries. If it was illegal in one place, it should be illegal everywhere. All those restrictions only applied to her, not other agents. She was too sick to see that.

She had spent years trying to locate Klast's cast out soul pieces, and she was finally starting to realize her nefarious role. She hadn't returned his soul. She had destroyed it. She simply fabricated a story about her heroics instead of her evil deeds because she didn't want to look at the truth. Klast's breed dogs were not trying to kill him off. They were saving him! They were casting parts of him out far and wide to stop *her* from taking his soul away.

"We are so stupid!" Peyton screamed, and she knew she was back to speaking Muthreney, the language in Hyphas, by the looks on her family's faces. "We undermined the lifeline!"

All this time she thought she was being sneaky, but somebody had to know what she had been up to and used it all against her. Some deeply ingrained program in her real mind or body had her snuffing the links. She had turned soulless before "giving" Klast back the second half of his soul. Soulless as in she had nothing to actually give him, and yet she'd given him something.

If Klast figured out her betrayal, he was going to hate her. He'd never talk to her again. There he was trying to secure an IB dog for her, but he'd stop trying once he learned she didn't repair souls. She destroyed them. What half soul had she put into Klast? Was it even his own? His was gone because she had killed it.

# 31

Igene seemed to not like a word Klast had said on the phone, but destroying evil organizations was his sole purpose in life. An organization like Sysmat was too much for him to ignore, especially since he had a dog connected to it now. He'd turned off the ear-destroying field and carried his pup across the invisible line while the thing trembled in his arms. Then he had agreed to help Klast look further for his lost dog. "Looking" meant that Klast was being used as bait.

Igene had been recording the encounter, so he had recorded Peyton over the phone mumbling incoherently. Klast was currently standing on a hill, repeating the sounds over and over. Not that he expected the deaf dog to hear it and come running, but there was more to it than that. The wild thing would have instincts. Peyton's soul had marked Klast. Klast was armed with the recording, a picture, and her mark waiting for the dog to find him.

Igene and his pup were standing downwind, out of sight. Bronze was circling the area, unable to stand still. He'd probably seen the crawling dog first, but he'd not done anything to mess up the plan. There she was, with blood dried on her ears, trailing down the side of her head, unable to stop herself from trying to reach Peyton. Her creamy coat was burred, tangled, and splattered in mud. She looked hungry and weak, which was unfortunate since Peyton needed better protection, and she needed it now. Deek stood right beside Klast, fur bristling as the dog crawled closer. Her eyes stayed on the threatening dog, while her heart moved her onward. To death would she crawl. It was a sad thing to see how far a body would go to satisfy the soul.

"Easy Deek," Klast told him. "She needs to get closer."

Then he'd sedate her. He didn't trust the shot that Igene had handed to him, but he did trust the one from Bronze. It was fabulous to have Bronze with him, if only for that. Klast never carried around sedatives. Too easy for something like that to be used against him, but Bronze had a couple of shots for emergencies.

Despite her battered state, Klast could only see the beauty of the dog. She was capable of killing. Capable of carrying out unthinkable missions without explanation. She desired to please the hand that fed her until now. Now she was confused and scared and torn between love and mind. She stopped halfway up the hill and collapsed to her belly. If she could whine, she would have. Klast wanted to rush down to her and scoop her up into his arms. He wanted to soothe her aches. He wanted to kiss her nose, and that scared him, too. He shouldn't be yearning for Peyton's dog. Not at all. He had his own.

"Come on, Muffin," Klast waved her forward. "Do you want to see Peyton?"

The animal didn't move. It was stupid for her to get any closer. Closer and she could be shot. She was wounded, but not dumb. She had seen Peyton already. While Klast would feel like the person the dog wanted to find, he didn't look like the woman. Therefore, the dog had to assume that something was wrong and that this was a trap. She would do anything to protect the soul of the person she loved, and once she made the connection with what she was looking at in Klast, she was going to charge up the hill and try to kill him. He had part of Peyton's... Wait! That's not how it was supposed to work! Peyton hunted him down by leaving part of her soul with him, but it wasn't supposed to be large enough for him to sense what dog she was going to fall in love with.

Klast shook his head. He'd worry about that part later when he talked to Peyton again. She'd be able to sort that out. He had to figure out how to get the wounded dog closer. She would not make the first move, even if she had come out in the open to reveal herself. If she charged upward, not only could she be shot, but Deek was there fit to pounce.

"You're going to have to lure her closer," Klast told Deek. "She'll see that I'm wrong. Easy as that. I have my soul, right? I'm starting to question this connection..."

He looked down at his silent dog. Deek was staring at Muffin communicating with his eyes a message of dominion over the man beside him. Deek said nothing about the current nature of Klast's soul. Not good. Peyton had given him half a soul from the void. It was supposed to be his. The other part he regained had come from his deceased clone dogs. He had felt much better after getting it, but he had still been unsettled, and Deek hadn't told him anything one way or another regarding what he could see.

There was never a moment that Deek smiled at him and said, "You have your full soul back."

"Deek?"

"Down!" Deek screamed as he lunged at him.

No! Deek barked and Muffin spooked. She went racing away even if she was weak. Klast went crashing to the ground as his leg buckled beneath him. The dumb dog! Bad, bad dog!

"Get off!" Klast screamed. He couldn't let Muffin get away! He needed to reach her!

"What's wrong with you?!" Igene screamed at him from below. "You fight with your bonded dog? First rule of the book, Klast. Always trust your bonded dog. What happened to you?!"

"Stupid animal," Klast mumbled as he tried to push Deek off.

"Stay," Deek snarled at him as he jumped off and went crashing down the hill.

Deek couldn't tell him what to do! He wasn't in charge. Klast made it up to his knees, only to find himself being shoved back over this time by Igene's pup. It pounced on him and pinned him, going directly for a neck hold.

"You're messed up, dude," Igene declared. "There is something seriously wrong with you."

"It was necessary to build mistrust between us to survive," Klast spat dirt out of his mouth. "Now get off."

"No. No owner should ever have a reason to mistrust his dog. There's something out there. Your dog told you to stay down. You're staying down."

"I hope you're recording this. Everyone will know how unsafe you are."

"People are going to see you fighting with your bonded dog. Shut up so I can listen. I'm not posting this. I have no desire to destroy you for what happened to you, but you will shut up."

Klast took in a breath to reply, only to feel the pup's teeth tighten on his neck. Message taken. He would not talk. He slowly let his breath out and focused on not talking while trying to keep his anger down. This was stupid. Nothing was here to get him. Igene had them in the back of some farm on a hill where they could watch Peyton's dog arrive. Deek couldn't have sensed anything that would warrant Klast being stuck to the ground like this. The dog was betraying him. Running off on him when Klast needed his help.

Klast wanted to shoot darkness from his hands; to bring in the power of the void to propel himself upward and away from the dog on his neck. But he shouldn't. He didn't lose control of himself anymore. He couldn't. The last time he'd spooked like this and shot the void through his hands, he had destroyed an entire building. It happened to be the building that Isabelle had been standing in. She had trapped him into marrying her. He refused and panicked. Big time.

He hated feeling trapped! He could storm into a pile of clone dogs set to kill him without wanting to burst the world apart, but get him stuck like this, and everything changed. Without the option to rush free, the option to shift, he felt a demon clawing at the back of his soul. Escape! Escape!

Klast clamped his eyes shut. He would not shoot the void. He couldn't shoot the void. He was going to trust Deek. He was going to trust the traitor. Trust that Deek had a better sense of the world than he did. Trust the dog that he loved more than anything.

More than Muffin?

Yes! He had to love Deek more than Muffin! He had to. Gosh. What was wrong with him? Where was Deek?

The ground didn't give him vibrations, but with his eyes shut, there was a colorful glow trailing off in the direction that Deek had run. Odd. Klast pinched his eyes tighter and focused on the line. He tried to yell when he felt part of his soul float away. No! He couldn't do this! He didn't have a blocker that stopped his body from moving! He wasn't blazen! He must have gotten it wrong. Peyton had no blocker. Her soul simply floated away and was taking his along with it this time.

Upward he went until he was left looking down on his trapped body. The colorful lights in the air got stronger now that he had disconnected. They would lead him directly toward Deek, but he didn't want to go there. He wanted to find where Muffin had hidden. He wanted to find Peyton so she could help him. He tried to drift in the opposite direction, only to discover that it was impossible. The line dragged on him, pulling him forward, leaving him no choice but to follow. How was this better? He had to break free. He had to!

An unreal sensation of gathering the void between his mortal hands tickled the back of his thoughts. Oh no! He couldn't bring the void when he wasn't controlling what he was doing. He had to go back! He had to return to his body to stop himself! Only it was impossible!

Hoping that reaching the end of the line would allow him to return, he pushed himself forward faster and faster in the direction of Deek. The dog would see him and then take him back. Klast hoped that Deek wouldn't spook too much to see him like this. Closer and closer. He could sense the dog moving before he saw him. He could feel a spark of Deek's emotions, and it struck Klast as amusing that Deek felt rather sure of himself instead of confused as Klast was. Klast got right next to Deek. His ears were perked, and he was chasing after something down a bean field that Klast couldn't make out. He paused, looked directly at Klast, and without a sound continued on his way.

"That was it? I find myself more broken than ever before and you run off?" Klast complained. At least the glowing sparkles had stopped. That would allow him to return to himself.

Find Muffin?

No. He shook the idea from his head and then opened his eyes again, unsure how he had made it back. One minute he was looking at Deek, the next he was here. Igene's pup still had him by the throat, but he could hear Bronze approaching.

"Klast? You in there?" Bronze asked.

"Where else would I be?" Klast said before he remembered he wasn't supposed to talk. The dog bit down tighter. He squirmed.

"Get that dog off him!" Bronze demanded.

"Ease up," Igene ordered, but the order wasn't to get the dog off completely. It only had the dog release his neck. The pup was still close enough to bite.

"Cedar said that you left yourself for a bit. I don't know… What's going on? Did you see your dad?" Bronze asked.

"I can't be near my dad!" Klast screamed, shoving himself upward with the force that had been gathering inside his fingers.

He had to get up! His dad was here! That's why Deek had shoved him down!

The ground beneath Klast exploded, sending chunks of the hill into his face and launching him perfectly to his wobbly feet. Igene's pup growled instead of whined as he was thrown through the air. Igene himself pulled a gun out on Klast as he staggered out of the way of the unknown force. Bronze raised his hands in mock surrender, but he wasn't really. He was just as ready to tackle Klast as any of them. His dog perched, ready to constrain Klast next.

"I can't be near my dad," Klast repeated, glancing around in search of him. It was no use. His father could shift in and out of a place on a whim. "I can't. He turned Peyton blazen. If he turns me blazen, then he has no need for Peyton anymore. I can't lose Peyton. Where is her dog? She needs her dog!"

This was the worst! All it took was one fatal stab and Peyton was done for. His dad didn't even need to stick around long. He could hop into the hospital room in Lexia and pop back out just as quickly.

"No idea what blazen means," Bronze answered, "but I got the dog. It's in the back of my trunk. Promise."

Bronze had neutralized Muffin when she bolted. That proved that Deek wasn't chasing her. He was running away from Klast. Running as if his life depended on it. Trust the dog. Klast had to make himself trust the dog. He looked down at the ground and the small crater he was leaving in his wake.

This was what he was capable of when under a mountain load of stress. He exploded things. The force was coming out of him without him even wanting it to. That made him feel reckless and scared at the same time. He'd worry about it later.

"We need to get Peyton and the dog together. Maybe they'll find a way to keep each other alive."

Klast took off toward Bronze's car. He ignored the whispering that came behind him as Bronze and Igene talked about him. Let them say what they wanted. He had more important things to deal with than speculation and rumors. He ignored the tickle in his nose. Then he ignored the blood that poured out of it. Peyton. He was turning into Peyton!

Deek had run off to safeguard the part of Klast's soul that he carried before anything worse happened to it. Klast had to save Peyton so she could save him. Again. He took another step wobbling against his vision turning black. The dark overtook him like a tunnel starting from the outside of his irises and traveling inward to the center until he was walking without being able to see. He took another step.

# 32

Beep, beep, beep, went the sound of a heart monitor. Peyton wanted to find it and chuck it across the room. She lifted her arm, only to feel a trailing line. IV. She was hooked back up to one of those. Did they have those in Lexia?

Her eyes shot open and her pulse skyrocketed. Beep! Beep! Beep!

This couldn't be. The walls were white. The hours that she had been asleep were posted beside her on a monitor. She should be done with the whole clone business! Yet here she was, waking up beside her doctor like it was a regular day in Sysmat.

"No!" Peyton screamed before clutching her throat. It was still raspy. She hadn't changed bodies. She'd simply been kidnapped again.

"Welcome back, Peyton," her doctor said, stepping closer to her and looking at the monitors even if he had nothing better to do than examine them while she had been asleep for... twelve hours and ten minutes. The last thing she remembered was Tim. It appeared that she had passed out after that. The doctor reset the time to show she had been awake for under a minute.

"I know you are not happy to see me, but I'm sure happy to see you. Some men in suits sprang me from a psychiatric ward because I'm intimately familiar with your case. You probably remember, but the last time we spoke, you told me to save a life. I did my best. How are you feeling apart from disoriented?"

She didn't answer.

"Take your time. Maybe I can answer a few questions before you ask them. We're in the Clydesdale Hospital near South Port. As far as hospital rooms go, this one is rather roomy, although it appears smaller with the other occupants."

What other occupants? She struggled to sit up to see. Turning her head only showed her a white wall and her monitors. Behind the monitors was a window on a far wall, but that's as far as she got.

"Your case has always been particularly interesting. You come and go sometimes looking like you know where you've been. From your expression, I take it that you were not aware you were sleeping for twelve hours. I didn't think that I'd ever find another person that matched your condition, but here you both are. Once the gentleman wakes up, I'm hoping he has something to say on the matter."

"Who?" Peyton rasped out. Annoying throat!

"They didn't tell me his name," her doctor came even closer and knelt beside her bed. That was a first as far as she could remember. "If I figure out his name, I'm not supposed to say it. I took his picture," he whispered. "Not supposed to. No images or recordings allowed, but I couldn't help it. This man was not like this a few days ago. I *know* he wasn't."

Her doctor held up his phone and Peyton's heart froze. Bzzzzz!!!! Her heart monitor screamed, alerting everyone within hearing range that her heart stopped. Klast. What had happened to Klast?! How had they both ended up in here on Hyphas?!

"Don't be too alarmed. I'm capable of keeping a person such as yourself alive. The man over there," he thumbed over his shoulder and Peyton's heart started beeping erratically again, "has gone in and out of himself about thirty times in forty minutes. Very unsettled. You never rush about that much."

"What happened?"

She got a shrug in reply and her first smile of the day. "All we were told was that we needed to tend to the patients. There's a dog in here too and a vet. From what I could gather, the surgery was a success. Reconstructed eardrums and vocal cords on the dog. The throat looked like it had suffered a dog bite years ago. The broken ears were new."

Igene had lied to them. Her dog wasn't born mute. Peyton sighed and failed at sitting up.

"Did you get the dog's name?" she asked in vain.

A shake of the head was her answer. Then her doctor started in on his usual questions out of habit. Peyton looked at the ceiling and refused to answer the Sysmat psychology.

"Perhaps you can shed some light on things," her doctor said once he got his previous programming out of the way. "The man in the other bed was attacked by clone dogs. Is what happened to you an attack from a clone dog? Your answer would help locate a cure."

She shook her head. Next thing she knew, she was looking at her monitor again and the time had changed. Asleep for nine hours and forty minutes. Not again! Her heart rate monitor started beeping, but her doctor didn't rush to her side. She could hear him on the other side of the room instead.

"In about another hour or so?" he asked.

"Yup," a female voice answered.

"And no one thought it a good idea to tell us anything about the IB dog? That thing could be lethal when it wakes up."

"That dog *is* lethal," the woman agreed. "I managed to locate it. It was bred by Igene Barker who sells in bulk to security companies. There are no records of the dog selling, so it still belongs to him. It should be alright, though. Everyone says that this guy right here is a dog whisperer. He can calm the worst and he spots the best."

"I know who he is," her doctor whispered back, "but he's not going to be much help this time."

"He just woke up."

"That wasn't him," her doctor answered. "Trust me. It wasn't. There's a reason he's strapped down to the bed and Peyton is not."

"No names!"

"Sorry. Hold on. Peyton is awake again. I need to ask her more questions."

"Your questions are annoying," Peyton croaked as her doctor approached her bed, along with a curly black-haired woman in purple scrubs. That would be the vet. She had a stethoscope around her neck and wore a paw print necklace. "Is my dog okay?"

It had to be her dog. Deek hadn't lost his hearing or his voice. Klast must have been the one to shift through the void and grab her to bring her beside the dog. Then either he or Bronze had arranged for the doctors. What didn't make sense was how Klast was strapped down.

"Is it your dog, honey?" the vet asked, casting a glance near Peyton's feet where the dog had to be resting. She looked relieved at the thought.

"Almost. Klast was going to buy her for me. What happened? Have you seen Klast's dog?"

Both doctors shook their heads, and neither one got upset with her for using names.

"Can you interpret what this says?" Her doctor held up his phone again. The vet crossed her arms about the break in protocol, but Peyton didn't mind. It showed her Klast again. He was indeed strapped down to his hospital bed and hooked up to so many monitors that he looked like he was dying. Peyton wasn't sure how to respond when the video started. Klast had his eyes open, and he looked aware, but what he was saying had to be his base language because neither doctor could understand it.

"Bad dog. Get back here! Stop running from me! The demon will rise. At least head toward Peyton so I can see if she's alright! You're going the wrong way! The demon will rise. My nose was bleeding. Must stop. Blazen. Unbelievable. Power of the void. Hey! The demon will rise."

The video paused as Peyton shivered. Her breathing was catching in her throat, but her heart was beeping a lot. The vet turned down the volume on her monitor.

"You said one of those phrases a lot too. Can you explain what it means? That last part. What is it?"

Demon. This was Klast's soul yelling through his mouth the things he couldn't get across otherwise. Yelling about a demon. Had she given him a demon? No. That wasn't right. She would know if she had been transferring around a demon. Besides, she was fairly certain that she had given Klast parts of her own soul. A little over half, to be exact. What one could repair, one could destroy. She'd tried to honestly save him by offering the only thing she had left which was her soul that could repair.

The demon then, had to be some other invasive soul that neither of their bodies liked much. It must have come from Jethro. He'd found or created some other demon soul that was bent on destroying the other souls it came in contact with probably for its own survival. It must not have its own body to walk back into anymore.

Where was Deek? She needed his opinion on this. What sort of soul was inside of Klast?

"If my dog wakes up—"

"Hold on," her doctor waved at her. He flicked his phone to a new recording. "Okay. Now go."

"If my dog wakes up before me, ask her to compare the composition of my soul with Klast's. If she can't figure out what she is looking at, then have her at least guess. Klast should have more than one soul. Two at the least. There could be a soul in there that doesn't have a body to return to. It's scared and cruel and eating away at him. He might also have fragments from past dogs. He's imprinted two dogs on a deeper level. No idea how many I've gone through, but I was imprinting clone dogs as a clone, stretching myself out all over the place. The phrase he keeps talking about claims there is a demon."

"When you wake up? Where are you going?" her doctor asked with a slight hint of excitement that he tried to constrain for professional reasons. Peyton smiled at him. She'd hated him, yes, but he had been trying his best to help.

"I'm going to see if I can figure out what I was trying to do when I moved my soul into my clones. I was working toward something. I was trying to repair Klast, but it looks like everything was twisted around and used against me. Things I did to save him rendered him vulnerable. I'm going to look at this from a different perspective. Be right back. I hope."

Peyton shut her eyes.

"Oh my gosh!" her doctor cried out. "She actually remembers! I think I'm going to cry. I'm really going to cry. I've spent years trying to help her remember where her soul goes."

"It was sixteen months," Peyton informed. She pinched her eyes tighter.

"Months?"

"Yeah."

"Who told you that?"

"Mr. Burma," Peyton replied as she snapped her eyes back open. She had to find him and stop him before that man found his son again. It would be nice if she had a body to use, but she was devoid of that right now.

"How long was I in Sysmat?" Peyton asked.

"Six years."

While she wanted to claim that her doctor would lie to her, she couldn't bring herself to do it. She herself had felt like it was five years at least. This fit her first thoughts a lot better than sixteen months.

"If you happen to see Klast's father, shoot him." He was a horrible liar.

"I'm a doctor!" the man protested.

"We don't carry guns," the vet told her.

Peyton's head strayed toward Klast even if she couldn't see him, only to be told that his gun had been taken away for safety purposes by the man who brought him in. Bronze. It had to be. Where had Mr. Burma gotten off to? Sysmat wasn't over because Jethro was still out there, using his technology against Klast. He'd done something to him like infect Klast with a demon. She had to find all traces of it so she could siphon it out.

Holding her eyes tightly shut, she wanted to hunt for traces of demon souls, but the sparkly lines rose before her, trailing her off in quite another direction as if she couldn't venture around until she found a piece of herself that was broken even after resting for a long time so she could restore her body enough to hunt again.

Peyton raced back through the void, back to Lexia. She zoomed directly toward Mr. Burma unable to keep herself away as if he was calling to her. She'd been lost to him now that Klast ran off with her back to Hyphas. Jethro couldn't reach her physically, but he could reach her soul. He was standing in a location that felt familiar when she arrived. It was an office with a stained-glass window of a flower to the left and a window of jeweled treasure on the right. A large gray desk rested in the middle of the room. Short bookcases housed books on the shelves and knickknacks on the top. Mr. Burma was crossing his arms, leaning up against the desk and tapping his feet simply waiting for her. The sight of him made her crash to a stop.

"Not too bad. I expected you slightly sooner, but my estimate of your lateness was wrong, so I guess that means we're doing alright."

"I don't work for you," Peyton heard herself say. Her voice amplified around the room from a system of speakers in the corners. She spun around to see them.

"Can you see me?" she asked.

"Not fully. That would require me being bonded to an IB dog. We both know how that worked out."

Peyton shook her head. "What are you doing?" she asked him.

"Not me. It's what you are doing."

She had to get out of here before he told her a lie. That's what he did. He lied, or bent the truth, or fabricated the impossible to complete some mission that she had been a part of and couldn't remember. Without all the facts, she was never going to come to the right answer. Hearing more lies would only confuse her thoughts more. Peyton took a step backward.

She would have rushed off right away except Mr. Burma pulled something out of his pocket that held her attention. It was a rounded disk, hefty like a compass. It had a large hole in the center like a donut, except that hole was filled with a moving liquid that by all accounts should fall out and wasn't. The liquid was green. The disk was black. She took two steps forward, trying to remember what it was. Her hand could feel the pressure of holding it as if her muscles could never forget.

"The experiments on this are finally complete, thanks in part to you," Mr. Burma told her.

Peyton glared at him. He hadn't said "his" experiments, but "the" experiments as if he wasn't the one orchestrating them. He was trying to make her think everything was her idea because he didn't want her to see the truth. Here they went. She had to hold to the small truths that she knew and not believe half the lies. She got herself ready. One: She would never knowingly harm anyone. Two: She planned to save Klast. Three: She would sooner die than betray any of that.

"You don't have to be scared of yourself anymore, Peyton."

She wasn't scared of herself. She could hardly move. There was nothing wrong with her apart from being too sedentary.

"You have looked long and hard to sort through the patterns of souls. Do you remember what you called them? Sparkle trails! All this time you have been learning how to read soul colors so that you could distinguish one soul from the next when you saw it. You could be like an IB dog seeing patterns and people in a way no other human can."

"When did you try to bond an IB dog?" Peyton asked him. He wanted to see souls. A part of her vaguely felt like Mr. Burma studied Klast for his ability to connect with IB dogs so well. She couldn't remember what all of that led to.

"Standing before one doesn't make one bonded to it, does it?" Mr. Burma asked her. "But you, you could bond any dog your heart desires."

Oh no. This was where it was going to get all twisted. Hold to the first truth. She wouldn't hurt anyone.

"You can pull out parts of the dog's soul and adhere them to yourself like weaving spider silk."

Forceful bonding by a monster. Not that she could remember trying anything like that, but it *did* sound like something she could do. All it took was a bit of yanking, and she'd have part of the dog's essence. The dog would see that and obey her. That could very well be how she got part of Shadow in the first place when his doggy heart would much rather belong to Klast.

"Sounds cruel."

Mr. Burma laughed at her. "No, dear girl! Not like that. Don't you remember what you've been trying to do this whole time? I'll give you a hint. It deals with an infection that has been in your soul."

He waited for her to answer, but she kept quiet. He was talking about *Mervolk* and skipping over the part where she could steal souls. She remembered bits and pieces of that part. She didn't have to be particularly close to anyone to steal a soul. All she needed was knowledge of what the soul felt like beforehand, and to gain that, all she had to do was stick part of herself to the person in question. To tag them for sniping, as Klast had once called it. She was a hunter. She was a destroyer. She had yanked out souls and turned people cold before.

There had to be more. She wouldn't hurt anyone without a good reason. Why had she been taking the souls out? She had to start backwards to go forwards. She had been taking out Klast's soul and killing it so there was room for something else to fit in his body. That part she was certain of before she had come to this conversation. What she had given him had felt light and joyful, not tainted and dark and ugly. Therefore, she had to conclude that she was double-crossing Mr. Burma successfully. He had no idea what she had returned.

"It's most commonly called *Mervolk*. A nasty substance that clings to strong souls and devours the body from the inside out. You have figured out that much, I hope."

What she had figured out was that living with *Mervolk* was painful. It didn't directly relate to Klast. They both struggled with their souls being torn apart, but in different ways. She was the one with *Mervolk* attacking her and her clones. Klast was the one with IB dogs pulling at him to shield him from what was *she* was doing to him. She had previously surmised that she destroyed half his soul while hunting it away from his dogs all under the guise of helping him. Had she been trying to get an IB dog away from Klast for Mr. Burma? He just said that he failed to imprint one so he could see souls.

"Do you have *Mervolk*?" Peyton asked to keep the liar talking so she could think.

"No, no, no. I don't have *Mervolk*. You had that. Don't you remember? You felt sick all the time. You could hardly keep your soul in your body. You were always drifting. Always far away."

Drifting was an interesting word. She didn't associate it with *Mervolk*. That was a clinging poison. However, her family said that her soul had drifted long before she was given *Mervolk*. She had been trying to find something that her soul craved.

Left on his own, Klast had tried to find her an IB dog. Maybe that's what she was after this whole time. She couldn't get out in Hyphas to find the dog for herself, but Klast could. The only way for him to pick the dog she couldn't locate was if she met him in person and attached some of her soul to him so he could feel the connection she failed to reach.

Heading after Klast was an interesting target, but if she took into consideration who his father was (Jethro Burma), and how Jethro had a Shadow clone locked away, she could assume that Jethro had *her* dog locked away too. The one that she kept trying to locate by leaving herself behind so much. She went after Klast because she hoped that he could reach the dog his father was hiding. Then Jethro used everything she was doing against her to take Klast down before either could finalize her plans to reach the dog.

Jethro had decided that she was too much of a liability and must have killed off her first dog if she was suddenly wanting this other creature that Klast had found for her. She doubted Mr. Burma would leave a known IB dog with a person like Igene Barker. It was highly likely that the first dog she had tried and failed to find was in Sysmat. With the recent invasion of the place, she had aided in the destruction of the very thing she was trying to reach. That sounded exactly like the sort of twisted thing she expected from the man standing before her.

If Mr. Burma didn't know about the dog Klast had found for her instead of for himself, then he wouldn't suspect that she understood what Jethro had already done to her. Why he picked her was a mystery, but it was probably a mystery to him too. She could imagine him walking around a dog arena with hundreds of pictures of children in his pocket, flashing them off to dogs until one howled in interest. Then, since she wasn't his child, it didn't much matter that she spent years being listless.

He had enough to go on so he could devise blockers for his own children to keep them away from Lexia. If they never went there, he was free to continue merging planetary technology so he could control souls on his own. Without someone to jump back and forth to guess what was happening, he was safe.

He stopped his children's shifting, all except for Klast, who discovered IB dogs and messed up his father's ideas. Or added to them. *Mervolk* showed up. One couldn't run experiments on souls without creating a weapon that would damage souls too.

"In any case, Peyton," Mr. Burma continued, "You have finally won. You figured out a cure for *Mervolk*."

IB dog acid. Mr. Burma wouldn't want her to figure that out. He wouldn't want her to know how to reverse what he had engineered so she could kill it when she wasn't able to shift. The disease had come from the dogs. It was reversible by the dogs. Once she was able to imprint her dog completely, she would be one step closer to ending those nosebleeds. Except... Klast had come down with something. Something new in his soul that he could only describe as a demon—an invasive substance. This was where Mr. Burma's lies showed the brightest. He let her believe that she had defeated him when all she had done was heard a lie.

Then again, she fully believed that the acid would work against *Mervolk*, and she still had the nosebleeds even after feeling like the *Mervolk* strain had left her. Therefore, the nosebleeds were not caused by *Mervolk* at all. She'd felt full and then emptier a moment ago. The bleeding had to be caused by the body trying to adjust to the accumulation and release of additional souls. She didn't need Mr. Burma to touch her for him to mess with her soul composition. He'd been doing it for years. He could simply snap some device and have her carry whatever soul he wanted. He could push some button and take it all back.

The item in his hand! He'd said it was perfected. As in, the device was capable of adding and subtracting from more than just her. He must have gotten to Klast, and either taken his soul out again or put something into it.

Jethro had made him sick! He had failed to stop his son before Klast revealed what he knew. His next plan was to stop him before Peyton managed to get Klast looking even deeper. Tragic. If Peyton was correct in that she had turned to Klast to stop his father, then she was correct that Mr. Burma had turned against his son to stop her from messing up his experiments.

"Congratulations, my dear. I see many more bright and happy moments in your future. This will only feel like a few moments for you, but it may take another full year before you get another body. The clone factory has been shut down on Hyphas, but there are plenty more places willing to pay for miraculous cures."

Mr. Burma tipped the device upside down.

No!

Peyton tried to grab at objects, but she couldn't break away. She had no physical form to hold a bookcase. She had no form with which to pick up the gun she spotted sitting on a chair. She had no power to stop herself from being sucked into the device in Mr. Burma's hand. Perfected. He thought he was trapping her entire soul away because she'd put it back together. Only he didn't know about the dog. He didn't know that Klast was ahead of him. He didn't know that she'd left part of herself with Klast. Peyton strained to hold her one thought that could save her from the madness of figuring this out over and over and forgetting it each time. Klast. Save Klast. If she did that, she'd save herself.

"See you soon, my soul destroyer."

That was the last thing she heard.

# 33

Nothing felt right. Echoes were beeping around his head, both close and farther away. One of them was extremely fast for a moment before hollowing out into a flat line. There was a tense moment where Klast thought somebody had died, but then the beeping picked back up and a feeling of titanium-thick determination flooded his body. Not going to die. The beeping was going to stay alive.

Something was staring him in the face as well, and he couldn't brush it away. His arms felt like lead. The staring felt like a dog, though. A rather intrusive one at that. Maybe Igene's pup was still sitting on him.

"Turn your peepers someplace else," Klast mumbled.

He wasn't on dirt this time. It felt like a bed beneath him. The beeping sounds continued, and a growl was the reply to his request. The dog's refusal wasn't the part that bothered him, it was the voice. He was pretty good at remembering dog voices. This one escaped him.

"Who are you?" Klast asked. He inhaled and then shifted his arms and legs about. Ouch. Still broken and beaten down.

"No," the dog answered him with a hint of giddy excitement.

Okay. He had to face it. Nothing good came from a sound like that. Klast opened first one eye and then the other. Muffin! Her brown eyes were staring at him hard, but she was smiling. Not because of him, but because she could talk again. Remarkable.

"You can hear again too, I take it? That must be nice for you, Muffin girl. A darling thing like you deserves that. Have you seen Peyton?"

"Yes!" The dog howled in happy triumph.

"Then why are you here staring at me? Go protect her. She needs you!"

"Yes. No," Muffin replied. "Deek soul, Klast soul, Peyton soul, Shadow soul, Tuff soul, Morgal soul—"

"What are you doing?!" Klast cut her off. She shouldn't know any of that. The only way for her to know dog names was if she was sifting through all of Peyton's thoughts. This dog had already swallowed through Peyton's soul. Muffin gave him a sharp growl and then went right back to it.

"—Phantom soul, Luke soul, Volt soul, Weston soul...."

"Stop!" Klast tried again. "Stay out of that."

"No. Many souls. Demon soul."

"Stupid dog," Klast told her. Then he swallowed. He could get away with saying something like that to Deek, but to this strange creature? He really shouldn't dare. "You're supposed to be helping Peyton."

"Peyton told her to help you," said another unfamiliar voice.

Klast looked to his side. That's where the beeping was coming from. He was hooked up to all sorts of machines and his heart rate was being recorded. If he wasn't mistaken about the data on the screen, he had died a few times. He groaned. Two people stepped into view. One was a man and another a woman he was rather fond of.

"Lakisha!" Klast sighed gratefully. "Get me out of this."

"Not this time. You've woken up several times speaking a creepy language, saying one phrase over and over. I'm starting to memorize it. It can't be good."

"The demon will rise," Muffin barked.

"You are such a creep," Klast told her. Then he winced again. He had to stop doing that! He was much better at controlling his mouth than this. "Sorry."

"Our other soul traveling friend is currently not with us. She dashed away and told the dog to examine your soul for her. Your friend was under the impression that you might have multiple souls about you."

"Dog souls, Peyton soul, demon soul," Muffin barked at him.

"I have a demon soul?" he asked Muffin so that the doctor and vet could not understand him. No need to get them alarmed. He was already feeling uneasy and his heart monitor was reflecting it enough, thank you.

"Yes."

"Good dog. Is it possible for my dog to take the soul out?"

"No."

"But he's an IB dog! It's what you dogs do! You suck out souls!"

"No. Share souls." Okay. He wasn't about to argue with an unknown IB dog, but he had been losing his soul for years because of the dogs. If it wasn't them, then what was it?

"Something other than the soulless has to be able to take out souls."

"Yes. Peyton. Peyton takes souls. Peyton gives many dog souls. Peyton demon."

"What?"

He understood what the dog was saying so it didn't repeat itself, but this was crazy. Peyton wasn't a demon. He didn't *want* her to be. The only force he knew to take down a demon was the void, and he didn't want to kill Peyton in that way. He'd already done it once, and that made him cry. He couldn't bear to do it again.

"Can Peyton take my demon soul out?"

As far as he knew, she'd never tried to take anything away from him, only give him soul energy, but Muffin here was telling him otherwise. Peyton had been taking his soul out and replacing it with dog souls.

"Yes."

"Will she?"

"Yes."

"What will that do to her?" Klast asked, knowing the answer before he got it. It was starting to click together again.

"Peyton demon. Klast kill demon."

"And then Muffin will attack Klast," he guessed. "Unless the Peyton I attack is a clone version so the real her remains alive enough to take my soul again. This is not fair. There has to be a way to fix this so that neither of us has the demon soul."

"Have you any idea what he's saying?" Lakisha whispered to the unknown doctor. He shook his head, but he appeared to remain interested all the same.

"Have I always had this demon soul?" Klast asked. He felt out of time to figure this out. There was a strange pressure urging him to hear something that wasn't talking. Some unsettled part in his heart was trying to yell.

"No."

"I got it from Peyton?"

"No. Peyton kills bad souls. Peyton wind soul."

Whatever that fully meant.

"Does that mean that she has a thin soul?"

"No. Small. Moveable. Strong. Hidden."

"You said she has a demon too. Can she kill the demon soul in herself?"

"No, no, no," Muffin barked at him. "Peyton demon. Klast demon soul."

Uh-huh. Muffin was trying to tell him that these were two very different things, only Muffin didn't have another word to describe the second part.

"Peyton blazen," Klast amended.

"No!" Muffin shook her head for emphasis. "Peyton de..." Muffin squared her feet again on his bed and stared at Klast's face again.

"Trapped!" she shouted while she wagged her tail, pleased with herself for coming up with the word. It felt like she'd taken the thing straight out of his brain. She might have done it too if Peyton had put more than her fair share of her soul into him. Her dog was devouring information from both of them. A scary thought, but one that he hoped was going to work for the better since it might make Muffin more compassionate than she could have been being raised as a killer.

"Hold on." Klast again tried to push the dog's face away from him and couldn't move. He grit his teeth, shook his head, and continued. He could not blow up. "You just said that I was to kill a Peyton demon. Now your word 'demon' is changing to the word 'trapped.'"

Muffin nodded and grinned at him. He couldn't help himself. Dog smiles were his weakness. One of his weaknesses. He smiled back and then tried to wipe the smile away, only to find his good arm still stuck! Geez, that was annoying. He heard his heart monitor spike a few times before he calmed himself back down.

Peyton demon. Klast kill demon. Peyton trapped. Klast kill trapped. That last part didn't make sense. However, dogs didn't always think in concrete terms, but rather in emotions and instinct. It was right versus wrong or command versus teasing. It was fun versus boring, and excitement versus sadness. Muffin was trying to tell him that a "demon" had trapped Peyton and she wanted Klast to kill it. He already had a good guess who the demon in question was. Mr. Burma had no use for Peyton's current rundown body.

"Where's Peyton?" Klast demanded.

"Right over there," the doctor answered before Muffin could. "She's fine. Been going in and out, but she's currently free of the thing that makes her speak that foreign language and nothing else."

What?

"Show me," Klast said.

"I was hoping that you'd say that. I have some questions. Can you remember your name?"

"Of course, I can," Klast replied.

"Excellent! Progress! What is the last thing you remember?"

"My nose starting to bleed. Can we get on with it? What thing traps her language? I need to know what it is."

"It's not quantifiable," the doctor told him, causing Klast to roll his eyes and strain against the straps yet again. He could shift out of this. He could blow the bands off him.

"You can see it on this monitor here." The doctor dashed off to drag a screen on a rolling cart over to him. "Over the years, I have come up with a method to track the changes in her fluctuations. I've isolated the variable to a single electronic pulse that usually pops up right before Peyton is scheduled to have a memory wipe. This time she arrived with several memories in place which I was happy to see. She also didn't have the electric signature here."

The doctor pointed to a line on the screen that he had colored purple to make it stand out from the other shades and colors around it. The line was a lot thicker at times and then it would vanish and come back up on the grid.

"Technically it's not an electric thing at all, but for simplicity purposes, that's what I call it. It's more in the form of, well, a soul. As you can see here." He flipped through his images. "These are instances where Peyton had no lines at all. It was during these times that she was essentially dead. Then she came back."

"After she died, there were several new lines," Klast pointed out.

"Yes. She would die and come back with new soul fragments tied into her soul. Most of the time, those were brand new souls apart from one recurring line that we have here. This is the line that I call Peyton." He pointed to a pink line that was consistently fuzzier than the others.

"Not to fill you with my excitement of discovery, but this other line here," the line was depicted in yellow, "matches perfectly with your recordings. The yellow line comes and vanishes just as quickly as she does. Here's an instance where I was talking directly with her and the yellow line vanished. Poof! It was gone as if she'd exploded it. She stayed awake the whole time and didn't seem disturbed that the soul was dead."

Klast looked at the screen impatient. Not that he wanted to give the doctor any ideas, but the man had to already know. The longer he dragged this on, the longer Peyton stayed trapped. Klast needed to help her already!

"Look, doctor, I know all of this already. Peyton was hunting down fragments of my soul. That was her entire mission. Tell me about the line that strained her ability to distinguish between dialects."

"This purple one," the doctor mused. "It may have had that effect on her, but that's not what it is. See, you arrived with the purple soul on you, and I can understand you perfectly again. You had a few moments of incoherent muttering in the mystery language and you were just speaking it right now with the dog who remarkably understood you."

"What is the line?" Klast asked him sharply.

"I always thought it was a sort of buffer that she brought in to shield herself from pain before the moment of the memory wipe."

"Describe the memory wipes," Klast sighed. "What happened right before? What happened right after? Was she awake when they came? Was she asleep?"

"Yes to both of those. Sometimes she was awake. Sometimes asleep."

"Torturous jerks," Klast muttered so that the doctor couldn't understand him. Muffin did. She gave a slight growl in agreement, but she didn't attack the doctor. That wasn't her current mission.

"Peyton was a rather interesting person when it came to those. As noted, she would always get this purple line. No one else pulled it in. She'd start speaking in the unknown dialect and then she would die."

"Every time?" Klast asked, concerned.

"Oh yes, but that was nothing unusual for her. She was always dying. Then she would come back, and attached to her typical scattered soul pattern would be a whole new string of soul lengths."

"How long could Peyton hold this purple line before she died?" Klast wanted to know. He had a very good idea what this purple line was. Deek was running from everyone and everything like his life depended on it. There was no way his father was going to catch Deek and shoot him so that he could destroy Klast's soul in one fell sweep. That purple line was the demon soul.

"Twenty-four hours. It was normally less than that."

What time was it? Klast glanced around at the monitors near him to tell him the time. There wasn't a clock, only a message telling him how long he had been in the hospital room under this doctor's care. Fifteen hours. That in itself didn't look good. That left him nine hours to live, but there would be extra time added to all of that for when he had traveled to this hospital in the first place, checked in, and waited for the doctor to be fetched. He didn't have much longer to live with the soul fragments he currently carried.

"Doctor, what you are witnessing is a soul-destroying technology," Klast told him. "That thing kills off whatever soul it touches."

"Which is why you will remain strapped to the table until the purple line has run its course," the doctor told him pleasantly. "It will be most impressive if you can remember your name after the attack is over."

He wouldn't make it back into his body when the line was over. This guy was nuts! The doctor talked about dying souls as if it was nothing. He must have desensitized himself to it all with the number of times he watched Peyton die on him. However, Klast wasn't Peyton. He knew that part of his soul was safe with Deek, but most of it was here with him slowly being eaten away. What was going to happen when the soul weapon reached the dog souls that Peyton had given him?

Peyton had grouped all the dogs he'd ever loved and fed them into him. Surely the dogs would feel the connection dying and they would strain themselves to replace it. They'd push themselves, trying to keep him alive while they slowly died along with him. He was going to kill his dogs. Again. Unless he could first rescue Peyton so she could take the impurity out. That's why Mr. Burma had latched himself onto Peyton. She was the only one who could stop him. He'd gotten her far too confused to remember how or what she was doing.

Think, think, think. Klast had less than nine hours to defeat his dad for good before he was officially dead, along with everything else he loved. The other beeping in the room turned into a long buzz. Klast tried to find it. Muffin pulled her ears back and whined.

"Not to worry. She always comes back," the doctor told them as he looked in the direction of the currently dead Peyton. Klast was almost glad that he couldn't see her. He'd seen her before while she was dead, and it never was a pretty sight. The emptiness that surrounded her felt wrong.

Bzzzz! Went the monitor. Muffin whined again.

"Any minute now," the doctor tried to ease the tension in the room as he walked over to Peyton and fiddled with the instruments.

Bzzz! He turned the sound off as he continued to work.

"Well," he said in a voice that failed to hide his nerves. "We still have her dog. You should have seen the animal when it woke up. She was so happy. She jumped right up onto Peyton's bed and howled herself backward!" The doctor laughed. "Scared herself with her own voice, she did. Then she rubbed her ears all over everything like a cat, surprised she could hear again. After that was over, she licked Peyton's face like peanut butter. The dog's not crying, so Peyton must be in here somewhere."

Klast stared at Muffin. Muffin stared back. They both knew the truth. Peyton wasn't coming back. Her soul had been trapped someplace else and her weary body hadn't been able to hold on any longer. Peyton was dead. A pond filled over Klast's vision. That had been his last hope. He was done for, and he couldn't stand to see Muffin waste her life away fully restored physically, only to be broken emotionally by a woman whose soul was forever lost. Maybe one day the dog would find it. One day. Klast hadn't the time for that.

"I'm sorry, Muffin," Klast told her, unable to wipe the tears from his eyes. "I want to die with Deek."

He couldn't let his other dogs die along with him. No way. Peyton had given him every resource she could to hold him up, but it wasn't enough if she couldn't be there to swoop in at the last moment. Klast would give himself up to protect the dogs. That was his duty. His mission. His job. His dad was going to head after Deek. That's where Klast was going to be, too. They would stand there before him and let him plow them over. Mr. Burma could be haunted by the accusation in Klast's eyes.

Klast had already started spreading the doubt about his father as it was. One day, Mr. Burma would face the consequences of his actions. He wouldn't be able to hide forever.

Klast closed his eyes and let himself use Peyton's soul to hunt down Deek's location. It was a lot harder to do this time around. Strained. Sweat came over him as he searched, trying to use shreds of a soul that couldn't respond anymore. He tried and tried. It had to be there! He heard Muffin pant along with him as if she was trying to help him find the honorable death he wanted. Everything stayed dark for the longest time. Then Muffin yelped. She bit onto Klast's arm so that he screamed right as he saw the sparkles.

There! He followed the line to where Deek was currently running and then dropped back down into himself when Muffin bit into his arm again. He couldn't knock her off, so he did the next best thing. Since he had a location, he shifted, dragging Muffin with him and ignoring the screams of his favorite vet behind him.

# 34

Peyton stumbled into the bathroom. She felt weird, but what else was new? Nothing apart from the fact that she was up and walking and could take herself to the bathroom. Funny how that simple action brought a smile to her face. There was a strange whisper against her soul as if a day ago she couldn't stand up on her own, let alone walk to a bathroom. Odd. Peyton paused to look in the mirror. Cinnamon hair swept to the side by her bangs. The longer locks traveled down to mid-back. She had a pointed chin and cashew brown eyes. The same as always.

"You have a mission in two minutes!"

That was the voice that had woken her up, too. He had her rolling out of bed to get ready in an instant. It was going to be another long day in the field. The last mission she had was to stop a man who had black eyes terrorizing a mobile park. Very nasty stuff. Everything he touched turned cold and frozen. Peyton had located the creep and her partner had burst him into a fine powder. They made a great team; her the finder, and him the savior. Still, sometimes she wished for a different sort of life.

"Peyton!"

"I need to pee first!" she screamed back. "Give a girl a minute!"

"Half a minute. No pruning."

"I'm not a bush!" she laughed back.

Jokes! Today might not be so bad after all. Fancy that.

She yanked down her pants and sat down, biting at her lip, trying to sort through the weird feeling in her heart. Was it her heart or her soul? There was a difference. One kept her alive. The other made her who she was. Soul. Totally a whisper against her soul, like another voice was trying to get through to her. She started to wipe and froze. What? There was a mark drawn on her leg. It wasn't the blue Sysmat mark. She yanked up her shirt sleeve to find the shoulder mark still there. That hadn't changed.

"Peyton!"

"Ugh!" she screamed back. "Give me the briefing through the door. I'm almost ready!"

"The briefing?" the voice laughed at her.

"Shut up!" Another joke. Dare she say he was flirting with her that time? My goodness!

"Anyone ever tell you that you're cute?"

"Anyone ever tell you that you're dead?" she snapped back. He was totally being a flirt! Must be some mission they had.

"This is an odd one. We need to find a stray dog."

"Fabulous! Nothing like a fluffy tail to pique your interest."

He did like dogs. He looked at them almost hungry when they passed them. It was a tad disturbing if she was being honest.

Anyway, what was this mark on her leg?? She rubbed at it, trying to take it off. It wouldn't move. If she had to take a guess, she was going to say that it was something she had put on herself. Something her whispering soul was trying to communicate to her by darkening the skin. Creepy. Gross. She hadn't time to worry about the language written there.

"It stole a soul."

"Klast shut up!"

"Why? What's wrong?" he asked her, concerned. "You okay in there?" He knocked on the door.

She took in a couple of deep breaths. No. She wasn't okay. Dead. Klast was *dead*. She felt it in her soul, and yet he was on the other side of the door. Something wasn't right about this. A few tears came tumbling down her face without warning. Oh gosh! She was crying because Klast was dead! But he wasn't! He was right there, the same as always. They were partners. They were the best team that anyone had ever seen. There had to be a truth in her brain that wasn't adding up. Where was the lie? She hated playing this game. Hated knowing that she was never going to win.

"Are you crying?" Klast asked, banging the door. He shook the door handle next.

"No, why?" she lied.

She'd deal with this later. Whatever it was. Peyton wiped at her eyes and finished her business. She splashed water on her face and wiped it dry, bursting out the bathroom and past Klast without looking at him.

"Come on, slowpoke!" she teased. "We need to go."

"You were crying. You can't hide it from me. I can sense your emotions better than anyone."

"Yes and why is that?" she snapped at him.

"What?" he asked her, stumbling back as if she'd slapped him.

It had never bothered her before. Some days it felt like her and Klast were the same person. Other days, it was like she didn't know him or herself. Today felt like none of those cases. Today felt completely different. Today felt like her soul was stronger than ever, and the Klast beside her was nothing like the person she had pretended he was. His teasing was actually funny. The emotion he had just given her almost *real*. Did that make her fake? Was he?

"Why do you sense my emotions like you feel them too?"

"I..." he shook his head. "Actually... I can't right now."

He looked down at his hands as if something was wrong with them. Then he glanced back up at her and smiled. It stopped her heart quite literally. She felt it pause and then contemplate what a smile from Klast could do to her. Safe. It started beating again.

"I heard you crying."

"Let me see your arm," she told him as she walked back toward him. She lifted his sleeve and looked at the blue mark. Sysmat agent. The same as always, yet never the same at all.

Klast stumbled backward. "Don't shoot me, Peyt!" he screamed.

"Peyt?" Since when did he call her that? "What's happening?"

Peyton looked around the underground bunker. This was where they had been since... Hum. She didn't have the answer to that. It probably didn't matter anyway. They were buried thousands of feet under the ground. It was a place no one could reach without shifting into it. They both had to use special devices to enter and leave. Her device was currently sitting on the coffee table right beside Klast's.

*"He doesn't need it."*

Peyton shook her head. That whispering! What was it? Of course, Klast needed the device to get out of here. Everyone did.

"Do you happen to, I don't know, have a secret gift of interpreting strange languages?"

"Yes," Klast answered her.

He rubbed at his arm where the mark was. He took in a few deep breaths and then rolled his shoulders, shook out his legs, stretched down to his toes, and checked for missing scars on his chest.

"Are you okay?" she asked him.

"I think I'm going to be. If you can live like this, I can too. Think we're the last ones?"

"The last of what?"

"The last to reach our mission for the day. You're being super slow!" he covered.

Despite his claim that it was time to go, he didn't head to the table for his device. He walked over to the bathroom and glanced in the mirror before looking back at her as if he too needed the extra assurance today that he still looked the same.

"Language? Go ahead and blurt it out."

"It's a picture." She shook her head at him. "I have to draw it."

"Draw away." He waved his hand at her, giving her permission.

Peyton stared at him, confused. Yeah, there was something different about him right now. Not a bad difference, but super different. He was standing right next to the drawer with the paper in it. He should be passing her the paper and pen instead of waving his hands about like he was clueless. Whatever. It was just a mood. He must have done some late-night reading that made him stuck in his thoughts today. He'd be back to normal tomorrow.

*"And normal would be?"*

Whatever felt right! Geez. Peyton stomped her way over to Klast. He looked at her concerned again as if he couldn't understand why she was slightly mad at him. He stepped to the side when she yanked open the drawer for the paper and the pen.

"Ah." He rubbed at his chin. "Right. Sorry. I'm in your way. Have you always had that freckle right there on the side of your chin?"

He rubbed at her jaw. She swatted him away, ignoring the way he grinned at her and the way it felt both frightening and amusing at the same time. She had to focus if she was going to get the picture right. Shoving closed the drawer, she placed the paper on the top of the narrow dresser. She drew the circle lines of it first and then the edges. Klast stopped staring at her to snap his eyes to the page. He glanced from it to her face and back again a few times before taking a large step back to give her space as if she was going to need it.

"Is it bad?!" Peyton wailed. "Just tell me. I hate waiting for things."

"Really?" Klast was back to smiling at her as if she had shared with him the name of her first crush or something. Stupid man. He was bonkers. For some reason it made her want to smile back at him. She frowned instead.

"What does it say?!"

"That's your name. Peyton Finch. You just wrote your name in the language of your birth. Do you remember any more of the language than that?"

"No." She bristled and crumpled the paper, leaving it on the floor.

He didn't say anything which was nice. Perhaps she did need a minute. Klast was normal. It was her that wasn't. She didn't have a birth language that she couldn't remember. She was born in… at… Her age was… Okay. She must have hit her head recently.

Peyton rubbed her temples, trying to focus on what things she could remember. One event only. Destroying that cold demon sucker. Great. It probably got to her before Klast blew it up. If she told him she was having memory issues, he'd turn her in.

She was fine. Totally fine. She gave Klast a shrug as if it didn't matter, and then went to grab her shoes. The only part of him that followed after her was his eyes. Why she could feel them traveling across her skin, she had no idea. This was weird.

"I'm going to ask you something you might not want to answer," Klast warned her. "Did you happen to find the image of your name when you were in the bathroom?"

"It doesn't matter."

"I'm taking that as a yes. Did you find a flash drive too or was that only the other you?"

"What is wrong with you?!"

Peyton grabbed her shoes and nearly threw them at his face. He wasn't smiling anymore, but standing there so calmly it unnerved her. There was a crisis going on and he was talking gibberish. There was no other *her*. She was the last one. The very last… How did she know that?

"*I told you.*"

Peyton stumbled backward, dropping the shoes. If she was basing her judgment on what felt right, she was doing a very bad job of it. She didn't feel like the voice was wrong, but there was a voice in her head and it wasn't hers.

"I'll take that as a no. Forget I mentioned it. It's going to be alright, Peyt. We'll figure it out."

"Don't turn me in," she whispered. She was doing a really bad job at acting normal. Klast had figured her out in five minutes.

"Me? Never. Don't turn me in. I feel weird too."

She nodded. "Maybe we ate some bad take-out."

He laughed at her. "Must have contained vinegar. Anything with that is rubbish."

She frowned at him again, trying to decide if she knew that about him. In all this time, had he ever told her something like that about himself? She knew so little about him it was impressive that she felt like she'd been in the same room with him for the last... year and a half?

"Was that here a moment ago?" Klast asked, pointing to a corner of the room that she had just glazed over.

Peyton turned to look again and stumbled backward for a second time. A dog! Not just any dog. An IB dog was standing there with a strange shifting device at his feet. How had a dog obtained a shifter? How did she know that it was a device that let him shift? It looked nothing like the one she used. This one had a large crystal smack dab in the middle of it as if that was its power source.

The silver dog himself was gorgeous. The fur looked soft and fluffy. He had black ears, and the brown on his legs looked like he had stepped into a vat of chocolate. He was also staring at Klast with a force she had never encountered before, even if the force felt safe and familiar at the same time.

"Is that the dog we're trying to find?" Peyton questioned. "And it found us first?"

"No," Klast answered, unable to take his eyes off the animal.

It smiled at him. He smiled back. Peyton felt her mouth drop open. Klast was looking at a dog without looking half-starved! A miracle!

"This is the dog we're trying to find."

He tossed her a tablet that had the mission details. Peyton inhaled sharply when she saw it. Creamy dog with one brown ear and one brown paw. It was an IB dog too, and even though the rest of her head was screwy this morning, she knew about this dog at first glance. *Her* dog. Too bad she'd never officially met her.

"No way!" Peyton rounded on Klast. She *felt* this dog. It was in her soul. She felt it! "We are not attacking this dog!"

"I was fearful that might be the—"

The director of the company flashed into view one moment. The next he was down on the ground howling in short-lived pain as the silver dog ripped through his throat. Peyton stood there in utter shock.

"Klast?" she whispered. There was nothing in the rule book that told her what to do if the director shifted into view and then died. On her bunker floor.

"Uh, huh?" he answered as he slowly walked closer to the crime scene.

That was Klast for you. She was of the mind to run and cower under a table. He was always the one to take that first step.

"Don't worry Peyton. I know what to do."

He was having all sorts of odd effects on her today. The gentle tone of his voice in the face of tragedy was enough to calm her down. For some reason, she believed everything he said. Normally theirs was a rush in, rush out situation. Except "normally" came down to a few feelings and one memory, now two, that were distressing.

"You'll remember it all soon. I have to get that soul stealer away from the director, and then I think we should get out of this place. Go get a smoothie. Get you back to Muffin."

"Who?" Peyton asked as she rubbed at her chest. It hurt. Not like indigestion hurt, but more like the pounding of something still trying to scream at her hurt. Peyton closed her eyes, trying to listen.

*"I love you!!!!"*

Wow. That had to be Muffin. The voice in her soul had a name.

*"Dog!"*

Dog. Right. Her dog. The one she felt an infinite connection to. Part of her knew Muffin wasn't the dog's real name, but the name was going to stick.

From now on, the cream dream was going to be known as Muffin. Where was Muffin?

*"In Klast's car. Deek drove. We are here to rescue you!"*

Klast knelt beside the dead director. He was facing away from her, but she could tell he was both smiling at the dog and grieving over the death. Out came a phone, a collapsible pen, and a set of keys from the director's pockets. There was a thin wallet and a key card. Then Klast revealed a black donut with a liquid middle. He tipped the item upside down.

All at once, something hot and burning flew out of the device and straight into her chest. Peyton screamed, trying to claw the strange thing out of her. What was it?! What was... Oh.

Images came flooding back to her. Clones. Finding Klast and his dogs. Shadow and Mr. Burma. Killing Klast. After all that work she had put into keeping him alive! He stood there and died! Now they were both clones. The very last hidden clones.

"You... died!" Peyton gasped as the tears came tumbling down again. She hadn't been wrong. Part of her soul was still crying for the both of them.

"I lived!" Klast protested. "We both lived. I shifted beside Deek and enjoyed his company before I got shot."

Peyton let out a slow breath. That's how it was. Imprinted creatures lived and died together, or suffered for years afterward if they refused to go down. She was a little nervous about all the negative side effects she had picked up and couldn't remember yet.

The astonishing part was how Deek had put Klast back into his clone so fast without her. It must have been one large gamble. Deek would have found the last of the hidden clones and then slowly released Klast's soul that he held, hoping that the clone version of him would soak it up. It was either that, or he had used a second soul stealing device that Jethro created to release Klast's soul back into him. Made sense if Jethro had trapped his son the same way he trapped her. His goal was to kill off the "infected" people so he could control their souls.

So, Deek had discovered Klast's fragmented parts to put his human back together. Then he had found a Lexian shifting device. Maybe he got help from Doctor Clark Manford. There. That sounded better. It all felt like a miracle. She wasn't fully dead.

"We destroyed Sysmat and the man who invaded it," Klast continued. "We stopped soulless and protected valuable dogs. We found two cures for *Mervolk* and discovered what blazen is. I think," Klast scratched his head. "I got a little confused by it all at the end. Your soul simply flies around..."

"If something else has a large portion of it, then yes, the soul will fly around and hunt for things. It's a very dangerous operation to take out a soul. You have to do so in pieces and replace the soul with something else, some other soul, or the body can't function. It dies. I had some deal with your breed dogs that I can't remember so I could take your soul. They probably thought they were saving you from me. Then I hunted it all back down and destroyed it. Your father used the soul casting to improve a soul capturing device he was working on—that pocket liquidifier. He was..."

Peyton looked over at Deek for the answer. She had tried to remember it all, but she hadn't been able to grasp everything either.

*"Jethro wanted to prove to Lexia that their myths were real. He was gathering data on soul dogs and blazen characters so he could create an army that couldn't be destroyed by the SD soul destroyer guns used on Lexia,"* Deek told them.

Peyton smiled at the smartest dog she'd ever met. She glanced at Klast to make sure he'd heard it too and then nodded in satisfaction.

*"He was making the soulless,"* Deek told them, *"and comparing them against being blazen. If he continued there'd be an army of both. I think he was going to take over Lexia with the army. He had a skewed notion that he'd be restoring the planet to a glorious state instead of an injured one by presenting living myths."*

That was spooky. Peyton already didn't like being the way she was. Imagine having a ton of people just like her mulling around unable to remember what they had been doing but knowing it was something dangerous and dreadful.

"Being Blazen means that another creature has your soul so that when you die from lack of soul, you're not really dead. Your soul simply gets released and travels back to you. The clones were necessary to hold the souls so that no one would mourn the fake versions when they died upon returning the soul they carried," Peyton explained to Klast.

He nodded.

"Right, and our death destroyed the demon soul that clung to our bodies and ate us apart."

"The demon was a disconnected soul. It was trying to take over your body. You should have survived it," Peyton sighed. The demon was the opposite of the soulless. A lost soul versus a body without its own soul. Both were awful.

"What do you mean survived it?"

"I tore you apart!" Peyton wailed. "Not Sysmat. Not your father. It was *me* because I couldn't remember what I was trying to do! I think the initial goal was to get you in a position to hold part of my soul so you could find the dog I couldn't get to. The first dog that turned me blazen."

"I think it died," Klast sullenly told her. "That's how you got free enough to move on to a different dog."

"Klast!" Peyton wailed. "Listen. Your dogs shared parts of their souls with you, but they can't take out soul material. I was the one taking it all out with that device your father had. When he found out, he found a way to use my scheme against me. Your breed dogs were the ones that kept letting me get in close because I tricked them somehow. Smelled like you or something. Your father wanted me to put the soul pieces I stole into a different dog to safeguard you and make you blazen, but I couldn't do that. I kept killing you off trying to give you my soul instead.

"Then Sysmat got me and everything became messier. I couldn't remember anything. I do think your father was trying to save you at first, only to turn against you in the end when he found you working with me. Maybe he thought Sysmat had wiped your brain too.

"Regardless, you should have survived the demon attack from your father, because instead of giving you your soul, I gave you half of mine. You would have lost the connection and died for a time, but then come right back as my soul repaired you. I don't know what happened to make it otherwise. It's all my fault for getting you involved in the first place. I was killing you!"

"Oh," Klast said staring off at the wall in thought for a moment. "I should have thought of that. I figured out that I had part of your soul, but I still thought that the demon would kill me. If not me then the dogs. I didn't want them straining themselves trying to keep me together when I was going to fail anyway. Plus, you had just died. The real you this time. Everything sort of felt over. I couldn't sit there and watch Muffin waste into dust, and I couldn't see any way to rescue your soul before I died next. I walked right into the path of my dad and let him shoot me to safeguard all my past dogs. He probably *did* think that I was mentally unstable. I didn't think far enough to realize that your soul would repair mine. Would it really?"

Oh gosh!

"I think so," Peyton answered as her heart thumped against her ribs painfully.

She knew it took a very certain determination and mindset to lose yourself for another living thing. It was a hard call to make. If the dogs hadn't added to him, then he would have bounced back, but he knew his dogs better than she did. Who was to say if they'd have let him lose his soul? Deek would have put up a fuss in the very least unless Klast wanted the event to happen. Tears welled up in her eyes that she blinked back. Klast reached out and tried to wipe them away, but they were already dry.

"Hey," he said gently. "That was my fault that time. You didn't kill me. You were saving all of Lexia. Despite how it has turned out, your intentions have always been good. I forgive you for forgetting even if that wasn't your fault. Please don't blame yourself. You don't deserve that. You suffered more than anyone for this already. The best thing to do now is move forward. There's a lot of good we can do. So many more dogs to train and lives to save. So many more souls to protect. I still think we should stick together. Birds of a feather and all that," Klast said giving her hand another squeeze.

After all she had done to him, he was still asking her to stay. That felt like a miracle too. Peyton looked down at their combined hands. Warm. The kind of warmth that had life breathed into them and a soul to hold them together. The kind that spoke of tenderness and hard work and sacrifice. The kind that would lift a fallen friend and patch together a mess. The kind that lived.

Peyton beamed.

"You have the most amazing eyes," Klast told her leaning in a little to view them.

Behind him, Deek started laughing. He howled something that made Klast blush. Peyton blushed. Muffin hooted into Peyton's soul. Klast itched the side of his neck with his free hand.

Peyton couldn't bring herself to let go of his other hand. Not yet. Just a little longer. Her other hand clenched into a fist to use the Sysmat technology, and the sparkle trail was back, pointing the way home. Home to where her soul could rest with Muffin.

She let go.

She was ready.

# 35

Klast rubbed his fingers over the palm that Peyton had been touching. It all felt so real, which went against the other thoughts in his brain that he was imagining everything. He wasn't a clone with a Sysmat mark on his arm. He hadn't just watched his father take his last breath in some secret room with no doors or windows. Deek wasn't hunched in a corner, staring at him like he expected Klast to grab his hair and shove his head into the freezer to scream. Klast had considered it, but he couldn't locate a freezer.

What he had found was a small living room with one sofa, two chairs, one coffee table, a set of drawers, and a line of cupboards that contained snack foods. He hadn't been hungry when he woke up, so he had skipped that stuff to peek into the one other room here. Peyton was in it. She hadn't looked tired, even if she was asleep, and she hadn't looked drained and sickly, so he assumed this was a clone of her. A clone that was alive. She'd not fully died on him!

Klast's chest had given an excited jolt before memories of yesterday had blasted him, showing how he had destroyed a soulless with Peyton. The memory was so real he couldn't refute it, but it felt like it didn't belong to him. Disturbed, Klast had moved to the coffee table that held three items. Two were shifting gadgets. The Sysmat kind with black boxes and blue buttons. One was a tablet that lit up when he had picked it up and it had detailed to him a new mission with its time. Believing he was functioning in some sort of dream, he had shouted at Peyton to wake up and get ready. It had all changed since then.

Klast rubbed at his hand again. Flesh and blood and bones. He wasn't injured. He looked like himself, and his muscles moved with strength, but his real self was supposed to be injured. He was supposed to be dead. He contemplated being stuck in an alternate reality, but he couldn't deny himself when pieces of his memory were filtering back to him, confirmed by Peyton who seemed more like herself today too. Yesterday she had spent the whole day scowling at him like she couldn't stand to be working at his side. Today she looked at him like they were friends. She trusted him with language questions that were secrets. She cried over him. She was returning to a more normal base state after a single day of being reawakened. That was a quick turnaround, and it scared him, because if she thought she was real, then he was...

It had been twenty-six days since the last time he remembered checking the date. He'd read the information on the tablet that morning. Twenty-six days ago was the day before he had ended up in the hospital with Peyton, where she had died, so it was twenty-five days since Klast had last seen Deek.

*"Wrong."*

Klast resisted smiling at the word in his head. Barely. Deek. The impossibly stubborn dog that was never going to leave him. Who would protect him no matter what form his conscience was inhabiting.

*"You made me leave you. I am still mad about that, but too happy that you remember me to snarl. I saw you yesterday. I snuck your soul back to you then. There's a faulty camera in this room that points directly to where I am standing. Jethro can't see me if I am right here."*

Can't or couldn't? One implied Jethro was still alive someplace. The other implied he was dead.

"Shhh!" Klast snapped, causing Peyton at the other end of the room to roll her eyes at him and Deek to tilt his ears down.

"I hope you said that to Deek because I said nothing," Peyton spoke. Then her face lit up. "I remember his name! And you never would tell it to me. I picked it up in the hospital when I was on the floor and you were telling him how to play with the hospital beds—"

"Shush!" Klast demanded again.

Peyton was programmed to carry on too quickly. She only had a split second to make half-remembered plans into reality. He, on the other hand, wanted to go back over everything she had just said and digest it.

He had been a soul without a familiar body for twenty-five days, because he had watched his father tip a device upside down, trapping his soul, as Jethro shot his son in the heart. Given how fast things had been happening leading up to that point, any number of things could have happened since. Klast needed to break it down into sections for his brain to process it all.

Peyton claimed she had destroyed him. She was helping to take his soul out and replace it with parts of his dogs and herself. She suspected she did this so that Klast would locate a half-imprinted IB dog that she had never met. His soul would spark with *her* soulful yearnings. With her constant memory wipes, she couldn't always remember where she'd left off, and her right from wrong got all jumbled. Klast wasn't sure if they would ever discover who her first dog was now that it was dead.

On the line of dogs. He had asked the impossible of Deek.

"I asked Deek to fake a connection to my father so that both of us wouldn't die," Klast stated, as the truth came rushing back to him.

Klast chose to sacrifice himself for his dogs, but he couldn't give up Deek in the same way. He'd told the dog to betray him, knowing that it was possible because Deek had done so before. Deek had spoken with Peyton. It was a gamble that Deek could do the same with Jethro, but since the man was working with soulless and blazen, Klast guessed that Jethro couldn't have an intact soul. There'd be slivers of himself missing, and one small sliver was all it took for Deek to put himself in there and save himself.

Deek had gone above and beyond. He had saved Klast next.

"You asked Deek..." Peyton trailed off and then scoffed. "Clever! Jethro was totally hinting that I should remember his attempt to get his own IB dog. You tricked him into thinking that he had the connection he wanted. Brilliant! He wouldn't want to shoot Deek if he could hear the dog. He'd protect the animal that was sneaking behind his back. You guys are the best!"

Peyton walked toward the squat coffee table in the middle of the room and picked up a shifter. Klast still didn't move. Not yet! He wasn't done centering himself.

"Wait."

"Slowpoke," Peyton teased him.

She pulled her soft hair to her left side and flopped down into a chair, where she looked up at the ceiling to wait impatiently. It was either that, or she was pointedly ignoring the dead body on the floor. That had to be it. She couldn't bring herself to look at Jethro. He was wearing a new black and brown pinstripe suit. The tailoring looked expensive. His dark hair was flattened on one side where it pressed up against the floor. The wide flare of his nose looked smaller that way. Jethro's gray-blue eyes, the same shade as Klast's, were looking straight ahead, eerily not blinking. His head was unnaturally turned from the rest of him. Klast swallowed and looked away again too. That was his dad. Unmoving on the floor.

It was so unfair! The way Klast could remember his father shooting him. The betrayal of a trust that never should have been broken. His father's brain had warped if he was capable of doing things like that. His betrayal was worse than Isabelle's, even if they were similar. Both were trying to claim his life. One of them had succeeded.

No. He was still here. He'd won.

Back to the demon that had been in his soul. Peyton claimed that her soul should have repaired Klast so that he didn't die from the soul-attacking demon. It was nice of her to attempt redemption, but this was yet another case where Klast felt she was entirely wrong. A blazen person could repair their own soul. He didn't trust that the soul could repair another person. What it could do was get out of the way so that his own soul could go back.

The doctor in the hospital had evidence that Peyton had died from the demon attacking over and over and then came back. It happened at the same time as the memory wipe. A little more of her was pushed out and put into a clone so that the new clone could be controlled. She wouldn't remember losing more of her soul because her memories were altered. That's what the demon soul was. It shoved out, not destroyed, souls. Then Peyton filled it all back in.

Klast had guessed that was what was happening to him. Part of his soul was being shoved out of his body by the demon to be put into a controllable clone. Jethro had already tried to lock Klast up in Lexia. Now that he could prove that Peyton was blazen, Jethro was using his advances on Klast to keep Klast from messing up his plans. A brain-warped clone was easier to control than the full force of Klast.

Therefore, the demon soul wasn't a lost soul without a body as Peyton suspected. It wasn't the remains of a soulless person without a soulless body. It was sentient and controlled. The demon soul was Jethro's own soul being shoved into other people to do his bidding. With a complication like that, it was very easy to see how Tuff and Morgal listened to Jethro. They had spotted this disconnected demon soul in Peyton, Klast, and Jethro. They were confused about what it meant, and they refused to follow Shadow's lead to cast their souls aside to protect Klast from something he couldn't see.

"The demon soul that was pushing our souls out was Jethro," Klast claimed, also doing his best to not look down at his father right now. He hadn't ended on best terms with the man, but the body being here left him uneasy with more questions. Peyton was purposefully suppressing thoughts on the matter for her own mental health. She wanted to be done with this. She wanted her life back. He understood that, but one of them had to face the facts.

"Jethro was someone we both knew. His soul felt familiar to us so it wasn't something we would have been alarmed about without that doctor of yours."

"Hmm," Peyton mumbled back. She looked down from the roof to stare at a wall instead.

Klast noticed how her hands were both clenched into fists. She was only half paying attention to him while she sniped out some other living organism. Her clone was doing the same thing he was—resorting back to what felt safe and familiar.

"Who are you looking up?" Klast asked, taking a step closer to her. He had a job for her. One that he would only trust her to do. He would not believe anybody else on this.

"Uh… Tim," she answered.

"My dad was trying to lock me up so he could control this clone version of me," Klast said slowly, unsure if she was really listening to him.

Deek had been with Jethro long enough to find Klast's trapped soul and move it into the clone. Klast's real body couldn't function, but this clone could. This had to be Deek's plan. Give clone Klast more of his soul so that Klast could fight back.

"My body could still be out there. The real me. The one with the broken arm, the broken leg, and the scratch down his chest. Can you find it?"

"No," Peyton answered.

Klast glanced toward Deek, which had him also looking across the fallen form of his father. That was yet another thing he had to get a clear answer on. Did his father have a clone? Was his father dead or was this a fake version of him that Deek had stopped?

*"Gone,"* Deek assured. *"No clones of Jethro. There were four other clones of Peyton and one other clone of you. Muffin and I destroyed the other clones and left you with the two clones that had the least number of conflicting memories."*

*"All by yourselves?"*

Deek rubbed at his nose with one paw. *"Hank and Tim helped."*

Klast shut his eyes and hung his head briefly. He'd have hated doing that. Hated harming anything that looked like a friend, or in Tim's case a sibling. In any event, that was where Deek's Lexian shifter had come from. Hank and Tim. Deek had found the two somehow to create a secret alliance hidden under Jethro's nose.

"So my dad is really dead?" Klast whispered.

That wasn't exactly a good thing. If Klast had been in charge, he would have learned how to use the memory wiping technology. He'd have made his father forget about blazen and clones. He'd have left the man to secure the planetary borders. Not dead. Jethro could keep his wife, Runette, company. Klast would have taken out the parts he didn't like about his dad to preserve the rest. Dead and Klast was going to have to explain that death. He was going to have to watch his family mourn. He was going to be haunted by the thoughts that he had led to his father's demise. Deek had passed a harsh judgment of death upon him too soon.

*"Modify his memory?"* Deek questioned. *"You would turn yourself into Sysmat? Destroy what you don't like and leave the broken rest? You take out the part of your father intrigued by scientific discoveries, IB dogs, and broken souls, and you take apart your entire father. It's who he was. Mine was a kinder sentence than destroying him and letting him live in agony. I wasn't going to leave him like Peyton."*

"Peyton's fine!" Klast snapped, angry at being compared to Sysmat. He needed Peyton to be okay, the same way he needed his father to be alive somehow. Jethro's soul could still be around. They could find it and bring him back.

Klast turned to look at Peyton and frowned. He doubted she would want to revive Jethro after everything he had put her through. Still, he moved to the chair she was on and shoved himself in beside her, aware of how their sides jammed together and the body heat gathered between them.

"I'm still a clone," Peyton whispered. "Without access to the medication, I die at the end of the month. I want to meet Muffin before that."

But... she.... Blast! They were both current clones. They both needed that medication stuff or they would wilt.

"Is my real body—!?"

He started to demand, unable to handle the thought of remaining a Sysmat goon forever, even if Sysmat was shut down. They wouldn't be telling him what to do, but they would never leave him. What he meant earlier when he said that he could live like this if Peyton did wasn't about taking medication to hold himself together. He was referring more to the fact that he had the Sysmat mark adhered to his arm. Peyton had survived removing it before by allowing her soul to drift between her real body and her clone long enough to come back to life. If Klast had a real body, he didn't need this clone one. He didn't want it.

"If I ever spot another clone of myself, I'm going to plain up kill him," Klast snarled.

"Not me," Peyton replied, sounding unnervingly calm.

"It's creepy! It's wrong. It's like you have access to memories that you never created and have new memories from this body that were never yours."

He had noticed the lack of a broken leg right away. No broken arm. No scratch down the front of his chest from Deek. His body felt familiar and alien at the same time. It was an extension of him, but not really him. All day yesterday he had felt like he was imaginary. Now that he felt more real, he feared going crazy. He was trapped! Trapped in a body that wasn't him! Could he even shift like this? Could he find the divide? Klast balled his hands into fists, tugging until he felt the dark matter pooling into his palms. He released the tension before he blew both of them up. Peyton didn't mention his experiment.

"I've seen myself through clone eyes before. While a little startling, it's not that bad," Peyton shrugged.

"I can't live like this."

There he said it. He changed his mind. If he had to stay a clone, he was going to turn psychotic. How many other clones ended up screaming their feelings out? All of them? All except for Peyton? Klast rubbed at his throat. The weight of his identifier necklace was gone. He wasn't wearing it because this clone version wasn't him. There was no circle on a chain giving his name in microscopic print in ten different languages.

"I'll miss you," she whispered so softly that Klast itched his ears.

Ugh. He had inherited ears that heard better than most people, and he was still struggling. She would miss him because he would be dead. Him. The only friend she had that understood even an ounce about what she was going through right now. She had to be having some of the same thoughts as him. This wasn't her. It wasn't right. She was an echo of her former self, not right in her skin. And yet she wanted to remain.

"How can you continue?" Klast asked her. Not that he was going to settle for anything less than his real body, but he wanted to understand why she could.

"I am a warden. I stand between the realms of insanity and hope. I protect the innocent from going through what I have witnessed. I will rise with the dawn and sleep with the stars, because if I can change one more person's life for the better, then mine has a purpose. One more person, Klast. Then one more, and one more after that."

The gumption of this girl. So selfless. He couldn't help but feel ashamed for whining about taking medication when Peyton Finch was thinking about saving universes.

"So you want to be a hero?"

"No, Klast. I am connected to a mythical, imprinting bodyguard dog. I am going to be a savior."

He blinked at her. This was sounding a tad too close to where his father had been going with all of this huffaballoo, and look where it got him in the end? The dogs were not everlasting. They were not mythical, magical beings. They were loving animals that happened to be intrusively loyal companions. Creating a blazen person was painful and wrong; the same as creating soulless. His father's experiments to bring about a myth were immoral.

"We may need to work on that." Klast stiffened as he spoke.

"Oh, and we shall," Peyton grinned at him as if she had won the argument. Her cashew eyes twinkled at him from three inches away.

It took Klast a full two seconds before it clicked. He'd said "we." He had told her, again, that he was going to stick around and help her just as she wanted. He had admitted that no matter how much he whined, he wasn't going to let her walk this fate alone to turn cynical and pigheaded, or worse, gloriously unholy. If she couldn't locate his real body, he would stagger around in this clone one as long as physically possible for Peyton and his dogs.

"But do I have my real body someplace?" he begged to know.

Peyton took in a long, slow breath and then rested her head on his chest. Klast turned more taunt. He thought he had been doing a really good job of not overdoing their close interactions today. He had been so thrilled that Peyton was alive, even as a clone, that he had wanted to hug her when he walked into her room that morning. He held back because the day before she was all business with little recognition. It had hurt to look at her and realize that she wasn't looking back.

It was a fascinating difference what the full soul could change. Today, she had looked at him several times as if she could peer at his soul inside and cherish him for what he was instead of who he appeared to be. Now she was doing it again, and it was dangerous because Klast didn't see his clone as his actual self. What did it matter if he traced the curve of her mouth with his eyes or compared the warmth of her hands to his? It wasn't really him doing any of that. It was the clone.

"I'm bad at…"

Keeping relationships? Starting relationships with a clone? How would that even work? She was destined to die. If they didn't secure the right medication, she was doomed just like last time. She'd turn soulless and freeze him. Klast clenched his teeth together as ideas flooded his brain. He didn't have to lose her. His father had learned how to craft clones. Klast could craft more Peytons to keep her alive. He'd secure the necessary ingredients for her medicine.

But was it fair to make her go through all of that on her own? Klast pictured her finding his real body. There he was lying on the bed in his home on Lexia looking sound asleep, hooked up to some monitor that kept him in stasis. He'd ask to be alone with his real body and Peyton would nod and wait for him outside his bedroom door. One of him would have to die. Would he kill his clone? Would he kill his real self and keep the clone so Peyton wouldn't be doing this alone? The choice sounded so loud and hard inside of his head. He wanted both. He didn't want her to suffer alone, but he didn't want to be like this himself.

"Maybe your body survived, too."

"Klast," Peyton sighed at him. "Muffin says Jethro and Deek were killing off the other clone versions of us on purpose. That's how the dogs know that we're the last ones. I know you don't want to hear it, but you died, Klast. I died. It's hard to adjust to this, especially because Jethro was your father, but he was done with us. I found a way to remember too much. I told you everything I could remember. We were an unfortunate pair that couldn't be. We destroyed the Shadow clone and stopped Sysmat. We cut off his resources. Picked at his experiments. What you are is what is left. I'm going to do as much good as I can with what I have left."

"Look again," Klast whimpered. "My body is out there!"

There was a large icy hand strangling his skull. Peyton was right that he didn't want to believe it. This wasn't him. It couldn't be him. He was going to go mad. He wasn't dead. He was alive.

Klast looked over at Deek to find the dog silently crying, staring back.

He wasn't alive.

Deek had been helping his father to kill off the clones, and then, when there was only one last living version of Klast, Deek had turned on Jethro and saved Klast even if he wasn't real. His doggy heart couldn't strike the final blow against the soul he loved.

"Does the medicine taste nasty?" Klast asked, trying to overcome the horror in his brain to accept his fate.

Peyton chuckled at him and took his hand in hers. He squeezed back really, really hard. She didn't flinch, even if he was crushing her bones together. He could feel them.

"What is a person but their collection of memories, feelings, and soul?" Peyton asked. "This is you, and you are real."

Deek had done the same thing Klast had done. At the last moment, Klast had told his dog to save himself, knowing how hard it would be on the animal to carry on in the face of the enemy. Deek was now forcing Klast to save himself as a version of the enemy. The last of the living Sysmat clones. Of course, he and Peyton wouldn't be able to stay here on Hyphas with everyone thinking they died or that they *should* die. They'd have to migrate over to Lexia and only sneak back this way to gather ingredients for their medicine if they couldn't locate it anywhere else. Being dependent on medicine was going to be rough. He was going to hide a few shots in unlikely places for emergencies.

"You know how to make the medicine, right?" Klast asked, feeling Peyton's gaze on the side of his face.

"Yes," she answered. "But it is nasty. I think I'll invent a pill form. That is much easier to take."

"Right, because you're a chemist."

It wouldn't be so bad. He could make this work. Given long enough, he'd get over the shock and start believing that he was real. Klast glanced back at Deek, ignoring how Peyton continued to stare at him. He should say something back to her like thank you or compliment her brilliance, only if he did that, he feared her seeing the truth of his thoughts. She was spectacular, and he thought she was gorgeous, whether she was a clone or not. It was harder to apply that same thinking to himself, but he tried to psych himself out.

Deek was still crouched in the corner, in the one area that the cameras couldn't see. Before him on the ground was the dead Jethro. If Klast brought his father's body to anybody, he'd have to explain why a clone was bringing him. Klast would have to face the fear that those on Hyphas would try to kill him for being fake. So, he couldn't publicly do anything with Jethro's body apart from abandoning it someplace, but then his fingerprints would be on it, and he'd be blamed. Where his body went would have to remain a secret on Hyphas. His mother wouldn't have anything to bury. No proof that her husband was dead. Rough.

Jethro's death would be different for Lexia. He was an important figure so people would go looking. If Klast buried him someplace normal, he'd be located, and Klast likely blamed. Jethro had to stay in a spot where no one else would look. Like right here.

"I think we should both agree that we have no idea what happened to Jethro," Klast said, risking a glance at Peyton. Her gaze turned from soft and comfortable to unsettled at the mention of the man.

"I can't tell anyone that I'm a clone," he explained. "I can't say that Deek killed him. I'd have to do both if we reveal what has occurred."

"So we make him look like a run-a-way lunatic. Plant some evidence that he got on the bad side of a memory wipe and disappeared on his own. I know where he kept his files," Peyton offered, "but I won't tell you until you take me to see Muffin."

Peyton's blackmail made his mouth hitch up. This was one of his favorite parts about gifting away a dog. He loved to watch that moment when two creatures vowed to trust each other forever. Loved to watch how they promised to safeguard their souls and lives. Loved to see the start of a beautifully electrifying friendship. Peyton could reach Muffin on her own with that transmitter in her hands, but he knew what she was doing. She was trying to draw him outside of his horror by giving him a task.

"At my car, you said?"

No sooner had Peyton given him the coordinates, than Klast had them there, pulling Peyton with him through the divide to the correct spot. His dark-green car, which he hadn't seen in a while, needed attention. There were a few new scrapes on the bumper. One side was completely scratched through as if his dog had missed a turn next to a metal railing. The back left window was jammed open at an angle, as if Deek had gotten frustrated with the controls to roll it down and had tried kicking it instead. The seats were scratched up, but that wasn't from his dog. That was from Muffin. The cream-coated creature was nervously pacing back and forth digging her untrimmed claws into the vinyl as she went.

Klast was about to mention that he could help trim those down, but he didn't get out a word before Peyton screamed. Danger! Klast reached for his gun (which was missing!), as he spun around trying to find the problem. Deek had parked them in a familiar spot; a campground where they had done a lot of training. All Klast saw were trees, dirt, and empty picnic tables in rows of flat spots. Had his eyes failed him?! He spun around again. Darkness rushed to his palms unwanted before he got his new nerves to chill. Nothing. Peyton's shout hadn't sounded like an excited scream, but it must have been, because Peyton was now running toward the car. Wow, she could get him going!

"That used to be a perfectly good seat!"

She pulled open the car door glancing around at the damage. "What happened to the… and the… and…" Her eyes scanned over what a nervous IB could do when desperately trying to reach its human. In retrospect, it wasn't that bad. Klast had seen worse. He opened his mouth to comment as such, but Peyton was quicker than him again.

"You are more beautiful in person," she trilled in such a way that Klast got goosebumps. He smiled as Muffin jumped from the car, knocking Peyton over so the dog could lick her face and roll on her. Both let out excited squeals, although Peyton's were filled with "gross" and "not the mouth!" Muffin howled out her joy sounding like she was shouting at the moon. Klast felt another dog's head sink into his right leg and then sit on his foot. Deek.

"They make some weird sounds," Klast voiced his thoughts as he continued to watch. Half the sounds Muffin let out were of various levels like she still hadn't learned how to control her volume. Peyton's words to her were mixtures of languages and jumbles of half words as if she couldn't decide if she was saying them or thinking them.

"I'm… not sad," Klast said, looking down at Deek. Klast sat in the dirt next and stroked Deek's fur, remembering the soft texture of the silvery hairs like he'd felt it all before even if his clone hadn't. His perfect, wonderful, best friend.

"What?!" Peyton shouted, jumping to her feet. "Fetch. Seriously? I throw something and you go get it and bring it back…. I don't know. For fun! You have to know fetch!" She glanced around, found a stick, and threw it. Muffin watched the low arch of the throw, her gaze landing on the ground before the stick did.

"Then you go get it," Peyton prompted.

Klast grinned. "She trained in weapon strategy, not fun and games. The only thing that dog is doing is analyzing the threat of a stick. You want her to fetch it, you have to make it more exciting. Like this."

He scooped up a bunch of sticks near him and held them up. "Each one of these is a bomb. If you don't bring these back in under a minute, Peyton goes boom."

He chucked the sticks outward laughing as Muffin scrambled around trying to remember which sticks out of the many were the bombs. Peyton shook her head and tried to help her, getting her all confused. Klast laughed at them. They were doing horrible at this training session, but his emotions swelled into a few tears. He didn't manage to brush the water onto his pants before Deek was beside him licking them off.

"It's just… I know how long and hard they worked for this. Now they finally have the real connection and I'm so happy for them," Klast told Deek.

And not jealous either. He was not standing there also wanting to hug Muffin. He didn't feel like Peyton had left part of her soul inside of him so she could force him to hunt down her dog. For once, he felt like the inside part of him was completely fixed.

"Funny," Klast said, ruffling Deek's head and flattening his ears while he did so to tease him. Deek lightly nipped at his arm for that. "Now that I'm not in my real body, I think I have my full soul. Do I? Am I whole, Deek?"

"Klast wonderful," Deek barked at him.

Klast nodded. Not perfect, but he was better. Part of his soul would always be with Deek. Peyton probably kept a sliver for herself. Or it was the reverse. She had a part of her on him so she could sparkle hunt him when she felt like it. Overall, he was improving. He no longer felt the strained gap where Shadow used to be.

"I might be able to look at a black dog and not want to weep," he admitted. That would be something. Deek licked his hand again. Then he jumped away to tell Peyton and Muffin that they had it all wrong. That made Klast question the sticks too because he was certain that the one by the picnic table had been a fake bomb.

"Boom!" Klast cried out making them all wail at him for causing them to jump. They were funny. He was still laughing his head off as he got himself into his car to inspect the damage. Apart from the seats, the inside was fine and workable. He started the engine, grinning when the others scrambled inside. Peyton dived herself into the back through the broken window. Her foot caught on the edge making him laugh even harder when she face-planted. They needed to work on some coordination there.

"I like it when he's in a good mood," Peyton told the universe. She pulled herself up unaware that he was laughing at her. "I thought we were going to infiltrate the office."

"Yup. Right after I hide this car better."

They were going to wish they hadn't come into the car with him. Klast laughed harder as he headed toward the perfect hiding spot. He was going to pin the car into a damp, smelly, cave that he'd discovered years ago during training. The car should barely fit meaning that there would be no room for any doors to open. There was no room for anyone to crawl in or out either. To move the car, they would have to shift in and out.

# 36

Klast blinked in surprise as they all arrived in the "secret" office that Peyton claimed held his father's research. Being night on Lexia, no glow came through the flower-patterned stain glass window. It was hard to see the treasure trove design on the second fancy window, but Klast knew its proportions well. He'd stared at it a long time the first time his father had shown him this room. It wasn't a secret. It also wasn't in the administration building but lodged among a group of accountants' rooms. Jethro said that they were quieter here, so he had his office two blocks over from where he worked. Deek walked over a small tile by the door and flipped on the lights.

When Klast was first here, he'd not skimmed the many books on the dark bookshelves because he wasn't capable of reading any of the titles back then. Now he didn't have a problem skimming between "Myths and Monsters" and "Quick Quadrilaterals." The many devices resting between the books were familiar to him as well. Spy gadgets, flashlights, media players, and trinkets from art fairs were evenly placed.

Peyton moved to the large gray desk in the middle right away. Muffin tagged along at her heel nearly getting kicked in the face. Deek was already sniffing all the corners as if making sure no one else had been in here recently apart from them. He looked up at the odd boxes wedged near the ceiling.

"Did he not explain those to you?" Klast asked as he walked to an opposite corner and read the model number on a box. Oddly not the latest model unless Jethro disguised new tech in old packaging. Deek shook his head. Jethro would have brought Deek here before if they were working together. For all the secrets of hiding clones, Klast had expected his father to hide his main office too. It was right here in plain sight in the form of his actual office.

"Those amply soul tech."

"They allow Jethro to hear what I'm saying when I'm talking to him in my soul form away from my body," Peyton added. "Is anybody good at guessing passwords?"

"X7Ijk*G9tv..." Deek barked.

Klast typed it in for her because she couldn't understand the dog speech anymore. Then he left her to rummage in the desk computer while he slipped out a thinner screen from between two books. He had spotted this on his first trip, but he'd never dared ask about it back then. It was a Hyphas tablet, not the sort of thing he would expect on Lexia, but something he hadn't thought too hard about back then. Deek helped him unlock it which only caused Klast to look around and wonder if he could identify where Jethro had hidden the transmitters that allowed such things as Hyphas phones and tablets to work way over here. Probably at some tower or other.

Klast clicked on a video link that was labeled "upload." He blinked, even if he knew exactly what this was and how his father had gotten it. His father could shift at will. He had shifted around to get different angles and stay out of Klast's sight when he recorded him. Already Klast was feeling tense, the fury boiling back up as he realized yet another truth against his father. It was his dad that kept getting footage of him and putting it up online. Klast had tried over and over to take down things that pertained to him. There was only one user that evaded him and kept putting videos back up, no matter how well Klast thought he had deleted them. "FightForIt." His father was the man sharing his secrets.

"The jerk," Klast mumbled as he watched through shortened breath.

His father had recorded Klast a few weeks back, running his dogs through a group training session. He didn't do many of those, and this one had been rough on them. Klast had set up an obstacle course, one that was designed for humans. He had his dogs work through it, noting where they failed, where they had to ask for human help, and how they overcame things in unique ways. The course had made Deek irate. He wanted to beat the course and couldn't do it alone. Klast had laughed whenever the other calmer dogs had sorted out an ingenious way to get around the constraints before Deek had. That only made it worse for him. After they had finished, Deek had insisted on running the course on his own. He created elaborate contraptions to help him reach objects designed for humans to squirm into. He'd not looked at Klast for two days after that.

Klast glanced over at Deek. The dog shook his head to clear it of the bad memory and put his focus on the shelves instead. Klast turned off the footage before it finished. There was no one left to share his footage, and no Klast left alive on Hyphas to film. It made him wonder if his pals there were crying about him. Nah. Bronze and Mike each had one of his dogs, and the dog would be able to tell that he was still around. So, he could go back around to see them sometime, swap training tips, and get the real news without facing the full media.

"Jethro was the one who kept stealing training techniques from me," Klast sighed.

"Not surprised," Peyton answered. "He tended to steal what he liked, didn't he?"

"Not always. He paid for it too."

Like the expensive printer that he had stacked beneath the desk. Klast sighed at it as he scanned the room again grateful that Jethro didn't decorate it with family pictures. This would be so much harder to say goodbye if Klast was looking at his dad's face.

"That should do it," Peyton declared as she wrapped up the folder she had been working on. "It's proof that Jethro was a little off trying to turn a myth into a reality and harming himself for it. I put it in a location that will be found soon enough, but not too soon by the rest of Lexia. All we need to do is pretend that we haven't seen Jethro in a while and that we have no idea where he was last. They'll think that he took it too far."

"He did take it too far," Klast replied. His voice wavered. It was going to take a while to get over the anger he felt and the grief that came along with it.

Peyton took in a couple of deep breaths, staring at the screen like she wasn't as aloof as she pretended to be either. Her hands curled into strangled fists and she panted, straining her soul. Klast sighed at her. She was searching. Trying to find Jethro despite all he had done to her. He'd be the first person she sought when she didn't know what to do since she'd been reporting to him. It would take her a while to get over this.

"At least the both of us can remember the good and the bad parts about him together. You don't have to hide anything from me. If you ever want to talk about it—"

"You know everything I can remember, and the rest of it I'm glad that I forgot." Peyton wiped at her eyes and pushed the send button. "I made it look like an emergency file that would send if Jethro hadn't logged in to his station in a few days. It will be okay."

She whispered the last part to herself so Klast didn't comment. He stared at the wall trying to figure out what he was going to do with his life now that it was vastly altered. Sure, saving others was on the list, but that was a guideline, not a quantifiable action.

"Klast?"

He glanced over at Deek, who was staring at a drawer intently. Klast rubbed at his ears, trying to decide if Deek had asked for him in or outside his head. The lines felt a little blurred right then.

"Both," Peyton told him as if she knew the question he was asking himself when he made such a gesture. "Now I know the answer to that too." She winked at Klast and then jerked to the side at something that Muffin thought to her.

"I can't hear him anymore!" she hissed at her dog. "I've simply had a similar reaction."

Proof that she couldn't hear his dog. Klast found himself grinning about that as he moved to the drawer that had Deek's interest. If it wasn't for the company he had, he'd be on the floor bawling, unable to make any progress. Knowing what his father had done, how long he had been betraying him unnoticed, made the air feel thin.

Klast pulled open the drawer and staggered backward. Suddenly Peyton was there holding him up, straining to look over his taller shoulders to see what had caused him to recoil.

"Oh," she said chipper. "I expected a gun or something, but this is much better. I finally get to see what that thing looks like!"

Her hands stopped bracing Klast up so that he took another wobbly step. She pulled out his necklace, the one he had worn ever since he returned from Lexia for the first time. The one with the round disk that said his name in ten different languages, including Lexian. His father must have shoved it in this drawer after killing him. Peyton squinted at the small letters and symbols and twisted the pendant around, trying to find "up." There was no up. The text wound in a circle so that the inattentive eye saw a swirl. Klast gulped. It was too close to the symbol that Sysmat had adapted as part of their logo. The swirl for the soul.

"I absolutely love it," Peyton declared. "Klast's soul."

Before he could stop her or protest, she laced the necklace around his head and tucked it down into his shirt. Klast stood there, willing himself to accept it.

"Please," Deek asked him silently.

It was hard! Klast kept telling himself that this clone was who he was now. That he was the clone. That he had to continue for the sake of his friends. It still felt suffocating. If he had to fight with being himself every minute of the day, he was going to go mad. It was going to take a miracle to get his mind over this hurdle. He stared straight ahead, ignoring everything around him while his head fought with itself. He couldn't move or flinch or anything. He felt numb all over as if he was trapped in a soul cage, standing for the rest of his life. That was until Peyton edged closer and planted a kiss on his cheek.

"When's the last time anyone told you how amazing you are? You are the strongest person I know. Brilliant, charming, and brave."

What? He was never charming. Against his will, Klast looked back at her, seeing the sincerity on her face. *Her* face. Not the face of a clone. He could accept Peyton. He should be able to accept himself. If Deek was the clone dog, he'd accept his dog without question.

"It's just... I need..."

"Space?" Peyton guessed as she flashed him an apology and turned away, pinching her mouth together as if rejected. She crossed her arms and looked away from him. If she had stepped away, he'd have screamed about being a clone; suffocated by no one accepting him when he couldn't accept himself. Turning around wasn't the same as shunning, though. She was the brave one.

*"Didn't start out that way,"* Deek reminded him.

Right. Peyton had dealt with living in clones for years. It wasn't that Klast was behind for feeling the way he did. She'd had a lot longer to get to where she was now.

"It's just…" He had to get down to the real part that was bothering him so he could step over it. "The mark on my arm!" he declared, pulling up his sleeve to look at the offensive blue symbol. "I am everything I despise."

Peyton pulled up her sleeve next to look at her arm and study the tattoo.

"Body." She traced the square. "Glad I have one of those that can help me accomplish my goals. Imagine being trapped, unable to move anywhere while the rest of you knows that there are things you need to get done. Things that only you can do. Things that the universe depends on you for." She shivered.

Klast knit his eyes together. Huh. He usually focused on how he hated feeling trapped. He hadn't thought much about how Peyton would have hated being able to move her soul around while her body remained broken and caged in a hospital for experiments. That was far worse than the cards he had been dealt.

"Soul." She ran her hands around the swirl next. "I am so glad that my soul is findable. Rent and it is weak. Together and nothing in the universe is stronger. You are incredibly strong, Klast. I've looked. You're a very powerful, beautiful…" Peyton blushed and then cleared her throat like she shouldn't have said that last word.

"Power," she covered, pointing to the two dots, "over death. It's a bit of an over-exaggeration because we both know how we can die, but the best legends have a bit of magic about them that sound unexplainable. Sysmat may have put the pictures together, but I don't see the company when I look at this mark. They were liars and thieves and devils. They stole people and souls and minds. Theirs should have been the mark of a demon. What they gave us was a reminder that good things can come from those trying to work evil. We are going to set this right, Klast."

He leaned into the words. There was no way he could survive this without Peyton reminding him over and over how to stand upright. She was right. The symbols themselves were not what had offended him. It was the actions of Sysmat that had. They could change the public mind about what the symbol represented by using it in a much better way. After all, the reverse had happened loads of times. People would take good symbols and turn them into scary cults. There. He had a firmer direction. However, without breed dogs the task of "right the universe" sounded too insurmountable after losing everything.

*"Muffin is cute,"* Deek whispered at him before sticking his snout into the air like he'd not said anything at all. Klast looked over at the restored creamy dog, his mind already contemplating what sort of pups would come about from two IB dogs who had both felt the divide and could live in multiple worlds seamlessly. Intriguing.

"You're right though. It needs a new name," Peyton mused, still looking at her arm, not his.

"Regalia, Burma, Owasinth?"

"What did you say?" Klast asked her, amused that the word had come from her mouth, and curious to know if she realized she was speaking Lexian.

"Owasinth. It's a shorter word, meaning the dedication one feels for protecting what is important. It's like loyalty, but deeper."

Klast nodded, smiling that Peyton was remembering how to speak. She'd be better than him soon because Lexian was his second language, not his first. He covered up the triangle point at the bottom of his mark and stared at the rest of it. A diamond with a soul and two dots of power. Power through the body and soul. It meant more to him that way if he took out the picture of death. That's what he was going to do. He'd start over with Owasinth, modified from Sysmat; an example of how justice and peace could be restored, not stolen.

"Deek thinks Muffin is cute," Klast snitched.

Deek jolted and rammed into Klast's leg. Muffin eyed Deek thoughtfully as if she'd consider him slowly, the way she was trained to analyze everything before she jumped in. Peyton giggled. Her face turned red as she looked at Klast, and then she was pointing back to the data.

"The soulless are kept in a nearby enclosure," she declared. "This file appears to detail how Jethro made them."

"Yup. We should put them out of their misery sometime soon," Klast agreed.

He wasn't looking at the screen though. He was looking at Peyton. She'd kissed him. He'd not let his heart contemplate attaching to a girl in a very long time. There were always the dogs to consider and the fact that he could shift. He had not found a person who would understand the separate worlds in his life and mind until now. What an unlikely situation he found himself in. His enemies had given him what he couldn't find. A small blessing from a large catastrophe.

"What are Hank and Tim up to?" he asked, trying to hide his real thoughts. Deek could hear them though. He stopped looking at Klast to stare at Peyton.

"They are setting up dog pens for you at your house in Lexia," Peyton informed him as she skimmed over the complicated medical information in front of her.

Klast nodded, feeling like he should do something more useful than standing there. He glanced around the office, at his father's organization, at the trinkets that would reveal how strained his father's soul had been. Klast wondered if his father could defeat a soulless in the end, but he put the question away as his gaze went back to Peyton.

Her red hair was curled at the ends below the shoulder blades on her back. Her head tilted slightly to one side when she studied. Her left leg bounced. Klast glanced at Muffin to judge the dog's mood. Fine. She wasn't feeling protective, so Klast let himself smirk. Quickly, so that Peyton wouldn't have time to react, he hugged her from behind, planted a kiss on her cheek, and shifted out of sight to go check on his house. He wasn't fast enough to escape Peyton's inhale and subsequent laugh or the way he felt his soul warm and glow as he moved through the divide to get his house ready for extra guests. Peyton and her dog were coming over!

His place here didn't hold the same charm as his Hyphas dwelling, but it was still amazing. The property touched the edge of the Lexian jungle providing him with new possibilities for dog training, and a much-needed splash of green against the bland atmosphere otherwise. Instead of a patio, the front entryway had two large fountains currently splashing recycled water. Birds scattered as Klast appeared beside them. The walls were tan stucco with green and blue tile inlays. The inside had some rather uniquely shaped windows and alcoves. It was mostly undecorated apart from basic furniture he'd gotten cheap.

Klast raced up to the front door and opened it with the entry code. He stepped inside to find both Hank and Tim trying to figure out what to do with a large red Kong that Hank was holding. They faced toward the wall, so didn't see him step inside.

"I still think it's a mini beehive. It should go outside," Tim insisted.

"Deek wouldn't want bees," Hank protested. "The bee breeds wouldn't be the same as what we have here anyway. It'd be an invasive species."

Klast laughed at them. "It holds dog treats," he informed as they spun around, hands moving to their guns. Funny how he felt no fear from the SD guns anymore. They wouldn't hurt him for long. He had Deek to safeguard him.

"Thanks for helping my dog. Sorry that you were asked to destroy clones of me. Must have been nasty and horrific. Deek says I'm the last one, so how about you don't shoot this version of me?"

"What's the password?" Hank asked, narrowing his eyes.

Password? Had Deek set up an identification system? Then not told him?

*"Klast has smelly feet,"* Deek provided.

Klast laughed. He could only imagine the guessing involved for Hank and Tim to learn that one unless they gave Deek something to write with.

"Apparently, I have smelly feet."

"Where's Peyton?" Tim asked, lowing his weapon first.

"At a facility learning secrets about soulless. I left Deek with her. She'll tell me when she's done and I'll—"

"I can move myself," Peyton declared, showing up right beside him with both dogs lodged in the crooks of her arms so that she was bent over trying to hold them. She pointed a finger at Tim.

"I have been meaning to tell you that I know it was you that ate the candy I hid behind my dresser. You're not getting away with that again!"

Tim blinked at her wide-eyed for a moment and then launched himself across the room to hug his sister. He probably thought she was the real thing, not a clone if she had back a few childhood memories.

*"We found a journal that Peyton had written. I read it to Muffin,"* Deek told him.

Klast failed to hide his mirth. They walked a delicate balance, but he wouldn't want to walk it with anyone else than the people and canines he had around him right now.

"You guys are the best," Klast declared. "Can't wait to start our newest business venture together: The Owasinth."

"That's my term!" Peyton protested. "I'll be the boss."

Hank slowly lowered his weapon. Klast gave him a thankful nod, which finally put him at ease.

"I think the dogs should be in charge," Klast teased.

Deek looked up at him, rushed to Hank to grab the Kong, and then barked for Muffin to join him. They shot off down the halls exploring, not interested in being in charge of anything more than securing the state of the house.

"Nice to have my soul patched back together," Klast commented. "It's like discovering how soft a bird's feathers are for the first time or realizing that you can't snap a handful of spaghetti as easily as snapping a single noodle. It's like being awash with awe standing before a colorful sunset. It's like..."

Klast pulled a hand into a fist, reflexively wondering which room Deek was in. Before he knew what was happening, a trail of sparkles appeared before his eyes, leading him right to the dog teaching Muffin how the tub worked.

"...interesting," Klast finished. He hadn't expected to find sniper tech in his wrist even if his clone knew it was there. This could be a useful tool. Good way to shift around without crashing into anybody.

"I need to treat you to dinner, Hank and Tim. It's on my to-do list for coming to my rescue the first time. I really appreciate it."

"You remember it all?" Hank checked.

Klast nodded. "Yup. No memory problems. Felt a bit odd when I woke up, but Peyton's good at helping me get over the mental bumps. You can come to dinner too," Klast invited Peyton.

Her eyes snapped up from looking at his curled fist to his face, flashing him a question. He nodded at her, and she stuck her tongue out at him as if she was telling him that she was always going to be better with the sparkle trail.

"Has she always been like that?" Klast asked Tim, laughing.

"She used to spit in my ear!" Tim complained.

"Only because you made it so easy!" Peyton claimed, even if she couldn't remember it at all. Tim shoved her shoulder. She stuck her tongue out again, declaring that she had grown up... some. A loud whirring sound from the bathroom had all of them jumping as Deek found the switch to flush the toilet. That was followed by both dogs barking out an alarm.

"Oh...!" Hank laughed. "Your plumbing is broken."

"Deek!" Klast shouted as he rushed down the hall to find the off switch. Just what he needed, a flooded bathroom. Leave it to a dog to trigger all the problems when he wanted to go out to dinner. Klast laughed his way to the bathroom.

His body ran for him, whole and strong. His soul worked for him, bright and true. His mind was still there unchanged yet smarter. His body, his heart, his lungs. Maybe he could accept himself like this after all. His nose. It started to smell the backup from the plumbing.

"It's just like you to make things smelly, Deek!"

Deek howled in glee. Klast heard him jumping into puddles of junk. He reached the door only to slam it shut and turn himself around, trapping the smell and overflowing toilet. He raced the other way to shut off the main valve for the water to the house. He wasn't going in the bathroom! Not with two dirty dogs playing in muck.

He heard Peyton muttering something about nasty things and how Klast was going to be the one washing up both dogs. He heard Tim pick a restaurant that they could all shift into at this time of night. He heard Hank call someone to say he was going out with a friend and would be back late. Muffin was laughing her head off at whatever Deek was doing to impress her. Klast focused on his heartbeat, seeing nothing but potential. After the darkness always came the light. He would rise on impenetrable wings, helping everyone rise with him along the way. How could he not when he lucked out with such good friends?

Souls united. Forever.